LI

A Trail of Shaman

Annie Kochert

Annie Kochert (signature)

Spirits Talking Press   Molalla, Oregon

F
Koc
c.1

Spirits Talking Press
P.O. Box 927
Molalla, OR 97038
1-503-759-4567

Printed in the United States of America

First Edition, First Printing

Kochert, Annie.
    Lineage : a trail of Shaman / Annie Kochert.
-- 1st ed.
    p. cm.
    LCCN 00-106659
    ISBN 0-9701860-0-2

    1. Prehistoric peoples--Fiction. 2. Kennewick Man--Fiction. 3. Archeology--Fiction. I. Title.

PS3561.O313L56 2000   813'.6
                        QBI00-901390

Cover by Sheila Somerville
Edited by Leona Grieve and Elizabeth Shannon
Design and layout by DIMI PRESS

Dedicated to and in memory of all my dads:
Valentine Kochert, Wes Summerlin, Kelton Neal
and especially my first mentor, Clarence Helmick,
whose blood flows in the rivers of my body.

ACKNOWLEDGMENTS

I start my thanks with Alan Frey. Here in the beginning, he gave me the boost needed to take pen (erasable pen) in hand. And to my mom, Elberta Helmick, Jim and Audrey Clark, Carrie Wiencken, Sue Parnell and Fran Hansen—all the backbone of encouragement. And not to forget, Jan Rouse, a Nez Perce friend, who allowed me to follow her along the Pow Wow Trail for three years.

I especially appreciate the diligent efforts of Marilyn Bloch, a former Molalla City Public librarian. She scouted and found volumes of useful archaeological material. Above all, thanks are in order to Leona Grieve and Elizabeth Shannon for cleaning up my text—not an easy job—again, thank you.

I give credit where credit is due—the Northwest archaeologists and anthropologists whose meticulous work leaves records of the past. Without their articles, reference books and professional reports we remain in the dark, and LINEAGE: A TRAIL OF SHAMAN would merit little basis. And on that note, a special thanks to anthropologist James Chatters whose examinations and studies of the Kennewick Man kept my undivided attention.

Others providing invaluable information were Lyon King, his knowledge of tattoos, Berry McPheison, of Game and Wildlife, who knows well the cycle of the salmon and Beulah Calica, Board Secretary for Warm Springs Indian Reservation, who shared her knowledge on gathering and preparing food plants.

FOREWORD

Kennewick Man

A 9,300 to 9,600 year old skeleton found in the summer of 1996 along the Columbia River at Kennewick, Washington—located just a few miles from the confluence of the Snake and the ColumbiaRivers. His affiliation to existing populations is unclear, however the scientific team who examined him found that his physical features mostly resemble the Ainu and the Polynesians. In **LINEAGE: A Trail of Shaman**, according to the bone evidence, the character Froom shares identical features and injuries with that of the Kennewick Man.

Ainu

Ancient population of people living on the northern Japanese Islands and until recently inhabited the nearby Kurile Islands. Their true origin seems a mystery—possibly southeastern Asian—possibly Eurasian — possibly Jomon— possibly a combination of many or nearly any existing populations of that time. Or just possibly their heritage is linked to the ancestors of Native Americans. Irregardless, the Ainu practice a belief thought to be the oldest continued religion in the world. Whatever their ancestry, the Ainu maintain impressive credentials warranting an 'early man' narrative.

Kurile Islands - Location of **LINEAGE: A Trail of Shaman.**

Marmes Cave

A cave excavated in the 1960's, located near the junction of the Snake and Palouse Rivers in Washington State and now under water as a result of Lower Monumental Dam. The cave boasted artifacts and human skeletal fragments dating as far back as 10,000 years. In my sequel, **LINEAGE: A Passage of Shaman,** the Ainu people will reach and be residing at this location.

Petroglyphs & Pictographs

All are located on the lower Snake River or within close proximity of the Snake River and the Marmes Cave. A good portion of this documented art is now underwater.

THE ABOVE INFORMATION PROVIDES THE SETTING, BOTH GEOGRAPHICALLY AND CULTURALLY. PLEASE REFER TO THE GLOSSARY AT THE BACK OF THE BOOK.

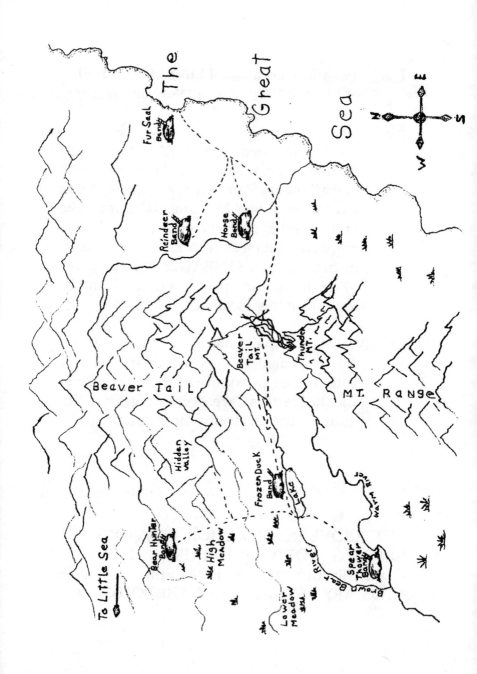

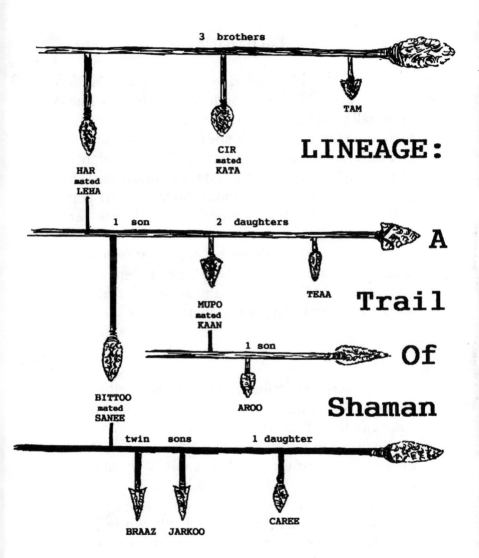

LINEAGE:

A

Trail

Of

Shaman

3 brothers

TAM

CIR
mated
KATA

HAR
mated
LEHA

1 son

2 daughters

TEAA

MUPO
mated
KAAN

1 son

BITTOO
mated
SANEE

AROO

twin sons

1 daughter

BRAAZ JARKOO

CAREE

PROLOGUE

Before the seas and rivers filled with water animals, Ceda married a condor and lived with him in the tall bluffs among his kind. Unhappy living so high up in the jagged cliffs, she fled to the lowlands. Her bird husband saw her trying to cross a mighty river that flowed into the Great Sea. He shouted an angry threat heard throughout the lands. "If you won't live up high with me, you'll live far below...forever!"

On his mighty wings he soared down and attacked, causing her to fall into the turbulent water and drown. At that very instant, all water creatures were born, and Ceda became their mother.

Man must pay tribute to Ceda by placing the heads of their catch pointed toward the place they were caught. This releases the fishes' spirits and allows them to return to her. After rejoining their mother, their spirits speak honorably of those who caught them, and Ceda is pleased.

When man pleases the water deity, she permits them to catch and eat her children. But when Ceda is angry with man, she withholds her children, sometimes causing starvation.

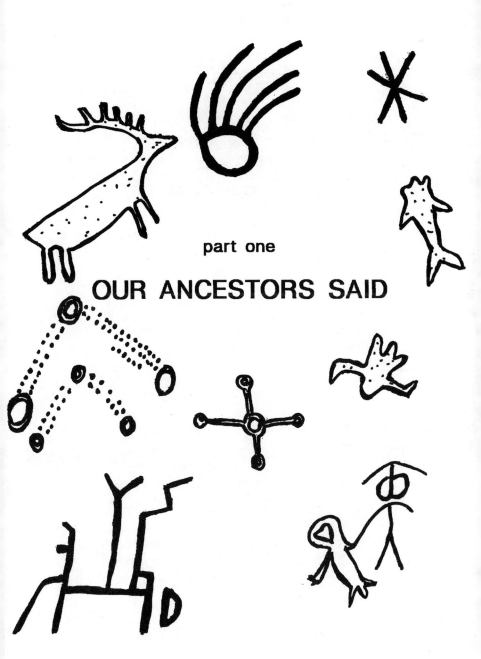

part one

OUR ANCESTORS SAID

A voice summoned him - but the meaning of the words escaped Bear Claw. The speech seemed vaguely familiar, and therefore comforting. Yet what he mostly desired was sleep.

The dark shelter felt damp yet warm, but nearly too small for them. Just a few more days rest and the two would begin their journey.

'Ya, Ho. You sleep the long winter sleep of a hibernating bear!' said Eagle Shadow to his dazed brother.

Eagle Shadow's words weren't words at all, rather the sacred silent language between identical twins—twins with neither scars nor birthmarks to identify one from the other.

'You'll gain your health, brother, for we come from a powerful lineage. Creator One Breath has deemed it as such. The blood flowing in the rivers of our bodies is the same red liquid which ran through the veins of the great tusu. OUR ANCESTORS SAID...

***

1

approx. 9,600 yrs B.P.

Bittoo dared not move. Something had awakened him. He dared not even breathe— but he had to. The earthen lodge lay heavy with the smell of dirt and smoke. He listened, straining his ears and heard his father's uneven snoring—nothing more. He remained perfectly still until his nerve allowed him to open one eye—then the other.

Slowly, he scanned the interior of the pit house. Even through the dimness his grey eyes spotted his sleeping father groping for the bed furs his mother had tucked tightly under herself. And nestled in the crook of his eldest sister's curled up body was Teaa, his youngest sister, noiselessly sucking her thumb.

Maybe a noise in his dream woke him, but he didn't remember dreaming. His hand flew to his nose-ring, hoping the loop would be enough protection should a dark lurking spirit attempt to enter his body.

Something had disturbed his sleep. But it seemed gone now...if it had been there at all.

He sat up, stretched his lean body and removed his sleeveless garment, quickly replacing it with a reindeer frock reaching to his knees. He wore only his inner leggings. Just a single set of clothing would prove sufficient for the short time he'd be gone. To guarantee his feet remained warm, the adolescent stuffed a thin layer of cotton grass in his seal skin boots. Slipping his feet into the comfortable boots, he hurriedly wrapped soft leather thongs around them, criss-crossing the supple hide where they met both in front and back.

He planned on going fishing, but now the urge was growing unusually strong as if something besides himself was driving him onward toward the ice. He clenched his jaws, a chill ran down his spine.

Does it have anything to do with whatever startled me awake? He now remembered hearing distant yet strange words when waking.

He stopped his preparations, and for the second time, sucked in his breath, holding the air until his lungs nearly burst. Had the voice called him a 'stupid boy'. Surely, he remembered wrong.

Grabbing his fishing spear plus the pack he readied the night before, he quietly climbed the crude ladder. Squinting, he saw that the clouds had dropped a boot-high of snow during the night. Standing on the last ladder rung, he gave a quick glance down into the dark pit house where his family slept and shuddered from head to toe. *Something did not seem right this day.* He pulled his wolverine-lined hood over his brown wavy hair.

Observing the fogless morning, Bittoo inhaled deeply, allowing the bitter air to sting his lungs. Both Thunder Mountain and Beaver Tail Mountain lay majestically covered in heavy snow. Thunder Mountain remained quiet, no smoke rising from its peak. The valley between the two looming mountains would soon be impassable. Spring would arrive before the snow melted, allowing travel to resume between the bands on the east side of the island and those on the west side.

He could barely see the nine large pit houses nestled on the ridge, overlooking Frozen Duck Lake. Deep snow drifts covered their domed roofs. The hidden ceilings were built with intertwined saplings and antler racks overlaid with sod. They varied only in size, like women's breasts.

A ladder stuck out through the smoke hole of each roof, most extending higher than a tall man.

During the time of the heavy snows, the poles marked the place of each lodge.

From behind him, came the crunching of heavy footsteps in the snow. He crouched, unseen, until a stranger carrying a cumbersome pack walked past, heading for the far side of the village. Quietly and slowly, he followed the man's fresh-cut path through the snow.

"Ya, Ho! Ya, Ho! People of Frozen Duck Lake!" the boisterous man began. He repeated his greeting while continuing to weave in and out between the pit houses.

As Bittoo rounded a domed roof, he saw both man and pack drop into the earth. Cautiously, he edged closer to where the man disappeared. The burly intruder had walked through Froom's roof, landing in the smoldering fire pit - his fur clothing badly singed and the collapsed ceiling destroyed.

Awakened by the commotion, the villagers gathered around the roofless dwelling, staring blankly through the billowing dust created by the fallen debris. Their eyes darted back and forth as a yelling match started between the two outraged men.

"You big nosed fool! You didn't build a strong roof! I nearly broke my neck!" ranted the intruder, brushing his bushy winter beard free of sod.

"You're as clumsy as a musk-ox!" exploded Froom, who had only heard stories of such a creature.

"It didn't need me to fall through it, your roof would've collapsed with the next heavy snow. And your marking poles are short! Who could see them...they hide under a snow drift!"

"Who are you?" demanded Har, peering down through the unsettled dust and breaking in on the argument.

"I'm Lant of the Spear Creek Band. I came to talk betrothal between my son and the infant girl of a man named Froom and his woman Patee. I brought many gifts for them," he replied, spitting dirt.

"We...are those...you look for," stuttered an embarrassed Froom.

The villagers burst into laughter as Froom, looking confused, swiftly swallowed his pride and anger. Someone in the crowd said, "This will be known as the day everyone laughed but Froom."

Ignoring the comment, greedy Froom attempted to find Lant a sitting place. He shouted at his mate to prepare a meal for their guest, then looked foolish, as everything, including their food, lay buried under antlers, melting snow and sod chunks.

Apparently realizing he just insulted the man he came to barter with, Lant also changed his attitude. He gave Froom a hearty slap on the back, then stated, "Friend, I think we should rebuild your roof before we talk."

Because Lant's statement caused an even louder roar of laughter among the people, Beaver Tail Mountain echoed the sound back at them many times.

Chuckling, Bittoo turned from the scene and using the butt of his spear as a walking stick, crunched through the snow's crust. He paused briefly to glare at the sacred bear skull lodged between a tree fork in the center of the village. The eye sockets were empty, the lower and upper jaws clenched so tightly together that he was unsure how such a dead animal could possibly convey messages on behalf of his band to the Land of the Souls. Yet it didn't keep him from being hopeful that somehow this deity would say good words for him, so this day he might catch many fish.

He continued down the ridge, only guessing if his feet were following the hidden path. Since no wind blew, he moved away from the unneeded protection of the sparse line of willow and birch trees which edged the cove, and continued on to fish in the center of the lake.

Today he hoped to pay homage both to the deity, Ceda, mother of all water beasts, and to the seven revered directions. If he accomplished this he'd also be honoring Creator One Breath—he who made all. And if he gained the respect of these and of other spirits before it came time for his vision quest, he'd surely be given a mighty spirit guide to assist him in becoming a fearless and proud hunter.

In order to achieve his goal, the fishing would need to be excellent. However the silver salmon were no longer running. A moon ago they swam from the Little Sea, up the lower Brown Bear River into the lake, then continued up river to spawn and die. Yet a few lazy ones, fat and firm, didn't make the sea journey, but chose to live in Frozen Duck Lake. He needed seven of these fish to accomplish his goal. He considered all this while chopping a hole in the ice with his father's short-handled chert ax.

He had seen both rites performed by adults and thought they could be duplicated; not realizing that never did anyone combine the two rituals. It was customary to pay respect to a single spirit, one at a time and in its own way. But Bittoo, still young and inexperienced, intended to do something taboo — something totally forbidden. Today, his dreams would be crushed and his life drastically changed — at least today, one spirit would try.

After casting aside the chunk of ice, he scraped the edges of the hollow, shaping it into a perfect circle, then emptied the contents of his pack: three lengths of sinew, ten dried strips of salmon skin, a small wooden scoop, a meager piece of well-done reindeer meat, and his warm gloves, which he choose not to wear.

Through a tear in the fish skin, he ran a length of sinew, wrapped it around the skin twice and tied the tendon securely. Holding the line in his left hand, he dropped the hookless lure into the frigid lake. With his right hand he held his spear, aiming downwards at the hole. Kneeling almost motionless, he watched the movement of the bait flicker from the slight current action. When the water calmed, he twitched the line to duplicate the natural sway of the lure.

Nearly transfixed by the lulling ripples, he failed to notice the salmon until it struck his bait. Startled, he jerked the line, and at the same time, thrust his spear at the disappearing fish.

Discouraged, he sat on the ice and spoke out loud. "You were an excellent fish!" he declared to the evasive salmon. To the mangled bait, he said, "You're a very good lure." Addressing his spear, he added, "You're a perfect spear with your side-notched barbs." Then berating himself, he said, "You have all these good things needed to catch fish and yet, you do not! You fish like a child who can't concentrate, and when Ceda gives you one of her salmon children, you insult her and give it back!"

Blowing on his hands to warm them, Bittoo pondered, wondering whether he thoroughly shamed himself. Deciding Ceda would be satisfied with his scolding, he returned to his fishing.

With a wooden scoop, he cleared away the clotting ice, opening up the hole, then rubbed a handful of snow across his face in an attempt to remain alert. He barely lowered the bait when a salmon of fair size circled the lure.

Gradually, the boy raised the line, and the fish followed the bait almost to the surface. His breath ceased while his heart beat even faster. He drove the spear into the silvery salmon. With both hands tightly around the shaft, he lifted the flopping, speared fish onto the ice. Slowly, he twisted the shaft back and forth until the embedded tip loosened enough to release his catch.

He reverently placed the unmoving fish behind him on the north side, paying homage to the first direction and with its head facing the hole in honor of Ceda. After catching three more salmon he placed them in their respective directions: south, east and west, and also facing the ice hole.

"Maybe I will catch seven salmon, one for each direction," he said excitedly. Then his voice lost its thrill. "But where shall I put my next fish in tribute to the direction 'above'? I can't just hang it in the air. Maybe I can throw the sixth one, which represents 'below' back into the water. But that could anger Ceda, and for many seasons she might not release any of her fish children. And what about the seven salmon representing 'myself'? Possibly I could just hold it."

His stomach grew queasy, his throat tightened. He hadn't thought his plan through, now harm might come to himself or others. "If I continue," he puzzled aloud in a sullen voice, "anything I do might be mistaken as dishonoring Ceda and the seven directions. Even quitting now would defile them...they'd be terribly angry at me!"

Confused about his situation, and not knowing how to reverse or correct it, he stared blankly into the blue-green depths of the frigid water. He knew one thing—something needed be done soon, or when it came time for his vision quest, he'd stay home. He wouldn't seek a vison quest if any spirits were displeased with him.

For an unknown amount of time, he sat, his mind blurry, until a loud harsh voice brought him to his senses. Looking around he saw no one.

"Stupid boy, gaze into the water!"

Peering up at him was a massive salmon, one of such immense size, it couldn't possibly fit through his fishing hole. Frozen with fear, his legs refused to react to his command to run.

"Boy, I am Ceda," the voice declared. *"Mother of all water beasts. You disgraced me and dishonored the sacred directions. A child playing with power is dangerous. There's earthly balance, and you've upset it!"*

As he stared into the pool, Ceda disappeared. The water and clotting ice began to form into eerie, uncertain shapes. Vague images, all in hues of whites and blues, twisted and pulsated, stretched and condensed. Abruptly, they revealed a grotesque scene—Frozen Duck Camp, void of hearth smoke, but engulfed in swirls of wispy fog, circling lodges like stationary dust devils.

Wailing and screaming arose from tortured throats, and bodies with extended bellies and hollow eyes lay where they had collapsed and died. Bittoo recognized his father's and sister's corpses overrun with scavenger birds picking at their flesh. His mother, Leha, appeared mindless as she rocked back and forth beside the lodge, talking with invisibles. Derk, their shaman, alive but too weak to stand, jabbed his carved walking stick into the side of a savage wolverine that feasted on his wife's decaying remains. In the distance, Bittoo heard the screaming of mountain cats and howling of wolves, inviting themselves to the carnage.

He strained to see the ghostly vision as it vanished in clouds of dense fog within the lake. He needed to see his village, to know if it was safe, needed to feel safe himself, but his eyes were locked downward.

"By withdrawing my children, there would be famine of such greatness, the people of the Frozen Duck Band would vanish like the mammoth to the Land of the Souls!" Ceda shouted as she abruptly reappeared. *"But Creator One Breath, creator of the seven directions and all within them declared me your spirit guide, and this time, I'm not allowed to punish you for being disrespectful. Your ancestors will remember you as a great tusu. Some will call you the Father of all Shamans,"* she relayed, her voice calming. *"Of your lineage, you'll be the first, followed by many generations of others with similar power. Your footsteps will leave a Trail of Shaman. However, it's your choice,"* the huge fish proclaimed as she submerged into the iced-over lake.

Bittoo's muscles, no longer paralyzed, relaxed

with such force he collapsed. Trembling, he struggled to rise, his head spinning, his eyes unable to focus. He wanted to run, but his feet slipped out from under him, and he fell, his head just missing the fishing hole. Total blackness consumed him.

As darkness started to fall over Earth Mother, Bittoo hadn't returned. Har feared his son might have fallen through the ice. Rushing and stumbling down the snow covered ridge, he stopped at the lake's edge and called to the boy. Receiving no answer, he carefully, one slow step at a time, listening for the sound of cracking ice, made his way toward a silhouette in the center of Frozen Duck Lake.

The dim figure looked to be in the exact spot where earlier he observed his son fishing. Cautiously, he made a wide arch around the form. Thinking he might be circling a wild animal, possibly a young bear or wolf, he pulled out his obsidian knife. But if it were an animal, it should have run. Yet, if it were his son, the boy should have answered him. He strained to see details of the form through the darkness. He made one full circle then noticed two distant figures carrying birch bark torches, approaching the lake. While keeping his eyes focused on the silhouette, he backed off the ice toward his younger brothers, Tam and Cir.

"Ya, Ho," whispered Tam, the youngest brother, presuming something of a serious nature was taking place.

"Your nephew fished today and is missing," spoke Har with a labored voice. "There's something or someone on the ice. It makes no noise. I don't think it moves."

Seasons of hunting together made further talking unnecessary. Cir swung wide to the right of Har with his loaded spear thrower in one hand and a bright torch in the other. Tam veered to the opposite side of his older brother. Proceeding in this arch-shaped formation, the three left an opening for an animal to escape.

Alert and ready for danger, the brothers gradually approached the form. They halted a spear throw away from what now resembled either a fur-covered animal or possibly a fur-covered boy. An anguished moan emerged from the fur heap as it suddenly began jerking uncontrollably.

"Bittoo!" responded Har, carelessly rushing toward his son, leaving Cir and Tam providing light from a distance. Each knew excessive weight in one area might cause the ice to break.

Cir studied the scene, noting the strewn contents of his nephew's pack and the four large salmon positioned with their heads toward a slight depression in the ice, which earlier must have been Bittoo's fishing hole.

Har knelt by his unconscious son, quickly scanning him for signs of injury. There was no visible blood nor rips in his clothing. "Son, you must get up," he implored, gently touching the boy's cold cheeks.

Tam moved a little closer, shining light on his nephew's face, but only blank eyes greeted him. "We must get the boy home," he stated curtly.

Har hefted Bittoo over his shoulder, stood with some difficulty, and with heavier steps, listened for cracking ice above his loudly pounding heart. To his far right walked Tam, lighting the way for the pair.

"Bittoo mumbles something about his fish," Har yelled back at Cir without stopping or turning.

Cir had already begun to thread sinew through the gill and out the mouth of one fish. Tying it securely, he used the first salmon as a stopper, and strung the remaining three on the same line.

Cir trudged behind his brothers, absolutely clueless that he carried something of great importance.

2

Word spread through the camp that Bittoo was in trouble on the ice. A concerned crowd gathered on the steep ridge overlooking Frozen Duck Lake.

"He went out early. Maybe he froze."

"No, it's not that cold."

"He was probably attacked by a bear or mountain cat."

"It's because he has no totem to protect him yet."

"Hush," scolded Kata, Cir's wife, placing her arm around Leha. "You speak foolishly and frighten his mother."

The rescuers grew closer, the torches casting enough light for the villagers to see Bittoo slung over Har's broad shoulder. Leha's hand flew to her mouth, stifling a cry. Kata gripped her sister-in-law as Leha's legs crumpled. The crowd shifted into silence, not as a result of Kata's reproach but from suspense and uncertainty: Was Har packing a live or dead body?

As the three crested the ridge, the villagers bunched around, almost halting the brothers' pace. Everyone seemed determined to discover the boy's fate.

"The cats will chew your bones!" bellowed Bittoo, unaware of his own words. "Ceda killed...in the water!" he continued, thrashing his arms against his father's muscular back, before passing out.

Startled by the boy's message, the crowd drew back. The only movement came from Derk, hastily shoving his way to the front. There's more here than just a raving adolescent, thought the shaman, remembering the nightmare he experienced the night before. He sensed a connection between his disturbing dream and Bittoo's mindless outburst.

Derk turned toward the lake, thinking the answers lay out there on the ice. His arm hairs and the hairs on the back of his neck stood on end. Waves of tingles vibrated just under his skin as they always did when he stood in the presence of spirits. "By Creator One Breath," he said softly. "I've never felt a more powerful force."

To himself, Derk muttered, "I fear, if this is an evil one." He moved apart from the others, watching with knowing eyes as the family of Har disappeared into their pit house.

With Tam's help, Har carefully placed his son's unconscious body near the dirt wall away from the fire, well aware that warming him too fast could be dangerous. "His breathing is shallow and his color is ghostly," he said, peering into the boy's handsome face.

Handling Bittoo's mittenless right hand, Har detected the white tell-tale sign of winter bite. Continuing his examination, he picked up the remaining hand, which still clutched a fishing lure. Not wanting to damage the flesh by prying his son's fingers open, he left the cordage and bait in the stiff fist. "Slide off his boots," Har directed Mupo, who knelt at her brother's side.

He inspected both feet thoroughly, then covered his son with a horse hair bed fur. Slowly he turned to his anxious family, who, except for Teaa, huddled in a semi-circle around the sick adolescent. "His feet are fine; his boot laces weren't so tight as to cut off the flow of blood. That's good. Nevertheless, his face and hands have pallor and his breathing isn't strong, although it's even. We'll know more by morning, woman," he concluded, smiling wearily at Leha.

Quietly, Leha walked to the rock-lined fire pit near the center of the lodge and added a stubby alder limb to the coals, while silently pleading to Grandmother Hearth. She looked over her shoulder, across the room, at her son. Was he still her son or did a black demon possess him? Because she was terrified, her face gone pale, the dotted tattoo across her forehead boldly stood out.

Without pausing, she marched to the dirt shelf where she kept her healing herbs. The lack of light made it difficult to check the contents of the leather pouches. Yet every herb held its own distinct odor. She sniffed each one until identifying the correct scent.

"I need bear fat," she announced, looking directly at Kata. "Could you borrow some? Ask Patee or one of the other women." Without waiting for an answer, Leha returned to the rekindled hearth. She'd stay busy, she wouldn't think about her son, black demons or any of it. She stole another frightened glance at Bittoo.

"I'll go with you and clean Bittoo's salmon," spoke Cir to his mate, as if glad to have an excuse for fresh air.

"I'll help too," Tam said and followed his brother and sister-in-law up the ladder, leaving Har and Leha time to talk.

Mupo looked from one parent to the other. But Leha and Har weren't talking. Both knew there was more wrong with their son than just winter bite. Hadn't he raved like a madman in front of the entire village? It seemed a very long silence for Mupo.

Although burdened with an unborn in her belly, Kata swiftly completed her errand. "Here's the fat," she said, handing it over to her sister-in-law.

Leha placed the glob of fat into a stone bowl. Already, the rock grew hot, and before the blubber melted, it began to sizzle and splatter. She fanned it with her hand, needing just a slow, steady heat to prepare the ointment for her son's hands and face. Because the herbs were too coarse, she deposited the dry leaves into her volcanic grinding slab and began to pulverize them—back and forth—back and forth, with loud exaggerated movements, until what she ground resembled dust.

Leha's thoughts weren't on her task. *What will I do if a dark, evil spirit rises out of my precious son? I'd need to save Mupo and Teaa...grab them and run...get*

them both as far away from their brother as possible. But
how could I desert him?

"Sister-in-law," Kata whispered warmly, gazing
into Leha's troubled face. "You didn't skim the
floating pieces off the oil, and you've skinned your
knuckles while grinding."

Tam's head appeared through the smoke hole,
making hand motions for his brother to join him
outside.

Har was reluctant to leave his son's bedside. But
in the quick flash of time it took him to study Tam's
facial gestures, he realized they had another serious
problem.

"All four salmon have roe in their bellies," Tam
divulged grimly when Har reached the top rung.

Confused by his brother's words, Har's
eyebrows nearly met as his forehead wrinkled.

"It can't be, it's too late in the season for spawning
fish."

"The fish haven't turned red like fish that plan
on dropping their eggs. Moreover, that's not the
worst," reported Tam, lowering his voice so he
wouldn't be overheard.

"Although they're all dead, many of the eggs
look like tiny fish...fishlings...already hatched."

"Impossible! Babies can't form inside salmon,"
snorted Har, whose skin began to crawl at the
likelihood of such a thing.

"These did," Cir revealed, presenting his brother
with the bizarre evidence.

Dumbfounded, the brothers gawked at the glob
of overdeveloped eggs, full of lifeless silver embryos
—miniature dead salmon.

Swallowing hard and nearly choking on his words, Har stuttered,"Something strange is happening that I don't understand." He paused, rubbing his stubby chin whiskers, took in a deep breath, let it out slowly and continued. "Earlier, Bittoo mumbled about Ceda, mother of all water creatures. Spirits are at work here. I think Bittoo knows the answers to this. Save the roe and the fish, dig a pit and cover them with bark and snow. They go against all of nature, but I'm afraid to destroy such a sacrilege."

During the night, as Har kept vigil over his ill son, he allowed himself to think about the roe. Its meaning lay far beyond his reasoning, although he sensed that the condition of the eggs stood for some future change. What kind of change, and how it would effect his family and his people, he could only guess.

It might just mean the silver salmon were going to start giving live birth. Since there were four fish, all the same, he doubted them to be just a freak of nature, like the two-headed fetus he cleaned out of a musk deer during the spring. Tomorrow he'd send for the shaman, but deep down, he wished Derk was already present.

Looking around at his sleeping family, he dreaded the idea of any changes. Cir and his wife, Kata, were sleeping together on the south side, opposite the hearth. They seemed a good match. She came to him from the Fur Seal Band, which made their home on the far side of the island bordering the Great Sea. Kata fit into the family from the beginning. Her little sister, Sanee, was betrothed to Bittoo. That too, Har felt would be a good match, and he intended to offer Sanee's parents extra bride gifts.

Cir, his middle brother, the tallest and leanest of the three, most physically resembled their deceased father. Bittoo was built like this uncle. Cir thought problems through slowly and carefully. When fast thinking was required, he usually accepted others' decisions. Nevertheless, he proved trustworthy and dependable, and Har felt confident when hunting with him. Cir also had a gift for catching animals, setting the snares in just the right places and effectively erasing any scent of man from around the traps.

When changing position and resting his elbows on his knees, his eyes fixed on his youngest brother, who slept soundly west of the fire pit. He and Tam were both stocky, with wide shoulders, muscular legs and ample body hair — both capable of growing generous winter beards. Tam's young mate died last autumn from too much bleeding. A woman's thing, though it wasn't known if she'd been burdened with an unborn in her belly. Tam was very young, only a slight six winters older than Bittoo. When Tam came ready for another lifemate, Har would pay the bride price and buy his young brother a new woman.

In the faint light, he saw his mate, sleeping with a daughter on each side of her slim body. Leha pleased him and so did his children. His daughters were a delight, his son was his pride. This he turned over in his mind, completely unaware of the smile that crossed his face.

His family led a good life and held status in the camp, but he suspected their lives were about to change. He'd rather everything remain the same than take the chance of their existence changing for the worse.

"Father and the girls are dead!" bellowed Bittoo, waking his entire family, including Har who accidently fell asleep with his head resting on his knees.

"Mother, we must leave here before Ceda kills us too!" the boy continued, thrashing his arms in frantic motion as though trying to ward off something only he saw.

Reacting promptly, Har pinned down Bittoo's thin arms. "We need to strap him or he'll do more damage to the winter bite on his hands," he said in desperation.

Quickly, Tam produced a narrow strip of worked reindeer hide. Har gently pulled his son's now limp body to a sitting position while Tam wrapped the soft leather thong twice around his nephew's torso and lower arms, just above the wrists.

"Mother, please! We must leave before the wolves come!" Bittoo implored loudly as Har carefully laid the boy back down on the comfortable mattress of furs.

Wide-eyed Teaa had listened to her brother's terrifying words stating she was dead. Then the young child, of just over three summers old, saw her father and Uncle Tam tie straps around Bittoo. Panicked, she dove head-first beneath her bed furs.

Mupo, seeing her little sister's need to hide from the unreal scene, lifted the heavy pelts and crawled in to reassure the youngster. "It's only a dream that Bittoo has. He'll be better tomorrow," she assured Teaa, trying to comfort herself as well. "You see...we're not dead." She gathered the tearful child to her.

"Ssh, ssh, son. I'm here," Leha responded solemnly to Bittoo's earlier words while cautiously standing near his head.

"It's obvious he hasn't any idea what he's saying," Har grumbled, shaking his head so hard his long graying hair swished across his face.

Leha's eyes grew round, tears ran down her fair skinned checks. Her son's words struck her hard — his voice not sounding like him, talking like someone crazy. Was a dark demon going to kill them all? Was he that demon? She knelt and hesitantly touched her son's forehead. "He burns up," she announced, sounding shocked at her own discovery. With a single movement, she jerked the tan hide off the feverish boy.

Her words sent the five adults into action.

Har again lifted his son, and Tam untied the knot and unwound the wrap to remove the boy's tunic.

Leha showed surprise, she wasn't at all sure she wanted Bittoo unbound. But in a breath of time, the two brothers secured his arms, and she applied the bear fat salve she prepared. The winter bite had now turned Bittoo's hands unsightly shades of purple.

Using two long bone scoops, Kata carried hot stones from the hearth and dropped them into a rawhide pouch that Cir had filled with snow. She then rummaged through her pack of fine sewing, where she kept the soft suede for her unborn baby's clothing. She selected a golden brown piece the size of two flat palms, dipped it into the cool water and slightly wrung it out, then walked to Leha's side and handed the wet hide to her sister-in-law, who gratefully placed it on Bittoo's sweating chest.

Kata removed the wet rocks, returning them to the coals. She continued, repeating the water-heating process, adding more heated stones and willow tree bark. The pregnant woman steeped the mixture until the hot water withdrew all the medicine from the bark. When cooled, she strained a small amount into a wooden ash bowl and delivered it to Leha. Kata and Har lifted Bittoo's head, while Leha spooned the untasty willow water into his unsuspecting mouth.

"He's not swallowing the medicine," Leha informed the others while trying to wipe up the spilled liquid from Bittoo's chest. No sooner did she speak than she brought forth a shiny smooth bone from one of her woman's healing bags. Putting the hollow bone to her lips, she sucked the bitter mixture from the bowl. While keeping suction on one end of the bone with her finger tip, she slowly trickled it deep into the boy's mouth. "Good, this time he drinks," she said in relief. "We'll give him more fever medicine later."

Leha pulled her sleeping robe next to Har who leaned with his back against the earthen lodge. She joined him in his sitting position, covering them both with the soft fur. She meant to stay awake until the rest of the family fell asleep, then discuss Bittoo's fate with her man. Her tired eyes searched the familiar dwelling, concentrating on its circular structure and many contents.

Little ringlets of smoke escaped between the top two ladder rungs, fading upward into the blackness of the night air. A large support post stood in the center of the floor and extended upward, snugly against the inside of the domed ceiling. The sturdy ladder had been secured at an angle to the support beam by using wet rawhide strips, which tightened steadfastly when they dried. When one reached the top of the ladder, and looked straight down into the hearth that person usually got a face full of choking smoke. And as often happened, when someone entered, mud or snow fell from their reindeer boots onto those sitting below, around the fire.

Leha was most fond of this portion of the pit house—underneath the ladder by the hearth with its rawhide pouches and paunches, sling baskets and drying herbs hanging from antler tines that jutted from the rafters. And here, the dirt shelf housed horn, bone, and shell spoons and ladles, wooden bowls, coiled and plaited waterproof baskets, bits of left-over food, her ivory fire starter kit, and other useful utensils. The fire where Grandmother Hearth, the fire spirit lived, belonged to her as all fires in all lodges belonged to the women who tended them. The only exceptions being the sacred fire pits of the shamans.

"Your thoughts are deep," Har voiced aloud, never having taken his eyes off his mate since she first sat down at his side.

"Our home is good," she replied, temporarily skirting the real issue. "You give us all we need."

"It seems unimportant when our boy is sick."

"He's possessed," Leha blurted.

"His strangeness may just be the heat of the fever, but if not, Derk can perform a ceremony to drive the demon away."

"You may think Derk can perform a miracle, but I don't believe our shaman capable of such a feat," she snapped. "Something happened out there on the ice, so horrifying it caused our son to be delirious. He screamed that you, Teaa, and Mupo are all dead, and Ceda intends to kill. And you know Ceda doesn't address humans. She sends her water children to do it for her."

In the filtered light, Har nodded in agreement, but Leha failed to see.

"Ceda doesn't disguise herself as an animal. Anyone can talk to deities, but they don't reply...only lesser spirits such as birds, fish, or other animals reply, and they don't claim to be deities."

Although her voice remained a whisper, her tone grew sharp. "Ceda did not speak to Bittoo...he did not see her. It's impossible, therefore I say his mind is deranged."

Har reached over and touched Bittoo's forehead. He reasoned there must be some truth to Leha's outburst, especially, when taking into account the hard evidence of the disgusting salmon eggs, which she knew nothing about. Even so, he was unwilling to give up on his only son.

3

For an immeasurable amount of time, Derk gazed into the nothingness of the night feeling the forces of power in the air. He stood captivated, thinking to do otherwise would be a terrible misdeed. The shaman was unsure whether he could pull away from its grip even if he tried. The entity represented authority. No, that wasn't correct. IT IS AUTHORITY!

The mysterious one first visited Bittoo, inflicting harm on the boy, and now the force was in his presence. He felt surrounded by it.He could almost sense the spirit mocking him, playing with him in some unnatural way only it might understand. This is a test, he decided. *"I must not cower."* With that, an enormous burst of wind knocked him to the ground.

Struggling to his knees took all his effort, but before he could push himself upright, a blast of hot decaying air threw him back down. The stench was of rotting fish, so rancid he retched.

At that very instant, he realized the entity demanded humility from him, and so, the shaman of the Frozen Duck Band spread himself face down in the snow.

Pressure from the violent wind continued to pin the middle-aged man, of thirty autumns, to the white earth. His heart beat forcibly against the frozen crust, and the deafening roar in his ears mimicked a multitude of demons pleading to be released from their own private torments.

As the snow began to melt under and around his prone body, he briefly wondered if this was the warm salmon wind that sometimes turned winter snow and ice into liquid. He choked on the slush collecting around his face, causing him to inhale a lungful of cold water mingled with air. Strangling, he rose to his knees, gagging on the foreign element while gasping for a clear breath. "I'm free of it," he mumbled aloud as his erratic breathing came to a halt.

Without moving his head, he scanned the darkness for any remaining signs of his unknown attacker. Just a cool breeze ruffled his wet hair. The smell of decaying fish had vanished. "Is this a sample of more to come?" he asked himself. "What are we in for?"

With callused hands, he felt the crisp edge of the snow and traced its contour. He pulled his hands back as if burnt. His mind could hardly grasp the evidence: The snow had thawed under him in a perfect human shape - his shape - and had melted clear through to the ground. He was kneeling in a pool formed by his own body and an unknown source of intense heat.

Scrambling out of the depression, he rushed toward his lodge, willing his logical mind to think. When passing Har's family dwelling, he overheard Bittoo's panic-stricken words begging his mother to leave with him. The shaman sped up his already fast stride until reaching the ladder and the security of his lodge.

"Good," he said aloud, talking to himself as was his habit. "My fire still smolders." He quickly peeled off his wet clothing, leaving them in a heap on the rush mat.

His woman snatched the garments and draped them over a ladder rung. She studied her man cautiously and silently.

"You can stay here only if you remain quiet, or you can go to your sister's hut."

His bossy words startled her, for he never ordered her in all their seasons together. She deposited herself on the bed furs to watch her man for clues which might unravel the day's strange events.

While still naked, Derk sprinkled cedar bark shaving onto the coals and deeply inhaled the aroma. Using his owl-winged fan, he slowly directed the smoke over the entire front side of his body. Next, he added more cedar and attained another mass of smoke, turned his back on it, and purified the rest of his frame while all the time softly singing praises to Creator One Breath.

He always felt clean and protected after smudging himself, but this time was different—he still felt vulnerable—extremely vulnerable. "I don't want to deal with this," he declared. "I don't know how to handle it, and I haven't any idea what I'm dealing with. By Creator One Breath, it should show its true self."

With an almost defeated attitude, he spread his white, sacred blanket of rabbit pelts over the ground and lowered his exhausted limbs onto the short furs. She Dog and her two overgrown whelps laid at the edge of the ritual blanket, awaiting a friendly pat from their master.

Last night, he experienced a fleeting dream where his wife lay dead outside their dwelling. He'd fought off a wolverine. The air throughout the village reeked heavily of death. Distorted bodies, men, women and children, lay scattered among the pit houses. Out of the corner of his eye, he spied a massive salmon, which vanished as fast as it appeared. So horrifying the nightmare, he awoke in a cold sweat and couldn't return to sleep.

He spent the early morning mulling over the ghastly dream, the meaning of which he failed to understand. Yet there was a message of enormous size hidden within its fiendish contents. Now, recalling the entire events of the day, he realized that everything happening, with him and with Bittoo, tied together in some morbid way.

He was the sole shaman for the Frozen Duck Band, and sometimes felt unfit for such an important role. His woman disagreed with him, often praising his deeds. Even so, this time he felt totally powerless.

Long ago, during a hunting trip with his father, the star people gave him the special gift to interpret dreams, visions and signs of nature. The first night out, he dozed lightly.

As a boy he desperately wanted to prove his hunting skills to his father, and the restless

anticipation of the hunt finally woke him. He sat on
the pine needle mattress, rubbing his eyes, wishing
for more sleep. The sky had exploded with a
magnificent display of shooting stars. He was
amazed by the show, wondering if there were going
to be any lights left for those in the Land of the Souls
when it finished.

Continuing throughout the latter portion of the
night, the stars had showered the hillsides with their
splendor. When thinking he could no longer keep
his eyes open, a flash of dim green light,
accompanied with a swooshing sound, then a loud
thud, disappeared a short distance from their
temporary camp. At the first hint of day, he busily
scoured the vicinity. His father found him sitting
on a decaying stump, staring down at a depression
in the earth.

"There's a star in that hole, father," he had stated,
flatly, unable to comprehend such a wonder
himself.The older man's right eyebrow raised high
on his forehead as he edged his way closer to the
spot. "Why do you call it a star?"

"I watched the fire balls until nighttime bordered
on daylight. One fell in this direction and when
morning came, I began to look."

Still skeptical, his father trudged through the
sparse underbrush until he stood directly above his
son. The tall man could see a rock the size of two
fists, resting in the bottom of the hole.

"There's warmth coming from it," the son
explained. "I don't know if the star will cool or
remain warm."

His father had gingerly placed his hand over the
hole, then swiftly yanked his arm back. "You're

right," he said, perplexed. He slowly passed his hand across the area again. "You've found something very mysterious. Are you sure it fell from the sky?"

"The darkness rained sky rocks for a very long time. Moon Watcher may be the only light left in the night sky. This one made a noise when falling and also when hitting the ground. I'd like to stay here to see if it cools."

He frequently thought about that day some fifteen summers ago, when he acquired a bit of the heavens sent by the sky spirits. He turned the crusty rock over in his hands, hoping it would give him a clue to the day's confusing events. "You're still a mystery to me, little star...where are your answers?" he said, placing the stone on the blanket beside his leg and dropping a short wooden branch onto the burning coals.

He ambled over to his woman, took a red fox bed fur from the pile she rested on and without making eye contact, slung the robe around his numbed frame and returned to his fire pit.

"I can do one thing," he announced as he studied the trench enclosing his hearth. A shallow ditch circled the hearth, marking it as the sacred fire of a shaman.

Taking a deep breath of confidence, he fumbled through one of his many medicine bundles and produced a thick leather pouch. Hastily shoving his feet into his wet boots, he scrambled up the ladder with only the robe around his shoulders, his owl claw amulet hanging from his neck, and the tiny bag clutched tightly in his fist.

He reached Har's lodge and stood outside for a length of time, composing himself as was expected of a holy man. He gazed into the sky through the endless space, where he imagined his star power originated. Then raising both arms, allowing the fur to drop from his shoulders, he cried out to the spirit who gave life to all. "Creator One Breath, I beg you to protect this dwelling and its people." As an afterthought, he added, "And the village of Frozen Duck Band."

He walked slowly, digging his feet deep into the snow, hollowing a narrow channel around the pit house. When completing one round, he removed needle sharp porcupine quills from his worn pouch. "I place the family of Har in the center of the sacred circle, and I shall scatter the armor of this animal for further protection," he said with reverence, finishing his short speech.

For the second time, and with less difficulty, he retraced his steps around the lodge, leaving the black tipped quills in the man-made furrow.

Hoping his medicine would prove adequate until young Bittoo could be questioned, he wrapped himself in the robe of fox, and with a new lightness to his gait, headed back to the refuge of his warm shelter.

4

The disoriented boy thought he heard chanting and a shuffling noise, but he couldn't be certain—his skull pounded. He lay very still, not knowing if he was in a safe place. Without opening his eyes, Bittoo sought out recognizable scents and sounds. Due to the warmth of an unseen fire and the odor of smoke, he realized he was somewhere indoors and ventured to open both eyes. He felt overjoyed, seeing his everyday surroundings. After taking a couple of strong breaths, his joy evaporated. From somewhere, a husky voice echoed familiar words.

"It's your choice, stupid boy."

Bittoo moaned and again inhaled deeply, trying to calm his overburdened mind. The loud throbbing in his head subsided, but there was agonizing pain in his hands. He couldn't get his arms to move and could barely wiggle his fingers. He willed his shoulders to rise, and as they did, his arms followed, tugging at the thongs. His exhaustive effort proved useless, only pulling the straps even tighter.

Attempting to sit upright, he rolled over on his right side, crushing his pinned hand.

Har's family was awakened by Bittoo's piercing scream. All eyes turned toward the now conscious boy, as Har and Leha scrambled to his side.

"You're conscious," his father stated, smiling down at his son's suffering face. "We've been worried."

"I don't feel well and my hands hurt dreadfully. Why am I tied? Did I go mad?" Bittoo stammered, finding it difficult to speak with such thirst and his tongue sticking to the roof of his mouth.

"Ah, he's still hot but cooler than earlier when we first checked him," Leha reported, reaching for the bowl that housed the fever-reducing medicine. She kept her eyes fastened on her son, waiting — hoping that something, anything in his manner might give her a clue as to whether he was truly demented. She spooned the willow liquid into his mouth then gave him a large drink of water from a stomach paunch that she removed from the support beam.

Har looked closely at the boy's face and saw no signs of winter bite, other than a reddish flush that experience told him would disappear and leave no lasting scars.

"My arms are tied, father," Bittoo repeated, still waiting for someone to give him an explanation.

"Bittoo, I'm going to unbind you but be careful not to bang or even touch your hands against anything. You have winter bite," Har revealed, untying his son's wrists with great care.

Leha's eyes grew round. Keep him tied up, she screamed to herself, he may be dangerous. Ashamed of herself for thinking such a thing, she remained quiet.

The family gathered at the head of Bittoo's sick bed and also saw the results of the boy's misfortune.

"Give me more light to check him," Har stated, his words sounding like a harsh command.

Tam disappeared outside and returned with a torch which he lit from hearth embers. Holding the torch at eye level so as not to burn the ceiling material, he angled the bright light, allowing Har to finish his examination.

"He's lucky," Har announced to everyone's disbelief.

"Husband, our son's hands are distorted with large, ugly blisters," Leha argued.

"The blisters on his left hand are filled with clear liquid rather than blood. That's a favorable sign. The blisters cover the hand, stretching to the fingertips. That, too, is a good sign. He broke most of the blisters on his spear throwing hand when rolling over and probably damaged the underneath skin. I've witnessed winter bite many times before. I don't think he'll lose his fingers."

"At the seal hunt, a man from the Reindeer Band had a black finger," Mupo stated. "His finger fell off before we left. He put the gruesome thing in his medicine bundle and wore it around his neck." She hung her head as though deeply embarrassed.

"Your brother won't lose his fingers," Har sternly repeated. "This could be important for you to remember...if blisters fill with blood, such a sign indicates winter bite of the worst kind. Bittoo's aren't filled with blood."

Little Teaa crawled between her Uncle Cir's legs, exiting directly at Bittoo's head. She pulled herself up as tall as possible, attempting to gain his attention and peered straight into her brother's dull eyes. "I be not dead!" she spat furiously at him, then burrowed into her mother's protective lap.

Astonished, and with his mouth gaping, Bittoo looked at each member of his mute family, then back at Teaa. "Of course you're not dead," he assured her.

"Mupo dead too. You say so," the youngster argued, turning her head to peer at her brother.

"I must have had a bad dream, little one," he lied bleakly. "I'm sorry you were scared."

"Your brother needs rest," Leha interrupted, shooing Teaa away. "And my stomach growls. I'll cook Bittoo's salmon," she said, wanting everyone to move away in case her son got crazy again.

Stunned by Leha's statement, the three men stopped dead. Quick thinking Tam replied first. "I prefer reindeer meat."

"That sounds tasty," agreed Har.

Finally catching on to why his brothers were asking for reindeer meat, slower thinking Cir popped up adding, "The venison is already cooked, and Kata and I should hurry. The two of us must check the snares we set yesterday before any trapped animals chew through the cordage or destroy my traps."

"You men puzzle me," Leha fussed, shrugging her shoulders. "When there's fresh fish, you want smoked venison, even though you've been eating reindeer for days."

The family gathered around the hearth on woven mats, eating a hasty meal. Teaa teetered on a chunk of tree limb, destined for the fire.

"I hate to leave," Cir told his relatives. "We'll hurry, but it may take us a couple of days, depending on the size of our cache. We covered a large area those two days when setting the traps...all the way down to the low meadow. But Tam should stay here this time. You may need him."

Tam and Har nodded in agreement.

After Cir and his mate left, the others quietly remained by the fire, each deeply occupied in their own thoughts. Har was anxious to question Bittoo, but the boy had fallen asleep.

Twice, he and and his youngest brother, Tam, made eye contact. Har noticed the concern on Tam's face and in his fidgeting behavior. Leha appeared the most distressed. She'd probably pack-up the girls and go elsewhere if she knew about the salmon's embryos. His woman would eventually be told, along with Kata, but only after he talked to both Bittoo and the shaman.

He wanted to believe the shaman capable of whatever needed to be done. Furthermore, with Kata carrying an unborn in her belly, he hoped Cir wouldn't tell her about the fish eggs while out on the trail. She might start her child pains with only Cir to help her, and there were many remaining moons before the baby was due. They already lost Tam's mate last autumn, he didn't wish to lose another family member.

"I should've spread more bear salve on Bittoo's winter bite before he slept...especially the hand with the broken blisters," Leha said.

She interrupted Har's and Tam's thoughts, they looked at her blankly, but didn't reply. Leha looked at them questioningly, shrugged her shoulders, then addressed Mupo. "If you cut meat for your brother, I'll fix something special. He can't use his hands. We'll feed him small morsels until they're better healed."

"Berries, mamma?" Teaa screeched, rolling off the log onto a scattering of wooden chips and slightly scraping her knees. "Me want berries!" she cried, jumping up and down, clapping, unaware of her scratched knees.

Leha tried to make her voice sound normal. "Yes, little one, if your Uncle Cir hasn't taken them all for snare bait, we'll feast on berries," she replied teasingly, walking to the dirt shelf housing her cooking utensils. "We'll eat blackberries, Bittoo's favorite," she added, smiling at her youngest daughter, knowing full well all three of her children favored the small dark fruit. And knowing full well her smile was false.

She squatted, pulled a hide covering back and all but her legs disappeared into a dug out storage hole in the side of the lodge. Her own body blocked the light, yet she always arranged the contents the same every fall and knew the placement by memory. Her trembling hands immediately seized the correct container.

She backed out of the storage pit and dumped dried berries into an intestine paunch. After adding water, she hung the mixture on an antler tine protruding from the rafters. By then, Teaa discovered her scraped knees and was cuddled in her father's strong arms.

"I be hurt," she whined, hoping for sympathy from her mother as well.

"Would you like a bite of Bittoo's deer meat?" asked Mupo, attempting to shift her young sister's attention away from her puny injuries.

Teaa wrinkled up her little nose in refusal.

"Father," a weak voice called above the crackling fire.

As the two brothers stood, Har gestured for Leha, and the girls to remain by the hearth.

She was happy to stay put, keeping the girls from their brother.

"Don't use your hands, son," the concerned man repeated, uncertain whether Bittoo even remembered being told. "Do you know what happened to you on the ice?" Har asked after he checked the boy's hands and touched his forehead.

"I know, father, but I don't understand. I wasn't dreaming, I'm sure of that," Bittoo moaned. "I went out early and caught four nice-sized salmon."

"Did you notice anything different about those fish?" asked Tam.

"Nothing uncle, just that they were big," Bittoo answered, giving no more thought to Tam's question. "There was this large fish, unbelievably large, much more so than the ones I caught. She said her name was Ceda. She stuck her head through the hole in the ice and angrily scolded me. She looked way too fat for the rest of her to fit through my fishing hole."

Har swallowed hard. "Are you sure she spoke to you?" he asked, but without waiting for an answer, he firmly addressed Leha from across the room. "You take the girls to the shaman's lodge. Tell Derk we need him. Stay there until he returns."

"Yes, Ceda spoke, and she was furious with me," the boy said, noticing his father and uncle exchanging glances of disbelief. "I'm afraid," he murmured.

"We found you unconscious in a heap, and you must have been there all day. That's why you have winter bite on your hands. Your face is untouched, because when we found you, your face rested against the fur of your sleeve.

"I tried to get up and fell."

Tam fed his nephew a meager three pieces of cut up venison. The boy refused the rest, so he placed the remaining chunks on the dirt shelf to the back side of Bittoo's sick bed. "It's a very unusual thing that's happened to you, nephew. If you need protection though, we'll protect you."

"Is there any protection against deities?" questioned Bittoo, his frightened eyes darting back and forth from Har to Tam.

"There's protection from bad spirits," Har affirmed, despite the gnawing in his belly.

"Ya, Ho. Ya, Ho." The voice of Derk blasted through the smoke hole, addressing the occupants. "I've been waiting to see you," the shaman wheezed as he awkwardly climbed down the ladder, unsure of his footing. He carried a bulky seal skin pack which rattled with each clumsy step he took.

Tam arranged the floormats and piled them with furs. The three men made themselves comfortable at Bittoo's side.

Derk placed his bundle in front of himself but left the container closed. "Yesterday, your father carried you off the ice. You seemed out of your mind and cried out some disturbing things. You said Ceda would kill, and the mountain cats would eat us."

The frightened boy nodded his head in agreement, before Derk even finished speaking.

"Start at the beginning."

Tam offered his nephew a drink of cool water, and after a brief pause, Bittoo began his tale, speaking rapidly wanting to get it behind him. "I went fishing and caught four salmon. I placed all four with their heads facing the hole in the ice, so their spirits could return to the water and rejoin their mother. I arranged them in accordance to the first four directions - east, south, north, and west."

"You offered Ceda's children to the four directions?" the shaman asked, aghast by the young man's confession.

"Yes, I wanted to catch three more fish in order to honor all seven directions," Bittoo replied, alarmed by the look on the shaman's face.

Hastily, Derk opened his pack and removed a dirty leather pouch packed between two halves of a shell. "Continue! Continue!" the shaman demanded, pressing the boy as he deposited cedar shavings into the clam bowl, spilling some on the furs.

Dumbfounded by the shaman's abruptness, Bittoo remained silent.

Derk found his owl wing fan and waved the feathers at Bittoo, indicating he expected the boy to finish what he started.

Bittoo looked at his father, pleading for help.

"He's terrified," Har said sharply.

Derk searched Bittoo's expression, discovering sheer panic. He reached over and patted the sick boy's shoulder then rose and went to the woman's hearth, lighting the cedar with a burning branch. "I must be patient, or the boy will remain quiet," he muttered to himself. When returning to Bittoo's side, he fanned the smoke with the feathered wing, sending the cloudy air over and around all three men, the boy and his sickbed.

"What happened next?" the shaman inquired in a slower and calmer tone, while putting the still burning clam shell between the boy and himself. He unwrapped his star rock and fondled the stone between his palms.

"A big salmon stuck its head through the ice hole and proclaimed to be Ceda, mother of all water beasts, accusing me of playing with power," Bittoo recalled. "I became speechless, she was so enraged." He paused, waiting for the shaman to comment but continued when Derk gave no response. "Then I looked into the water and saw Frozen Duck Camp. People lay dead everywhere. Ceda said she'd starve us by not granting her water children to be caught."

Har growled at the possibility. Over half the band's food source came from the water. It'd mean slow starvation.

"But Ceda admitted she wasn't allowed to punish me this time, because Creator One Breath wouldn't permit it," he added.

Tam and Har looked perplexed, but the slight smile on the shaman's face indicated relief. "At least we won't starve to death any time soon." Derk laughed, creating a less somber mood.

"Ceda told me I'm to be a great tusu, and my children's children's children, for many generations, will be great shamans. She gave me the choice of whether to walk the path of power or not. If I do, she'll be my spirit guide." Derk grew thoughtful as he went over Bittoo's amazing words. His eyes ceased to focus as he tugged at something from his memory.

"This is impossible," Har said, clearly uneasy with his son's account. "Ceda is a deity, she doesn't talk with mere men, and she doesn't become anyone's spirit guide. You're being tormented by a black spirit."

A lump caught in Bittoo's throat, one that he couldn't swallow. He attempted to pinch himself in hopes of waking from this nightmare, but his injured fingers wouldn't move.

Expecting some type of guidance, everyone stared at Derk. He shrugged his shoulders. "I don't profess to know the mind of a deity whether it be the sky deity, the earth or the water deity. I've never talked to one, nor heard of anyone who has. But night before last, I dreamed a similar event and witnessed our people dying. I even beat a wolverine with my walking stick." He watched Bittoo closely.

"I left that part out, but I saw it too," Bittoo acknowledged, still keeping quiet about seeing Derk's dead mate. He looked deeply into the shaman's eyes. "So you dreamed what I saw before I saw it?"

"Almost," the shaman replied, gently blowing on the cedar which had nearly died out. "For just an instant, I saw Ceda, but we didn't talk. Was my woman dead in your vision?"

The question took Bittoo off guard, and for the second time, he could only confirm by nodding his head.

Satisfied the boy was telling the truth, he proceeded. "There are many things we must consider. I believe Bittoo experienced a powerful vision, and it appears Ceda is now his spirit guide. He'll be a shaman of strong medicine with a deity as his totem, and according to her, so will his offsprings. Because of my dream, I believe his story." His facial expression grew serious. "The boy provoked her. Even though she's unable to punish him now, there may be another time."

"She called me a stupid boy. I'd rather have a normal animal spirit!" Bittoo blurted, the words flopping out of his mouth before he could stop them.

"Don't talk rashly," Har pleaded with his son. "You'll make her hostile."

"That's true," the shaman stated, looking directly into Bittoo's eyes. "It's no longer a matter of what you want, but a matter of what is best for the entire band. The mother of all water creatures implied she'd destroy our village. I suspect if Ceda is rejected, she might follow through with her threat."

"How do we appease her?" asked Har.

"Besides Bittoo following the path of a shaman, I'm uncertain," Derk replied. "I guess she didn't make that clear. Is there anything else? Did you forget to tell us something?"

"I told you everything," Bittoo answered.

Tam cringed, dreading the words he felt compelled to say. "Cir and I cleaned Bittoo's salmon. The fish were all female with roe in them, yet none of the four had turned the red spawning color."

As Tam went outside, the shaman quietly rubbed his battered rock.

"We stashed his catch in the snow. There were eggs in the salmon, but most of them have developed into small fish...inside their mother's bellies!" Har explained excitedly.

Bittoo shrunk from his father's words. He didn't believe them. The statement seemed too outlandish —too unreal. Maybe if he went to sleep, he'd wake up and every thing would be normal.

"Nothing surprises me now," the shaman replied suddenly as an uncontrolled twitch in his face caused the star symbol tattooed on his upper cheek to dance and give evidence of his true feelings.

Tam returned, holding the salmon at arms' length as if afraid he might become contaminated. They remained fastened with cordage that ran through their gills. He placed the baby fish and eggs in a shallow woven basket which he thrust at the shaman.

"I've never heard of such a thing!" Derk said as he fingered through the embryos. "They really are miniature salmon! Has anyone else fished in the lake since Bittoo?"

"Froom fished, very early this morning and caught one female salmon. When he cleaned it, I saw nothing unusual about the roe," Tam recalled.

"What does she want from us?" Har asked of the holy man.

"She follows Creator One Breath's instructions, although I don't think she's very happy about doing so. For some reason, it must be important for Bittoo to become a shaman, and not a hunter, as he wishes.

Except, I can't see the significance of these baby fish,"
the shaman responded, rising to his feet to examine
the four mature salmon which Tam held.

Derk handled each salmon dutifully and
thoroughly, turning them over and even peering
down their mouths. "You overlooked something
when you cleaned these fish," he said, a smile
crossing his face. "I understand now...even if it still
seems impossible. These four salmon aren't female.
Look at the blue-green color on their heads. They're
males...all of them. The adult salmon represents
your son, and the baby fish represent his offsprings.
This indicates the promise Ceda gave the boy. Bittoo
is destined to be a tusu, the beginning of a new line
of powerful ones." He looked over at Bittoo. The
boy's eyes were closed.

With doubt racing through his mind, Tam walked
to the hearth and inspected Bittoo's catch. He slowly
turned the thong in his hand, causing the heavy line
to twist. The light of the fire shown on the salmon's
scales and produced flashes of silvery specks. He
believed the shaman saw the colors whether they
were there or not, for the holy man possessed a rare
gift for seeing things no one else saw. And the
shaman had always been correct.

Astounded by the shaman's statement Har stared
at the man without even seeing him. It was a
momentous claim Derk made and his words would
surely change all their lives. Earlier, he felt the
change might turn out to be a disastrous one. Yet
now it sounded rather promising. But why chose
Bittoo? The boy never once showed any desire
toward following the path of a shaman. Har looked
at his sleeping son, then at Derk.

The shaman rolled the star around in his hands, grateful he remembered to bring the mystical rock. When anything needed interpreting, the answers came to him more easily and clearly with the sky rock in his possession. But many questions remained unanswered. Even so, he felt relieved to have a successor. No one else in the band appeared gifted toward this work. True, two young men and an adolescent girl expressed a desire to become shamans. None of them seemed especially talented in that direction though, plus none had been counseled by their spirit helper to follow the sacred shaman trail.

His teacher had been Noork, a wise old soothsayer, who took him under instruction soon after finding his falling star. Noork passed shamanistic secrets onto his legacy. He soon discovered that much of the ancient knowledge he inherited, wasn't his to use. He could only pass the vital secrets down later to his apprentice.

Now that student lay in a bed directly in front of him, and Ceda proclaimed the boy to be a great tusu. He would be willing, even content, to turn his duties over to Bittoo once the boy learned the ways. But there was a nasty churning in his gut—something wasn't right—something was very much wrong. *Why is a holy man with such power needed at this time?*

5

Gaaf fidgeted with the fringe dangling from his medicine pouch. Recently, he completed the ornate bag, and was rather proud of it. Soon, the small satchel would replace his infant sickness bag that all children wore until they became of age. Next spring he'd seek his vision quest, hopefully filling the new pouch with sacred totem items to help him become a skilled hunter.

He worried, for not all young men who sought their vision quest returned home. And some returned home without ever having a vision. Well, he and Bittoo made a pact. They meant to go out together, then separate, keeping in shouting distance of one another. That way they expected to remain safe from predators, but more importantly, both of them decided not to come home until each had been visited by their spirit brothers. Returning to the village without experiencing their quest and proving their coming of age would be too shameful.

Each spring, all six bands living on the island met at the Great Sea to hunt seals. The six bands made up the Clan of the Ancient Humans. The Fur Seal Band was situated closest to the hunting ground, and his fiancee and Bittoo's fiancee both belonged to that band. And both young women were expected to be at the hunt.

Last year, neither of the girls foreheads were tattooed with the blue dotted marks along the hairline that indicate the coming of age. Life seemed full of trials designed to bring shame upon one's manhood, the girls coming of age first was surely one of them.

As he studied Bittoo's fluttering eyelids and his facial gestures, he wondered if his friend was experiencing a dream or was Bittoo truly possessed by something evil, like many in camp were saying. If a dark demon lived in Bittoo and wouldn't leave, then much would change. For sure, they couldn't strike out together for their vision quest. But worst of all, what would happen to Bittoo? Would Bittoo ever be the same? Would he lose his best friend?

Three times he inhaled large amounts of air and three times he exhaled slowly. His hands felt clammy. He leaned closer to Bittoo - but not too close. A twinge of panic caught in his throat. "Ya, Ho," he whispered.

"Ya, Ho, Gaaf," Bittoo sleepily replied, appearing pleased to see him. "Where's everyone?"

Gaaf's jaws flopped open. "Ah...tonight the...ah...story-telling began. The villagers are...ah...squeezed into Froom's dwelling." His eyes showed fear as he studied Bittoo.

"Thank Creator One Breath, they didn't come here." Bittoo heaved a huge sigh of relief.

"The entire camp...ah...wanted to start the story-telling at your lodge, in hopes that...ah...you might explain what happened on the lake. You shouted some pretty bizarre things. Ah...everyone's frightened. But Har and the shaman refused to let them come near you."

"Good." Bittoo grinned broadly. "No one else needs to know."

"Oh." Gaaf's shaky voice echoed disappointment. "I...I only slipped away to see if you were all right."

"My hands have winter bite...almost useless." Bittoo raised both for Gaaf's inspection. "But father says they'll heal."

"You're fortunate the damage is only temporary. I worried when seeing your father carrying you on his shoulders. And no one told me anything." Gaaf's eyes darted toward the exit. "Should I go now?"

"No, don't go. But stop staring at me like I'm going to bite you or something. I won't bite, and I won't explain to anyone else, just you. I'll go mad if I don't tell someone who'll understand me."

"Are you well enough?"

"My father, my uncle and the shaman care less how I feel. And what happened makes no sense at all. The shaman maintains it was my vision quest." Bittoo's voice rose as he looked into Gaaf's face. "But I didn't seek a vision. I didn't prepare for one. I did not deprive my body of food or drink nor sing any spirit songs. It's unreal!"

Gaaf's eyes grew large. "What's unreal?" He wiped his sweaty palms on his fur tunic.

"When fishing, a large, ugly salmon talked to me in a mean voice, showing me a picture of the village with almost everyone in camp dead."

Gaaf's mouth dropped open. He wiped his hands again.

"Don't try to picture it, it looked too horrible!"

Gaaf closed his gaping mouth.

"That fish even called me a stupid boy and became furious because I didn't pay proper homage to her. She expects me to become a tusu, and she called herself Ceda."

"Is that possible? Ceda governs all water creatures."

"The shaman thinks so. Earlier, after waking, I heard her disgusting voice, again, calling me stupid. And the other morning, I think she summoned me out of my sleep and lured me onto the ice."

"Maybe, Ceda plans on haunting you...chase you around until you give into her wishes."

"She said I could be a great tusu, and my future generations will also be holy men."

"That's an important honor. If that was actually your vision quest, and Ceda is your totem, then you can remove your nose ring. You have the protection of your spirit totem now and no longer need it."

"She makes me think I need protection from her. It shouldn't be this way," Bittoo said bitterly. "My desire is to be a hunter, not a shaman. I fear her and think she dislikes me. Ceda wanted to punish me, but said she wasn't allowed. The water deity may bring her vengeance against Frozen Duck Camp, otherwise why did she show me all those rotting bodies? The whole thing makes me crazy. Ceda says I can make up my own mind, but I'm not given a choice, not really."

"She traps you like an animal!"

The boys remained quiet for a very long time, each mulling over Bittoo's few options.

Eventually, Gaaf broke the silence with words he hoped would help his friend. "You don't need to make up your mind tonight. Maybe not for many days. Put it off as long as you can and see what happens."

"I could try that," Bittoo answered, sounding as though he felt slightly better.

"If you did become a shaman, your life would be good. Holy men are provided for, receiving many presents for their services. Everyone listens to them. No one does bad things to a shaman. People are afraid to."

"Shamans are pampered too much. Look at Derk. He's required to take either a guard or his dogs with him for protection when he goes beyond camp."

"That's the way with all the shamans in all the bands."

"When he hunts, he's never allowed to take risks. Shamans are always situated behind a boulder or tree as if they're hiding. They never get in the middle of the action. No holy man will ever become a great hunter if he hides."

"Already we're hunters, and we make a good hunting team," Gaaf boasted. "Remember the wounded mountain cat you and I stalked and killed?" He hesitated then asked, "What about our plans to journey around the island?"

"We'll still go and explore everything on the island and visit the other five bands before the time comes for us to take mates. We'll discover new places and do new things. And hunt every day we're gone."

"And get away from here." Gaaf's face lit up. "You know, shamans travel. They roam more than anyone. Derk takes some very long journeys. He spends much time with other holy leaders in their villages." The statement proved inspiring, and Gaaf looked pleased with himself for thinking of it.

"Derk must have wonderful adventures," Bittoo reasoned sullenly.

"Something else bothers me. This spring we planned to go on our vision quest together. But you already met your spirit animal and received your vision. As a shaman, you aren't permitted to go with me when I seek mine," Gaaf concluded.

"What others want doesn't matter. I'll go anyway. Even if I must sneak away. We have through the season of the heavy snows to figure out a plan."

Gaaf wavered, then slowly and clearly, in an earnest tone, spoke up. "If you decide to follow the path of a shaman, I'll be your guard."

Bittoo studied his friend's set face. The two had always been close friends. They often talked of becoming a pair of accomplished hunters whose feats would be boasted about around the fires of all the bands. Yet now, Gaaf seemed willing to set aside his dreams to protect him.

"I'd like that," Bittoo said, looking directly into Gaaf's eyes. "With you, I'd feel safe." He cleared his throat, put his mouth near Gaaf's ear and whispered, "But I'll never walk the trail of a shaman."

6

Earlier than usual, a crowd gathered for the story-telling. The night before, they met at Froom's lodge. Tonight, the villagers were jamming into Har's dwelling. Har didn't want his son exposed to the close scrutiny which seemed bound to happen this night. He feared for his son's life. The boy appeared confused and much too weak, however it would be highly rude for him to turn his neighbors away again, since he and the shaman did just that the previous evening.

Outside the pit house, anxious people huddled in groups, swiftly wagging their tongues while waiting their turn to climb down the worn ladder. Ceasing their chatter and one by one, they hastily descended into the hut. Their eyes scanned the lodge for a glimpse of Bittoo. When spotting him, they sat cross-legged on the floor as close as possible to the boy lying on his sickbed.

Like sentinels, Mupo and Gaaf sat side by side, directly in front and at the head of Bittoo's bed,

positioning themselves so no one could see his face.
"The entire camp is here," Mupo informed her
brother. "I'd count them, but I'm unable to count
that high."

"They're too shoved together to count anyway.
They look like a herd of cornered horses driven into
a box canyon by mountain cats," stated Gaaf, causing
Mupo to giggle.

"I resemble a cornered horse," Bittoo reasoned.

"The villagers don't expect you to tell your story
first. Such a request shows bad manners. Later, you
just pretend to be asleep. We can shield you from
their view, and they'll never know," Gaaf said.

"You two better not go to relieve yourselves. If
you move away and those mountain cats see me, I
won't be able to keep a straight face," Bittoo
informed them, stifling his laughter.

"Ssh," Mupo muttered, "you're going to be
overheard."

"I feel over herd-ed, by all these cats!" Bittoo said
in a fit of laughter.

Mupo reached around and slapped her palm
over her brother's mouth. "If my fist goes down your
throat," she teased, "you really will be hoarse."

Bittoo choked over the joke, and gasped deeply
for air while Gaaf hung his head, and clenched his
teeth in an effort to regain his composure.

Har and Derk watched the swarm of people who
gathered in the dwelling. They were the only
spectators standing and from their vantage could see
Mupo and Gaaf screening Bittoo from the curious
crowd.

"Their strategy might just work," Har mused,

nudging the shaman.

"I hope so, since I don't think our bandsmen should be told, not until we're positive they're not in any danger from Ceda. Already they whisper that Bittoo's possessed by a dark demon."

"Our people will react badly if they suspect Ceda, a mighty deity, has threatened to starve them," Har replied, adjusting himself against the support beam, then adding, "Possibly we should show them the roe from Bittoo's fish."

The shaman climbed part way up the narrow ladder before speaking. "I've given the matter some thought". He perched snugly on a rung. "Yet I'm unsure. If the boy made amends and erased the hard feeling between himself and Ceda, the situation could change entirely...that's the solution...the answer to this madness. And he must become a shaman."

As customary during story-telling, the children lined the front row. The excited youngsters seemed unaware of the heightened mood of their parents, who sat bunched tightly together on mats and hides, unable to move without poking the person next to them. The small open space left between the spectators and Bittoo was reserved for the story-teller.

Mupo clenched her hands, obviously uncomfortable with so many ill tempered people peering in her direction. Gaaf kneeled next to her, his arms crossed tightly against his chest. One after another, he stared-down each set of adult eyes which glared at him for blocking their view of Bittoo.

"Coort! Mammoth!" shouted a little girl. Her words disrupted the heavy atmosphere caused by the onlookers.

"Mamut! Mamut!" yelled Teaa and another youngster.

The three impatient children sat side by side, slapping their knees and giggling with anticipation. Coort's story-telling antics gained him a reputation as the most sought after narrator in Frozen Duck Band—the young ones always captivated, the adults amused by his abilities. When he last told the story of the great mammoths, he used a combination of the light from the fire and his nimble hands, casting shadows of monstrous sizes against the walls of the pit house.

Coort flaunted a long nose, a thin mouth that sprawled across his chin, and eyes which slightly protruded, giving him a frog-like appearance. The story-teller's ungainly looks added merit to his mastery of sagas, whether he depicted them as comedies or tragedies. He stood on his oversized feet and gave an enormous smile, extending from ear to ear.

"Mamut! Coort! Mamut!" prompted Teaa in her shrill voice.

"Our ancestors said," Coort began, as his bulging eyes slowly scanned his audience. "When the water sunk very, very low, large, big giants lived on our lands." Coort stretched his arms out wide to demonstrate the greatness of the beasts. "They wore a mass of shaggy hair," he conveyed, ruffling his own tangled locks, then bending his lean frame forward, touching his hands to the ground.

"Shaggy hair," a little boy repeated, ambling to his knees and messing Teaa's hair.

"Och!" she cried when his fingers caught in a

snarl. "Top that!"

Coort walked on all fours, portraying the gait of a mammoth. He swaggered from side to side, illustrating the heaviness of its bulk. "I'm a mammoth with two long tails," he said loudly, so all could hear. "A tail at each end!"

The children shook their heads at the thought of such a sight.

"No two tails," corrected Teaa.

"Yes, two tails," Coort declared. "And I have two ivory tusks...much longer than my two tails." He raised his arms, using them as tusks and playfully attacked the youngsters, causing squeals of pleasure among the little ones and a roar of laughter from the older onlookers.

Instantly, Coort's guise changed, he became serious. He knelt down and jutted his grim face into a boy's face—nose to nose. The startled child cringed. "What did the mammoth do when he spied the people of the Frozen Duck Band?" Coort demanded sternly.

"He ran far away," answered the boy.

"You're correct," Coort replied, turning his back on his audience and again mimicking the lumbering walk of the giant beasts. He swished his rear-end back and forth in exaggerated movements, and for the first time the observers noticed a long makeshift tail trailing out of his leggings and dragging on the ground.

Coort clumsily walked straight into Mupo and Gaaf. Going backwards, he retraced his prance and became tangled in his imitation tail. It yanked out of his breeches, and the story-teller went sprawling to the dirt floor.

A frenzy of animal calls rose from the crowd. The highest form of appreciation a performer could receive was when a spectator imitated the sound of his spirit guide. The noise grew piercing, the children plugged their ears and along with their parents, howled, growled, and chirped their favorite animal noises.

For lack of room, some adults found themselves unable to clap their hands or pound on their knees in approval. They didn't know whether Coort purposely or carelessly tripped on the tail but not knowing added to the allure of the drama.

"Me tell tory. Me tell," Teaa shrieked when the room quieted.

"Yes," Leha said, giving her daughter permission to do so.

Teaa stood and faced the audience. She looked at them, and for a breath of time, lost her bravery.

"You'll be fine," Leha stated, encouraging her little girl and glancing across the lodge to see if Har was watching.

Teaa gazed at the ceiling, ignoring the now friendly faces and the giggling of her playmates. Still peering upwards, she started her tale. "Long time go."

"Psst. You must begin properly," Leha whispered.

Teaa gave her mother a look of disapproval. Frustrated, she puckered her mouth into a pout and demanded, "What?"

"First you must say 'My ancestors said', then go on with your story."

"Me nancestors say," she blurted loudly, with a renewed sense of confidence, which delighted the crowd.

"That good, Teaa," two of her friends acknowledged together.

"This is her first story-telling," Har bragged to the shaman as he strained to hear his daughter's words.

"Ceda live with birdies," Teaa said softly, observing her attentive audience for their reaction. "High up," she explained, raising her short arms over her head.

"Move over a bit," Bittoo requested of Mupo and Gaaf, so he could peek between them and watch his sister.

"Ceda run way an fall in water. Splash!" she added, holding her nose, pretending to swim. The crowd laughed hysterically.

"She be fish then," Teaa informed the assemblage, in a tone that implied they were hearing this revelation for the first time.

Many silently chuckled, concerned now, that if they laughed out loud, they would miss what the girl said.

With her pudgy hand, Teaa made a slight gesture toward her brother's sickbed. "Bittoo see Ceda," she excitedly divulged, pointing in his direction. "She call him a tupid boy."

Wondering if they heard correctly, the suspicious group shifted forward. Teaa seemed as intrigued with the spectators as they were her, but the crowds uneasy manner slipped past her understanding.

"I think Bittoo tupid too," she said mischievously. The adults remained still, but the children in the front row giggled and rolled playfully on their sides in delight.

With their bodies Gaaf and Mupo closed the gap which allowed Bittoo to observe his sister. "It's time to fake sleep," Gaaf said quietly to his friend.

Teaa took the cue from her playmates, whose interest seemed comical. As if only speaking to them, she continued. "He be tupid," she alleged. "He say me be dead. He say Mupo dead. Me not dead!"

"What are you talking about?" shouted Froom, his voice full of anger. He and the entire group were connecting Teaa's strange story with Bittoo's mysterious incident on the ice. This was why they came. They'd been left in the dark far too long.

The shaman slid from the ladder. Suspecting things might get ugly, he and Har warily stepped around the sitting bodies, working their way toward Teaa, who seemed visibly shaken by Froom's harsh words.

Answering Froom, she stammered. "He say...Ceda no give us fish and all die...no more people."

"What's this child mean!" demanded Froom, just as Har reached his daughter's side.

Har swooped up Teaa and handed her to Mupo, then turned, facing his irate visitors. Alarmed by the events, the men began shouting, and the scene appeared to be getting out of hand. Tam joined his older brother and the shaman, forming what he hoped looked like a striking show of strength.

Mupo placed Teaa in Bittoo's care. The horrified child quickly disappeared beneath the bed furs, snug against her brother's back, and gripped her arms around his neck.

"I need you in the morning," Bittoo said, addressing Gaaf while attempting to loosen Teaa's strangling hold.

"If we're going to starve, I think we ought to know about it!" Froom bellowed above the turmoil and the shaking fists. Patee tugged at her husband's clothing, apparently wishing Froom would consider the safety of their baby she held.

"You give us an explanation!" yelled the band's most courageous hunter.

"Yes! Yes!" echoed many other voices.

Barc squeezed in beside Har, directly infront of his son Gaaf.

"We're not a pack of wolves fighting over a kill," cried Har, trying to instill some semblance of order.

The shaman took a step forward and addressed the band. "There's no real problem," he claimed, emphasizing the word 'real'. "Bittoo experienced a vision. Part of the time he's been delirious. We don't know everything yet," Derk related, misstating the truth to some degree. "When he's well, we'll hear the complete story."

The shaman remained firm with his teeth clenched. The tattoo on his check twitched in spasms while his fiery brown eyes dared anyone to defy him.

Froom stood. He seethed, his face turning red.

Bittoo flinched then held his breath, wondering if Froom would challenge the holy man's words. Surely, Froom realized the unhealthy results of doing such a thing. A conflict with a holy man was unheard of, yet Froom who sometimes didn't seem to belong to the clan often did the unexpected.

Froom remained quiet, collecting his thoughts, until he realized that all eyes were drawn to him.

Embarrassed and humiliated, he stalked out of the lodge. One by one, the people of the Frozen Duck Band rose and streamed after him.

'*Are you still sleeping?*' *Eagle Shadow asked his twin, sending the question directly from his mind to Bear Claw's mind.*

*Without issuing a sound his sibling gave a faint reply. '*Your story-telling buzzes in my head like bees swarming their hive.*'*

Eagle Shadow thought his brother's statement amusing, yet he was greatly alarmed by the weakness in his twin's words. If he hadn't been concentrating, he would've missed his brother's noiseless remark. Now, he was unsure whether Bear Claw would remain with him or enter the Land of the Souls to live with their ancestors.

'*Whichever path you walk, brother, I want to walk it with you.*'

His earnest request brought no response.

***

7

Derk broke free of the dense underbrush and emerged into a partial clearing on the bank of Frozen Duck Lake. Both the snow covered ground hiding root snags, and his cold condition hampered his progress. He sat forcefully on a downed limb that looked capable of supporting his weight and flogged himself with his arms, attempting to spur warmth into his frigid body.

He longed to be in front of the fire drinking a bowl of hot lichen soup, his heaviest robes and his dogs keeping his feet warm. The canines begged to tag along, but they would've violated the ground by their mere presence. He broke an age old rule by leaving camp without the protection of man or dog and then wandered much further than he intended. But last night the situation with Bittoo nearly got out of hand, he desperately wanted to find a solution before it turned into a crisis. He expected guidance from his sky spirits and hoped to entice their aid.

In the darkness of early morning, he had slipped away from the village unnoticed and hugged the lake's shore until sunlight replaced the light of the moon. He took little account of the distance he traveled, but diligently remained steadfast in his plight.

The area he sought needed to be unspoiled, clean of any animal or bird signs. He even went so far as to reject a tract tainted by a few withered leaves and twigs. After relentlessly foraging a good portion of the early morning, he selected a location for his morning cleansing ritual. The space was the size of a large pit house. On its surface, the crusty snow glistened with playful dancing spirit-lights.

It wasn't his custom to perform the ritual in snow, as other shamans did during the winter. It appealed to him very little. But with Ceda threatening the extinction of the village, and Bittoo making no moves toward becoming a shaman and thereby rescuing everyone, he felt compelled to execute a greater effort at self discipline. He shivered when recalling rubbing the snow over his naked frame in preparation for the ceremony.

He had worn his most magnificent robe for the occasion. In his head, he began by creating a drum rhythm, allowing the magical beat to take over his entire body. There was only a strange, primitive pulse as the cadence surged through his veins. Slowly, he stood, blind to his surroundings. He felt protected, as if in a cocoon, and thought he must have resembled one too, with his arms hugging his sides and the long white feather cloak engulfing him.

With a sense of weightlessness, his body rose above the ground. His whole being moved to the strong, primeval cadence, which seemed to come from the seven directions, including within himself. Gracefully, he spread his winged arms, dipping and swaying, his movements becoming so slowed the motions couldn't be seen. He was unaware of anything but the music and his natural yet unfamiliar dance. His outstretched arms supported the cape that from the back surely appeared as an eagle soaring through the sky.

Remembering no other details, he awoke as though in a trance but elated with an awareness of accomplishing a great deed. He studied the area where he performed his sacred rite and saw no impressions to indicate he disrupted the region. The snow-covered ground remained as pure and unmolested as he originally found it.

His morning ritual had been overtaken and replaced by an unknown rite. "But never mind," he marveled to the emptiness, "I walked with the spirits...even if I hovered just a breath above the ground!"

The village was barely in view, and he could make out a voice here and there. His plan was to follow the bank to the willow trees and cut up the path to camp and to the warmth of his lodge. "I find sitting easier than rising but remaining inactive is dangerous in this cold weather. I must head home." He took a few difficult steps on partially numbed feet before spying Bittoo and Gaaf leaving the path and venturing onto the lake. The holy man braced himself against a young fir tree and watched.

Struggling with the weight of four salmon and a cumbersome basket, Gaaf distantly lagged behind.

Bittoo slowed his pace, keeping his eyes downward, scanning each area where the snow's crust looked disturbed. He was searching for his fishing hole where he encountered the water deity, three days ago. Not finding it, he moved on.

He glanced back at Gaaf and saw that his friend was trembling. *He's as afraid of meeting Ceda as I am.*

Bittoo knew he must again face the mother of all water creatures. She proved a real threat to the people of Frozen Duck Band. If there was some way of compromising with her, he would. He still didn't intend on becoming a tusu, a holy leader. His path was a hunter's path. Even if he did follow the path of a shaman, how could he work with such a hateful spirit guide? He felt terrified, dizzy and sick.

"This is the spot," he informed his friend, pointing with a loosely bandaged hand at a trampled section of dirty snow.

Gaaf squinted against the sun's glare on the white lake. "It looks like something happened here."

"There...right there," Bittoo gestured again. "See the round impression? That what's left of my fishing hole."

"Hmm," moaned Gaaf, who appeared less than courageous.

"We need to clean the snow back...away from my original hole and then cut through the ice at exactly the same spot," Bittoo instructed, using his feet to sweep away the white substance.

"Will she be here?" Gaaf asked, setting to work.

Bittoo no longer felt the cold or his painful hands, nor did he hear his friend's question. He also trembled. "Place the fish together, facing the water."

Gaaf finished his task and stepped away. Bittoo sat with legs extended, straddling the deep recess and waited for his fate. Perhaps he should have brought his fishing gear and reinacted his earlier experience with Ceda. He didn't know the secrets used to summon the spirits and worried that he was about to commit another sacrilege.

"You said I have a choice," he began, forcing himself to stare into the calm water. He cleared his throat.

"You whine," came a reply. *"You're the only one to be chosen by the deities, and you're the only one throughout all time, refusing such a role. You're not worthy of such a title, but it's not my choice."*

Bittoo shrugged his shoulders. "What choice do I have?"

"You have the choice of being selfish or not."

"I brought back your salmon children and respectfully placed them so their spirits can return to you."

"Your shaman has wisdom. Learn from him. The adult salmon represents you as the Father of all Shamans. They are mine...just as you are. The miniature salmon represent the future shamans of your lineage. I give them to you in your honor."

Not knowing how to respond to a gift that repulsed him, Bittoo changed the subject. "Will my people be harmed?"

"This is bigger than you or the people of the Frozen Duck Band."

"Can someone else be the Father of all Shamans?" Bittoo blurted, wishing as soon as he asked the question that he hadn't spoken.

"Your rudeness angers me!" she rebutted. *"Can't you understand, you stupid boy?"*

Bittoo felt weak, close to losing his nerve and his stomach contents. He wanted to put his swollen hands over his ears and run as rapidly as a mountain cat.

"You're mistaken to think you can hide from me. In your lifetime, there'll be such changes that only a powerful tusu can insure the preservation of the Clan of the Ancient Humans, and at that, only a select few from each of the bands will carry on the name of the clan...many shall perish."

"But I'm ordinary," Bittoo stubbornly protested. *"You're strong, and the spirits recognize your strength. Would a weak boy resist me this long? Would a weak boy find the courage to challenge the demands of Creator One Breath? Oh no, he picked wisely."*

Bittoo made no reply. Ceda seemed to talk out of two mouths, calling him stupid and selfish, and then claiming him strong, and saying Creator One Breath had chosen wisely.

"The salmon of which you so wrongly violated, won't exist. If you don't call them, they'll forever avoid the mighty river."

"Our salmon are numerous," disputed Bittoo, thinking the water deity still talked foolishly.

"The time shall come for you and some of the people to separate. You and your lineage are their only hope. Your gifts are hidden, but they're numerous. Many from the spirit world stand ready to help. We don't want to see the people vanish from Mother Earth."

"All bands are happy and do well where they are. Earth Mother is generous, and we mostly laugh during the time of the Starvation Moon."

"What happens when a wave hits the beach?"

Puzzled by the question, Bittoo remained quiet and nervously pushed a strand of wavy hair from his blank face.

"One small occurrence alters Mother Earth forever. And in turn, that single happening brings many changes into being."

"The water action carries in sand or takes it out," Bittoo answered. "The waves also bring in much to use. We eat sea-weeds, make rope, turn the cordage into nets to catch fish and... !"

"You're that wave," the voice interrupted.

"Pick someone else...someone worthy," Bittoo appealed, shrinking at the idea of so much responsibility. "If I fail...," he stopped, realizing what the consequences of such a failure might be.

"Only you've been chosen as keeper of the clan. It's much too early for the spirits to reveal when."

"You speak of choices when there are none," Bittoo argued brashly.

"Normally, you give much thought to everything you attempt. Your decisions aren't hasty. That shows wisdom. With wisdom comes power. Over many seasons, your medicine bundle will fill with power objects. The bear and the white fox will aid you. Add to your bundle, and when you can see the spirit of the wind, then you'll possess the knowledge needed to be worthy."

"I see the wind. Everyone sees the wind."

"You see the leaf floating through the air. Can you see what carries it?"

"No," he mumbled, his voice barely audible. Glimmers of knowledge flashed through his mind. The suspicions seemed obscure, fragmented at first, even irrational and unthinkable. Yet the pieces joined together perfectly. Yes, this issue is more than the survival of the clan and the placement of the salmon, he reasoned to himself.

His conclusion frightened him more than anything ever did—far more than his first meeting with Ceda. He grew faint again, but with all the false courage he could muster, he unveiled his sorrowful but startling findings to the water spirit who awaited his decision. "If the people perish, then so will the spirits. The spirits can only exist as long as people exist...people who believe in them."

Wearily, he walked toward the shore ahead of Gaaf. His friend fell two paces behind, carrying only the tightly woven basket of tiny fishlings. When Gaaf had reached for the four larger salmon, intending to take them back to the lodge, Bittoo shook his head vigorously, indicating he wanted them to remain where they were.

"Did you see her?" Gaaf asked. "Bittoo, was she here?" he quizzed, even louder.

"I didn't see her," Bittoo uttered quietly.

"Were you talking to yourself?"

"I talked to her. Didn't you hear her voice?"

"I heard only you." Gaaf caught up with his friend. A tear lay frozen on Bittoo's red cheek.

A tremendous sound stunned the boys. They swung around facing the direction they came. A mighty burst of lake water spewed high into the air, but not a drop landed back onto Mother Earth.

"It doesn't fall!" Gaaf bellowed above the deafening roar. "The water only goes up. What's she doing?"

"My guess is, the mother of all water creatures wants you to know of her presence and the shaman too. He watches from the bank."

"She goes to great lengths to make her point," Gaaf stated loudly, appearing pleased that a deity would bother with him.

"She knows if I'm to be a tusu you'll defend me, so you need to be a believer."

Bittoo didn't notice that a number of people had gathered on the ridge. Ceda was putting on her display for them as well. If she couldn't coerce the stubborn boy into following the trail of a shaman, then perhaps the reaction of the horror-stricken villagers would be persuasive.

"Look at it! The geyser sucks back into your fishing hole!" Gaaf barked in alarm as the pitch-lined basket slipped from his trembling hands.

The spouting water reversed itself, and in the time it took for three long breaths, returned to the lake.

"Bittoo, she accepted the mature salmon you left for her. They're no longer lying beside the hole."

Gaaf's discovery didn't surprise Bittoo. Ceda already decreed that those fish represented him, and he belonged to her. "Of course," he responded curtly.

The two young men paused until convinced Ceda had completed her performance. Uttering not a word, they looked blankly at one another, then continued toward Frozen Duck Camp.

"Stupid boy!" came a mocking shout from behind them.

"I heard that!" Gaaf exclaimed, briskly quickening his stride.

8

Enraged eyes glared at Bittoo as he walked through the camp. Hushed accusations were being whispered. The men made distance between Bittoo and themselves. The women and children frantically disappeared into their shelters.

Bittoo could hear their moaning, their shrieking. He didn't blame them for being terrified of Ceda, but why did they look so hostile at him. He had done nothing. If anything, he was Ceda's victim.

He halted at the entrance of the shaman's dwelling and whispered to his loyal friend. Gaaf nodded his head and started to leave, but instead, reeled around to face Bittoo. "I now understand why you don't take off your nose ring."

Foregoing the customary greeting, Bittoo admitted himself into Derk's lodge. In bleak silence, he dragged his sagging frame aimlessly to the far side of the dirt room. Drained of strength, he huddled at the shaman's sacred fire.

He's on the verge of a decision, thought Derk, who rushed back to camp ahead of the two boys to warm himself across the room at his woman's cooking hearth. His teeth chattered against the smoothly worn bowl as he eagerly drank down its warm contents. Bittoo looked defeated, close to exhaustion, the boy's head and shoulders drooping so low he cast a headless shadow against the earthen wall.

Derk was biding his time, hoping the situation wouldn't turn unmanageable. He needed a strategy. What could he do if the men of the village became violent? At all cost, Bittoo required protection. Something told him this adolescent held their future. What must the poor boy be feeling with nearly the entire camp and the water deity angry with him? When darkness falls, he might be able to sneak Bittoo out and hide him in the woods. And for Bittoo's own safety, should he try to leave the lodge alone, Derk felt determined to convince him otherwise.

Froom concerned him the most. The unreasonable man possessed a raging temper , and he had been painfully degraded the night before at the story telling. Yes, Froom is a danger, and might provoke others into irrational behavior. It seemed likely just a matter of time before Bittoo fell prey to him and his followers, unless Har and Tam returned first, or if he devised a plan to prevent such a disaster.

Earlier, before entering his underground hut, he held enough foresight to stop briefly and convey his wishes to Bittoo's Uncle Tam who also saw Ceda's immodest display. If all went well, Har, the boy's father, and Tam were already on their way to summon two of the most powerful shamans in the

clan—one brother going south to the Spear Creek
Band and the other north to the Bear Hunter Band.
Running, both men could reach their destinations
by dusk, and should there be a bright, guiding moon,
the brothers might arrive back at Frozen Duck Camp
by morning with the others.

He carried two stubby branches over to add to
the sacred fire where Bittoo sat. His sullen visitor
made no attempt to look at him, nor did Bittoo seem
to comprehend his presence. Perhaps the young
man's thoughts were lost in the middle world.

A few times he'd been in attendance when other
holy leaders underwent this remarkable event. They
always felt inspired after experiencing its magic. As
a neutral place, between the human world and the
world of the souls—man's and spirit's logic could
meet in counsel. Deciding the time wasn't right to
interrupt his guest, he returned to his unfinished
soup.

As usual, he felt inadequate, his star power too
weak for him to determine the proper steps to take.
Together though, he kept faith that the two great
shamans could help. Yet as strong as these holy
men's magic was, he recognized all their power as
being only a lone star in the sky compared to Bittoo's
potential power.

He set aside his empty wooden bowl and in the
light of the two fires, eyed Bittoo from across the
room. One of She Dog's pups lay with its head on
the boy's crumpled lap. Although tired, he was eager
to remain awake and alert. He worried his visitor
might leave if he fell asleep.

Now and again, Derk overheard upraised voices
coming from outside. It was quiet now. Full of

suspicion, thinking Bittoo possessed, his own mate bolted up the ladder when Bittoo first entered.

He stacked a pile of comfortable pelts opposite the boy at the sacred fire, then eased himself down onto the soft mound. If he drifted off, he was now close enough to hear Bittoo when he withdrew from the middle world. "Poor boy, he's not so much a guest in my dwelling as a prisoner," the shaman mumbled to himself, picking up his star rock and tracing its edgeless contour. The smoke added to his already dry eyes—his lids closed—his rock slid into his lap.

As before, Derk soared in his robe of feathers, only this time he flew high, just below the clouds. He looked up and saw the billowing fluffy masses leisurely drifting to the east. They welcomed him, he felt drawn to their peaceful call. Napping in their folds might be pleasant, but he perceived an urgency —something unexplainable summoned him in the direction of the morning sun.

A slight breeze caught him, sweeping him far from home. He flew above the Beaver Tail Mountains with its narrow canyons drowning in the melting winter snows. A startled flock of geese lost it's formation when spotting him intruding upon their domain.

From his vantage, he spied three villages, all belonging to the Clan of the Ancient Humans. The two southern camps were located half a days walk inland, and both appeared nearly deserted, but there was a great busyness in the camp of the Fur Seal Band which sat perched high on a bluff overlooking the Great Sea. It was the time of the birthing seals, and hordes of clansmen, from all the six bands, gathered to hunt the animals on the ice for their hides, fat and meat.

He studied the people closely, at first not recognizing anyone. He circled the camp four times before picking out similarities between the people below him and those whom he knew. The first familiar face turned out to be his niece, whose mate belonged to the Reindeer Band. She looked older, almost as old as he did.

Next, a man with a shaman's mark on his cheekbone caught his attention. The tattoo, in the design of a fish, wasn't one he'd seen before. Squinting at the stranger, he tried to pull some remembrance from his mind. No shaman wore such a sign. He watched the stranger suspiciously as the man wandered through the overcrowded village. Bandsmen greeted the middle-aged male, presenting him with gifts which he graciously accepted.

Derk flew closer to Mother Earth, getting a lung full of smoke from an outdoor cooking fire. "Look up! Look at me!" he shouted, not knowing whether he made himself heard. The outsider stopped to look around, but saw no one calling him. He slowly raised his head and found himself staring into the eyes of a gigantic bewitching bird.

"Bittoo, it's you!" cried Derk from above, as he recognized the tattooed shaman.

Derk jerked himself awake only to see the identical set of startled grey eyes fixed on him through the crackling blaze of the sacred fire. "I dreamed," he declared, realizing he just received a glimpse into the future. He glanced down and smiled at his rock which rested on his lap. For sure, Bittoo would become a shaman—his dream foretold it. He expelled a huge sigh of relief.

"I also dreamed," Bittoo acknowledged, but with a tone of doubt to his words. "I dreamed, without being asleep."

"If you weren't asleep, you journeyed to the middle world...a hollowed place reserved only for shamans with special vision. Did you see Ceda?"

"No, but she may have been present. The spirits of the great brown bear, the wary white fox, and what might have been the mammoths of old were there. When leaving that place I found myself as a shaman, many seasons from now. I strolled through the camp of the Fur Seal Band and heard someone shouting from above." He studied Derk's face. "I gazed into the sky and saw an enormous fowl. It looked purer in color than the white clouds floating around it." His eyes gleamed with wonder. He pointed at Derk "The spirit bird was you!"

The two sat quietly digesting their unusual experience.

After a time, Derk broke the stillness. "There's a link between us, a very strong link."

Bittoo leaned forward so as not to miss the shaman's message.

"Four nights ago, I dreamed about the destruction of our people, and you also saw that destruction when Ceda first came to you on the lake."

"Was I in the middle world then?" Bittoo asked, interrupting the shaman.

"No. That time, Ceda came to you in this world, which makes me think she must be desperate.

Normally, she, as the mother of all water creatures, would send one of her children to become your totem. Did you call her?"

Bittoo weakly shook his head. "No. At least, I didn't mean to."

"Then I think she waited for the opportunity, which you provided for her when you went fishing. But just now, you came back from the middle world, seeing the same images as I just did, however I was asleep...dreaming. Our power is connected somehow, or maybe Ceda just needed me to confirm your story, so our people will believe you." After a long pause, Derk continued. "Do you know any reason for Ceda to be so determined? She seems driven."

"There's a chance many in the clan will die. You dreamed it too. Supposedly, my becoming a shaman is important to whatever is going to happen." A bitter taste invaded Bittoo's mouth, causing his stomach to churn violently. "I'm not so sure the water deity cares much about the clan, except without us to pay homage to her, she'll cease to exist."

"As absurd as your reasoning is...it makes sense. I came to the same conclusion but hoped you knew of some other explanation. So even the deities are threatened. That's scary, but the ancestors said it happened once before."

Gripping his star in his hands, the shaman stood and paced back and forth between the two fire pits and around the ladder. Restlessly, he talked to himself in a low inaudible voice. His woman had returned, but he ignored her.

Finally, he thrust his stone in Bittoo's keeping, stepped over to the dirt shelf, and returned with a large leather bundle. With great care, he unwrapped the hairless hide, exposing a collection of items. "These are the ritual objects of the holy men...once the shamans of the Frozen Duck Band," he explained almost lovingly. "They're to be passed down, always, from one holy leader to the next."

He separated the articles, wiping each one as if it were thick with grime. "These are two fangs from a sabertooth cat. They belonged to a long forgotten seer."

"Was the sabertooth a deity like our bear is now?"

"No, there's no such legends, but these treasures held very strong magic for the ones who used them." Derk caressed the yellowed teeth, each tooth stretching the full length of his hand. "The remaining teeth on the amulet are that of a bear. Noork, my mentor, strung and wore them."

Bittoo reached over and touched a tooth.

"Every relic here holds its own power...some even used by more than one holy man. When I go to the Land of the Souls, don't bury my sky rock or my owl talisman with me. They should be placed in this bundle forever and be treated with great respect."

"But why keep them?"

"A shaman can select any of the medicine objects to help him commune with the spirits, or he may find his very own. None of these worked well for me, but they may become a power source for you. A shaman must guard and protect these, for they're divine and possess the true strength and the fate of the band. Nothing else we own is more valuable."

Impressed, Bittoo picked out three ordinary finger-sized stones from a pile of many similar shaped ones.

"If you notice, all those are covered in sacred red paint. Paint made from the blood of the seer who used them. He was an esteemed healer."

Bittoo's eyes locked on the stones, his stomach continued to turn. "Paint...made from the blood of a human who's very much dead?" He placed a hand over the pile, lightly stirring the smooth pebbles with his fingertips. Hidden underneath lay a longer black-grey stone. The boy's hand began to tingle, sending waves of vibrations up his arm. His breath caught in his chest, and he quickly jerked his hand away.

"Ah, you feel the power."

Bittoo crossed his arms but didn't respond. Instead, his eyes fastened on two other objects. "Are those also the teeth of some long extinct animal?"

"Those are small pieces taken from the tusks of the vanished mammoth. They're the most ancient things here, and we're the only band left with any of its ivory."

To see them more clearly, Bittoo moved closer to the flames. "What's scratched into them?"

"On each is carved an outline of the huge animal. We weren't always called The Frozen Duck Band. Before that beast became extinct, we were known as the Great Mammoth Band, and the mammoth was our deity."

Bittoo joined Derk on his heap of furs. "I don't remember hearing of such a tale."

"It lives only in the memories of the shamans. There's a cave somewhere in the cliffs of Thunder Mountain where the holy ones gathered generations ago, and conversed with the mammoth spirits. That's how the story got passed down, and I believe it, except the mammoths and their spirits are dead now.

The mighty creatures can no longer protect our people. I keep the pieces, so we don't forget."

"It could happen again." Bittoo quivered at the enormity of the situation.

"Yes, if all water life dies, then Ceda would also perish. Or if all our people die, she too would expire, for lack of anyone left to worship her. She'd cease to exist either way."

"She said something about a place where there's no salmon, and said I'd be needed there to call them."

"By Creator One Breath, you'll possess strong medicine if you call salmon into empty rivers! Since your spirit guide, your totem, Ceda, dwells in the water, she'll assist you. Gather power objects from that source, and it'll be helpful for you to eat mostly water creatures. Your magic will be stronger if you do. Pay proper homage when doing these things. My medicine comes from the sky, so I have my star and my amulet, and of course, my feathered robe."

"There'd be much to learn," the boy responded seriously, his voice low.

"And much to teach. Eventually, you'll be the one doing the instructing."

Bittoo felt a chill go down his spine. *Not me. I walk the path of a hunter.* He shook his head. *Something will happen to turn this all around.*

Derk strode past the ladder and peered out the smoke hole. Moon Watcher was half way across the sky—half the night had already passed.

Using a clam shell, he spooned soup into a bowl for his bewildered guest.

9

Gaaf held the ladder stable while his feeble grandfather gained his footing. The boy watched closely as the crippled man descended—fixing both feet on the same rung before gaining the confidence to step down to the next one.

"Ouch!" yelled Gaaf as his legs buckled out from under him. He'd been struck across the back of the calves with a heavy walking stick.

The nearly blind man used the staff to feel his way through camp. He had memorized the village well. Except, when something was out of place and in his way, it often received an accidental swift whack. And Gaaf was out of place.

"Move," grumbled the aged hunter, who, rather than admit to his faltering eyesight, pretended to have hit the boy on purpose.

"It's me!" cried Gaaf, hoping to ward off another painful blow.

"Of course it's you," snarled the prideful old one. "No matter whether it's you or someone else, you're still in my way," he declared, obviously annoyed because he couldn't identify his latest victim.

"You've attacked my grandson, you blind bat," rose a voice from within the dwelling.

The blind elder mumbled something to himself, lunged his walking stick forward until the wooden cane clashed with the ladder pole, took hold of the creaking structure and went below to join the others.

The four old men grew up together, played together and hunted together.

They'd been born in Frozen Duck Camp, and here they expected to die. Now their tired frames pursued two functions—sitting around discussing old times and sitting in counsel. Tonight, the white-bearded elders sat in counsel.

"Har should be present," gummed Coort's toothless grandfather.

"I sent my granddaughter to summon him," stated the blind one. "She scoured throughout the village, even asking his woman, but Leha wouldn't tell the girl where he could be found."

"Too many peculiar things are going on in this camp. Har can help us decide what must be done. We need to find out what he knows. After all, whatever is happening, involves his son."

"Where's our shaman, Derk?" wheezed the fourth elder.

"My granddaughter says the shaman is with Bittoo, communing with the spirits. Both have departed from their bodies—journeying to another place. Derk's woman is afraid to interrupt."

"Then I'm certainly not going to disrupt them. I

won't be responsible if the shaman's soul is incapable of returning to his body," said Coort's grandfather.

There was nothing, as yet, for the elders to decide. The men whose wisdom had, so far, never failed the band, were without a plan. The fire crackled softly, but their failing ears heard nothing. They gawked at one another—as well as their four sets of worn-out eyes could gawk.

There was much being discussed in Froom's lodge. He'd called a secret gathering of his young hunting companions. He purposely excluded Tam, also their age, but Tam would've rejected any such meeting. Even so, Bittoo's youngest uncle hadn't been seen since earlier that day.

"Why did you ask us to sneak into your dwelling?" Coort asked, fearing the reply.

Froom looked at the men's serious faces, hoping he was doing right by confiding in them. "We must do something about Bittoo."

"Why? It's up to the elders to decide what to do."

"I stood outside the pit house where the old ones counsel. They're baffled and sitting in silence," one hunter revealed despairingly.

Froom intended to approach the issue cautiously, but he couldn't hold his tongue. "Do you men want your families to die? They will, if we don't act."

"Nonsense," claimed Coort. "We can't take the matter into our hands. It's much too serious."

"That's exactly what we must do." Froom's voice began to rise. "And the only thing to do."

"What if a dark spirit isn't possessing the boy?" Coort asked. "What if the invisible one is a powerful spirit animal? We shouldn't interfere with a person and his spirit guide."

"This entity isn't a spirit helper!" Froom exclaimed, shaking his head in disgust. "Do your spirit guides threaten to starve the village?"

Nervously, Coort scanned the lodge but didn't focus his bulging eyes. "Everything you say is true, for all of us heard little Teaa's words. She said the fish would disappear, and the people would die."

"What kind of spirit brother makes such a decree?" Froom asked as he began to see the discussion going his way.

"I think a demon has entered Bittoo's body," another hunter stated flatly. "But I'm not going to meddle."

"You saw the water spout. Some are claiming the boy performed an evil deed, dishonoring Ceda, and for revenge, she placed a whale in our lake. If that is so, the sea whale will devour all our fish. Then what? I'll tell you what." Froom paused long enough to catch his breath. "We'll be exactly where Teaa said. We will all be dead!"

"Don't forget, whatever it was, demon or spirit guide, the strange entity called him 'stupid'."

"Bittoo violated the spirits, and our people are going to pay for his mistake." The hunter's lips formed a snarl. "But our place isn't to interfere. Wait for the elders and our shaman."

"And if there is a whale in Frozen Duck Lake," Froom said, his face red with frustration, his nostrils flaring. "How long until the rest of the fish are eaten? We can dispose of the boy, then if the thing is a demon, maybe it'll die along with him. But if the entity is his spirit totem, it will be pleased that we destroyed the boy who did wrong against it."

Coort looked at Froom in disbelief. "My heart doesn't permit me to be a part of this. But because we go back many seasons, and you once saved my life, I won't reveal what's been said here." He glared at Froom, his tone somber. "I hope, friend, you change your thinking. I sometimes wonder if a dark spirit lives in you."

Leaving Froom brooding and refusing to be a part of any scheme, the hunters departed the lodge. They were sure that by sunrise, his temper would cool, whereas the troubled man would most likely disregard any fool-hearted plot. With their ill-natured friend Froom, that's how it had always been.

He crouched. For the better part of the night, Froom squatted beneath a matted wolf hide, his eyes sharply watching the entrance to the shaman's pit house. He was furious with his friends for deserting him. The bunch of them acted like spineless jelly fish, floating aimlessly with the current. Sometimes he felt like an outsider even among them, but surely after completing his plan, that would change. For by himself, he intended to resolve the problem, so the people wouldn't perish. With the boy dead, the spirits would have no reason to take their wrath out on the villagers.

Soon after the shaman's woman returned to her hut, She Dog with her two pups bounded outside. The whelps romped noisily, burrowing into the white powder, causing the soft snow to fly off their multi-colored fur. Bent on a sniffing quest, the mother dog ignored their antics. Every object in camp met with the canine's keen sense of smell until she came near the tree which housed the sacred bear skull. She stopped, stiff-legged, baring her teeth, the hair on her neck and back standing on end.

"Get away, mutt," hissed Froom, attempting to form a ball of snow to throw at the intruder, then thinking better of it.

His words caught the attention of the pups who grew bored with their game. They crept over from behind and nosed at the wolf hide covering the man. Thinking the novel-smelling fur should be included as part of his territory, the male pup lifted his leg. He sent a stream of warm, yellow urine down the hide and the boots which slipped out from under the robe.

"Good girl," Froom said sweetly, changing his tone and strategy toward the large female. He held out pieces of dried venison, however the cautious dog kept her stance. When the pups joined their mother, Froom offered them the meat. They found nothing threatening in the gesture and gulped down the chunks of savory food.

With her small ones following, She Dog slowly backed away, never taking her eyes off the peculiar man, whose scent smelled of death—the same strong killing odor men threw off when preparing for a hunt.

Moon Watcher glowed with a brilliance that made it necessary for Froom to remain hidden under his musty camouflage. His shifty eyes, now the only part of him exposed, darted suspiciously back and forth with each new sound: people snoring, children whimpering, and occasionally, adults coming out to relieve themselves. All were sounds that caught his notice and began to wear on him. Earlier, he heard voices coming from the shaman's lodge, but now it remained quiet, as did the rest of the village.

The longer the night grew, the more erratic his thoughts became. He observed the smoke from both smoke holes. The opening without a ladder vented the shaman's sacred fire. The other smoke hole vented his woman's hearth. When the smoke of both reached above the domed roof, they merged, creating what appeared as menacing demons, dancing intertwined. He took the transparent figures as omens dictating the ruin of all he ever cherished.

He felt strongly determined never to go through the pain of humiliation again—like he did at the story telling. Bittoo was the cause of his shame, and he found it difficult refraining and not rushing into the shaman's lodge and grabbing the evil boy. He thought of himself as a hero, ready to pay homage to the invisible spirits—by giving them the young, evil troublemaker.

So many things had developed this night, Bittoo was unable to sleep. Near dawn, after the shaman fell asleep for the second time, he decided to return home to get the healing salve for his blistered, oozing hands. He surfaced from the pit hut.

In the last few days, his life had changed and changed for the worse. He felt cheated. Even his people hated him. Ceda was truly stealing his life away. How could he ever become a hunter? Yes, he'd learn to hunt even if he needed to sneak away to do it. But how could he oppose Ceda? Would she retaliate? Would the salmon ignore their lures? He might be able to trick Ceda into thinking he was walking the shaman path. Maybe he did have a choice.

He trembled remembering the glaring horrid looks that yesterday the men of his band shot at him when he walked to Derk's lodge. He stopped briefly using his fur sleeve to wipe away a tear. He wasn't their enemy. It was hurtful to think the villagers, the people he loved, were turning against him. Didn't they realize how terribly frightened he was?

When half way across camp, he heard footsteps fast approaching from behind. He hesitated, his breath catching in his chest—he swung around. There wasn't time to yell nor to defend himself.

The crazed man struggled to drag the unconscious boy to the center of the lake. Bittoo bled from the temple where the flat side of the flint hatchet struck. Was Bittoo already dead? It would probably be easier to dispose of a lifeless body than one fighting him, for he didn't relish wrestling with the boy while holding him under water. He chopped wildly, reopening Bittoo's fishing hole.

"What are you doing?" cried the shaman, startling Froom, whose swings sent ice chunks and splinters in all directions.

"Saving us all!"

"You're mistaken!" the shaman answered, now sorry he made She Dog stay home.

A line of clansmen moved down the trail to the bank. Tam arrived, and with him many from the Bear Hunter's Band. Toward the back of Tam's group, a stocky individual with much body hair emerged. His dress was of unsewn furs, tucked and tied together, giving him a fearsome unkempt appearance. He stomped onto the ice as if daring the mass to crack under him.

His loud commanding voice carried loudly across the lake. "You will not harm that boy!" the mogur of the Bear Hunter Village ordered.

The mogur moved forward, unwinding a lengthy braided cord that wrapped many times around his shoulder. At the other end of the thick thong, an eager female bear took advantage of her newly extended leash. As next autumn's sacrifice, she weighed little less than a human adult. Her paws and jaws harbored sharp weapons, capable of ripping a person apart. The impressive animal represented the most powerful of all the clan's deities. To harm her before the bear festival would bring on the worst kind of vengeance. These creatures ensured the clan's good hunting season and were responsible for carrying messages from the people, to the Land of the Souls.

"You go against everything we stand for," insisted the mogur, who, by Tam's earlier words knew what had transpired at Frozen Duck Camp.

"I'm saving us all," the assailant repeated, frantically shifting his gaze from man to beast.

"By Creator One Breath, you'll destroy the entire clan," interpreted the shaman, his expression hardening.

"Bittoo's the one who brings disaster down on us. The spirits will rejoice with this boy dead." In the morning light, Froom could make out the large purple scars streaking across the mogur's face and see the vacant area above his lips where a nose belonged—all resulting from tragic run-ins with revered bears.

"Bittoo will help us. Ceda wishes him to be a shaman, a tusu, but the boy resists her commands," the esteemed mogur declared, not overly convinced he believed his own statement and finding it difficult to declare Bittoo a holy man, let alone a great tusu.

Froom tried to pull information from the foggy reaches of his mind. The hunter was unsure whether he could kill the brown bear if the creature attacked. But should he manage to accomplish the feat, then it would still mean instant death for him—buried without ceremony and buried in a pit underneath the bear's body. If the beast killed him instead, the creature would be destroyed, and her furry corpse placed under his. Both outcomes horrified him. He feared dying under those conditions, for he'd be unwelcome in the Land of the Souls. As a spirit who was an outcast, he'd become a dark demon.

Much was transpiring and the mogur's keen eyes spotted it all: Tam worked his way quietly across the far side of the lake, attempting to sneak behind Froom. The mogur saw Bittoo's arm move slightly— although it may only have been a muscle twitch. He also detected a change in Froom who still held the boy captive.

The mogur jerked at the leash, hoping to create a much needed diversion. The partially grown animal rose on her hind legs, sinking further into the snow. Tilting her broad head and growling deeply, she flashed her piercing teeth with drool trickling from the corners of her mouth.

The bear's interest wasn't jarred by the tug on the thong or by the scent of Bittoo's blood—she caught wind of a faint fish odor around the hole, remaining from Bittoo's earlier salmon catch, and she needed little prompting from her captor to react.

"You aren't a holy man and don't understand these things!" the mogur bellowed, his stare piercing

Froom. "We don't slaughter our own kind. Such an action is forbidden! If that boy dies, you won't be permitted to join our ancestors. Your black soul will walk Earth Mother forever!"

The mogur's words stung Froom, but his immediate worry was the foaming beast stretching her leash taut, attempting to plunge forward. Surely, the mogur wasn't strong enough to hold the animal back.

Yielding to his sense of survival, and keeping at a safe distance, he cautiously eased his way around the mogur and the aroused bear. Defeated, and with his head cast downward in shame, he skirted past the shaman. He lowered his weapon, which had suddenly grown heavy.

When nearing the embankment, he came upon Har, flanked by the medicine seer, plus other new arrivals from the Spear Creek and Bear Hunter Bands. Har appeared clueless as to what just occurred and gave Froom a quick questioning look, then let him pass. Strangers and friends alike backed away, giving him ample room to retreat.

Reaching the crest of the ridge, Froom stopped in his tracks. Lant, from the Spear Creek Camp, his daughter's father-in-law to be, blocked the way. The sizable man stared in disgust, his expression firmly set, and after several lusty breaths he allowed Froom to withdraw.

The clansmen watched as Tam carried Bittoo off the ice-covered lake. For some, it was a familiar scene.

Froom reached his empty lodge. He frantically collected his only spare clothes, a basket of dried roots, strips of smoked meat, his fire starting kit with extra tinder, plus a pouch which housed his flint knapping and mending tools. What didn't fit into his pack, he hurriedly wrapped in a musk deer hide. His obsidian knife was already strapped around his waist. Loosening the leather band, he added his hatchet.

"When will you return?" Patee asked, alarming her mate who didn't hear her enter.

Shrouded in both shame and anger, Froom remained quiet. He looked long at his devoted woman and infant daughter before leaving their earthen dwelling, carrying his spear thrower and the heavy load.

Lant spied. He saw when Froom entered his shelter. Patee followed shortly afterward, toting their small child. A brief time later, he observed Froom stealing from the lodge. The disgraced man left by a well used trail and without words, disappeared through the forest.

Lant had a vested interest in this family, the little girl especially. Many seasons from now she'd become his son's mate. Already, he gave them a generous bride price. Now, he was concerned about the child's welfare. "Woman!" he cried out, standing at the entrance to her pit house. "Do you have enough stores to last through the season of the heavy snow?"

Patee looked up, her face smudged with tears.

"Good, I'll be back to fetch you and the girl before the Seal Birthing Moon."

"Froom will come home," she whispered, and as she uttered those words, her deep sorrow was acknowledged by yet another female.

Thunder Mountain belched a thick grey ash cloud from her agitated belly. The dark flume carried eastward with the wind in the direction of the Great Sea. The ground shifted, just enough for the ice on Frozen Duck Lake to shatter in all directions. The cracks split, reaching the shoreline, forming a webbed pattern, and at its center lay Bittoo's unmolested fishing spot.

The ancestors said that a quaking earth resulted from a huge underground fish shaking its tail.

10

Derk's woman never appreciated her hearth as much as now. She stared at the jumping flames, pretending to pray to Grandmother Fire. She finished her prayer long ago, except, in order to appear mannerly, she remained with her head cast down. But a person couldn't fake such a stance forever—she'd pretended to be praying for as long as seemed reasonable.

She felt incapable of controlling herself any longer—the hideous woman caused her to laugh, which was unforgivably rude. The mogur's mate squatted directly across from her, with a wide, black band outlining her lips. The silly female actually believed the absurd marking enhanced her beauty. She raised her eyes, while biting hard on her tongue and peered at the woman without fastening her eyes on the ugly face.

"I think others will tattoo around their mouths too," the woman admitted as she moved her head in primping gestures.

"Oh," was the only response Derk's woman could mutter.

"I did it to clarify my position as the mate of the great mogur. But after the women of my village saw me, they also desire to make themselves more beautiful for their men."

Not trusting herself, Derk's mate quickly shifted her attention back to the fire pit.

"Maybe you'd like to improve your looks in the same way?"

She felt a giggle emerging and hoped, no prayed, for a distraction. None came. She bit down even harder on her tongue, then shot a glance at the three holy men from across the lit room.

The heat of two fires was affecting Derk. He perspired heavily, although usually the added warmth didn't bother him in such a way. "I've told you both all I know, and all I experienced."

"Our ancestors say that tusus are the greatest, most powerful of any shamans," quoted the medicine seer.

"Yes, but can you honestly recall a single story about one who lived among our clan?" quizzed the mogur.

"Never," stated Derk, finding the fact surprising.

"There aren't any legends because there haven't been any tusus. And there will probably never be any," the mogur said, the tone of his words sounding final. He didn't intend to change his mind.

"If Bittoo said Ceda called him a tusu, then I believe the boy," Derk replied curtly, unwilling to let the matter drop.

The mogur's expression didn't change. The scars across his face pulled the skin tight and prevented most muscles from moving, but his deformity didn't keep Derk from catching the blaze that fueled in the mogur's eyes.

"Perhaps, Bittoo will be the first of them," suggested the medicine seer who hadn't yet noticed the mogur's unyielding attitude.

"We should concentrate on getting this boy healthy," spoke the mogur who disliked the direction the dialogue was going. He loathed the idea of there possibly being a holy man with higher status than his own. His apprentice seemed lacking, and he himself, although not old, felt the effects of his multiple injuries. He imagined a shift in power if Bittoo lived.

"Some say Ceda put a whale in the lake, and the whale sent up the geyser of water through its breathing spout. Those people also think the whale caused the earthquake by thrashing its tail..all because Bittoo angered her. Others say a dark demon is lurking, and Bittoo is its target." Derk paused briefly then added, "But I believe it was Ceda."

Attempting to end the bleeding, the medicine seer pressed sticky wads of spider webs into the open wound, then bound Bittoo's head with a soft strap of unused buckskin. "The rivers of his body have lost much blood. The strike to his head was brutal, and if the boy lives, he might not be right."

"Then where will we be without him?" asked Derk in alarm. "I didn't watch him closely. He should've been given the same safeguards as all shamans. I bring evil upon this band," he said, suddenly riddled with guilt.

"What about that man, Froom? Lant saw him leave camp. Is Bittoo still in danger from him?"

"That one has a temper," Derk admitted. "I'm not sure what to expect of him."

The mogur opened his mouth to speak, but bickering from outside the dwelling interrupted his thoughts.

"Me go see Bittoo," declared Teaa, her mind firmly made up.

"You stay out here! He's with the holy men. They'll make him better," Mupo explained.

"No! Me go!" the child argued, slowly easing around her older sister. "Bittoo dead."

"Our brother is not dead. They would tell us if he were."

"Me fix him better den," Teaa squealed, raising her hand which clutched something hidden. Doing a fast zigzag past Mupo, the small girl jumped backwards onto the ladder. She roughly bounced down on her rear, whacking each rung as she went, and hitting the ground with such force, she went tumbling.

She pulled herself up and limped over to the sacred fire. Acting not the least bit threatened, she scowled at the three speechless men, then turned toward her brother who lay on a thick bed of sleeping furs. His heaving chest, seemed to satisfy her.

"Dis be Bittoo's. It fix Bittoo," she proclaimed dramatically, thrusting an object at Derk, then scampering back up the ladder.

Derk held up the sweat-soiled bag which contained ashes from Bittoo's mother's hearth, plus remnants of dried milkweed. "It's Bittoo's childhood sickness bag. He's fortunate to have it back." He placed the worn pouch in the boy's lifeless hand.

The men were amused by Teaa's braveness, and the unusual way she gained admittance. They chuckled lightly, but from across the shelter, at the woman's hearth, Derk's mate burst into an overdue fit of laughter.

Noise outside continued even after Teaa's exit. Menacing clouds rolled in, building up, still as yet incapable of making the final thrust which would carry them through the mountains. Speedily, the men felled trees to cage the bear.

Midway through the day, the mogur, relieved to escape the earthen lodge, set out to inspect the work. He found their efforts exceptional, as he knew he would. Built of stout alder logs, the structure stood on four strong poles driven into the earth. The bewildered, female bear had just been lowered into the cage when he arrived. He watched as the tired clansmen fastened a layer of logs for the roof and secured them by placing heavy rocks on its top. Although only a temporary winter home for the animal, the enclosure seemed sturdy enough to last many seasons.

"Ya, Ho," Gaaf said as he caught up to the mogur who was returning to the shaman's lodge. "Bittoo may need these for his healing...some of the eggs and the baby fish found in the salmon he caught."

"So these are the famed fishlings," the mogur stated sarcastically. His face turned grey, his features stone-like. "Is this a joke you boys are playing?"

Gaaf glared at the mogur for asking such a thing. With disrespect and courage, he turned and stomped away from the ignorant man and his ignorant question.

The mogur was shaken by what he saw. The gummy roe appeared in various stages of hatching. Some, already hatched, remained bonded to their embryo sacks. They certainly look real. He didn't have an explanation for the unnatural things. "Oh, yes," he said in a low voice. "I feel my power slipping...right into the hands of that injured boy."

As he approached the entrance to the shaman's pit house, he found himself wading through piles of sea and water objects left by the villagers for Bittoo. Some were beautifully carved, while others were untouched and natural. The presents were a magnificent array of regalia, a great honor to any holy man.

What the gifts stood for angered the envious mogur. Had the people changed their minds about Bittoo? Surely not. Maybe the villagers hadn't really accepted Bittoo as a tusu at all, maybe they were taking precautions like he intended to do—so that no matter whether the boy turned out to be special, or whether he was found to be possessed by evil, they'd be spared—either way. Yes, they must be taking precautions—a smart thing to do.

"We prepare for the healing rite," Derk explained when the mogur rejoined them. He'd whittled sharp points on the end of willow stakes then carved the opposite ends and left finely curled shavings clinging to their side.

"We should strive to restore his wholeness now, rather than wait and let him die. Trying to bring Bittoo back from the Land of the Souls might prove too difficult, perhaps even impossible," claimed the medicine seer.

"Nothing is sure. But you're wise," replied the mogur, wishing he wasn't in the middle of this. "The spirits dislike releasing someone who's died, and usually the dead one is content in the afterlife and unwilling to return." He felt his prestige wavering, but what choice did he have? He must do the necessary thing for Bittoo, just in case the predictions the boy reported came true. The survival of the clan concerned him the most. He'd put Bittoo in his place after the boy got well.

To the antler tines jutting from the rafters, the medicine seer attached tiny leather pouches of pulverized gall bladder extracted from former sacrificed bears. When digested, the powder had healing properties, but none he thought would be helpful this day. But because the powder came from the revered bears, it also boasted spiritual powers, and spiritual powers were greatly needed this day.

Carefully, so as not to destroy any of the delicate curls, Derk pounded the ritual sticks into the ground. He drove one complete circle of sticks into the earth around Bittoo and his sick bed, while the remainder he placed throughout the lodge.

Amid the bundle, housing the power objects of earlier seers, he found the red healing stones. While he placed the blood covered rocks around Bittoo's lifeless frame, the mogur discharged a handful of soft yellow pebbles into the embers.

The fire spit and flashed in resentment, filling the air with a pungent odor and a mass of blinding dense smoke. The heavy vapor escaped overhead, signaling to the villagers the beginning of an important ceremony—one which indicated that interruptions weren't permitted. Rarely, did a clansman desire to disrupt such an event.

Derk worried. Did he have the stamina required to perform such a rite? He knew that when depleted of strength a person became more susceptible to demon possession.

As if answering Derk's thoughts, the mogur said, "When we combine our energies, we'll be stronger."

The mogur, the medicine seer, and Derk took their places. Hunkering on the north side of the fire pit sat the mogur who represented the highest deity form—the bear. His position in life and around the flames corresponded with the earth and the mountains —whence live the bears.

The medicine seer positioned himself opposite the mogur and to the south. He was one with the element of fire—its fury and energy.

Derk sat at his rightful seat, east of the sacred pit. His sky rock appointed him, many seasons ago, as a holy one connected with the air.

Unconscious, Bittoo lay directly across from Derk on the west side of the sacred circle. His motionless body drew its power from the water.

Thus the most powerful of all forces, Air—Fire—Earth—Water, were joined together in Derk's lodge. Four directions, four elements and four holy men. Never before did they remember a ritual being so balanced—so charged with power.

The three men placed green boughs of cedar on the burning flames. Cleansing smoke filled the room, purifying the shelter and those within its confines. The branches twisted and cracked, surrendering, which soon, the holy ones knew they must also do.

Derk passed a branch of mugwort to both the mogur and the medicine seer. The ancestors once said that mugwort was the first plant Creator One Breath put on Earth Mother. Therefore it was known throughout the clan as being stronger than any evil.

The mogur held a length of stuffed seal intestine, containing trance-inducing herbs. Every season he made new linkage by properly cleaning and tying off one end of the gut, then inserting the potent dried roots, leaves, or bark and tying another knot before adding more. This paunch contained ten preserved plants, each separated by a knot—each poisonous if improperly taken.

With reservation, the mogur ran his hand over the intestine paunch which held his lethal plants. His features remained stoic, masking the turmoil within him. Where his hand stopped, he cut off a section of the stuffed gut. He did this three times, presenting Derk and the medicine seer with the first two segments and keeping the last for himself.

Nervously, the medicine seer poured sea water into a bleached mussel shell, took a portion of the herbs and washed it down with the salty liquid. He handed the water pouch and ribbed shell to Derk and the mogur, who repeated the process. The mogur, sitting next to Bittoo, refilled the white shell and placed the shallow container at Bittoo's side. None of them relished the deadly trance-seeking plants. But the demanding spirits craved the food as a means of communication.

The three men clasped hands. While the mogur grabbed the boy's ankle with his free palm, the medicine seer tightly clutched one of Bittoo's thin wrists with his other hand. Air, Fire, Water, and Earth —bound together by a human chain. They'd make their journey together, strengthened by their unbroken circle.

"Ya, Ho! Ya, Ho!" cried the mogur pleadingly. "Unseen spirits...join us. Bring your healing knowledge to this young tusu. He..." His voice trailed as his eyes glazed over. The herbs had begun their magic work—his words dwindled into vague mumbles.

Seeing the mogur's condition, Derk finished the man's request. "Ya, Ho! Ya, Ho! The boy is young...deserving to live. You named him Father of all Shaman, a tusu!" His stomach revolted against the strong plant, the sea water and his fear. His eyes refused to focus. He concentrated, staring at Bittoo's face, and lost his thinking pattern. He devoted his energy to reason, and his sight blurred once again. He closed them both briefly and resumed his plea. "Ceda, water mother. Do not desert the clan!"

The blaze of the sacred fire erupted uncontrollably. An immense single flare rose upward, leaping above the seated men. Slowly, it dwindled, presumably spent of its mischief. But unable to remain in its confines, the flame danced over the hearth and clung to the earth, spreading low and flowing. The blue heat crept between the holy men, then brushed against Derk. He flashed his eyes wide, expecting to be burnt, but the rolling hot blaze turned its course.

The medicine seer saw the smokeless fire demon with its surging heat as it closed around him, but his eyes remained shut to the rest, sparing him from seeing his body reduced to hunks of roasting meat.

The mogur and Derk screamed silently. They smelled the horrible odor of the medicine seer's burning skin. The fire absorbed into the seer's body, leaving blackened flesh which peeled——cooking off his bones. Derk, still clinging to the medicine seer's hand, felt the charred hot meat shrink under his touch.

No longer were the holy ones in control of their speech. Their thick tongues seemed incapable of forming the assurances they wished to convey to one another. Derk owned the presence of mind to squeeze the two hands he still held. The mogur responded with a hardy grasp, however the medicine seer's answer came as a faint movement in his fingers. The circle hadn't been broken, though as with Bittoo, the medicine seer was now a fragile link.

Bittoo in his defenseless state seemed the obvious one to attack, yet the sinister fire demon had assaulted the medicine seer. Fear, fear was the explanation, the mogur concluded. The dark one feared Ceda, and the reason could only be because Bittoo was her special ward.

Derk saw crashing sounds. He wanted to pluck them out of the air, except the mogur held tight to his hand. If he could just free himself, he might snatch and strangle the noise which hurt his temples. The loud sounds now bore a flavor—sweet—so sickening his mouth salivated, sending slobber down his chin. Why couldn't he hear the sounds? Was his hearing gone? He strove to concentrate.

He knew the ritual herbs bore the ability to cause such a mix-up of senses. Easily, he could break the medicine seer's grip and snatch the irritating noise, but such a reaction might leave the frail seer defenseless, susceptible to the malignant one. It was a trick! That was it. The evil one wanted him to let go of the medicine seer. He put added pressure on the seer's fleshless palm. No matter what, he'd hold on tight!

It seemed to him that the entity was resisting an assault on Bittoo. It must either be fearful of the boy or of Ceda, the boy's protector. Clearly, the wicked being wasn't going to confront Bittoo directly, only indirectly, by way of the rest of them. Apparently, the medicine seer was attacked first, since earlier, he used his healing knowledge to help the boy. Derk turned his head, discovering a glint of the same understanding in the mogur's eyes.

The mogur pondered over the selection of the herbs they digested. All his magical plants contained the properties to summon the entities from the invisible world, except not a single deity or any other spirit helper from the Land of the Souls had, as yet, come to aid them. Maybe, he alone witnessed the demonic fire-being which consumed the medicine seer. Observing through blurred vision, he saw the seer—a skeletal figure who continued to cling to both Derk and Bittoo.

A slow chilling fear overtook him as he sensed something entering the lodge. He tensed while his eyes darted back and forth, striving to catch a glimpse of the unknown intruder. The unidentified was coming for him—he knew it—he knew it for sure.

Full of terror, Derk viewed a spirit manifest above the sacred hearth—a brown creature that took the form of a magnificent bear, yet with feet and hands of a human. As the ghostly image became clear, he noted the expression in the mogur's eyes changing from fear to joy, then back to fear.

As if unaware of the serious situation, the

creature pranced light and playful until growing tired of its own games. Abruptly, the graceful beast altered its moves, turning into a cruel looking demon. Its human-like fingers transformed into long, deadly claws, savagely striking out at the mogur. The aggressive monster tore open lengthy slits over the man's torso. The blood ran fast, first drenching the mogur's tattered clothing, then his sitting furs.

The mogur squirmed in his own pool of red fluid, but still kept his handhold with both Derk and Bittoo. Seeing this, the maddened beast severed the mogur's head in one swipe. With blood dripping claws, the demon scooped the mogur's head hollow and placed the empty skull upright in the fork of a tree branch rising from the fire. The mogur, with flesh remaining on his face, stared at Derk through two vacant sockets.

No longer capable of watching the grisly scene, Derk shut his wet, salty eyes. He concentrated on the sky people and his treasured star rock. He wished his tongue might loosen and allow him to sing his power songs. In his mind, he heard a vibrating chant, and in his body, he felt a renewal of strength. If only he could attract his spirit guide's attention, persuade it to cleanse the shelter of the evil ones, and restore Bittoo's health.

A soothing brightness shone through his thin eyelids, radiating warmth and caring sensations, like those occurring in the past, the many times his spirit guides had visited. Yet still fearful, he refused to peek at the being. His tactic proved useless, the illusion penetrated his closed lids. The entity presented itself as a beautiful semi-transparent woman who held a golden star in one palm and the dim, hazy moon in her other.

He desperately needed to believe in the vision. But since the previous demons impersonated the mogur's and the medicine seer's spirit helpers, he distrusted and firmly rejected the woman and the soothing comfort she offered.

The spurned female viciously threw the star and the moon into the dwindling fire. As she did, her face and body began to age, then distort. Her hair whitened and thinned to a few wispy clumps, while her face grew grotesque with a jutting sharp nose, deep set stabbing eyes and leathery wrinkled skin which sagged like a string of long beads. Heckling and mocking, the sorceress circled Derk, grabbed at his shoulders and slithered into his body.

The possessed man jerked violently as spasms wrenched through him. Draped in blood, the black spirit slowly drifted out Derk's gaping mouth, carrying his dismembered organs. The hag punctured his unattached stomach and sent its foul contents splattering over the four holy ones. Greedily, the hideous cannibal devoured Derk's pumping heart and immediately disappeared through the smoke hole, trailing a lengthy section of human entrails.

On their own, the battered men had endured the ravages of the worst of the demons. Temporarily defeated, unable to break the circle of hands, the three dark phantoms had departed.

A spray of refreshing water drenched the exhausted men. Replacing Bittoo in his sick bed, lay an enormous salmon, flopping wildly. The mogur now gripped the slimy tail of a fish, instead of the boy's ankle. The medicine seer found his hand hooked through one of its gills.

The men couldn't believe a black spirit was actually assaulting the holy young tusu. They were finished, totally beaten. If they let go of the fish in order to defend the boy, they'd break their power circle, which until this time, had kept them all from perishing.

The three watched and held onto the phantom. The spirit did nothing, except slowly decrease its movements. The men had limited energy left to continue. Nonetheless, the unbending mogur devised a simple final plan. He wouldn't allow the salmon to return to the water—he intended to hold onto the scaly fish until it suffocated. After that, he'd be depleted of energy for the healing rite and at the mercy of any dark entity which chose to dispose of him or of Bittoo.

He wanted the fish demon to suffer as he, Derk, and the medicine seer just suffered. If possible, he'd gladly slit open its soft underbelly and joyously watch the vile being spill its slimy guts over the sacred fire.

For an extended amount of time, the three seeking revenge watched the salmon, refusing to let go—refusing to break their circle of power. As the demon's activity gradually lessened, the holy ones' senses gradually increased—the fish gulped for breaths of lake water, and their vision returned. Its silvery scales dried stiffly, and Derk's speech improved. It turned rotting black and still they held onto the demon, refusing to break the circle. When the fish faded, becoming almost transparent, Bittoo could faintly be seen. The boy and the evil one, both hazy figures, appeared as a single merged form.

Awareness crossed the mogur's eyes. Realizing the awful truth, he swiftly broke his forceful hold on the dying salmon and studied his empty palm as if his hand just did something deplorable without his permission.

Following the mogur's example, the remaining men also freed their cramped hands.

"I've just attempted to kill the water deity," whimpered the mogur, sickened and remorseful of his action. "A dark demon wouldn't have restored our sight and speech, let alone our strength. It must be Ceda."

"And the boy!" Derk exclaimed, as the outline of the deity vanished altogether, leaving only Bittoo on his hill of sleeping furs, exactly as he lay when the ceremony started except now conscious and alert.

Perplexed, Bittoo studied the three holy leaders. The medicine seer's clothing hides looked charred with holes and his hair singed. Derk's mouth streamed blood, and hanging from the mogur's shoulders was his unsewn garment, sliced and stained red. A puddle of thin blood surrounded the mogur. And each one, including himself, was thoroughly soaked, doused in water that held an obscure yet familiar scent.

*For a very long time, his feeble brother hadn't
stirred. Surely, Creator One Breath was looking over
Bear Claw since his weak body still felt warm.*

*To no avail, Eagle Shadow tried to dismiss the
horrible thoughts which consumed him. How could
he live on Earth Mother without his identical twin?
They were truly just a single person instead of two.
If one of them died, it'd be as though one half of a
human journeyed to the Land of the Souls and the
other half remained with the living.*

*The idea seemed dreadful, so Eagle Shadow forced
himself to continue with his story-telling. Whether
his brother understood his words, he didn't know.
But he needed to keep occupied and send his own
ghastly thoughts into the hidden depths of his mind.*

***

11

He'd do it. He hated to, but he would. Such
a thing was expected. But he felt himself
being forced. Forced by the shaman, forced
by his father, but most strongly forced by his spirit
helper. "She's not my helper. She's anything but a
spirit helper," Bittoo spat out loud. "I'll do it because
I fear for the safety of the clan and because I fear her

threats." He drug his feet while trudging through camp.

From a measurable distance, he inspected the abandoned bear cage. Snow had filtered through the spaces between the roof beams, accumulated inside, and covered the solid wooden floor. Unmolested icicles, their tops as large around as one of his thighs, encased the entire frame, giving the appearance of a double set of bars, constraining its absent captive. The pen stood empty, used for a brief two days before the Bear Hunter Band had hastily packed up and marched back to their camp.

"Ya, Ho," Bittoo said absent-mindedly, after entering Derk's earthen dwelling.

Derk anticipated that today might be the one when the adolesent returned. During the moons of the heavy snows, routinely, Bittoo passed many days and nights with him, learning the knowledge of the ancient shamans. When the boy's head spun with the vastness of their unfamiliar practices, he gathered his winter sleeping robes and crawled home for long dismal periods, remaining at his own fire, absorbing the new wisdom.

"Ya, Ho," Derk and his woman rendered together, their voices sounding as one.

Vigorously, Bittoo stamped the snow from his new seal skin boots and resumed his regular place to the west of the sacred hearth. "Why did the mogur direct the bear cage to be built, if only to use it a short time?"

The question amused Derk. He wanted to chuckle, but decided such a response might be inappropriate. It was for Bittoo to decide whether the mogur's actions were humorous or not.

"Do you know?" the adolescent inquired louder, wondering whether the shaman heard his question.

"The mogur intended to remain through the time of the heavy snows. So the men built the enclosure. His people even brought ample provisions to stay."

"Then why did they go?"

"The mogur fears you because your spirit guide is too powerful for him. He would've stayed longer if he hadn't tried to kill Ceda. During the ceremony, we were terrorized by demons that at first pretended to be our spirit guides. The mogur assumed the fish was another evil one disguising herself, so he attempted to strangle her."

Bittoo laughed heartily. The shaman joined in, until warm droplets of water rolled down his chin.

"It's good the incident happened in such a manner. Although the mogur said nothing to me, I feel sure he considers you his rival. As a tusu, you're regarded more highly than he."

"Then, I should be wary of envious holy men," Bittoo said hesitantly, thinking it just one more unexpected obstacle in the never-ending craziness that had befallen him.

"It's doubtful you need to be uneasy where the mogur is concerned. He won't plot against you now. He broods too much about Ceda taking her vengeance out on him. He's probably in his pit house creating new rituals, and hanging elaborate talismans in her honor. If anything, the mogur will stay a safe distance from you, but when that becomes impossible, he'll be overly nice."

"You mean," Bittoo laughed, "if I visit the mogur, he'll do almost anything for me?"

For a brief time the question went unanswered. Derk thought hard about his reply. "I think that just about anyone would do just about anything for you. But they would rather keep their distance. No one knows whether Ceda or a demon stalks you, and what might happen next. And no one understands you."

The smile left Bittoo's handsome face. It seemed odd that clansmen might do more for him than they would normally. It was funny yet sad. Most everyone in Frozen Duck Band seemed afraid and avoided him. He'd spent much time this winter learning the ways of a shaman, ways he hoped never to use. *But I do these things only to please. I do everything to please. By Creator One Breath...someday I'll resist.*

Sleet furiously assaulted the shelter's roof, adding to the sad mood of its occupants. Thoughts turned to the hunters who left early in the morning darkness. It should've been the end of the Starvation Moon, but this winter was everlasting. Some families completely without stores, relied on their fellow neighbors for daily handouts. Loose clothing concealed flesh hanging from bony frames. Children silently pleaded with sunken eyes. If meat wasn't obtained soon, the people of Frozen Duck Band would boil and eat their sleeping hides.

"After today, you'll be forever connected to Ceda, mother of all water creatures," conveyed Derk. "Or did you change your mind?"

"I haven't changed my mind."

"Will you remove your nose loop?"

"No," came Bittoo's firm response. He still distrusted his new spirit helper. Sure she'd protect him from outside harm and restore his health when necessary, for as long as it benefited her. She named him tusu and the Father of all Shaman, except in reality, all was a pretext for her survival. Her concern was for herself, her own mortality, and at any time, she might turn on him. Therefore he intended to keep his nose ring in place as protection against her.

Derk and Bittoo had indulged in this same discussion two or three times during the bleak winter. The boy, steadfast and secretive, never explained his reasons. Once, without results, the shaman suggested Bittoo transfer the loop into his medicine bag.

"I can't influence you to do otherwise, but continuing to wear your nose ring suggests you lack faith in your spirit helper."

"It's best I do it this way," Bittoo insisted, determined to follow his strong sense of survival.

"You..." Torrents of unyielding sleet battered the domed roof, drowning the shaman's reply.

She Dog's male offspring playfully attacked a stack of sleeping fur. Determined, the gleeful whelp tried to catch the bouncing ice pellets, which gained entrance through the uncovered smoke hole. His lunge left him deeply sunken in the center of the fluffy pile of furs, unable to find his melting prey.

"Get," scolded the shaman, then turned his attention toward Bittoo. "When are you going to take that pesky canine home?"

"He should grow a little more before I separate him from his mother."

"The pup has been weaned for a whole two moons."

Bittoo stubbornly dropped the subject. His reason for not accepting the dog at this time was one he didn't care to divulge.

Before Derk placed dried wood onto the fire, he arranged tumbled river stones in the coals. "Since we can't agree on the dog or your nose ring, perhaps we should prepare for your shaman's mark."

Bittoo removed a small stick from the fire and drew two lines in the soft ash, one arching upward and one arching downward—one end connected while the remaining two ends crossed.

"That's a fine sketch of a fish. Easy for me to copy, too," Derk said pleasantly. "It looks remarkably like the one you wore in my dream." He handed Bittoo a rawhide pouch filled with water and strips of birch bark. "You should boil this solution before we proceed."

He followed Derk's instructions, adding the smooth rocks to the mixture, removing the stones and adding more after the liquid finished sucking the heat from them. Before it readied, the chore grew tedious, but the additional time provided him a chance to think—and plan.

A stone bursting in the fire jarred his thoughts to the present. He suddenly realized his mind had been elsewhere, as if he weren't the least bit troubled with what was to follow. Sweat trickled down his brow, even though he turned clammy cold. He hung the tacky pouch from an antler tine to cool, and keenly eyed Derk, opening a small rawhide container. Inside lay six obsidian awls rolled individually in pieces of soft buckskin.

The shaman selected the tiniest of the shiny obsidian punches which resembled a large porcupine quill. First, he submerged the sharpest end into the hot liquid and followed up by tightly winding nettle fiber around it, allowing only the tip of the point to peek through.

He waved for Bittoo to stretch out near the fire. He cleansed the boy's right cheek with a soft rabbit hide dipped in the hot bark solution. "Bite down hard, and whatever you do, don't move or I'll accidentally slice you."

Unspoken alarm crossed Bittoo's face. *I want to be anyplace but here.* The point looked as deadly as any weapon he'd ever seen. He clenched both his jaw and his fists, waiting for the jab of pain.

Concentrating, Derk swallowed hard. After sucking in his breath, he punctured the boy's skin with a swift accurate tap of the obsidian point. He began his efforts on the underneath line in order to eliminate blood streaming from above. Thinking he'd be proud if the tattoo turned out favorably, he pierced Bittoo's cheek with steady, even raps.

He paused briefly and wiped the blood away with the saturated hide before starting again. This time he endeavored to make conversation, for he'd seen a tear squeeze loose from the corner of Bittoo's eye.

"Once, many seasons ago, the mogur implored Noork, my mentor, to apply the tattoo of a bear claw on his face. I remember seeing the sacred mark...truly inspiring to look upon. One might think it pleased the bear deity, however two seasons later, a sacrificial bear ripped open the mogur's face, straight through the tattoo, even tearing off the mogur's nose."

Bittoo gagged on saliva dripping down his throat. Derk stopped for the second time and allowed the boy to rise. Bittoo's color turned white, and his body shook. After clearing his throat, he laid back down.

"I'm almost finished," the shaman assured him, feeling immense pride in Bittoo for his bravery. "And I'm almost finished with my tale." He continued, without missing a single stab.

"Where was I? Ah yes, the mogur's blood had drained swiftly out the rivers of his body, and some clansmen say they heard the souls of the dead calling for him. The elders urgently sent for the medicine seer and the holy men from other bands. Of course they saved him, that's evident, but for many days, the medicine seer expected him to die. When he survived, the clansmen gave all the credit to the mogur and none to the seer, or even the other spiritual leaders. The people said the mogur's powerful spirit guide, brought him back from the edges of death."

Derk hesitated, inspecting the lines of bloody dots. The outcome satisfied him. He reached into the warm coals with a bone scoop, and one at a time, lifted out three rocks covered in black soot. "Just a little longer," he said but realized Bittoo was unable to hear. The boy had passed out.

When the stones cooled, he thoroughly scrubbed the wounds with the blackened rocks, until the charcoal lay evenly distributed in the holes of Bittoo's skin.

Bittoo exited the shaman's dwelling midway through the night. The sleet had ceased, leaving an unwanted gift, a treacherous layer of ice shrouding the trampled snow and everything else it could conquer. He stood still, admiring the bewitching scene and hearing the occasional snap of a branch, breaking from the excess weight of ice.

He did it—he actually did. He allowed Derk to mark him with a shaman tattoo, while all along, knowing he'd hate it. He thought of the tattoo as a temporary thing. But how could it be removed?

Gazing upward, he caught a glimpse of Moon Watcher's face disappearing behind dark, fast moving clouds. "I bet you dislike having your vision blocked," he murmured aloud to her. "What are you doing when I can't see you?" he questioned seriously, wanting and half expecting a reply. "I wish I could hide my face like you're doing right now." He rubbed his chin and for the first time, felt soft whiskers. His eyes brightened. Someday, he'd be able to grow a beard and hide the unwanted tattoo. His smile grew wide. He wouldn't leave his face bare as other shaman do.

From somewhere ahead of him came a steady crunching noise—made by a human walking slowly but deliberately choosing his footing. He realized that the person was larger than himself. When the individual stepped down, breaking through the ice and snow, the sound was loud—whereas he knew his steps made much less commotion. His Uncle Cir would be glad he was able to determine this.

Moon Watcher's face shone through a break in the clouds, allowing Bittoo to catch sight of a male, burdened with a difficult load. The man failed to call out a greeting which seemed odd. All hunters knew to make themselves recognized when entering the village.

In the darkness, Bittoo saw the man's silhouette move near the fringe of the encampment where the first two dwellings meet the forest path. The intruder bent at the waist and lifted a large object from around his shoulders. Appearing to place it on the snow, the man stood upright, and as though frightened, turned and fled into the woods.

Bittoo went forward, making as little noise as possible. Again, he thought his uncle would be proud of him, this time for his almost silent tread. He was within a spear throw from where the man took flight when Patee's, soft and beseeching voice startled him.

"Froom is that you?" She lit a bark torch, waving it high in a wide circular motion.

Bittoo quickly sprawled on the ice covered earth. He lay among a scattering of alder, pine and cedar fire wood. Patee walked to the forest path and with ample light, vanished through the trees. He felt somewhat responsible for the woman. Horrible things could happen to anyone alone in the forest at night. But what if the man he'd seen was Froom? Would the lunatic try to kill him a second time if he got the chance?

He pulled himself to a sitting position, observing Patee's torch-light moving sluggishly through the timber. Maybe, she was having a secret meeting. It took a clever and hardy man to live alone during the moons of the heavy snows. Especially when he wasn't prepared to do so as was the case when Froom left camp in the fall. Surely, Froom hadn't been returning for food throughout the winter, because Patee seemed to have plenty when every one else's stash was nearly depleted. He assumed, as did others, that she'd been sharing Froom's uneaten portion with her hungry neighbors.

He decided to wake the shaman and turn the mystery over to him. Derk remained the only man in camp, except for the elders. Before he could rise, the torch-light began moving in the opposite direction, back toward the village. Quickly, he crawled to the rear of Patee's dwelling and on his tip toes, peered over the domed roof.

The woman wandered into the clearing, carrying her head and torch low, and walking the walk of someone who bore a sad heart. By plunging the butt end of the torch into the ice crust, Patee freed her hands. She removed her woman's knife from her waist strap and knelt down.

Bittoo's blood pumped fast, he held his breath. Patee was about to harm herself. Immediately though, he saw her intent and released his breath: The gutted corpse of a spotted deer was spread before her.

His mouth watered as he imagined a large, juicy chunk of the roasted meat. Maybe the band's hunters will be as fortunate as Patee's phantom visitor. He wanted to help her skin and cut up the deer, but was unwilling to expose himself, then she would know he had been spying.

For Bittoo, it seemed he'd just gotten to sleep when he heard Patee's shouting voice. "I have cooked venison! Come!" Groggy, he touched his painful cheek, then noticed Father Sun streaming through the smoke hole. Quickly forgetting how savory, fresh meat tasted and how empty his stomach felt, he drifted back into a restless slumber.

A full day later, he woke, this time to joyous cries of laughter. Derk looked in on him twice while he slept, checking the tattoo for signs of fever and puss. The hunters returned after rousting a bear from its winter sleep. The animal's den was among the roots of a giant cedar tree. Cir discovered the burrow the last time he trapped near the low meadow, so he received the honor of thrusting the first spear.

The women were quick to inform their mates about the musk deer which appeared at Patee's lodge, but no one, not even the children, asked Patee who gave her the buck. Everyone appeared reluctant to cause her shame. After all, she unselfishly shared the meat and marrow throughout the hungry camp.

12

With mixed emotions, Gaaf followed the path that skirted the western edge of Frozen Duck Lake. When reaching its fork, he planned on taking the trail north. Only two handfuls of days had passed since the hunter's victorious return. In that amount of time, the weather drastically improved. Except for the northern slopes and the mountains where glaciers leisurely clung, the warm salmon wind speedily melted the build-up of winter snow. The camp had turned into slippery muck, but in their cheerfulness, the villagers saw it as the beginning of abundance, an essential condition before roots, berries and game became plentiful.

The time of the heavy snows turned out to be a lonely season for him with Bittoo stuffed away in either his or the shaman's lodge. When he did see his boyhood friend, Bittoo seemed sullenly preoccupied. He missed the carefree times they spent together and missed having someone to confide in. He wished he could relate his fears and dreams to his friend, for today he embarked on the most important, yet frightening, event of his life. He was headed for a private region, two days from camp where he hoped to be given a spirit helper.

Late yesterday, he'd begun his fast. This morning, rising early and with reservation, he went to the shaman's hut. There Derk purified him with fragrant smoke. Being cleansed was the last thing he remembered. But Sun Father shone high in the sky when he departed the lodge, which meant he stayed with the shaman the entire morning. The shaman had placed him in a trance then smeared the red ochre clay over his slackened face.

With difficulty, Gaaf ignored his growling stomach. After all, he'd been much hungrier just recently, during the time of the Starvation Moon. Barc, his father, had nourished him with bear meat, knowing strength was necessary for one seeking a vision quest. Barc would've given him a fatty portion, except the bear used up its massive fat reserve during its winter sleep.

He carried his bed fur, fire-starter kit and three short spears for his spear thrower. To eat when on his vision quest was strickly taboo. He brought his spear thrower for protection. After his vision quest, while on his way home, he intended to hunt and forage for food. If he returned in time, he'd join the bandsmen journeying to the Great Sea for the annual seal hunt.

He quickened his stride. All the same, he deeply wished Bittoo were with him, the way they always planned. Of course, exposing a tusu to such a venture could prove dangerous—such an undertaking was forbidden.

Had he turned toward Frozen Duck Camp, for one last look, he would've seen the villagers watching his departure and also caught sight of Bittoo harboring a mischievous grin.

The following morning, alone in the lodge, Bittoo realized he must hurry. He tied cordage around his sleeping fur. Inside the bed roll, he wrapped the necessary items, but unlike Gaaf, he hid both his spear thrower and spears inside his furry pack.He inspected the support beam. The timber looked bare without his leather spear-case hanging from its peg. Hastily unbinding his bulky pack, he withdrew the spear-case. After removing the short spears, he hung the leather container at its rightful place on the pole, feeling confident that his family wouldn't notice its missing spears. He left his two long spears resting against the post, thinking their absence would be obvious.

Looking and listening, he warily crept up the ladder rungs. If done just right, his family would think he was at the shaman's lodge, and the shaman would think him home with his family. Maybe he'd be fortunate enough and return to camp before anyone realized his absence.

A loud disturbance from across the camp caught his attention. Since not a single person roamed the grounds, he assumed everyone was drawn to the ruckus. Unable to believe his luck, he bolted toward the woods, performing a head-on assault into the underbrush, stopping only long enough to make sure he hadn't been observed. His heart throbbed in his chest and up his neck, blasting heat pulses through his head.

His strategy was to strike out through the forest, until crossing with the northern trail. He might be seen following along the bank of the lake as Gaaf did. But the noise in the village, which so nicely allowed him to sneak away, had still not subsided, and his curiosity got the best of him. He edged his way, crawling on his belly, in the opposite direction he needed to travel. He squirmed though the foliage until seeing the villagers and clearly hearing their voices.

"She hasn't anyone to provide for her or the child, and her stockpile of food is used up," proclaimed Lant of the Spear Creek Band.

"Froom will come home," responded Patee.

"Then let him find you at my lodge," voiced the burly man in an unyielding tone.

Bittoo suspected as did every one else in camp that Froom had secretly provided meat during the times of the heavy snows. Who else could it have been? Yet it wasn't known if Froom still lived. He might have died right after leaving the last deer for Patee. An accident may have befallen him, moreover if Froom still lived, the man could as easily fetch his woman at the Spear Creek Camp. Froom may even feel less humiliated among the villagers of that band.

Actually, Bittoo didn't care, he never wanted to see the evil man again—for surely, Froom would try another attempt on his life. And Lant was a man of his word—the man came back for Patee as he'd said. However no one would take her by force.

"My daughter and I will go with you," Patee said in her soft voice. "But Frozen Duck Camp is our home, and someday we'll return."

Bittoo caught the expression on the woman's face, already she looked homesick. He felt sorry for Patee, but with her gone, perhaps Froom wouldn't come around and he'd feel safer, that is if Froom still walked among the living.

He snaked his way backwards, seeking denser forest cover. Except for his face, his complete front side was mud-smeared. He jerked around, thinking he heard someone moving behind him. Remaining still, he held his breath until his lungs resisted.

After a short time, which seemed eternal, he stood, partially hidden against a fallen cedar tree. He judged the camp to be a safe distance away, and whoever or whatever startled him was either gone or apparently not aiming to be harmful.

He adjusted the leather straps which held the bed roll against his back. They had caught on snags and loosened. Soon, when reaching the other path, he'd untie his bed fur and retrieve his weapon.

In the late afternoon, he took a well deserved break, resting on a large basalt rock, overlooking a swollen stream. The trail, so often used, lay stripped clean of vegetation. He slipped and slid in brown mire the entire day and chuckled aloud when seeing evidence indicating Gaaf experienced equal difficulty walking the same route. His friend even left a grimy hand-print on the rock where he now sat. Fidgeting, he peeled the nearly dried hunks of mud from the front of his seal skin tunic, then tossed them into the fast running water.

Five moons earlier, he promised Gaaf they'd go together, and now, he was keeping that pledge. Gaaf would surely be surprised. It'd be impossible to catch up with his friend who already had a full days start, so he'd join up with him in their special valley.

He stood and studied the marks on the ground. He might save time by determining the spot where Gaaf or anyone else recently crossed the flooding stream. The high rushing water from the snow melt made the usual crossing treacherous. Any other season, it wasn't an obstacle. During periods of low water, a person could take a long running start and jump across. But when a person misjudged, that person received a refreshing drench. This he knew by experience.

A number of sunken boot prints headed upstream while only one smeared set of human tracks followed the riverbank downstream. None of the travelers backtracked. He pursued the group of footsteps leading up river, not just because more clansmen plainly went that way, but clearly Gaaf's shorter bootprints overlayed all the other ones.

The tracks led him to an uprooted pine tree, stretching from bank to bank, over the frigid water. Allowing for easier foot traffic, earlier travelers removed the top branches from the log. The remaining boughs hung off the sides, bouncing wildly, yielding unmercifully to the whims of the swift dark rapids.

With well placed tiny steps, Bittoo walked the soaked log. Loose bark broke away under his boots. He held his arms straight out at shoulder height, maintaining balance, until reaching the opposite shore.

He felt free. Freer than he thought possible. He wished never to return to camp. No longer did he hold even the smallest control over his life. No longer did he make decisions for himself, and no longer was he a normal adolescent. He envied his friend

Gaaf. But for now he felt free, if only for a short time. How comicial it'd be to sneak back into camp with Gaaf and find out that no one noticed he ran away.

At dusk, Bittoo exited the tedious trail, scouting a location for a safe sleeping place. He choose a spot against an embankment, underneath the graceful flowing boughs of a spruce tree.

Twice in the dark of the night, he heard something making its way through the woods. Both times, he yelled loudly, trying to startle and frighten the intruder. But each time, the response came as total stillness. Any variety of animal would've bolted when hearing such a loud human voice and made a great deal of noise when fleeing.

Maybe his uninvited guest belonged to the two-legged species. He threw dirt on his tiny fire and waited for the unknown. He slept fitfully, although he hadn't planned to sleep at all.

At dawn, he savored a few bites of smoked salmon while scouring the area for clues of his nighttime visitor. He found broken twigs and trampled ground leaves. Neither sign proved helpful in solving the mystery but only confirmed that something disturbed the area quite recently. There wasn't any fur, hair or spoor with which to identify his uninvited guest.

He pushed on, wanting to reach the valley before nightfall. Two summers ago, he and Gaaf tagged along with the women to pick blackberries at the largest thicket they ever saw. The brambles covered a gigantic meadow and slowly, over time, encroached upon the forest. Trees and bushes had fallen victim to the heavy vines that sent their strangling tentacles high into the air, scouting for prey. On the outskirts of the thicket grew robust trees, unsuspecting of the first vines which enveloped thorny arms around their bark.

Curiously, they decided to skirt the dense briars just to see how widespread the entanglement truly was. He started in one direction and Gaaf went the opposite. They set out to walk until they met on the other side. Failing to achieve their goal, they returned at nightfall, stating the thicket proved too large to hike around in one day, and apparently it stretched far over the ridges in both directions.

They rose early the next morning with a new plan. Small animals had burrowed through the berry thicket, leaving a maize of tunnels, most barely accessible. Being without their winter mittens, they wrapped protective leather over their hands, plus bound thick layers of hide around their bony knees. Undetected, they crawled single file into the brambles.

He had led the way, but when running into a dead end, both turned about, which put Gaaf in front. They found evidence of rabbits, raccoons, skunks, fox, and feathers of various species of birds and gave no thought to the chance of meeting anything hostile.

A considerable bulk of time elapsed before they entered a clearing. With their good sense of direction, they exited on the opposite side of the massive berry patch, exactly where they hoped they would. Both were badly bloodied and scratched.

In awe, they explored their new surroundings. The small secluded valley was canyon like, with high cliffs on every side, except for one end, the opening overgrown with blackberries. The east bluff of the canyon harbored a spring. Its water trickled out through the rocky basalt, creating a crystal clear pool with no visible drainage. Neither he nor Gaaf told anyone about their find and vowed to return when the time came for their vision quests.

If only life was as simple as when he and his childhood companion found their private playground. They'd been joyous and lighthearted. He still aimed to live much the same as he always planned, hunting and fishing and going on journeys with his friend, Gaaf. Maybe not as often as he wanted, but he intended do those things regardless of anyone's criticism.

Derk could perform all the rites and rituals for the band. After the shaman died, and only if there was no other way, he would take over those duties. Meanwhile, he expected to be tutored by Derk. Anyone scolding him for placing himself in risky situations would need to adapt. Most of the time, the villagers politely avoided him. They seemed leery of the strong spirit that tormented him and unsure of what it might do. He too was unsure, but he knew it to be Ceda. If he could just finish whatever she held in store for him and get on with a normal life. She told him that when he saw the spirit of the wind, it would be time. He was always trying to see it.

Deep in thought, he almost passed the narrow footpath which led to the blackberries. Had he stayed on the main trail, he would've promptly reached the village of the Bear Hunter Band.

He wondered if Derk were correct when claiming that the mogur was actually a distant ally. Perhaps, the mogur had spied on him during the night. He withdrew the cruel allegation soon after the thought entered his mind. Besides, the mogur wouldn't be alone; he was required to travel under the protection of either his dogs or his apprentice. And two intruders in the brush would create more noise than he heard. Perhaps, he and Gaaf could take a side trip to the Bear Hunter's Camp after Gaaf finished with his spirit search. It might be amusing seeing the mogur's reaction to him.

He considered himself clever, refusing the male pup Derk gave him. If the animal became homesick, it may have scampered back to Frozen Duck Camp and alerted the villagers of his absence.

He arrived at the canyon well before dusk, elated to have returned to the tranquil hide-a-way...so much so, he didn't feel the rigors of his brief two-day journey.

Slowly, he sauntered to his right, heading for the pool and a drink of chilling spring water. He peered through the scrub trees, hoping to locate his friend. The lush valley floor was cluttered with willows, fern and moss, while spruce and fir trees meagerly dotted the rocky cliffs.

He dropped his bedroll onto the damp ground. Before sleeping, the fur would be thoroughly inspected and shook to remove the thorns it harbored. Laying prone on Earth Mother with his head over the edge of the clear pond, he scooped handfuls of refreshing liquid into his mouth.

After splashing his face with the tantalizing water, he sat up and continued his search.

He didn't call out for his best friend as such an action might disrupt Gaaf's ritual. If Gaaf's power

animal appeared soon, they'd have plenty of time
to explore together. But if his friend's spirit guide
was slow to manifest, then he'd spend the time by
himself. He ignored the other possibility—what if
Gaaf didn't receive a vision, and the spirits ignored
Gaaf's plea?

Happily, he spotted his friend sitting below a
jagged overhang, straight across the canyon. "Ah,
this is excellent. I can stay near the pool and watch
him." His main purpose now was to safeguard Gaaf
while his friend was in a trance and vulnerable to
outside harm.

By nightfall, he had scrounged enough dried
wood to last till morning. He moved his gear onto a
slight incline, a spear throw away from the pond,
where the ground felt less soggy. Tomorrow, he
planned to collect leaves to place underneath his
sleeping robe. Such a bed cushion would allow him
to rest more comfortably.

He unpacked his sleeping robe by lifting one
furry end and letting the contents roll to the ground.
From the scattered items, he hastily snatched his fire
starter kit. And within a breath of time, he'd created
a dust that smoldered. He dropped the drilling stick,
and speedily but artfully added parched tinder,
while lightly blowing on the mixture. When the
tinder caught fire, he placed twigs on the tiny flames,
then even hardier twigs until the little fire burned
and accepted short stubby branches without dying.

The next morning, he woke to a pair of startled
wood ducks hurriedly flying from the pond. A rush
of loose rock tumbled from the cliff's face directly
above the pool, causing high splashes of water and

a muddy pond. Without taking his eyes off the steep bluff, he slowly loaded his spear thrower, then remained motionless for a very long time before deciding it was safe. Looking across the canyon, he saw Gaaf, still sitting as stately as a tree.

He checked around the pond to see whether there'd been any early morning visitors, but other than the duck tracks, there weren't any fresh prints. Whatever ventured atop the cliff had probably kept the wildlife away. Now, he not only needed to worry about the elusive intruder above him, but where to set snares for the small game, so he could get food. By tomorrow, his stash of smoked fish would be eaten, and Gaaf would be famished after his vision quest.

The first part of the day, he stayed busy, making and setting traps the way his uncle Cir taught him. Normally, the task would take a short while to finish, however much of the time he spent scanning the bluffs with its many rocky outcroppings, jagged overhangs and small shadowy caves.

Lacking anything to do by mid-afternoon, he rested on his sleeping furs and studied the changing formations of the clouds.

The huntress was frightened by the odor of smoke that assaulted her nostrils, then alarmed by the pungent smell of another of her most dreaded enemies—a two legged beast, that suddenly interrupted her early morning prowling. For the very first time, she was glad to be barren with only herself to look after. She was accustomed to the hardships of motherhood which left the body weak and thin. This season, her muscles were firm and her coat sleek and golden tan.

The area wasn't her usual territory, yet the terrain rang familiar. Perhaps she'd been this way in her infancy. Somehow, even before cresting the ridge, her senses informed her of the water pond on the valley floor. But before getting near the base of the cliff to crouch in-waiting for her next meal, she detected the dreaded smoke. It took her by such surprise, she clumsily knocked unstable rock down the mountain slope.

Throughout the day she watched the boy, unable to understand his doings, and unable to reach the water hole to drink. When the boy ceased his activities, she undertook a different approach. Following the ridge away from the human, she dropped down to the valley bottom near the blackberry thicket. His repulsive scent was stronger in the canyon bottom. She wondered if the human's flesh tasted different than it smelled.

Hidden among the bushy willows, she skillfully worked her way toward the stranger. Cautiously watching him, she prowled closer and closer, always staying concealed. For a very long time, the human hadn't moved. Every muscle in her frame anxiously prepared for the easy kill. She scrunched down, shifting her weight to her back haunches in readiness to spring.

A fast whishing sound hummed past Bittoo, causing an air current to streak past his face. His eyes popped open as a spear bounced off the cliff rock directly at his side. Instincts taking over, he sank flat against the ground. He heard the rustle of bushes and the snapping of branches - someone was beating a hasty retreat.

Shakened, he seized his knife from his waist strap and waited. Someone had attempted to kill him. Most likely the same person who stalked him when he first left Frozen Duck Camp, and then, back in the forest the night before last, and the one who'd been on the bluff.

Again, there were sounds of movement. This time faint, as if someone was withdrawing but carefully choosing his steps.

Concerned for Gaaf's safety, he shifted his gaze across the valley. With a bed fur under his arm, his friend began his trek across the canyon. Bittoo gave the hand-signal for danger, and Gaaf swiftly ducked behind a sizable boulder.

Unable to see the problem from his vantage, Gaaf scampered up the bluff. Part way up, he turned and studied the valley floor. The willows grew thick in places, however nothing among the scrubs stood out as abnormal. He made his way down and over to

Bittoo. "Ya, Ho. Whatever was there is gone now," he reported.

Trembling, Bittoo pulled himself to sitting position and reached for the deadly spear. Its obsidian point had shattered when striking the cliff's surface. He turned the weapon over, and just below the wrapping, which held the spearhead to the wooden shaft, he spied four familiar man-made marks, three slashes and one dot.

He glared at the weapon with the tell-tale marks. "So Froom still lives!"

"You three must leave the lodge. Sho," Leha insisted gently, addressing Har, Cir, and Tam. "This is a delicate matter, and the presence of men is strictly forbidden."

No further prompting was necessary, the brothers readily escaped up the wooden ladder.

"Is it time?" the shaman asked, walking over to the trio who emerged from Har's dwelling. He eyed Cir's nervousness.

"My middle brother will soon become a father," Tam revealed, his voice full of amusement.

"And does Bittoo break a taboo and stay inside during the birth?" asked the concerned shaman.

"He's not in your lodge?" demanded Har, overwhelmed with the sudden knowledge that his son was missing.

13

The people of the Bear Hunter Band studied the young men as the two marched into their camp. Ceda had supposedly appointed Bittoo a great tusu, the Father of all Shaman, but the villagers had their doubts. Even so, they were familiar with shamans but completely unfamiliar with tusus. Only in legends were there predictions of such a mighty spirit leader. And what could be expected of a tusu wasn't clear. Certainly, Bittoo didn't act like any kind of holy leader that they ever knew, although now, the boy did harbor a shaman's tattoo on his cheek. Even those in Bittoo's village remained afraid of him. They feared associating with someone whose spirit helper or demon threatened to destroy their village with starvation.

And they were also frightened. While at Frozen Duck Camp, their mogur, seemingly out of fear, ran from Derk's lodge, where he participated in a healing ritual for Bittoo. In a terrified state, the mogur gathered up his people and hurriedly returned home. The rumor spread that he nearly strangled the water deity whom he claimed to be Bittoo's spirit totem.

In his earthen dwelling, the mogur had remained distant and closed off throughout the season of the heavy snows, the Starvation Moon, and even now as the time of the Seal Birthing Moon grew near. He'd seemed indifferent and unconcerned about their spiritual needs. The only ones having contact with him were his woman and his apprentice Luun.

Bittoo and Gaaf rounded the mogur's dome roof, startling a sleeping dog tethered to the ladder pole. The vicious animal leaped toward Gaaf, but Gaaf stood beyond the dog's short rein.

"Ya, Ho," Bittoo called, hoping the occupants would restrain their canine and invite them inside.

"Go away," answered Luun. "The mogur doesn't want to be disturbed."

"I can't see anyone! I'm talking with the deities," claimed the mogur, his voice raspy and frail.

"I'm Bittoo, the great tusu," he bragged loudly, winking at Gaaf and rolling his eyes. He thought it funny to call upon the holy one, owing to the fact the scar-faced mogur thought Ceda's powers stronger than his own, and the man feared the deity so. The whole thing rather amused him.

A charge of long silence enveloped the pit house. Bittoo and Gaaf looked disbelieving at one another, as did the three occupants inside the quiet lodge. The unyielding dog stood his ground with his guard hairs upright. Growling, he held the two at bay.

"Should we leave?" Gaaf asked.

Frowning, Bittoo shook his head.

"Get that mutt and let Bittoo in!" the mogur ordered, straining his words.

Luun bolted up the ladder and held the animal firmly by the neck. As Bittoo descended into the shelter, Luun viewed him suspiciously until Bittoo returned his hardened stare.

Bittoo broke into a large forced grin and mannerly addressed the occupants. "Ya, Ho."

Gaaf followed his friend into the pit house and caught him by his sleeve. "I don't like this," he whispered. "A dwelling with three mistrusting people and an entrance guarded by a vicious dog. There's no escape."

"Let's get the mogur's reaction. It might prove interesting, considering we haven't seen him since he nearly killed my spirit helper. I won't push things too far...just keep your eyes on Luun, he's really jumpy," Bittoo replied quietly as he watched Luun stealing down the ladder. "I think he fears I'll do something bad to the mogur."

"Ya, Ho," greeted Bittoo for the third time as he worked his way toward the sacred fire.

The mogur made an attempt to rise, but he looked in a weakened state and incapable. Bittoo dodged various talismans of shells and dried fish fins hanging from the antler tine rafters. It alarmed him to see the mogur looking shriveled and unstable.

The mogur rested among a large pile of sleeping robes on the west side of the sacred hearth, the side reserved for those who received their power from the water. It seemed a peculiar position for the soothsayer, whose power came from the north.

Like an animal, on his hands and knees, the sickly man crawled north of his fire pit. "Join me," he said, his heart beating rapidly in his meatless rib cage. "Sit at your rightful position."

Life was ebbing from the mogur's thin body. Bittoo thought he understood why. He lowered himself on the furs, a rush of shame flooding him. He had intended to playfully badger the middle-aged holy man, expecting his host to be very gracious even to his smallest wishes. But the mogur clearly looked ill and most likely because he still feared the water deity. The man's eyes deeply sunken, but wide and round, seemed filled with panic at the presence of his unwanted guest.

Bittoo felt embarrassed and ashamed. He'd spent much of the cold season learning the ways of the shamans, only aiming to store the knowledge in his head, nothing more. He hadn't planned on performing any rites or rituals for others, yet the great mogur required help—and very soon. The man looked close to death.

"I came to thank you for saving me from drowning when Froom drug me onto the lake and nearly killed me. I'll forever be obligated to you." The corners of his mouth curled in a warm smile. He could see the mogur letting his breath out and appearing more relaxed. "The mother of all water creatures is grateful." He only guessed that Ceda might appreciate what the mogur did.

Seemingly filled with pride, the man's grey eyes twinkled. Abruptly, their brightness faded. "I tried to choke Ceda!"

"She's too powerful for you to have succeeded. The mother of the water knows you thought she was a dark spirit."

"My behavior has made my heart heavy. Soon I shall die. Either I'll turn into a black demon or enter the Land of the Souls. But because of my actions toward Ceda, I believe my soul will become a dark and evil spirit, always tormenting the people of the clan."

In the dim light, Bittoo glanced over at Luun and Gaaf. Luun's facial gesture took on a slight smirk. No, maybe he only imagined seeing the smug look across the apprentice's face, for surely, Luun didn't wish the mogur to die and become a dark demon. But it seemed certain, without help, the mogur would soon die.

Unrolling his pack, Bittoo strew its contents on the ground. He reached for his large clam shell. His hand touched Froom's broken spear and a shiver of fear shot through him. He ignored his impulse to wrap the weapon back up and hurry off toward his village. "You've hung numerous talismans in Ceda's honor. It must please her."

"She doesn't show herself to me. I've beckoned her for a very long time, but the mother of all water beasts snubs me. She still hasn't forgiven me for my deplorable conduct."

Bittoo's stomach burned, and he smoldered with rage as his mind raced with a clear image—the truth of the matter. *Oh, but she has forgiven you. Ceda not only forgave you, but she planned for you to try and strangle her. She realized you'd later become demented, lose your strength and be on the verge of dying. And she knew I'd be compelled to exercise the duties of a holy one, performing a healing rite to restore your health...something I vowed never to do. And it was her plan, not mine, that I sneak away from Frozen Duck Camp and end up here.*

Bittoo wanted to explode his anger. Gaaf's earlier words, 'she traps you like an animal' rang in his ears. He sat for a very long time with his teeth clenched, his eyes pinched shut, feeling utterly and hopelessly trapped. If only he could shrink so small that he could hide.

"We'll call on her together. She will cure your body and your mind," he declared, knowing the mogur would recover, no matter what ritual he performed. For Ceda feared he might never follow the path of a tusu if the ceremony failed, and the mogur perished.

"I'm too weak...not strong enough to endure such a difficult healing ritual."

"You won't die," promised Bittoo, trying to control the fury he felt towards Ceda for tricking him so.

The apprentice moved to the mogur's side. "He needs to wait until he's strong before he calls upon the spirits. In his fragile state, a spirit can cause his death."

"We'll journey to the middle world. I'll carry him if necessary. Because if he does nothing, he will die!" Still infuriated with Ceda left him little patience for Luun, who was either overly protective of the mogur or didn't understand the urgency of the situation.

"The demons might enter his body if you take him there," Luun harped, keeping his voice and facial expressions calm.

"Hush, I taught you better." The mogur shook a bony finger at Luun. "Even if you haven't achieved the feat of entering the middle world, it's well known that only benign spirits meet with mortals there, but only when those spirits wish it. Evil spirits fear and never venture to the sacred place." The mogur had little breath by the time he finished scolding his apprentice.

Bittoo felt a twinge of sympathy for Luun, who, just two winters older than himself, seemed to genuinely care for the mogur. Yet he wondered if the apprentice, with so little knowledge, were truly destined to follow in the footsteps of the mogur. "Do you have any sacred sea water?"

"In the paunch, but the liquid dried up," the mogur whispered. He pointed to the container made of deer stomach, resting near the his fire pit.

Bittoo regarded the empty paunch. Inside, a light crusty film clung to its walls. He ran his hand across the white substance then tasted his fingers. "First bring me river water," he demanded, "then everyone leave the mogur and me to ourselves."

The mogur's mate abandoned her woman's hearth and presented Bittoo with the water. She smiled at him, obviously thankful he came to help. The broad tattoo around her lips portrayed an enormous grin. She shuffled up the ladder behind Luun and Gaaf.

Gaaf remained outside the mogur's hut. He'd allow no one to enter the dwelling, especially Luun. Something didn't strike him right about the apprentice. He wasn't sure what. He watched the furry dog that still protected the entrance and probably wouldn't permit him to go in alone. He thought about his new spirit animal. Under his breath, he sang a plea to his white fox spirit helper to shield him from this offensive apprentice.

"I should take part in the ritual," Luun informed Gaaf. "I'm practicing the ways of a shaman."

"This is between the mogur and the tusu," Gaaf rebutted. "You're not welcome."

Speechless, Luun shot Gaaf a look of disapproval. Gaaf could tell that Luun loathed his interfering. Perhaps Luun felt a little jealous of Bittoo, whose powers would soon heal the mogur. After Bittoo accomplished this healing, he'd forever be considered the most famed of all the holy ones. He had great faith in his friend and little in Luun.

Attempting to distract Luun, in order to keep him from joining the two holy men, Gaaf scourged his mind for something to say. "Bittoo's lucky to be alive," he finally revealed. "The tusu was almost killed."

Luun's brown eyes strained. "Would Ceda let it happen?"

Gaaf didn't have an answer. He shrugged his shoulders. "We've just come from my vision quest. Bittoo camped across the canyon. A spear went flying past him, just missing his face. We didn't see anyone nor did we find any foot prints."

"Why does someone want him dead?"

"The spear clearly has Froom's marks on it. Three slashes and one dot," Gaaf said. "Bittoo carries the weapon. Maybe, later you can see it."

A half smile played about Luun's lips, giving Gaaf a chill of foreboding. Why? Again he wasn't sure but felt deep down that he should've kept his mouth shut about the spear.

Bittoo poured the fresh water into the empty storage paunch. He whirled the container around, sloshing the water until the dried film dissolved. He sipped at the liquid and detected a mild salty taste.

Satisfied with the solution, he poured the entire amount into his clam shell.

Carefully, he pulled the mogur to a sitting position, stuffing hides behind and to the sides of the tottering man in order to keep him upright.

"Peer into the water and we'll travel to a place where only those with special vision go, and there we will converse with spirit helpers."

"I've tried to visit the place to communicate with Ceda, but she eludes me. I find myself sitting in a void without entities of any kind," the mogur related sadly, his eyes swelling with tears.

Bittoo placed the clam shell between himself and the mogur then reached over and held the man's quivering hands. "Don't let go of me. I'll carry you there, and my strength shall flow from me into you."

The two sets of grey eyes watched the liquid as it slowly moved inside the shell. It rippled like water being taunted by a gentle breeze. The motion embraced the shamans, and they swayed with the movement of the salty mixture. The two bodies lost their heaviness and floated just above the ground.

When the water stilled they looked down at its clear surface. A vivid picture took place in the waters depth—a worn mountain path wandering through a dense forest. Bittoo, still grasping the mogur's hands, let himself be drawn through the sacred water and into the vision.

Bittoo stood beside the mogur in the center of the trail which extended north and south. He was undecided which direction led to the deities, so he chose the northern route because the mogur always received his powers from the north. They walked through the quiet woods, hearing nothing and seeing not a single animal.

Finally, a white fox scampered onto the path and without fear spotted the shamans. With a flick of its tail and ears, the fox gestured for the two to follow. Bittoo recognized the animal as Gaaf's new spirit guide and a warm rush of confidence engulfed him.

They arrived at a rolling meadow, thriving with golden yellow flowers and littered with a maze of tall grass. The vibrant fox disappeared into the woods and reappeared with two young kits. The three frolicked together, unafraid of the humans who penetrated their special domain.

Loud thundering noises came from the far fringes of the colorful field. Bittoo looked at the mogur, whose eyes filled with terror.He jumped to his feet and tugged at the frightened man, pulling him behind a stand of firs. They peered from behind the scrawny trees. A swelling cloud of dust blocked their view, while the strange sounds grew deafening.

Until the air began to settle, the two feared the ghastly ruckus came from a chorus of dark, wretched demons. Possibly, he and the mogur hadn't entered the middle world, rather some unknown place. They continued to watch as three magnificent creatures, large ancient mammoths, stood upright and descended down the path.

Bittoo recalled seeing another such grand creature the first time he visited the middle world. The mammoths were once the spirit deities of Frozen Duck Band, and before the beautiful beasts died out, his people were known as the Great Mammoth Band.

Amazed with the grandeur of the massive giants, he sent a silent thanks for their presence, then stood and pursued them. When they reached the opposite side of the meadow, the hulking creatures vanished.

He led the mogur to a knoll where the path meandered for a short distance through the forest and suddenly ended at the sea. The wind erupted, bringing the bite of the salty odor inland. Bittoo sucked in the refreshing, wholesome air and for a breath of time, felt at peace with his surroundings. *Show me the spirit of the wind...I want to see it.* His eyelids fluttered, and their heaviness caused them to close.

"*Stupid boy!*" roared a gleeful voice in the breeze.

For a considerable length of time, no sounds came from the mogur's dwelling. Luun, Gaaf and the mogur's woman strained to hear. The mogur's smoke hole was idle. Finally, concerned about Bittoo and the mogur, they quietly entered the lodge. In the dimness, they saw them lying on the bear robes with their hands touching.

The woman lit a birch bark torch and presented it to Gaaf. Softly, he circled the sacred hearth. Both men stirred. The mogur sat upright.

Bittoo rolled on his back and beamed up at Gaaf. "Ya, Ho," he blurted then rolled back onto his stomach and regarded the mogur. A lump caught in his throat. He motioned for Gaaf to lower the light, so he might inspect the mogur's face.

The mogur ran his hands over his cheeks and above his lips. Everyone watched in disbelief. His woman began to cry, blinking as if she wasn't seeing clearly.

No longer were there wicked scars across the mogur's face. Even his old shaman's tattoo was unmistakably distinct on his upper right cheek. But most incredible of all, his nose had been restored.

The mogur stretched out on his fur, as if believing himself to be demented or dreaming.

"Ceda healed your face," Bittoo said excitedly.

"Am I dreaming?" The mogur stood without assistance, rubbing his legs and arms. "I'm even strong."

As Father Sun rose to greet the Beaver Tail Mountains, Luun woke before the others. Scooting near Bittoo, he fumbled among the tusu's belongings. His hands found Froom's broken spear. He traced its outline and the markings with his fingertips, then hastily replaced the weapon.

Without making noise, he left the earthen lodge, striding casually until he ventured out of sight of the village. Thinking no one could see him, he raced wildly towards the stream that cut through the trail leading to Frozen Duck Camp.

Jumbled thoughts stirred in his mind. Until both Bittoo and the mogur lived in the Land of the Souls, his own status remained low. He just wished the lunatic Froom had already succeeded in killing Bittoo.

He had studied under the great mogur and knew him to be the most hallowed of all the shamans in the Clan of the Ancient Humans. The mogur's power came from the majestic bear deity. But the mogur recently neglected the regal animal, turning his attention toward the water deity and totally avoided the people of his band, including him.

Before yesterday, the holy man seemed close to death. Now, the mogur had long to live. And he didn't relish waiting to become mogur of the Bear Hunter Band. Until yesterday, the people would've gladly followed him—since the mogur hid in his dwelling ignoring their spiritual needs.

He foresaw the holy leader's death as his chance to become renowned, perhaps more so than his teacher. If only Bittoo hadn't restored the mogur's health. But Bittoo's magic proved mighty, and now he wouldn't become the mogur of this band until many seasons into the future, after the mogur died of old age. He could never kill the mogur himself, since they both shared the same bear totem. The spirits would strip him of his powers for committing such a horrible deed.

Breathless, he stopped to hold his aching sides. He peered down at the ground and discovered he was leaving very plain boot prints in the mud. Departing the trail, he angled off into the forest. His westward tread would land him just above the fallen log that the people used when crossing the stream during high water. He walked as lightly as possible through the underbrush, thick with moss and lofty sprawling ferns, their green foliage growing as tall as his chest.

He spent two long seasons with the ailing mogur inside his pit house, a stuffy, dismal and frustrating time. This was the first day he'd gotten away, yet he was unaware of the fresh, inspiring air and felt unconnected with Mother Earth. The only sounds he heard was his heart thumping while frantic thoughts whirled in his head.

He reached the base of a ridge and clambered clumsily up its wet bank. From the crest of the embankment, he looked down, satisfied with his position. After settling on the carpet of cool moss, he took four stubby spears from his quiver and removed his chert knife from his waist. He felt fortunate to own so many spear points made of obsidian. In the past, most of his were made of chert or jasper, and only an occasional one made from this shiny black rock. Luckily, his spears looked almost the same as the one Froom used in attempting to kill Bittoo.

He despised Bittoo. The young tusu called on the spirits and healed the mogur. Not only that, he hated Bittoo for becoming more worthy of being a holy man than he could ever be. His desire was to become the most powerful of all living shamans. His plan might take a long time, but today would be its beginning. When finished, he'd be the most sought after holy leader in all the clan.

With great care, he used his sharp knife to cut into the shaft of all four spears. Over the marks of three dots, one below the other and the third to the side, he transformed the markings into three gashes and a solitary dot. He admired his work, then glanced down at the creek.

Sometime after Father Sun reached its peak, Bittoo and Gaaf would cross the stream on their journey home. When Bittoo made it half-way across the long log, and unable to defend himself, he meant to use his spear thrower to hurdle a spear deep into the tusu's chest. Next, he'd reload and plunge the second obsidian point into Gaaf. The idea seemed foolproof since both would probably venture together onto the overturned tree, there becoming easy targets and nearly incapable of using their weapons.

When finding the bodies of the two adolescents, it'll be seen that the spears belong to the crazy man, Froom, who twice already tried to kill Bittoo.

No one would blame or even think anyone but Froom could have executed such a cruel deed. After all, murder was nearly unheard of among the clan. But then, maybe Froom wasn't of the clan—he did look a little different than most, and he certainly had a temper all his own.

Surely, the mogur would relate Bittoo's earlier tale about how one of Froom's spears just missed Bittoo. But if not, still the bandsmen would find a spear in both bodies, plus the broken one in Bittoo's pack, all with the same three dashes and one dot which they'd immediately recognize. Everyone in the clan would know that Froom murdered the two. That is, everyone except himself, and of course, Froom—wherever he might be.

Luun stood and stretched, facing the Beaver Tail Mountains. Before long it would be midday. Father Sun hid behind hazes of clouds but sometimes pushed the white blurs from his view and beamed at those on Mother Earth. At first, Father Sun cast lengthy shadows, but now they were short. Soon there'd be no shadows, informing him that it was time to conceal himself.

He turned around and caught a glimpse of three men approaching the swollen creek from the south. He thudded flat against the ground, peeking between clumps of ferns. The men looked vaguely familiar but were not from the Bear Hunter Band. The roar of the fast running water made it impossible to hear them talk. The strangers stopped rather than walk the log. They appeared to be checking the tracks near the rushing stream. Five days had gone by since the last rain, and everyone who followed the trail still left footprints. He sighed deeply, hoping the three would cease to read the human signs—for on the other side, further down the path, they were sure to find his bootprints.

Anger shot through him—anger at himself for walking in the mud, and furious with the three newcomers who might discover his tracks.

Father Sun had emerged and there weren't any shadows, and if the strangers didn't leave soon, Bittoo and Gaaf would also reach the creek, making it impossible to kill them with three more clansmen present.

Fondling his medicine bag, he attempted to draw strength from the bundle by holding his totem objects. The hide felt soft, both inside and out, allowing him to feel the contours of the bear claws and teeth within. With his other hand, he traced the tip of one of his sharp projectile points still lying on the ground. While he squeezed the brown bundle and tightly clutched the knife-like point, he became aware that the power of his spirit bear was working: The men mounted the log, made their way to the opposite shore, then disappeared into the woods, heading in the direction of the Bear Hunter Camp.

The bear claws in the bag jabbed his palm, and the spear point sliced the other. Pride for his spirit guide swelled in his chest. Raising both arms, he graciously thanked the bear deity for its help. Blood dripped on his face and ornate leather tunic. He wiped his hands over a layer of moss and squinted at the painless thin wound cut by the edge of the obsidian blade.

When the bleeding subsided, he slipped two fingers into the holds underneath his spear thrower and placed one of the newly marked spears on top of the device, holding the weapon in position. He knelt and sang his power song, ready to jump up and hurl the deadly spear.

Father Sun moved slowly though the sky. Afternoon shadows cast new obscure shade patches. Luun didn't see the clansmen until they reached the northern bank of the stream. He counted five in all and wished this unwanted group would hurry on, so when Bittoo and Gaaf arrived, he could carry out his flawless plan.

With his idle hand, he shaded his eyes and studied the travelers. Seized with frustration, his body shook with spasms. He dropped his spear thrower and hit his fists against the earth. The group crossing the rushing creek was the same three strangers from before. With them walked Bittoo and Gaaf.

part two

TWIN SPIRIT

SINGLE SPIRIT

***

Bear Claw felt himself dropping into a black void, a void he feared there'd be no withdrawing from. Spirits beckoned, ready to skirt him away to live with the ancestors—the spirits his brother spoke of. Wanting to say farewell to Eagle Shadow seemed too difficult a chore for his mind to convey. If only he could sing a power song and strengthen his soul, but even those holy words wouldn't come—his mind had grown pitted with emptiness.

Eagle Shadow was alarmed. Fragmented thoughts flowed from his sibling's mind to his. His twin was dying and the saddened brother close to tears. He possessed no healing skills. There seemed little to do except chant a sacred song to properly send his twin to the Land of the Souls.

When he completed the song, he would resume his story-telling. Bear Claw might like that.

***

14

Twenty years later

Squealing with delight the small child snatched the bola from her father's grip. A chunk of drilled walrus ivory was tied to each end of the five nettle strands. The opposite ends of the strings were tightly bound together around a wad of straw, creating the handle. The girl clutched the adult sized weapon, letting the string and its polished ivory weights smack painfully against her ankle.

A thick crust of ice hugging the shoreline had entrapped a small flock of colorful teal ducks. Tiny youngsters with their parents scrambled down the lake path. Had food been in demand, the grown-ups would've crept upon the distraught fowl, but the time of the heavy snows had been short. The band breezed through the Starvation Moon with spare provisions, their clothing fitting taut, much the same as before winter began. So the imprisoned ducks were at the mercy of the anxious children, who through their inexperience would lose many more birds than they captured. For sure the trampled bank would be littered with greenish feathers, and both disappointed and elated muddy youngsters when the slaughter finished.

"If you lean your body back like this, you won't strike yourself," the man demonstrated to his daughter.

"Like a tree ready to fall," replied the bright child.

"Hold the base firmly and at arms length, then twirl the bola." He positioned himself at her back and grasped her thin wrist, rotating her hand. The bird killer whirled, picking up speed. "When I let go, just keep spinning."

The little girl's serious expression turned to joy as she continued to manipulate the device on her own. Her pale grey eyes gleamed with satisfaction. Her mother stood a few paces away from the wildly swinging weapon, ready to dodge whenever necessary.

Attempting to give further advice, her father
added, "When you let go of the bola..." His words
hung in the air. Just as the youngster tilted her arm
sideways, she released the weapon. The awkward
angle sent the cords downward, wrapping in a
tangled confusion around her bare legs. Instant red
welts criss-crossed her flesh.

Leisurely, Gaaf watched the spectacle from
above, his legs dangling over the embankment as
he reclined backwards on his elbows. "Do you
remember an earlier time when your three children
and my son took part in the same event?"
No reply.
"She's a determined one." Gaaf chuckled aloud.
"Look, she tries again." He peered over his shoulder.
His friend faced the lake as if watching the show,
but Bittoo's eyes seemed unfocussed."You worry too
much." Gaaf said. "Sit and be amused. It appears
we have a bold group of new, little hunters whose
skills may soon be superior to ours."
"I stared in my clam shell all night, asking Ceda
to send me a vision. I even filled it with the last of
my sacred sea water." Bittoo sighed with disgust.
"You and I are grown men with children...our sons
almost old enough to take mates. Yet Ceda's only
response was to call me a stupid boy." His arms
dropped to his sides in defeat.
"The water deity forever provokes you. You
don't stay in your lodge or even around camp to
perform the duties of a shaman, a tusu. You expect
Derk to do it all. You still wear the nose ring of your
childhood. This irritates her, and she refuses to help

you in your personal life. You're too stubborn. It's a test of wills, and someday she'll break you."

Bittoo's jaw set firm. Since Ceda first came to him in his youth, his life had become a nightmare. Always she manipulated, tricked him, pushed him into the role of a tusu. He swallowed hard. What devious thing would she do next? Would she bring her wrath and strike at his children? "Because of Ceda the people are against me...they don't know which way to turn."

"You lost your chance. When you were young and healed the mogur, everyone believed in you, but after that you ignored the shaman path, and the clan grew suspicious again of both you and Ceda."

"They don't know what she'll do next and neither do I. Everyone fears her and because she's my spirit guide, they fear me too...so much so, one nearly murdered me. Froom is still out there somewhere," stated the tusu flatly, his features tightening.

"Yes, but your sons are safe from harm. They have each other and their exceptional gift. Besides the villagers say Froom lingers mostly around the Spear Creek Band. They say during the seasons of the heavy snows, he brings provisions to Lant's lodge, leaving the meat outside when no one is watching." Gaaf stood and faced his friend.

"I haven't seen even a glimpse of him, not for many seasons, though occasionally I sense him spying on us. At times, the hairs on the back of my neck stands up, facing Father Sun, yet I'm unable to detect the reason."

"But Froom has no motive to hurt your twins."

Bittoo doubted his friends words. "Only if Froom still hates me. My two boys make easy targets while on their vision quest."

"Does clan blood flow through Froom's veins?"

"I sometimes think that reptile blood runs through the rivers of his body."

"And he's still consumed by dark demons?"

"Yes, he's still possessed. Otherwise the demented man would've claimed his woman from Lant's lodge long ago."

"Perhaps he stays away because his shame runs deep for attempting to murder you when you were young."

"I doubt that. He tried to kill me...twice. Remember? He's probably sorry he didn't succeed."

"At least no one still thinks the spirit which first visited you was a dark demon. Everyone seems to believe it was truly Ceda."

"Does it matter...does it truly matter? She acts evil with her threats to withhold her water children and cause us starvation and talks about me leading the people to a new land. Since everyone thinks Ceda is angry with me, most don't associate with me, believing she'll become angry with them if they do."

"You don't want them befriending you. If they did, they might request your services...rituals and stuff. And of course, that wouldn't set right with you."

He couldn't get mad at Gaaf. His friend spoke true. The only rituals he performed in his adulthood were with his family, Gaaf and Derk.

"You're grey hair will turn white if you continue to dwell on this. Let's bundle up our sleeping robes and join our fathers and your uncles on their hunt.

Your father and my father are much too old to be climbing the north face of Beaver Tail Mountain. Now that, I worry about!"

The moderately used trail followed the contours of the upper Brown Bear River. The walkway not much narrower than an animal path, allowed access to drinking holes. The trio traipsed single file, with Gaaf leading the way and his son bringing up the rear. Bittoo's dog, Raccoon, scampered through the lush underbrush, returning briefly to sniff at her master's heels. After determining Bittoo's well being, she'd run off again.

Bittoo found it difficult to pull out of his dour mood. Gaaf and his son Piika sought to draw him into their conversations, but he felt confident that something horrid would soon take place. He couldn't shake the foreboding heaviness that surrounded him.

"It's a good thing we aren't hungry," said Gaaf lightheartedly. "All our blundering has surely scared the game into the Bear Hunter's territory."

"Then they'll have favorable hunting today," Piika joked. "And maybe, even invite us to the feast."

Bittoo said nothing.

Gaaf heaved himself onto an uprooted fir tree blocking their way. He straddled the rotting bark, facing the direction they'd just traveled.

Engrossed in his own thoughts, an unobservant Bittoo ran smack into his friend. "Sorry," he expressed, looking directly at Gaaf.

"Did it occur to you that if anything happens to your boys...probably the two people you treasure the most on Earth Mother...that Ceda's prediction can't come true?" Gaaf's voice sounded stern. "She said out of your lineage, will come a new line of shamans. With those boys dead there won't be anyone to carry on that legacy. They boast a special power never before heard of. Ceda, and most certainly Creator One Breath, put them on Earth Mother for a purpose."

Startled by his friend's blunt truth, Bittoo studied Gaaf thoughtfully. A slight smile quivered at the corners of his mouth, growing into a broad, toothy grin. "Did I ever tell you, my most trusted friend...that long ago the water deity told me...no, instructed me to secure the help of the mammoth, the bear and the white fox spirits?"

Gaaf's eyebrows raised.

"So far I've neglected the bear spirit, and since the mammoths died out, I've been unable to call-up their ancient spirit. I fear it no longer exists, and I didn't know what she meant by the white fox spirit until that wily animal became your totem."

Gaaf smiled, as if grateful his companion was pulling out of his glumness. "Of course, you never told me!" He laughed. "You didn't want me to know she ordered you to listen to me!"

Piika watched the two cheerful men then interrupted with a tinge of urgency in his voice. "The air is getting heavy. Fog or rain will soon be on us."

Bittoo and Gaaf looked skyward, but saw only the tree tops. Gaaf swung his legs over the downed log and set a faster pace for the group. They hoped to reach a spot upriver, where hunters occasionally camped for the night. From there, they could easily reach Beaver Tail Mountain on the following day.

Raccoon, with her banded brown and yellow fur surrounding her eyes, joined the runners, playfully nipping at Piika's leather trousers. Weary of Piika's swift but gentle kicks, the canine darted through the brush and emerged ahead of the men. Although their odors weren't fresh, her unfailing nose revealed that the older men, Har, Cir, Tam and Gaaf's father, Barc, had traveled the same upward trail.

"I hear your betrothed has fleas in her bed robes," Bittoo teasingly shouted back at Piika who was just two summers older than his own sons and promised to his daughter, Caree.

"And I hear they jumped off her father's ragged bed furs onto hers," replied Gaaf's good-natured son.

Gaff raised his arm, signaling alarm. The group stopped, short-breathed, and concealed themselves behind broad tree trunks with low boughs. Raccoon barked in earnest. After rounding the bend just ahead of them, she disappeared out of sight.

They edged their way through the timber in time to catch a peek at a male brown bear crossing in the shallows of the swift running river. With each lumbering stride, the bear's loose skin rolled gracefully as if unattached.

"You'll tangle with the wrong bear someday," Bittoo said, stroking his dog.

"Luckily, the she-bears still winter in the dens with their cubs, or else Raccoon would already be bear meat," Piika commented.

"The beast has rummaged through the fire pit looking for bones left by Har and the others," Gaaf said as he walked into the small camp. "At least he didn't damage the lean-to."

Gaaf and Piika foraged for firewood while Bittoo relined the cooking pit with rocks. Earlier their women packed enough dried food for their outing, but the men intended to kindle a fire for warmth and as a precaution against predators.

Raccoon found an undevoured bone still full of juicy marrow and snatched the blackened fragment from the cold ashes. In warning to the vanished bear, the dog snarled as her teeth bit into the leavings.

The shelter consisted of a square wooden frame and two poles holding up the front with the back of the assemblage resting against a knoll. Interwoven green fur branches covered the roof.

"We'll see fresh snow on the mountain tonight," Gaaf stated. "I wish the four, old hunters had waited for stable weather."

Har, Cir and Barc remained motionless. They anticipated some movement and a command from Tam, Har's youngest brother, when he reached the rocky ravine. Volunteering for the most difficult work of the hunt, Tam left the group at first light with instructions to work around the base of the mountain. When finding a way up the incline, he was to head west, hoping to drive the sure-footed goats directly into the waiting men.

All winter, Har thought about this hunt. He wanted to obtain a white sacred fur for his son's rituals, even though Bittoo owned two white hides of infant seal skin. Late fall would have been the choicest season to secure the lavish coats of the goat. But most of all, he craved something special for his grandsons when the boys returned from their vision quests. And two identical goat horns would make very special presents, indeed. He'd make tinder containers out of the pair, with straps for easy carrying and a closure to keep the shredded bark and grasses dry.

They sat posted in a line with Cir high above and Barc stationed far below him. With only their heads visible, they remained as still as the rock outcroppings they hid behind.

Har could barely see both of his companions out of the corners of his eye. He needed to move his head to see them well, but dared not do that: Goats possess the sharpest eyesight of all the creatures he ever hunted. Not only did the agile goat enjoy keen hearing and an acute sense of smell, he was positive the handsome animals could taste the scents that drifted in the air—the very reason why very few hunts were successful. Earlier, he and the others deceptively rubbed the unscraped hide of a ground squirrel over their exposed skin. The rodent was one variety of animal sharing the high region with the nimble goats, and hopefully, its rank stench would override the odor of the men.

The lower, north flank of the mountain looked void of snow, and as Har anticipated, there were head ferns growing in rock crannies and lush patches of bear grass to lure the goats. Last night so as not to alert the rock climbing animals, he and the men slept huddled in a small confining cave without a fire, and with just their robes and each other's bodies for heat. If they were fortunate, something would happen very soon. Tam had already been gone half the day.

He removed his fingers from the two holes of his spear thrower. After holding the device most of the morning, his entire arm ached. He worked his palm, then rubbed the flesh vigorously with his other hand, all the while scanning the distant tundra slope.

Squinting, he saw four white specks fixed on the horizon. Unsure of trusting his sight, he briefly closed his weary eyes. When reopened them, he again observed the white dots, however now there were two handfuls of them. Sighing in relief, he slid his hand back into the finger holds of his weapon.

Someone stirred at the base of the far cliffs below the goats. He spied a snatch of moving color. It wasn't the agreed upon strategy for Tam to drive the game from below. If such a plan were tried, the skittish animals would most likely head over the mountain summit and out of the hunter's reach. From the east, Tam was to lag a set distance behind them, so as not to appear an immediate threat, yet threatening enough so the bearded animals would leisurely graze toward the three armed hunters.The domain of these hoofed creatures was hazardous country for humans, with vertical bluffs of loose rock. The three crouching hunters watched patiently as their unsuspecting prey grew nearer.

Har could now make out Tam's silhouette standing in much the same place he first located the goats. Tam's actions didn't make sense, but apparently changing locations a few times from far below the creatures, then back to the far side of them was working effectively. His little brother must be part mountain goat himself.

The shaggy goats reached the far side of the ravine, and as if taunting the invisible hunters, they lingered on its crest, nibbling at the bear grass. The largest of these sly animals shot an inquiring stare in Har's direction, then seemed to dismiss any ideas of danger. With little effort, it stepped over the edge of the canyon, the remaining mountain goats followed his lead. They worked themselves further down the steep decline, until the men were unable to see them without moving nearer to the rim; this was Tam's cue to advance swiftly to the eastern fringe of the cliff, for Barc to proceed to the bottom and Cir to angle to the top of the narrow but deep ravine.

When Tam reached his destination, he nodded to his awaiting companions. From the four directions, the men closed in on the animals. They stood for a breath of time and looked down upon their quarry.

Too late, the goats realized their plight. Har held his weapon upright, lifting the spear thrower over his shoulder. With a whip-like motion he sent the projectile hurtling toward his target. His accurate aim struck the largest animal in the the throat. He quickly reloaded, placing the spear on the wooden device with its upper surface flush against the protruding notch.

Three other goats went down. Each of the hunters hit their mark—getting what they came for.

Unaware that the danger had passed, the remaining goats panicked and sought escape through the gaps between the four men.

Tam reached the bottom of the ravine first, pulling his broken spear point from the one he killed. "Those clouds look threatening. Let's get off this mountain," he said, while slitting the throat of his kill.

"We'll never outrun this storm. It's dangerously near and moving fast." Har looked at the slain animal resting at his feet. He knelt by the goat's head, admiring the prize set of horns—perfect for his grandsons. The meat wouldn't be tender; the goat had lived too long and grew tough over time. But that wasn't important; he came after the curved horns. He counted the rings encircling the horns. There was one ring for each finger on both his hands and one for each finger on an additional hand. If he tallied correctly, this magnificent creature was the same age as his twin grandsons.

The warmer air stirred as the storm front began to push it from the region. Barc watched while his breath became visible in the air. "There's no time to return to last nights shelter, where we left our sleeping robes."

"There's a cave near the crest...over there." Cir pointed toward the north side of the ravine where he'd awaited the hunt. "I ran so fast coming down the canyon, I almost fell into it from above."

"It suits me," Tam agreed. He hoisted the heavy carcass, which was double his weight. The goat rested around his neck with all four feet draping over his chest. Holding the legs, he heaved himself to a standing position.

By the time the bandsmen walked the short distance to the cave, a scattering of dry snow had fallen. In defiance, wind gusts seized the white powder. Snow swirled and danced ill-temperedly, unable to find a place to reside.

The cave proved to be only slightly larger than the one in which the travelers previously passed the night. After gutting the carcasses, they ate of the fresh organs. Tam preferred the liver, while Har and Barc favored the bloody heart. They smiled at one another with red smeared grins.

The wind blew forcefully, howling a warning through the ravine.

"We might be here more than one night," Cir deduced as he sliced a bite-sized piece of goat tongue.

Har crouched beside his kill. With his sharp obsidian blade, he expertly cut the hide away from the goat's body. When finishing the task, he used the knife's edge to scrape the meat remaining on the underside of the pelt. "Tonight will be cold. Am I the only one who'll own a sleeping robe?"

Abandoning their banquet, the three men's attention turned toward securing warm furs. Har chuckled to himself. His companions had all been young men when they last ate the meat of the goat. While relishing in its unique flavor, they almost forgot their peril.

"If we had only made it down to the treeline, we would've found firewood," Tam said with regret.

Har reached into a niche of the cave's rocky wall, drawing out nesting material from a packrat's den. "We have kind friends here who left us gifts," he reported, pulling out twigs and bark. He checked another crevice and found more sticks.

Standing, he located a dark recess tunneled into the mountain. Tossing a newly acquired piece of wood into the hole, he waited for a response. When none came, he raised himself up onto the ledge and snaked his way into the black hollow. Squeezing through the littered opening, he came into a roomier area. Cautiously probing with his spear thrower, he discovered chewed bones and scrub branches. He pushed the dusty piles of debris through the crawlspace and onto the cave floor.

The snow dropped thickly, and the angry wind

whipped the white substance into their cozy shelter.
Before the sun set on Beaver Tail Mountain, the
stranded men realized they were facing one of Earth
Mother's worse spring storms.

15

The noble hunters woke early to find a snow drift covering the narrow cave's entrance. Cir peeked out a hole before hitting the drift with all his might. The others laughed as the feathery snow fluttered in all directions, and Cir's lanky frame went sprawling to the hard ground.

"Did you think you were knocking down an ice sheet?" Tam asked jokingly.

The men gawked at the scene before them. The sun shone hazily through a thin veil of clouds. The snow reached nearly to their thighs. Struggling through the powdery covering wouldn't be an easy task.

"I say we head out before another blizzard hits." Barc looked at Har to see if his friend agreed.

No one spoke. They rolled up the new white shaggy hides, boosted the stiff bodies of their kill onto their aching backs and struck out toward the village.

The four trudged a very long time, but covered very little ground. They leaned against a boulder, pausing to take a break. Not until then did Har remember to ask Tam about his previous stalking method.

"Why did you dart to the bottom of the slope, then rush back up and prod the goats along from the side...going back and forth? I grow exhausted just thinking about your strategy!"

"I only herded the animals from the east. Someone hunted below me. But I assumed he was Barc, although I didn't get a good look at him."

"It wasn't me, but I caught flashes of someone hugging the rocks below...or thought I did."

After taking time to digest the information, the three turned to Cir and in unison asked the hunter, "Did you see someone?"

Cir shook his head. "I was stationed too far away to see anyone at the base of the slope."

"So someone spies on us, or perhaps tracks us like game," spat Har.

"Likely there was more than one intruder...Bittoo and Gaaf thinking their fathers too old to climb Beaver Tail Mountain. They believe our minds are daft since we insisted on making such a venture," Barc stated with humor in his tone.

A tremendous roar interrupted the discussion. For a split instant, the men stared in absolute horror. They said nothing. Each fled at full speed—straight down the surging mountain toward the treeline in hopes of finding protection. They rolled and tumbled, sliding unmercifully.

Earth Mother broke lose with a fury the seasoned hunters had dreaded but hoped wouldn't come. She unleashed her vengeance: rocks, boulders and an avalanche of snow and ice upon the four faithful men who always treated her with the greatest respect.

Bittoo and his companions stood in the treeless charred remnants of what had been a beautiful section of woods. The devastation was the spirits way of providing for man and beast. Lightning, apparently struck a tree, spreading fire northward. The sky spirits eventually drenched the flames with water to keep the blaze from traveling over the entire mountain range.

"We should come back here when another moon has passed," Gaaf suggested. "The hunting will be excellent once Earth Mother turns this into a grassy meadow."

"The game should be plentiful," Bittoo agreed, smiling.

Raccoon crawled on her belly. With tail between her legs, she wedged herself between her master's feet.

"We could..." Lines crossed Bittoo's face. "We could... listen!"

Piika seemed unable to catch the tusu's meaning, but he looked alarmed because the expression crossing Bittoo's face showed fear. "I hear nothing."

"That's the problem. Even the birds are quiet. And see this dog." In a breath of time, Bittoo assessed the situation—Ceda—her vengeance was somehow at work. He jerked his neck around, and faced Beaver Tail Mountain, knowing how vulnerable the four, old hunters were.

The violent quake knocked them to their knees, but still they watched the horizon in disbelief as a torrent of rock and snow rushed down the distant mountain. Far off, the unwavering slide billowed, like clouds moving swiftly along the earth's surface. For someone not comprehending the situation, the scene might seem beautiful. But for Bittoo, Gaaf and Piika, the sight before them represented the most ghastly of nightmares imaginable.

They rose on unsteady feet and bolted up the path toward their loved ones. Deep in their hearts, the trio hoped to run into the old men returning down the trail. Despairingly, they reached the northern slope. Raccoon led them over the unfamiliar terrain, darting wildly, discharging short desperate yelps of concern.

The slide did little to alter the first area they came upon. Raccoon disappeared into a rock shelter. Before the others could enter the recess, she dragged a spotted deer hide out into the open. Gripped in her strong teeth the dog shook the robe vigorously.

"That belongs to grandfather," Piika said excitedly.

They examined the contents of the small shelter, finding a total of four sleeping furs and as many traveling packs.

"The old ones intend to return. We could wait here for them," Piika said to his father.

Thoughtfully, Bittoo mulled over the situation. They could wait as Piika suggested—at any time, the elders might shuffle back for their belongings. For sure, if at all possible, the aged hunters would come back and retrieve their packs. But it was also conceivable that the men were in the region of the slide and required assistance.

Loud serious barking broke their concentration. As Bittoo came out of the shelter, he saw Raccoon disappear eastward over the rise. At a cautious pace, the men followed the determined dog. They watched as she tracked the scents of the missing men. Finally, the group reached the devastation. The destruction spread as far east as they could see. Unable to find the men's trail, Raccoon whimpered. Bittoo grabbed the panting dog by his fur, forcing the unyielding animal to rest with them.

When the trio regained their wind, Bittoo released his grip on the dog. They wandered along slowly, waiting for Raccoon to pick up the familiar odors. Choosing their steps, they became ever mindful of the unstable snow, rocks and boulders shifting under their feet. The dog led them to a single skinned and gutted goat carcass with both horns removed.

"Look! Someone's down there!" Piika raced down the ravaged slope with Bittoo and Gaaf behind him.

From far below, a solitary figure gazed up at the group, then as though frightened by the three intruders, vanished through the woods.

"Where's he going?" Piika shouted back at Bittoo and Gaaf. "Wait!" he yelled at the man. Piika tripped and fell, rolling over Raccoon who had stopped abruptly in his path. Hurriedly, the boy pulled himself to a sitting position. His eyes bulged and his stomach heaved. Next to him, on top of the cold earth, lay Har's stiff body. The man's opened eyes stared skyward, his gaping mouth filled with snow. Piika looked sick and incapable of warning Bittoo of the tragedy.

Bittoo flinched before kneeling silently at his father's side. Tears flowed unchecked down his face and onto his father's lifeless chest. He touched Har's cheeks, and with shaking fingers, scooped out the snow lodged in the dead man's mouth. He stood looking bewildered when realizing that someone had dug his father's body out and placed it on top of the snow. He stumbled down the high mountain toward Gaaf and Piika, who stood at the first stand of timber, marking the beginning of the treeline. Barc's body lay wrapped around the crooked trunk of a fir tree. The force of the slide slammed him backwards against the disfigured tree, breaking the hunter's back.

"Have you found the others?" Bittoo asked. The two didn't hear his question. He repeated his words but received no response from his grief-sticken friends. He scanned the landscape and further into the trees, spotted Raccoon digging in the debris. Rushing to the site, he saw two hands protruding through a mass of rocks. He recognized the slender palms of Cir. Those hands once taught him to set snares and traps and to track the most difficult of animals. Madly tossing the stones, he sent them flying in every direction. In his mind he knew his uncle lay dead, but in his heart he wished for a miracle. Gaaf and Piika joined him in his useless effort. Cir's frame was crushed and his bludgeoned face unrecognizable.

Bittoo stood, his attention turning toward his youngest uncle. "Tam!" he screamed as loudly as possible. "It's Bittoo, your nephew! Come back!" Bewildered, he stared at Gaaf. "Why did he run from us?"

"Perhaps he's injured his head and is confused," replied his childhood companion.

The worried trio started out in the direction Tam fled. "Where's my dog?" asked Bittoo.

"She raced down through the trees ahead of us," answered Piika, his voice sounding weak.

The ground vibrated with an aftershock. Gaaf seized Bittoo by his shoulder. "Let's get off this mountain before the whole thing comes down on us."

"After we find my uncle," Bittoo declared, unbending. "And then we must take the bodies home."

Gaaf shook his friend. "You aren't thinking straight."

Bittoo jerked himself loose from Gaaf's grip. "Just a while longer."

"There'll be more tremors. This mountain will take our lives too."

"Tam needs us," argued Bittoo.

Piika watched the disagreement. "I don't want to leave my grandfather's mutilated corpse to the mercy of mountain cats, wolves or even another earthquake. They all required a proper burial to insure they reached the Land of the Souls."

"I know Tam needs us," stated Gaaf, "and the men should be buried, but we're no good to anyone if we die. And we'll be in even more danger if we get caught up here after dark."

"You leave then," snarled Bittoo.

Gaaf stood close to his friend, so close Bittoo's hot breath crossed his face. "If you and my son were safe at the village, I'd scour this mountain until I found Tam, but many seasons ago I pledged to guard you with my life. Whether you like it or not, you're the great tusu, Father of all Shamans, and I'll drag you off this slope if I have to."

16

Unlike most young men of the clan, Jarkoo and Braaz were undecided on a place to go for their vision quest. In fact, rarely did the two talk about the upcoming event. There seemed little need to discuss the matter as each sensed the fear and anticipation the other one felt. This ability to understand one another's emotions was a gift given to them from Creator One Breath, along with other unique skills. But it wasn't so much that they understood each other's emotions, as they most often experienced identical feelings and thoughts.

The people of the Frozen Duck Band considered the twins to be quiet and shy. But the bandsmen knew nothing about the active conversations that went on, back and forth, between the young men's minds. The bandsmen treated the boys like they treated the boy's father, Bittoo—with quiet indifference. Unable to comprehend the mysterious nature of the three, they suspiciously stayed clear of the trio whenever possible. Yet being shunned allowed the twins time to themselves—ample time to perfect their special abilities. Jarkoo and Braaz enjoyed talking and usually did a considerable amount when together or among their family.

"We'd make faster progress if we were hares," Braaz complained as he broke loose from a maze of vines and underbrush. He sat cross-legged and waited for his brother to clear the entanglement.

"Getting to our destination might be easier if we weren't carrying these ritual sticks. I just broke more curls off mine," Jarkoo informed his brother. "This isn't a normal vision quest, otherwise we would be choosing our own location, and Derk wouldn't have insisted we bring the prayer sticks."

"Shamans don't experience normal vision quests. Our father didn't and neither did old Derk."

"Yes, but their spirit totems first came to them when they weren't expecting them. We seek out our spirit helpers. If we were truly supposed to be shamans, wouldn't our totem animals have come to us?"

Braaz stretched his aching body. "Surely, the spirits decided on a place for our ritual. Didn't it seem odd that we never spoke of our vision quest? And that something inside ourselves keeps driving us up Thunder Mountain in this remote area, yet neither of us knows why or even where we'll end up?"

"Two days away from the village seems too far away for a quest."

"I sense we're close," Braaz stated uneasily.

Jarkoo also believed they were nearing their destination, however the words from his twin added reassurance.

Weak and hungry, they rose and continued up the trail-less mountain, making slower progress than when first leaving Frozen Duck Camp. They rested again under a fir tree.

"Do you feel a strangeness?" asked Braaz.

Jarkoo peeked between limbs and brush. "Yes, I no longer have a desire to push on. Surely, we're not expected to await our animal spirits under this tree." Jarkoo's gaze followed his brother's pointing finger to a small opening in a nearby cliff.

Excitedly, the two raced over to the bluff, then scrambled up the small, dirt hill to the hole. Braaz peered inside the recess. "It's a large cave. At one time or another, the entrance must have collapsed in on itself."

"Look at this." Jarkoo wiggled it, trying to dislodge the branch-like object from the compact soil. Unable to pull it out, he dug the discolored bone free with a sharp edged stone. Above him, Braaz widened the opening to the cavern.

"The cave is full of bones," an astonished Braaz reported.

Jarkoo abandoned his endeavor and shuffled to his brother's side. "What animal could possibly have been so big?"

"There had to be more than one. Look at the size of that bone pile."

With their fists, both adolescents hammered their ritual sticks into the soil. Jarkoo crawled through the entrance and slid on his buttocks to the cavern floor. Braaz copied his brother and landed disheveled at Jarkoo's feet.

"Whatever they were, the beasts were certainly monstrous." Braaz circled the heap of discolored fossils. He was unable to comprehend such animals, let alone touch the eerie pieces. "Maybe they died of starvation when the face of the cave gave way."

"Anything that large could have walked through the earthen closure as easily as we walk through a spider web."

Braaz squatted, resting against his heels. Cocking his head this way and that, he examined the heap. "I think these bones were purposely brought here. On top of the mound are long arched ones. Those may have been tusks, because just under them are large curved bones, probably broken ribs. On the bottom, there seems to be gigantic skulls...not just one but many."

Layer by layer, the twins removed the heavy rubble until exposing a dirt floor. Grimy and tired, they sat in its midst with the circular pile of bones surrounding them.

"Someone used these bones to build a dwelling. Over time, the leather which held the shelter together rotted, and the structure broke down," Jarkoo concluded.

"This is a holy sanctuary. That's why we've been led here."

"In the time of our ancestors," Jarkoo stated, "this must have been a very powerful place."

"Perhaps in the time of our ancestor's ancestors, because I don't know of any animal so huge."

The twins woke the next morning, surprised at finding themselves still in the middle of the deposit. The night before they'd been fascinated with their find, and neither remembered retiring or even thinking about going to sleep. Their hunger pains had vanished along with their thirst. Their pale eyes had grown accustomed to the dimness, allowing them to see a great distance into the cavern.

"This is not a comfortable place...inside the womb of Thunder Mountain," Braaz whispered.

"I think the spirits safeguard us," Jarkoo conveyed. "At least I hope so."

The twins stood and stared into each other's familiar face, seeing what they always saw when looking at their own reflection in the lake. They appeared the same, yet opposite of one another. Both harbored grey eyes, the identical handsome features and long wavy brown hair. Jarkoo's hair parted on the right side, and his small mole lay directly under his right ear. He was right-handed, whereas Braaz bore the identical characteristics, but all situated on his left side. Always, they pulled the crown of their hair backwards and secured the locks with cordage. The tactic not only concealed their parts,but also hid their moles so the villagers couldn't tell them apart. Often, they carried weapons in their opposite hands which confused everyone except their family members.

Silently, they proceeded into the deep interior of the cave. Soon, only pitch darkness greeted them. Compelled by an unknown force, the pair continued through the abyss. After a while, a bright light shown at the tunnel's end. Together, they walked on until the radiant glow engulfed them with such a brilliant gleam, they were blinded. Jarkoo and Braaz stood motionless, waiting.

Finally, a compelling voice echoed from the now fading light. Transfixed, they watched as a large prehistoric animal lumbered toward them. From its size, the twins knew the creature to be the exact breed of animal whose bones they had found. Its body reminded them of a bear, only many times larger and with long shaggy hair, swaying as it walked.

When noticing the beast harbored what looked like a tail at both ends, they recognized the animal as the ancient mammoths in the stories they'd heard since early childhood. Any other time, such a creature would frightened them. But this was their vision quest, a test of manhood, and this long forgotten monster beckoned them in a trusting manner.

She stood in front of them, ever watchful with her small beady eyes, then lowered her massive head to scoop them off the ground. The young men rode, each in the curve of one of her ivory tusks. Effortlessly, the beast turned and treaded into the dazzling light, which dulled in intensity with each step she took.

Spread in front of them was their village and Frozen Duck Lake. At first glance, all appeared as it should be. The boys saw their grandfather, Har, and a few other kinsmen and bandsmen they knew, yet most of the people were total strangers. The entire scene seemed the reversal of their village, as if it were a reflection in the water.

The setting proved delightful. Everyone looked happy and content, but no one appeared to see or hear the newcomers. The boys gave up their calls and gestures to enjoy the peacefulness. It was nearing the time of the Salmon Moon. In the village, many of the occupants worked, repairing drying racks for the fish. Seemingly unaware of his grandsons, Har walked in their direction, placed two striking goat horns on the ground and backed away.

The boys wanted to wander through the camp, but the beast withdrew and headed back toward the dark tunnel. Communicating through her mind, she conveyed a disturbing message. "I'm your totem. When you eat my flesh you will live," she said sadly as she lowered the pair.

Jarkoo and Braaz watched as the stately mammoth turned and re-entered the white light. They gave a slight bow in reverence to their new totem spirit. For a length of time, both did nothing but stand in awe of the majestic creature—the essence of their vision quest, their passage into manhood. Then they discoverd the pair of beautifully matched goat horns lying at their feet.

The twins left the cave the next day, after spending one more night amidst the sacred bones. They wished to remain longer in the sanctuary, but Derk instructed them to return shortly after obtaining a spirit helper. It was customary for the shaman to interpret any unclear messages received during a vision quest and also for the holy one to introduce the adolescents to the villagers and declare them 'men'.

Instead of bringing home their ritual sticks, each carried a curved goat horn, larger than any either had ever seen. They cherished the objects and secured them tightly to their waist straps.

"I never thought our totem would give us something from the spirit world," Jarkoo said, his eyes sparkling with wonder. He examined the horn, even though he'd studied the piece many times already.

"I was surprised, but long ago, Derk's sky people gave him a star, and the water deity gave father the salmon with the baby fish in their bellies. Gaaf dried them for father, he stores them in a satchel. So I guess it's fitting for us to receive a gift."

"But why is it from a goat when our totem is a mammoth?"

"I don't know, nor do I understand why our spirit helper is an extinct beast. The mammoth was beautiful though, and noble." Braaz's voice filled with overwhelming tenderness for the creature.

Early in the day, the twins found a deer trail which ran much the same direction they were headed. The path made for an easy and fast descent. They crossed Warm River and still the trail obliged them by angling downhill.

Jarkoo stopped in the middle of the track and waited for his brother to catch up. "That's the second tremor today."

"The first one felt somewhat stronger," Braaz announced.

"I'll feel much better once Thunder Mountain is behind us."

"Our ancestors said that earthquakes are the result of a large underground fish shaking its tail. Does that mean Ceda, the mother of all water creatures, causes them?"

Jarkoo shrugged his shoulders. "I don't know whether father's totem, Ceda or Earth Mother's mischief causes them."

By mid afternoon they forgot about the minor quakes, so when chancing upon an unexplored waterfall, they made an early camp, and played in the cascades, allowing the water to flow over them. Exhausted, they fell asleep without eating.

The following day, the boys continued their journey home. "We should come across the trail between the two mountains soon," Braaz said matter of factly.

Jarkoo had a faraway look in his eyes. "During our vision quest, did we visit the Land of the Souls?"

"I think we experienced a dream."

Jarkoo paused, collecting his thoughts before continuing. "Grandfather Har, Tam, Cir and Barc aren't dead, which means we didn't visit the real afterworld." He grabbed a branch from a bush as he walked by, stripping the stem of its leaves, then opening his hand, let them flutter to the ground.

"It looked as I expected the Land of the Souls to look," Braaz stated. "We've always been taught that the hallowed place is the reverse of our home here on Earth Mother, and everything there was the exact reverse...turned around. Here, it's almost the seal birthing season, yet it was nearing the Salmon Moon in the Land of the Souls."

Jarkoo didn't appreciate his brother's reasoning, even though the same idea crossed his mind. "Yes, but ever since we were born the people have been frightened of us. Never before has anyone given birth to more than one baby. We look alike, yet opposite, so they believe one of us is dead and is a spirit that came back from the Land of the Souls. Except the villagers are uncertain as to which of us is alive and which is dead."

"They've always mistrusted father, afraid Ceda would refuse to give them any of her fish children and cause the clan's extinction. Then after we were born, it gave them more reason to fear. But at least our sister is normal and is treated well."

From behind, Jarkoo reached over, playfully jabbing his brother in the rear. "I think it's you, brother...you're dead. See, you stumble along so slowly, I'm about to run you right over."

When reaching the main trail connecting Frozen Duck Camp to the Great Sea, the twins perched in the middle of the well-used path. They settled where each could see a considerable ways in both directions. Thoughtfully, they ate the last of their provisions.

"Father was right to keep his childhood sickness bag and to continue wearing it along with his nose ring. One can't have too much protection. I plan to keep mine." Jarkoo sounded very firm with his decision.

"The villagers will laugh at you behind your back. They'll say your spirit helper is weak, and you take refuge behind your boyhood talisman." Braaz stated a fact Jarkoo had already considered. "Though it's difficult putting my trust in a mammoth, an animal totem which no longer lives on Earth Mother."

"Then I'll wear my child sickness bag, but remove my nose ring and put the loop in my new medicine bag." Jarkoo realized his decision affected both himself and his brother. For if he were the only twin without a nose ring, everyone could tell them apart. But he read bits and pieces of his brother's mind and knew Braaz was thinking similar thoughts.

"At least our totem acted friendly...not like father's spirit guide who constantly badgers him when she finally does talk to him...which she seldom does."

"The mammoth seemed sorrowful, as though she knew something so grievous it hurt her to her soul."

"It doesn't matter if the villagers make fun of me behind my back, because they'll have even more to say when learning our totem is a long dead mammoth."

Their brows wrinkled as both heard voices coming from the east. They scurried up the embankment until recognizing the familiar gaits of their father, Gaaf and Piika.

"Ya, Ho," yelled the boys, waving their arms excitedly. The twins ran toward the trio but halted short when seeing the heavy way the three carried themselves. Jarkoo and Braaz understood something dreadful had transpired.

"Ya, Ho," replied Bittoo, overjoyed to see his sons safe but unable to express the happiness he felt. "There's been a terrible accident." He put an arm around each son, drawing them close. "Your grandfather, your Uncle Cir and Barc are dead."

Bittoo took an extended breath, allowing his sons to comprehend his message. "They were caught in an avalanche. Tam is still on the mountain...but injured. He ran from us."

A knowing looked crossed the twin's faces. Jarkoo opened his mouth. "Father, our uncle Tam is..."

"...dead too," said Braaz, completing his brother's sentence, as each often did when speaking with others.

Bitooo raised truthful boys and knew they wouldn't lie or even joke about such a thing. The twins possessed unusual powers. Although he didn't know how his sons came to such a conclusion, they wouldn't make such a statement unless it were true.

"When the aftershocks are over, we'll go back and recover the bodies. We must make sure their spirits don't hover in this world and are welcomed into the Land of the Souls. We'll need your help." He looked steadily at his boys who often perceived more than mortal men. The pair maintained a reassuring calmness.

"All of them...grandfather, Uncle Cir, Uncle Tam and Barc are content and already reside in the afterworld," the twins stated at the same time.

Bittoo's face went pale as his eyes, turning downward, saw the two splendid goat horns lashed to his sons' waists.

"The horns are gifts from Grandfather Har and our spirit totem," revealed the twins together, raising them high for their father's inspection. "Grandfather presented them to us in the Land of the Souls."

17

Caree sulked out of Frozen Duck Camp, her brown eyes and delicate upturned nose aimed toward the ground. She kept to the river path until it met the trail which ran through Whistling Wind Pass, connecting her people and the peoples who lived east of the Beaver Tail Mountains. Departing from the junction, she walked into the cool green forest and slumped down on her knees. She dug a shallow hole and took the saturated cotton grass from between her legs. Putting the wadding in the ground, she covered it over.

She began her woman's bleeding four days before and felt joyless ever since. Soon, she'd go through the pain of the woman's tattoo across her forehead just under the hairline, and next, be expected to take a mate. Her man was to be Piika, Gaaf's son. They'd been betrothed since she was first born. Truly, Piika had proved to be a masterful hunter, a kind male and almost as handsome as her twin brothers, Jarkoo and Braaz. Yet she felt unprepared for such grownup experiences.

She despised the idea of abandoning her father's lodge and living in another, although staying in her own village pleased her. Jarkoo and Braaz were her best friends even when they teased her to tears. Her Grandfather Har and her Grandmother Leha, showed their love and comfort whenever she needed soothing. She felt a deep affection for her mother, Sanee, but with her brothers and her father she felt an even stronger connection, one she couldn't describe.

On the day of her first woman's flow, she'd been by herself near camp, collecting firewood. Each day since, she wandered a short distance into the surrounding timber and picked spear head mushrooms among the fallen decaying trees. If only she'd gone with her father, Gaaf and Piika, and gathered the large white mushrooms which grew at the edge of the melting snow. But she was absent from camp when the men decided to follow her grandfather, uncles and Barc up Beaver Tail Mountain.

So far, no one knew about her bleeding, and that was the way she wanted to keep it. In the future, when having her moon blood, even though the occurrence marked her passage into womanhood, she was determined to spend as much time as possible away from everyone in order to keep a secret.

All the males of her lodge had departed camp and she felt lonely. Her twin brothers left first, seeking their vision quest. They would reach manhood before returning. Grandfather Har was the next to leave. The old man went hunting goats. Her father, Bittoo, worried about Har climbing the steep cliffs and decided to pursue him. Every one of the men took the same trail when leaving the village. Unfortunately, she couldn't determine which route any of them took when they reached the fork in the trail. During the next few days, she planned on returning right where she stood, until they came home.

She settled on a bed of pine needles and rested against the tree. Collecting a handful of dried needles, she decided to braid the long spikes. Normally there'd be three needles in each cluster, rather than five. Not for many days had she smiled such a broad grin nor shown such a sparkle in her eyes. She rose to her feet and inspected the tree's brownish red bark for damage.

On the south side of the pine, she found a large injury cutting deep into the tree. Seeping resin oozed from the wound. With her fingers, she scooped up the sap and put it in her mouth. The sweet taste pleased her. She ate slowly, savoring the flavor of the goo. One mouthful was all she intended to devour, for an abundance could harm her system. Tomorrow she'd bring a container and take the remaining sticky sap home to her mother, who'd most likely store the bulk of it in one of her medicine satchels.

Her curious nature sent her weaving in and out among the trees, seeking more of the tall pines. A large cone fell directly in front of her, its unripened spines unopened. She identified the cone as the type which harbored the largest edible seeds, as big as her fingernails.

She returned to the tree nearest the path, and again, sat in the cushiony bed of needles, waiting for the men. Leaning against its trunk, she drifted off. When her head slumped, she jerked it up, then for the second time fell asleep.

A fluffy tailed, grey squirrel scampered across her lap. Her eyes snapped open, but she didn't stir.

A sleek black and white skunk ambled over one ankle and sniffed greedily at her leather trousers. She tried to remain relaxed as the hungry creature gnawed on one of the bone beads at the end of her boot lacing. Alarmed, she wished she had climbed the tree rather than sat under it. As long as she could remember, animals had been drawn to her. Some she learned to tolerate, such as rabbits and squirrels, but many others she dreaded to be near. Last berry season, on two different days, a bear and a mountain cat came within throwing distance. Both vigorously sniffed the air, carefully watching her before they left.

She heard the distant sound of singing. It grew closer until she recognized the off-keyed voice as Derk's. When the startled skunk waddled away, she hid behind the tree to observe the shaman as he strode past her, taking the right fork into Whistling Wind Pass.

Derk stopped short when he finished his spirit song. With merriment in his tone, he turned around and as loudly as possible, bellowed back in the direction he'd just come from. "Ya, Ho, Caree!"

Embarrassed for getting caught spying on the shaman, Caree's cheeks flushed red. She remained in the cover of the woods.

Derk had felt uneasy ever since experiencing an unsettling dream after the men of Har's lodge went away. His interpretation of the dream frightened him, so he hoped to locate Bittoo, the twins and Har's group of old hunters.

It worried him to know that he remained the only shaman in camp. The future of the people was based on holy men. And all of his successors were gone at a time when the giant fish who lived underground violently thrashed her tail, causing the earth to tremble.

The damage to the lodges in camp had been slight. The first and strongest quake rattled the earth, swaying the domed roofs. The antler rafters teetered back and forth, remaining steadfast in their foundations, despite an occasional earthen clump falling out of the roof and into the dwellings. A clod of ceiling dirt fell into the shelter directly in his hearth, dousing the sacred shaman's fire.

His dreams were bad omens, very bad indeed, as was the smothering of the divine flames. For days now, the tattooed star on his cheek continued to twitch; he was powerless to arrest the erratic tic. "By Creator One Breath, what's happening?" he asked aloud.

He wanted to pretend that he didn't understand the meaning of his dream. "True," he said, as though he talked to someone. "It was full of disaster. Surely, not all of the men are dead. Creator One Breath, don't take those shamans to the Land of the Souls, take me instead!" He felt overwhelmed by his appeal to the great one, who created every thing and every person. Nonetheless, his words came from his heavy heart.

Winded of mind and air, he sat on a rock to rest, one hand held his mystical rock, and the other clutched his owl claw amulet hanging from his neck.

Over and over, in his dream he watched as a mountain of snow and rock wiped out the lives of a number of men. Clouds of moving snow blocked his vision until he couldn't see clearly and was helpless in determining which men had perished.

Caree no longer felt embarrassed for watching the shaman without making herself known to him. In fact, she expertly edged her way through ferns, fir, and pine trees, keeping well out of sight of Derk. When he began talking to himself, she grew curious as to why he blabbered so. She crept near enough to make out a few of his words. Terror ran through the fibers of her being.

After the shaman stopped muttering, she hunkered down silently and strained her ears, wanting him to continue his one-sided dialogue. She listened intently, too intently—ignoring anything else which might prove a hazard.

A movement caught her attention. The pesky skunk trailed her again. She couldn't imagine why the night creature was roaming around during the daylight. Quickly, she pulled out her woman's knife. Cutting the remaining bone beads off her lacings, she threw them toward the smelly animal.

Apparently grateful, the offensive skunk paused and relished the treat, but walked right up to her after eating. Not aiming to startle it or make her presence known to Derk, she held her hand tightly over her mouth and stifled a scream. The fearless varmint explored her boots for even more savory beads. Obviously disappointed, it sauntered back into the underbrush.

She composed herself and looked over at Derk, only he no longer sat beside the path. She emerged from the trees and ran eastward down the trail and around the first bend, where she collided into the him.

Derk's forehead and nose wrinkled. "By Creator One Breath, you smell a little foul." He laughed and was glad she joined him. Now he could think of more pleasant things, even though her aroma was certainly less than pleasant. He wondered if the girl had listened to his earlier outcries concerning her father and her brothers.

"Who's gone to the Land of the Souls?" Caree asked courteously, holding back her anxious feelings.

Derk always felt a compelling need to protect the girl, not that he ever remembered her being in jeopardy, but because there seemed something very special about her. Something that still hadn't shown itself. "I'm not sure who died...maybe no one."

"You're a good interpreter. The sky people gave you the gift to explain signs that others don't understand. You're keeping something from me."

The shaman rolled his star rock between his hands. This wasn't a conversation he wished to continue, as he felt positive some of Caree's family had been killed. "Most of the time the spirits allow me only bits and pieces of information. I don't see all things."

"Will you tell me what you know?"

"I know I'm going to walk down this trail. Today, I'll run into your grandfather, uncles, father or brothers." He promptly left Caree and resumed his walk. He turned to tell her that she was too far from home, but she was gone. When he looked straight ahead again, he saw a number of men walking in single file toward him. "Ya, Ho!" he screamed, thankful that at least some of the males from Har's lodge came home safe.

That evening Caree joined her solemn father and brothers when they gathered at the shaman's lodge.

The men congregated around the sacred fire, while she remained across the room with Derk's mate at the cooking hearth. Derk's woman added rabbit to a pit in the ground, lined with heated rocks and a thick layer of lichen. Quietly, Caree watched her cover the hare with more lichen plus a layer of stones extracted from the blazing fire.

When finished, the woman discarded her bone scopes and peered into Caree's mournful face. She opened her arms wide and embraced the anguished girl. Droplets of tears fell from Caree's eyes, her body quivered. The woman held Caree even tighter, gently swaying back and forth.

When Caree calmed, she sat upright, wiping the moisture from her cheeks. It was painful to think that so many men were gone from her lodge. Guilt consumed her for not staying with her Grandmother, Leha, and Great Aunt Kata, since both just lost their mates. But her mother stayed with them tonight, and she would be a comfort.

It surprised Caree, for all the times she'd stolen into Derk's dwelling after her brothers and father, none of them ever told her to go home. Usually, the shaman glanced up at her as she descended down the ladder, but he never spoke a word. No one ever commented about her presence. She guessed they knew she eavesdropped on the conversations going on at the shaman's fire. True, she only caught shreds of what they discussed, which caused everything to seem even more confusing.

At no time, did she ask the holy ones to clarify anything they said or did. They might banish her from the lodge if she inquired. But always, she sat silently and listened.

This night should be a special night for her twin brothers—the most important night of their lives. Derk would hear about their vision quest, interpret its meaning and pronounce them no longer boys. But four able-bodied men were killed in the avalanche, and now she had no idea what would transpire among the ones sitting at the holy fire.

18

"Ya, Ho, shaman," came a tired old voice from outside. The newcomer declined to gain entrance until invited.

Derk recognized the man and felt overwhelmed with gratitude at his arrival. "Ya, Ho," he replied and stepped over to the ladder to steady the structure. In what seemed to him as all pomp and glory, the mogur from the Bear Hunter Band entered the pit house. Directly behind him came the medicine seer from the Spear Creek Band. Only on one other occasion had he felt such happiness in seeing the two holy leaders.

The mogur and the medicine seer had run into one another on the trail west of Frozen Duck Lake. Some of their bandsmen traveled with them—all headed for the Great Sea to hunt the fur seals with the western bands. Many people from Frozen Duck Camp planned to join them. The holy leaders thought the long exhaustive trip might be their last, and even this one might prove difficult for them.

When first reaching Frozen Duck Camp, a group of villagers had crowded around the holy men, giving them the appalling news about the avalanche and the deaths it caused.

The mogur was concerned about his friend, Bittoo. When merely a boy about the age of the twins, Bittoo performed a healing rite as he lay near death. The young tusu saved his life, and he felt obligated to him ever since. Though never had he heard of Bittoo taking on any other holy duties, but he knew with all his being that Bittoo was the tusu and Father of all Shaman.

And someday, something dreadful would happen, and only through Bittoo's wisdom could the Clan of the Ancient Humans be saved. An inner knowledge he possessed told him this was so. And now he was on a mission to tell all the other bands. When he left for the Land of the Souls, everyone in the Clan of the Ancient Humans should realize that the time grew near for them to follow this great tusu.

The four holy ones took their places around the fire—the same locations they took many seasons ago after Froom savagely attacked Bittoo.

Jarkoo and Braaz stood, looking bewildered, not understanding where they belonged at the sacred hearth. Each of the four directions were already represented—one by each of the holy ones who were already seated. Even so, they were confused as to what direction their new spirit deity stood for. When the mammoth once roamed the earth, the beast would've been associated with the northern direction, the same as the bear deity where the mogur sat. But now, the animal was deceased and only lived in the afterworld. Possibly, their totem represented the sky on the east side. They looked at one another with the same perplexing thoughts running through their minds.

Derk peered up and caught the twins' blank look. He patted the spot between himself and the mogur, a direction which placed the boys not quite east and not quite north, but in between. It pleased them, and they joined the circle of shamans.

Jarkoo started the tale. "We stumbled on a cave and inside..."

"... we found bones which once belonged to giant creatures."

"It appeared that someone made a hut out of them, but long ago the bindings must have rotted, and the bones fell into a heap," the twins conveyed, at the same time.

Derk nodded his head in wonder. "The ancient shamans of our band passed down a story of such a sacred dwelling. But no one ever found it...until now."

The account fascinated the mogur, and the boys' way of speaking a marvel to him. They completed each other's sentences and even said the exact same words at the same time— feats that suggested each knew what the other was thinking. He reclined on a soft stack of furs and listened.

"The first night..." Braaz said.

"....we slept in the middle of the pile, but neither of us remembered going to sleep. Just waking up."

"When we woke, we walked further into the dark cave..."

"...and before long saw a blinding light streaming in, ahead of us."

Excitedly the two reported, "When reaching the opening, a mammoth stood waiting for us. She swiped us off our feet and carried us in her curved tusks." Both Jarkoo and Braaz suddenly looked uneasy.

The medicine seer shot a quick glance at the mogur and saw the surprise in his eyes. The seer seemed a little apprehensive with the boys' story and the odd manner which they related it.

Bittoo understood the mood of the medicine seer and the mogur, and was glad to be present when both of them learned of his sons' rare but exceptional gift. But he could tell the boys had more to share—more than they felt comfortable telling. What he didn't realize was that no matter what—the other three holy men would stand behind him, and of course, he stood behind his sons.

"She took us to the Land of the Souls," they claimed timidly.

Bittoo smiled, proud of his boys. The mogur's surprise threw him into a coughing fit, and Bittoo pounded lightly on his back.

"It was a vision, a dream," said the medicine seer as he restlessly ran his hands through the lush hair of a silver fox pelt. "No one enters the afterworld unless they're dead."

"When your mother gave birth to you two, people of the clan believed that one of you was really dead...a spirit," alleged the mogur.

Bittoo's eyes glared as his nostrils flared. "I didn't father a spirit!"

"No, I didn't mean to imply that I give credit to that rumor. I just don't understand."

"The furthest place a shaman has ever gone is to the middle world, although not all holy men possess the powers to go even there. Have we ever known two people who are identical or appear to comprehend what the other is thinking?" asked the medicine seer.

"What you've forgotten, is that Ceda once told Bittoo he'd be the father of a lineage of great shamans. By Creator One Breath, I swear that even though the circumstances are unusual, it's meant to be!" snapped Derk.

"Yes it's meant to be," declared the mogur. "Is there or has there ever been another holy one who could have restored my health and my disfigured face? I think not. I don't comprehend, but I do believe in Bittoo and now his sons. In fact, I go to the Great Sea to express the same to the shamans there."

"Let's hear what Jarkoo and Braaz have to say," added Bittoo, delighted with the mogur's statement. He motioned for the twins to resume their account.

"At first we thought we entered the afterworld, the Land of the Souls..."

"...but then we saw grandfather...."

"...Uncle Cir, Uncle Tam and Gaaf's father, Barc, so we assumed we were dreaming."

"Later, when we ran into father on the trail, he told us that the ones we saw in our vision quest were really dead," Jarkoo related, without his brother speaking with him. "Only then did my brother and I accept the reality...we had visited the afterworld."

"Except, father still thought Uncle Tam was alive."

"But we also saw Uncle Tam in the Land of the Souls...."

"...and then father realized that Tam was also killed in the avalanche."

"Grandfather gave us a set of goat horns. We brought them back," they testified in unison.

"Before finding the bodies," Bittoo said, "I came across a skinned goat. The horns had been removed. That's why my father went hunting, to get one for each of his twin grandsons. The beautiful horns journeyed to the Land of the Souls with my father, but they returned with my sons."

Mysteriously, a wordless dialogue shot back and forth between each set of shamans' eyes.

Addressing Bittoo, the mogur stated his opinion. "When you were but a boy, you were given more power than any shaman I knew of. More than I possessed or ever attained. Your power is in you somewhere, even though you seldom chose to use it."

"Or maybe there wasn't any need to use his power," added the medicine seer, now running his fidgety hands through his white hair, tinged with the old age yellow.

"I look upon your boys, and I'm amazed. The story of their vision quest is potent. I listen to them and hear their words, speaking together as if they were only one person. Never have I seen such a magical gift. The water deity spoke the truth when she proclaimed you to be the father of a lineage of mighty shamans."

"She spoke the truth," affirmed the medicine seer. "But the mogur and I fear for your safety, and now for the safety of your sons, unless all the shamans and everyone who make up the Clan of the Ancient Humans understand that you're the great tusu. Sometime soon, they must believe and listen to you."

"That's true," agreed Derk.

The mogur cleared his throat. "I remember when she first declared you a tusu. I grew jealous of your power, because our people looked upon me as the greatest of shamans in all the six bands. I didn't desire another taking my place or outshining me. I wasn't thinking and considered only my own interests ...not those of our people."

The mogur's declaration touched the twins. They'd never heard how he felt—no one ever mentioned it. They only knew their father, as an adolescent, was saved by a healing rite which the mogur and other shamans performed. And soon after that, the mogur had been healed by a ritual their father performed. Nothing was ever said about the mogur's envy.

"But I didn't see things that way until after you restored my health. We waited all these many seasons, thinking you'd show the clan and walk the shaman's path. Except for you curing me when you were young, you remained idle."

"There's been no reason. Derk does everything a spiritual leader should do for his band. Ceda will alert me when the time comes. When I see the spirit of the wind, I will know," Bittoo reasoned politely.

Derk chuckled to himself. Ceda expected Bittoo to do more than learn the ways of the shamans from him and sit around waiting for the wind. There always seemed to be a struggle between her and the tusu.

"The medicine seer and I go to the gathering at the Fur Seal Band where we'll convey your greatness to all. What we fear is someday other shamans...envious shamans won't follow you or may even attempt to harm you. You stayed in the background without displaying your incredible skills or your wisdom."

"Because of this, some clansmen may regarded you as weak. However, some shamans may actually know of your greatness and see it as a threat to them and think you too strong," the medicine seer deducted.

"We'll try to gain unity between the spiritual men of the clan. We hoped that Derk and you would journey with us to the Great Sea and meet with the shamans there." The mogur looked at Jarkoo and Braaz. "Just now, we witnessed the powers of your sons. It looks as if they, too, have been hiding their abilities."

Jarkoo refused to look at his brother. He would smile too broadly if he did. Few knew they experienced the same thoughts and were able to speak the same words together. But none, not even their father, knew of another of their skills—one they still kept to themselves.

"I've just lost my father and uncles. I'm saddened beyond words...this is a grievous time for my family. We also lost Barc, therefore we need to think whether this is a time for us to leave. The avalanche took two elders from the Frozen Duck Band...Barc and Har. Derk's the only remaining elder."

"We feel deeply for you. Perhaps your pain is less severe with the knowledge of them already reaching the Land of the Souls," the medicine seer said with sympathy showing on his face and in his voice.

From across the room, the mogur's apprentice leaned against the support pole. Caree's eyes were on him when he came down the ladder, but the others, deep in discussion, hadn't noticed Luun. Luun's ears were sharp, however, he missed much of what was going on. He eyed Bittoo, and his hatred for the shaman nearly overtook him.

Again and again, over his adulthood, he stalked the tusu. Never once finding the perfect opportunity to pierce Bittoo with a spear that bore Froom's marks on it. Always, he carried the hidden weapons, as he did today.

He tried to concentrate on the shamans' conversation, but his mind wandered. Time was running out. The mogur grew old and wouldn't live through many more seasons. Then, it would be his turn as shaman of the Bear Hunter Band. Yet Bittoo still stood in his way, for when Bittoo became the shaman of the Frozen Duck Band, the entire clan might give him the highest respect of all the holy men — that is if the mogur were successful in persuading them. Such a situation wasn't acceptable. He wanted to be the most revered shaman in the entire clan. His head filled with the torturing thoughts of being second in line, and he missed everything being said concerning the twins. He slipped up the ladder, determined to devise a plan.

The camp of Frozen Duck Band appeared in utter clamor and turmoil. Numerous bandsmen were already preparing for the trip to the Great Sea when Bittoo came home with news of the avalanche and the four deaths. Now the villagers made ready for a burial feast. Without such a meal, the departed ones couldn't enter the world of the dead. In such cases, they might become dark spirits.

When a feast was prepared, the elaborate meal took on a double importance. Even if the people

knew the four dead men already lived in the Land
of the Souls, it was still necessary for the food to be
eaten by Bittoo and Gaaf's family members. In that
manner, the deceased then took the food to other
departed ancestors in the afterworld—the ancestors
of those who fixed the meal.

Luun walked through camp ever watchful of the
proceeding. The new arrivals from the Spear Creek
Band and the Bear Hunter Band were overly helpful with so much needing done. The camp, overcrowded, burst at its seams, and the aroma of roasting meats, roots, and simmering soups teased his
taste buds.

Deciding it important to determine where Bittoo
lived, he sauntered in and around the lodges. He
came upon a small group of clansmen sitting around
an earthen hut, some with their hands full of food.
He peered down the smoke hole and saw people
crowded tightly together. Joining the ones outside,
he listened closely to their small talk.

The young woman squatted on the ground with
her arm around her small daughter and a tightly
coiled basket brimming with cooked cattail sprouts
resting on her lap. When young, her favorite play-
mate had been Teaa, Har's youngest daughter. Now
Har was dead, and she came to show her respects in
hopes that her food gift would reach her own parents who dwelled in the afterworld. She truly missed
Teaa who lived at the Fur Seal Band. In a day or two,
she and her man would travel there to hunt seals. It
would probably be her duty to inform Teaa of her
father's and uncles' deaths.

In the darkness she found it difficult to see who was sitting in the crowd, waiting for a turn to enter the lodge. A man just sat down beside her, but he hadn't spoken to anyone.

"Mother, don't be ashamed," whispered an unfamiliar female voice. "Bittoo's family holds no grudges."

"I hope not," replied a more matured voice.

"Patee, is that you?" asked the young woman.

Before the older woman could respond, a stream of people exited the pit house.

When the lodge nearly emptied, the ones who waited in the darkness worked their way down the ladder with their edible burial offerings. Luun remained outside but scooted close to the entry in order to overhear those inside.

A middle-aged woman lingered near the support pole, while the others greeted the three female occupants of the dwelling. Their voices mingled and fused together, annoying Luun since he was unable to make out anything being said. He'd grown curious and a little baffled when earlier hearing a woman say something about Bittoo not carrying a grudge.

A brief hush fell over the group inside, and two women rushed over to the woman who hadn't joined in.

"Patee, we're glad to see you," said Kata.

"We missed you so," Leha added, putting her arms around the woman.

Luun racked his mind. Throughout the seasons, there had been mention of someone named Patee, except he wasn't pulling the remembrance from his brain. He listened further, but again, everyone talked at once.

He gazed into the sky. The stars and Moon Watcher were nowhere to be seen, making it difficult for him to devise a night attack on Bittoo. He now knew where the tusu lived and the probable route he would take through the lodges when departing Derk's dwelling. What he hadn't been able to determine was a place to conceal himself—a spot where the could throw a spear and not be seen.

It remained a mystery whether Froom still lived. Many seasons had passed since anyone mentioned the man's name. It was vitally important that Bittoo's enemy still walked Mother Earth, for the short stubby spears in his own quiver were disguised as Froom's. "I remember who she is," he whispered to himself. "Patee is Froom's mate who went to live at the Spear Creek Camp many long seasons past, after Froom tried to drown Bittoo."

He was elated. If Froom still lived, he most likely was in the immediate area. Long ago the whispered stories stated that Froom never roamed far from Patee, even though he seldom encountered her face to face. Rumors flew that Froom even hunted for her, leaving meat outside the lodge she currently called home.

Now, this night, after killing Bittoo, the people of the clan would surely believe Froom committed the murder. That is, if they thought the crazed man was truly still alive.

Luun wandered through camp until coming upon a handful of men roasting strips of meat on an outdoor fire. One man from his band, he recognized, the others were strangers. Someone shoved a pronged stick and a hunk of raw venison in his hand. Grateful for the food, he collapsed onto the hard ground and pierced the meat with the green willow branch, thrusting it over the coals.

"This is Luun," spoke the man from the Bear Hunter's Band. "He's the mogur's apprentice."

"We were talking about the avalanche and the mysterious man who ran from Bittoo and the others," divulged a stranger. "At first, Bittoo, Gaaf and Piika assumed the person who fled was Tam, because his body hasn't been found. For some reason, even though they didn't discover Tam's lifeless form, all of them are convinced he's dead."

"But no one explained to us why they believe Tam perished," said the man directly across from Luun.

"If it wasn't Tam who fled, it had to be Froom. We can't figure out who else would bolted from them."

Luun's heart pounded in his chest. Not wanting to appear overly interested, he calmed himself. He pulled the meat off the forked limb only to see he'd been so intrigued with the tale, he burnt one side and failed to cook the other. "Does Froom still live? A long time has passed since I've heard anything about him," he quizzed coolly.

"He's living. He wanders in the mountains and during the seasons of the heavy snows provides for Patee."

The talk changed, but Luun lingered around the pit as if to show interest in their small talk. He thanked the men for the meat and ambled away. When out of the light of the fire, he discovered that the sky was twinkling with stars and Moon Watcher was gaping down upon the camp. "It's an omen," he deducted. "The light is dim enough to hide behind, and yet, bright enough for me to see my mark."

He headed back the way he came. No one was up and about, and even Bittoo's lodge was quiet and seemed empty of visitors. He saw a direct line between the entrance to Bittoo's dwelling and the woods. He explored the thick forest until finding a fast way to escape once he killed the great tusu. The way would prove easy when returning to the camp where he could pretend to be fast asleep.

Sleepily, he waited. Moon Watcher and the stars slowly died out—replaced with a hazy glow in the east. He wondered how many other times he endeavored this same feat—remaining in hiding, waiting for the right opportunity. Soon, the sky would be lit and his obscured place as well.

He heard talking and stepped back into the dark shaded foliage, and at the same time, he raised his spear thrower.

Seething, he lowered the weapon to his side. Bittoo, his twin sons and daughter were walking so closely together, he couldn't get a clear aim.

He angrily snapped the readied spear over his knee. Enraged, he stole into the density of the trees, making his way around and back toward the village. Someday soon, he'd accomplish the deed.

Like sudden lightning out of the sky a very amusing thought struck him. Since Patee was in camp, Froom must be lurking somewhere close. Most likely, Froom would strike Bittoo dead. And the job would be finished.

Bear Claw didn't understand any of the information shooting through his sluggish mind. He sensed his brother had been speaking for a long, long time—maybe an eternity—he was incapable of telling. His vigor was fading, his mind cloudy. He didn't wish to desert his beloved twin. From the beginning, they proved inseparable.

He'd fight harder to pull himself out of the engulfing darkness. More sleep might benefit him—yet maybe not. If resting in that manner again, he might never wake.

A far away voice was calling him. It wasn't his brother's familiar voice because he heard the words with his ears rather than his mind. He wouldn't give into the coaxing of the invisibles. Instead he'd listen intently to his brothers distant voice, even though he no longer comprehended the words. He'd block out the voices coming through his ears.

***

19

The little girl skipped through the crowded camp looking for her playmates. Her loose brown hair bounced with each springy step.

At the first lodge, everyone was missing—the smoke hole covered over with a thick coarse hide to keep the rain out. Sadly, she remembered her friend went with his parents to the Great Sea.

She scampered over to three more dwellings, and even though the busy pit houses looked full of people, the shelters were empty of children. Like herself, her playmates must have been sent outside, out of everyone's way. Being ushered outdoors delighted her, especially now with so many newcomers in the village.

She guessed her friends might be at the old deserted lodge at the edge of the camp. It was their favorite place to play grown-ups. Sometimes, she pretended to be the mother, and at other times, the child. She liked being the mother best of all. She made good mud patties. Whoever lived there before left many fun cooking items, like the grinding stones and rock hearth. Most everything made of skins lay rotted or chewed up by rodents.

She walked around the domed roof and nearly stepped on a sleeping man. Jumping backwards, out of reach, she watched the newcomer. He lay soundly sleeping in all his clothing, with his bed fur heaped on the ground.

The stranger snored, much like sky thunder, with his chest heaving up and down. She squatted on her heels, holding back a giggle. Mischievously, she picked up a long twig, running it back and forth in the dirt. His lips vibrated against themselves each time he pushed out a breath. She continued to observe the man who looked much older than her father, wondering why anyone would sleep this late.

Timidly, she moved the leafed twig up to the man's face. He sucked in a big gulp of air, rubbed his palm across his nose, and with his eyes still closed, rolled over on his side toward her. She scooted further back.

The stranger's eyes fluttered and popped open. He sat up quickly, glaring at her. "Who are you?" Luun asked crossly when seeing the tickling stick the girl clutched in her hand.

Startled, her mouth jolted wide. She couldn't reply, but her short legs flew into motion, and she bolted for her lodge, dropping the twig along the way.

Luun shook his head and ran his hands through his bushy hair, then rubbed the scratchy stubble on his chin. The previous night came flooding back. Again, his attempt to dispose of Bittoo had failed.

Thinking the mogur must be expecting him, he spread his sleeping robe down flat in order to place his belongings inside and roll the hide around them. A frown loomed along his brow when he grabbed his quiver. The leather container seemed much too light. He rummaged through the bag. Three spears were missing, besides the one he broke last night and left where it fell. He inspected the two remaining weapons. Both had his marks on them. The only spears absent were the ones which bore Froom's markings on their shafts.

His hands trembled with the knowledge that someone stole them. Whoever it was, the person must surely realize he tried to kill the tusu. "No, that doesn't make sense," he mumbled. Maybe, the little girl played with the spears, even though he knew she didn't leave with them. He searched around the abandoned pit house, but found nothing.

If the weapons had slipped out of the quiver when walking through the woods, he would've noticed their absence before going to sleep. But just in case, he trampled through the underbrush in hopes of finding them. He reached the spot where he'd waited for a good shot at Bittoo and not even the splintered spear he broke in half was there.

He made his way back to his bed roll. Was it possible that someone saw him, last night, hiding in the forest? And why would anyone steal only the spears without his marks? Whoever rummaged in his pouch found five spears—three supposedly belonging to Froom and two belonging to him. His remained and Froom's were taken. Maybe the thief recognized Froom's and figured things out. Maybe by now, the entire camp knew of his evil-doing.

He shuddered at the overwhelming possibility. If the people of the clan had grasped the situation, he'd soon be forced to flee into the mountains and never again live with the band. How frightening that might be—living somewhere in the wilderness under the harshest of conditions where the wild man Froom also dwelled.

Composing himself, he took many slow deep breaths before gaining the courage to join the holy men at Derk's lodge.

Forgetting to announce himself, he entered the earthen house and made his way to his teacher's side. The mogur, who was eating out of a raw hide pouch, gave him a disappointed glare. Earlier, he had been hungry, but he felt too jumpy and had lost his appetite. Food was the last thing crowding his thinking. He needed to disguise his nervousness—at least on the outside—his insides felt all in a jumble.

Derk's mate passed a wooden bowl brimming with cooked brown lily bulbs under his nose. His mouth watered from the smell of the food, which in turn, almost caused him to retch. Politely, he refused her offer.

Bittoo and his sons were absent, but he gave the appearance of listening to the mogur and Derk as they talked among themselves. His gut told him that neither of the holy men knew anything about the spears, or they'd already be furiously confronting him. However, the person responsible for taking the weapons might soon inform them. He was determined to devise a story which in no way could place either blame or suspicion in his direction. "When do we leave?" he inquired of the mogur. The mogur was either ignoring him or didn't hear his question. He sat in silence.

Derk pointed at Luun who for a considerable amount of time, had remained listless and unresponsive.

"Have you heard anything we said?" pressed the mogur.

Luun jerked to attention—ever mindful of being addressed. "No," he stammered.

"What's the problem?" asked the mogur. "You sit as if in a stupor." So many issues plagued them at present, he hoped his apprentice wasn't going to add to their problems.

"Nothing much, just something rather odd happened last night."

"How odd?" Derk asked.

"When I went looking for a place to bed down..."

"We wondered why you didn't sleep here."

Luun ignored the statement and continued with his made-up tale. "I stumbled over some short spears...spear thrower ones, out near that empty lodge. No one was there to claim them, so I put them in my leather pouch. I figured to ask around today and find their owner, except the spears were missing from my quiver when I woke."

"You're right, that is odd," the mogur grunted, happy Luun's tale was only unusual and not serious. For some time now, he'd been carrying a bad taste in his mouth for Luun. Thanks to Creature One Breath, the middle-aged apprentice wasn't, as yet, the holy leader of the Bear Hunter Band. Luum seemed to always think of his own self-centered gains.

For sure, when returning home, he'd start training another apprentice and hopefully, live long enough to tutor him well. Last night, Luun hadn't even sat in counsel with them. "How many spears were there?"

"Four, all obsidian."

"What marks were on them?" the medicine seer asked.

"I didn't see the marks." He felt a little uncomfortable again. He'd become very hot, and suspected his outward appearance might give him away.

"Did you touch them, run your fingers over their roughness?" the mogur asked.

"No, I was tired. It was dark, and I didn't identify them,"he lied again.

"The matter seems trivial," professed the mogur, waving his bony thin hand, indicating he wanted to drop the issue.

Derk regarded Luun. One advantage to a shaman's lodge was the two smoke holes, which during the day let in an abundance of light. By chance, the mogur's old eyes seemed incapable of seeing the red flush that now colored Luun's face, and the beads of perspiration rolling down the man's forehead. Luun appeared as though he were acting —ignoring his sweaty condition. He was being deceptive, not wiping the perspiration from his face. What reason could he have for being sneaky?

Luun was satisfied with his false account concerning the spears. Now, no one could ever prove he'd been in possession of the deadly weapons all along. Everyone would think he found them, including the one who took them, if that individual ever made himself known. Another attempt on Bittoo's life would have to wait. He was pleased with himself for telling such a wonderful covered-up story. He felt suddenly famished.

"Ya, Ho!" rang three voices in unison. Jarkoo was the only one to make his way down the ladder, which he did, skipping every other rung. As he approached the sacred hearth, and caught Luun's face in a ray of sunlight, he exclaimed, "You look sick!"

"Your eyes aren't adjusted from coming indoors," Luun blurted back. "I'm fine." More than fine, he said silently to himself, if you just keep your mouth shut, trouble maker.

"Which twin are you?" inquired the medicine seer.

"Jarkoo," he informed the group of shamans, as he knew even Derk couldn't tell him and his brother apart.

"Where's your father?" asked the mogur, his tone sounding disappointed.

"He's waiting for me. We're going to Beaver Tail Mountain to bury the bodies and find Tam's corpse."

"The tremors have ceased," Derk declared.
"You'll be safe. Who's going?"

"Father, Gaaf, Piika, Braaz and myself."

The mogur cleared his throat. He'd gotten misty
thinking about the awful accident and the men who
came to such a tragic fate. "If you take the trail
through Whistling Wind Pass, we may run into you.
We leave in two or three days for the Great Sea."

"We have three less hunters in our lodge. Gaaf's
lodge has one less hunter. Father and Gaaf decided
some of us will go hunt seals. I don't know who.
When the decision is made, they'll be glad to travel
with you to the Great Sea and will meet you on the
trail."

Gaaf and Bittoo were overly winded by the time
they neared the area devastated by the avalanche.
Both men feeling compelled to reach the region, allowed their sons to set the grueling pace. They
plunked onto the ground, panting. "You two go with
Piika, he can show you where the bodies are. Gaaf
and I will catch up soon."

Gaaf searched his friend's face. "The snow has
nearly melted since we were here five days ago."

"With the snow gone, Tam's remains will be
easier to find," Bittoo whispered, then raised his
voice. "Since this accident, you, your woman and
Piika are by yourselves. It's certainly lonely and
seems very empty in our lodge now. It's probably
the same at your lodge. I invite you to live with us.
No longer will the shelter be called Har's lodge. From
now on, it'll be Gaaf's and Bittoo's lodge."

Gaaf choked, his emotions nearing the surface.
He opened his mouth to speak, but one of the twins
was frantically beckoning to them.

They scurried over the dangerous terrain and down toward the tree line, passing the spot where they remembered seeing Har's body. Bittoo was sickened at the thought of some vicious animal dragging the corpse off and devouring it. They reached the three boys who stood around a large pile of rocks.

A yip and whimper came from a nearby stand of twisted trees. In wonderment, Bittoo spied his dog, Raccoon, tethered to a skimpy limb. Braaz raced down and with his sharp knife, cut her lose. Happy to be with her master, the dog leaped on Bittoo, almost knocking him down.

While Bittoo gained his balance, Raccoon wiggled over to the mound, layed down and whined. Perplexed, the tusu looked at the carefully placed stones.

Draped respectively on the very top of the pile were four familiar medicine bags. Confused, no one said a thing. But all understood that this was a grave. A grave which housed, Har, Barc, Cir, and Tam—a grave dug and erected with extreme care. Someone cared, but who?

20

Caree had climbed a very tall fir tree, carefully making her way from one limb to another until she gained a full view of Frozen Duck Village, the lake and the trails leading to and from the camp. Shaking, she teetered as the treetop tilted, its upper scrawny branches too flimsy to support her.

Clutching her childhood sickness bag, she wondered if its power could possibly help her now. Just two handfuls of days had gone by since she started her women's bleeding, and already she should've replaced the tiny bag with a new grown-up medicine bundle. Keeping her womanhood a secret seemed shameful. High up in the tree, so far up, she must surely be near the spirits, and surely they must be unhappy with her. But she wanted a glimpse at Whistling Wind Pass and the trail which Piika and her twin brothers took.

She missed her brothers and even Piika, which rather amazed her, never remembering a time when she missed him as much as Jarkoo and Braaz. Lately, she felt a new kind of warmness toward Piika which she unsuccessfully tried to dismiss.

All three had traveled to the Great Sea to hunt seals. If only she'd gone with them, but no one asked her. No one said they were going. She had assumed they went with Gaaf and her father to bury the bodies, nothing else. But her father and Gaaf returned to camp alone. If she were with the twins and Piika now, she would be visiting with her Aunt Teaa and Aunt Mupo and feasting on a variety of sea creatures, including urchins which she prized above all salt water food.

When she was born, Teaa, her favorite aunt, lived in the same lodge and lived there for many turnings of the seasons. Whereas Mupo, her other aunt, took a mate and had already moved away to the Fur Seal Band. Mupo's son couldn't speak, therefore he talked with his hands. Her poor Aunt Teaa remained barren.

Caree let go of her sickness bag and used both arms to hug the tree. She closed her eyes, allowing herself to sway rather than fight its movement. She felt a oneness with the massive growth, envisioning, picturing all which the ancient fir must have seen, long before she was born, even back to the time of her ancestors.

Her eyes bolted open. How long she'd been hanging onto the graceful tree—she was unsure. What an unusual thing to do—lose track of time while clinging to a treetop. She began her descent, wondering if the tree were capable of understanding things within her. If so, the stately fir knew her secret.

When nearing the ground, her heart nearly stopped. Two wolves, one white and one black, stood at the base of her tree. Straddling a sturdy lower branch, she waited. Her first thought was to throw a fir cone at them, except the cones grew too far out on the limbs for her to pick. Instantly, she was grateful the cones grew out of reach. If she had acted on that impulse, they may have turned vicious.

The wolves seemed to have nothing better to do than keep her pinned in the tree. Watching them, she judged the pair as much larger than any she'd ever seen and therefore more threatening. Their hair had the thickness of winter fur instead of ratty, spring fur. The hair on the black one shone with luster.

All her life animals flocked to her, this time, she was frightened. No one knew of her whereabouts, she had traipsed off again. She shut her eyes, trying to think. When opening them the wolves were gone. But caution warned her to remain on the limb in case they suddenly returned.

She should be home helping her mother and the other women of the lodge as they prepared for a root gathering journey. Not that the family would venture far from home, probably one or two days walk from camp, except their trip would last two moons, about the same amount of time which her brothers and Piika would be absent.

Quietly, she crept down the tree, afraid the wolves' keen hearing would detect her movements unless they were a very long ways away. She reached the ground and saw where the male urinated on the trunk, causing a muddy mess on the ground. The animal had claimed the tree as being a boundary of his territory. "You can just have this old tree," she muttered to herself while heading toward the village. Cautiously, she watched, her eyes darting back and forth, for she might be going in the same direction as the wolves.

She rushed into camp, then slowed her legs down as if nothing seemed the matter. Approaching the dwelling, she saw her father and Gaaf, each striking at large jasper rocks with their rounded hammerstones. She observed at a distance as the men continued to whack at the beautiful red and golden jasper, chipping until the objects bore a general shape. Next, they used antler tines to flake the edges of their new projectile points.

Hoping to find a good but unwanted spear point, she moved closer, her eyes searching the ground among the leftover pieces at the men's feet. She couldn't find a suitable one—the two men had wisely chosen rock nodules which housed no inner defects, and both Gaaf and her father excelled at making the sharp weapons. There were no discarded ones.

Her father completed his slender point and shook out the thick protective hide he'd draped over his lap. He spied his daughter and gave her a stern look, one which suggested she'd been absent too long and should be helping her mother.

Caree ignored his gaze, asking, "Do you have a spear point that I can have?"

Curiously, Bittoo glanced at her. Someday she'd become Piika's mate, maybe even before the time of the heavy snows if she began her woman's bleeding. He didn't like her roaming from camp by herself, which he deemed very careless. Once, he saw a mean-looking silver-grey badger casually following her until she reached the openness of the village. Another time, four or five blue jays circled her head in a friendly manner. He was unsure as to why she insisted on owning a spear, but it seemed a sensible idea. "Why do you want one?"

"I'd like to carry a long spear, not the short kind that's used in a spear thrower."

His three children were the beginning of the dreadful legacy Ceda once spoke of. When his twin boys were born, he knew them to be shamans with unbelievable powers. When his daughter came into the world, he looked upon her for the first time and knew without question, although it surprised him, that Creator One Breath had also gifted her with remarkable power. His sons showed their ability from the start, always speaking the same words at the same time. Whereas Caree hadn't, as yet, emerged into the status of a holy woman. Her time drew near, he won't inquire any further about her need for a spear. Perhaps when she experienced her moon flow and became a woman, her destiny might unfold. "I'll make you one and show you how to use the weapon, if you want."

She smiled mischievously. "I can throw it and hit my mark, too."

Apparently hoping for a demonstration, Gaaf provided her with one of his long spears. She grabbed it by the wooden shaft, feeling for the weapon's balance, then rolled and bounced the finely made implement in her palm. Hefting the hunting spear back and over her shoulder, she swiftly and accurately threw it, piercing a discarded piece of leather quite some distance away.

She walked over and pulled the spear out of the ground. The pierced scrap of hide clung to the point.

She made her way back and handed Gaaf his weapon. No one spoke. Both her father and Gaaf looked as though they swallowed bad water. She kept her sight on them, thinking her father was possibly angry with her.

Bittoo was dumbfounded, astonished and even proud, as Gaaf seemed to be. He shook his head in awe and burst into a hearty laugh. Gaaf joined his friend until he held his sides and tears clouded his vision.

Hearing the comical racket from inside the lodge, Sanee, the girl's mother, climbed half-way up the ladder. She seemed unable to make out the reason for the men's roaring outburst, even so, she developed a contagious giggle.

Bittoo overheard his woman, turned toward her and announced, "Our daughter is an accomplished markswoman. I suspect that our boys and even Piika gave her numerous lessons."

Father Sun cast a shred of light as the group departed Frozen Duck Camp and took the northern trail, heading for the high and low meadows. It was cool, a comfortable day for fast walking, loaded down with oversized packs and many baskets.

Caree was the youngest traveler, so the adults set a steady and rigorous pace. By the end of the day, the group expected to arrive at the root gathering grounds, no matter how many steps Caree needed to take for each step of theirs. Bittoo walked behind, and Sanee and Great Aunt Kata, directly in front. Surprisingly, Derk and his mate, who treaded behind Gaff and his woman, kept up very well considering their age.

Sanee constantly turned around, checking on Caree. She wondered what her daughter might do with her new spear and hoped as they walked, Caree wouldn't carelessly jab her in the back with the sharp weapon.

At dusk, they reached the outskirts of the high meadow. Twice, the rain drenched the group and never once did Father Sun peep through the mass of clouds and smile down. Caree removed her large burden basket and fell exhausted onto the still soggy ground. Her father had carried her bed fur pack for the latter part of the day. She sat watching as everyone else prepared a temporary camp.

When shuddering with cold, she rose and hastily gathered enough firewood to last the night. She continued heaping her arms with dried branches and sticks so by the next evening, after digging roots and bulbs all day, there'd be no reason to repeat the chore.

After finishing her task, she crumpled by the unlit fire. At a distance, she heard her father and Gaaf talking but was unable to understand their words over the business of the camp. She no longer felt cold, rather very hot, and if owning a fire-starter kit, she would have kindled a fire just for its light.

Once again shame flooded her, for always a girl was presented her own kit when she became a woman. The cooking hearths within a lodge belonged to the females who lived there. And Grandmother Fire Spirit resided in the women's hearths. Probably the fire spirit was another spirit displeased with her for not revealing her status as a woman.

She stood and ventured into the trees toward the two familiar voices.

"One of us needs to stay awake tonight. They followed most of the day, always staying in the undergrowth."

"What did?" Caree asked.

"A pair of wolves—one white and the other black."

"I saw nothing."

"The animals trailed to the side of us, but behind you. Too bad I insisted Raccoon stay in camp with your grandmother."

She crept back to the shelter, listening for any sounds the wolves might make and feeling terribly foolish for going into the woods with no thought of taking her new spear. The description of the wolves fit the two which earlier kept her up the tree. Her father's dog Raccoon could have given warning if the wolves were lurking. But she had seen those wolves, and Raccoon wasn't any match for them.

Everyone clustered around the newly made fire, situated just inside the entrance of the large lean-to. The night looked starless. They brought in all the provisions and baskets—under the covering and out of the threatening rain. Caree fell asleep while the others remained awake, deciding their next day's plan.

When she woke, everyone around her was busy. The four women helped one another with the baskets each would carry on their backs.

Sanee handed her a handful of dried venison, then assisted her with a large conical basket. "You and I will cross the open field until reaching the stream. There we'll turn west, looking for bulbs. The other women are going to forage in the low meadow...Gaaf and Derk keeping guard over them.

We're expected to return to camp when our baskets are full or before sunset. Your father stays near you and me."

During the time of the heavy snows, Caree had made four useful baskets. Two baskets for serving food, the third, sealed with pitch, to heat water, roots and meat in. She lugged the fourth, a loosely woven basket, on her back.

In one hand, she held her spear and in the other, her digging stick. All three ignored the plants they normally would've dug and briskly rushed toward the creek. The dark clouds hadn't produced rain since the day before.

"Your father said we didn't need another man to watch over us since we now have a daughter capable of throwing a spear and hitting her mark," Sanee said half-heartedly.

"Yes, but can this girl strike a moving target?" jested Bittoo.

Caree took her father's question seriously and answered with a snap to her voice. "I haven't any idea. I've never tried. I wouldn't enjoy killing some animal just to find out." She closed her mouth tight when realizing how abrupt her words sounded.

Sanee and Bittoo were both a little taken aback by Caree's curt reply. Inwardly they both snickered. The girl hardly seemed herself.

Sanee made a wide berth around a massive bed of leeks. Caree and Bittoo followed her lead. "The patch is much bigger this season. We'll make a point of coming back during the hot weather."

Without slowing his steps, Bittoo bent at the waist and pulled up one of the immature stalks. Along with the plant came a young tiny bulb. Caree wrinkled her nose and made a face when her father bit into it. She disliked the flavor of uncooked leek. Its aroma didn't please her either. In the past, when they dug them, everyone smelled as bad as the plant.

Next, the trio fell into an area which at first was only sparsely dotted with corydalis plants, but the further west they walked the thicker the plants grew. Sanee and Caree dug the bulbs, putting the entire supply into Caree's basket. When the container grew heavy, Caree turned and tracked back to camp.

She sat in the dirt. Since the bottom of her willow basket rested on the ground, the straps around her shoulders came loose. She wiggled her way out of them. Already, two piles of bulbs lay in the shelter. Apparently, Derk's group arrived, then departed right before she showed up. Slowly, she tipped her load and carefully dumped them.

Her father would worry if she didn't hurry. But distant thunder rumbled, and cold rain pelted at Earth Mother, driving her to stay under cover. Far away, she glimpsed a hopeful blue sky. She huddled in the lean-to, watching the ugly black clouds rolling and tumbling, moving speedily across the sky. The wind grew strong and scary. Cracks of loud boisterous lightning darted above—way too near.

Surely, the wrath of a spirit was punishing her. She must have made the sky people angry, for they certainly knew about her moon bleeding. She shut her eyes tightly and plunged a finger in each ear.

Even though her mother and father were probably crouching under a large fir tree getting soaked, she wanted to be with them. Water dripped from the roof, working its way through the compact boughs. Droplets landed on her head. Opening her eyes, she discovered that the bulbs were getting wet. She moved just a bit to avoid the water, then peered upwards. The clouds had turned from black to grey, and the sun was struggling to penetrate them. It was raining heavier further into the meadow, but only a fine mist fell on the small encampment.

Hunkering down, she waited for the worst of the storm to pass. She was astonished at the volume of bulbs already harvested. How could they get so many home? And how many more would they dig? Perhaps they'd dry the bulbs here, at camp, rather than take them home to prepare. Maybe they could all go home early.

She began to feel panicky, knowing that corydalis bulbs were a favorite food of bears. Besides eating the bulbs as all bandsmen did during the winter, the Bear Hunter Band fed the cooked bulbs to their sacrificial bears. And this was the season when wild bears feasted in the fields. And yesterday, two wolves had stalked them. Why did her father send her back to camp without his protection? This outing wasn't safe, for too many men, her grandfather, uncles, brothers and Piika, were not here for protection.

She began to cry, quietly at first, then loudly, her stomach and chest heaving with each wretched sob. Her eyelids puffed, turning an unsightly red while her nose stuffed up, forcing her to gasp air. Rivulets of water flowed into the shelter, and she sat crouched in a puddle, her seal skin boots saturated. Grabbing her cumbersome basket, digging stick and spear, she dashed out of the lean-to and flew in her wet soggy boots to find her parents.

Sanee's basket was only partially full when the sky opened up, bursting with a torrent of water, hail, lightning and thunder. She had found refuge under an overhang, jutting out from a low cliff while she waited for Bittoo's return. He had trailed their daughter to the edge of the field, scanned the area for predators, saw her enter the lean-to, then returned. They both had waited until the storm subsided before hurriedly heading for camp. When they arrived at the place where the woods turned into the green field, Bittoo stopped in his tracks. Unable to halt quickly enough, she ran into him.

He pointed to a brilliant rainbow arched high above and ending in the meadow. They watched, unaware that Derk and his group also watched but from the south end of the grassy field.

Bright red formed the outermost band followed by orange, yellow, green, blue, indigo with violet being the inside color. The rainbow was the most stunning and vivid any of them ever witnessed. At the end of the arch, a dazzling white light glowed, almost hurting their eyes, making it impossible to see where the rainbow touched the ground.

21

Derk knew. Deep in his heart he knew. He knew because his power came from the sky people, and directly in front of him he watched their magnificent display — a rainbow the likes of which he'd never seen before, one that hid a purposeful meaning within it, somewhere.

His most recent dreams had been full of beautiful colors as the ones that now sucked in his vision. And every dream included Bittoo with his twin sons, except each time, the colors, the exact same ones he now saw before him, settled on and embraced Bittoo's daughter Caree.

Many long seasons had past since Ceda first declared Bittoo a tusu and the Father of all Shaman. He hadn't expected all three of Bittoo's children to inherit this precious gift. But now each of them were blessed by the spirits. Somehow, this magnificent rainbow was heralding the news. Caree was chosen—chosen for a destiny, the same as her brothers and her esteemed father.

The beautiful rainbow began to fade. The light at the ground faded. Surprisingly, Caree sat on the ground where the rainbow just ended—as though in total peace, her arms around two wolves—one black, one white.

Derk felt dizzy, weak. Something wonderful had transpired — another piece fitting together just as Ceda first proclaimed to Bittoo. 'Of your lineage, you'll be the first, followed by many generations of others with similar power. Your footsteps will leave a Trail of Shaman.' The foretelling was happening before his eyes. He felt a part of its greatness.

Looking across the meadow, he eyed Bittoo and Sanee, both walking toward their daughter who remained seated with the two striking wolves. Slowly, Derk struck out for the girl. Gaaf marched at his side with a spear thrower in position to destroy at least one of the peculiar acting wolves which nuzzled with Caree. Both men noticed that Bittoo carried his spear thrower low as though he had no intention of using it.

Fear gripped them. Fear for the girl gripped both sets of loved ones who made their way toward her. Wild wolves appearing tame might prove dangerous. But maybe they'd been sent by the spirits, the same spirits which properly chose young Caree.

Derk and Gaaf halted when seeing the ears of the black male twitch as it detected their advance. Following Derk's and Gaaf's cue, Bittoo and Sanee stood perfectly still.

Caree noticed the strange figures slowly advancing on her—two forms from the west and two from the south. They looked human, only all four were

completely surrounded by colors—colors of the rainbow, beautiful hues of red, green, blue, and yellow,
ornate shades and tones. These rainbow people were
watching. She'd been basking in the radiant colors
at the very end of a rainbow. And the ones converg-
ing on her were enveloped by those very same colors.

The wolves stood back to back, each one facing
two of the ghostly forms. They seemed to sense her
apprehension. She tried to focus on the center of the
silhouettes—their hair, faces, bodies. Unable to identify them, she closed her eyes, as she often did when
even the least bit troubled.

She remembered leaving the encampment to find
her parents, then spotting the rainbow and wondering if she could actually find its end. It appeared to
terminate in the grassy field, so she rushed forward.
The rainbow remained still, not moving as she always heard they did when anyone ventured toward
them. She stepped right into its enchantment.

The spectacular colors had consumed her, giving her a sensation of composure and wisdom. A
voice which came from within her said that she was
being given a gift, one allowing her to determine
the wholeness and goodness of people. The curious
message startled her, yet she'd always felt an emptiness, like something inside her was incomplete or
unfinished. In the past, she tried to fill the void by
listening to everything being said around the
shaman's sacred hearth, and it helped. No one
scolded her for eavesdropping. So maybe, all along,
they knew, and maybe, she knew too that someday
she'd be one of them.

Opening her eyes, she saw the four beings for
their true selves—her parents, the shaman and Gaaf.

She ran her slim fingers through the fur of both wolves, giggling as she did. The large animals were friendly, rather than aggressive as she'd earlier thought. Her hand brushed the bulging sides of the white female. Her belly, filled with babies, wiggled under Caree's touch. "You go now, little mamma, you have better things to do," she said, her voice full of affection.

The wolves, unfamiliar with her words, comprehended her tone and the odor Caree emitted, which told them she no longer felt in jeopardy. Mother wolf nuzzled her wet nose against the back of the girl's hand before following her black mate into the woods.

Overwhelmed with what they just witnessed, no one moved toward Caree—they gawked. She had sat at the end of a rainbow, which glowed a white dynamic light, one so strong she became invisible until after it faded. Then she had remained resting on Mother Earth, with two very fine looking wolves ready to defend her.

Caree was also in awe of the unexpected developments, and with the understanding she was no longer the same person. Now, she had a purpose and a responsibility. Unsure whether to laugh or cry— she did both.

"I think the wolves joined me as soon as I entered the rainbow."

Bittoo, Caree, and Derk huddled around the sputtering fire while the remainder of the group stretched out on their sleeping furs further inside the shelter. Marveling, Bittoo looked at his daughter.

"The rainbow lured me, and it consumed me. The colors and white light folded around my body like a nurturing mother wrapping her arms around a needy child. I felt comforted beyond anything I ever experienced. The colors gave me a new wisdom. It came from the sky people."

Bittoo was amazed with his daughter, not only her experience but the words she now spoke. They didn't sound childish. His little girl had grown up, fast, even though she hadn't as yet began her woman's flow. He eyed her as she dragged a fur to her sleeping place.

"The girl's power comes from the sky people. She saw spirit lights," Derk revealed smugly. "My power is also from them, however they honor me with a different gift, a gift to decipher. When I join the people in the Land of the Souls, give my star to Caree. No longer is my sky rock required to go into the bundle with the other sacred articles that once belonged to our shamans...the ones just waiting for a holy leader to come along who can use their power. Caree is the one to use it. And let her wear my amulet." He fondled the owl's claw amulet around his neck. "I plan to live in the sky in the afterworld, I won't need these things."

Bittoo heard the shaman and watched the light of the fire dance across his pleased face. Derk seemed as proud of Caree as he was.

"In such a very short time, all the children with your blood flowing through the rivers of their bodies have been appointed as holy."

"Yes, I know," stated Bittoo. "All is happening as Ceda said."

"Your offsprings are pleased with their positions," Derk remarked while adding barkless wood to the fire.

Bittoo shook his head in agreement. "Power suits them."

"Does it still not suit you?"

"The role of a shaman doesn't appeal to me. I still prefer to walk the path of a hunter, like my father, rather than walk the trail of a shaman. Even my spirit guide doesn't suit me. She's been spiteful from the start, and now she's vindictive," said Bittoo harshly.

"Times are changing. You've studied under me and learned well. You taught me more than I taught you...but this was with words only. You, the great tusu, Father of all Shaman, haven't applied your skills. Seldom do you fill your clam shell with water and view into it to see the visions your spirit totem might privilege you to view."

"Ceda doesn't always oblige me when I do."

"No spirit gives away all the answers. We work with what they release to us, which is more than we had before. It's our duty as holy leaders to learn from the deities. It's our responsibility to our people."

"Our people haven't needed me, they have you," Bittoo spurted out.

"I say again, the times are changing, and the time is coming when more than ever the Clan of the Ancient Humans will require your knowledge."

"I always knew that day would come, the day I'm to lead the people to some mysterious land, though I wished to be on better terms with Ceda before then. But now I know there's no such thing as being on better terms with her. If the people die, if they don't get to this other land, then apparently she'll cease to exist. If she dies so do all the water creatures...at least that's how I see it."

"Stubbornness held you back," Derk informed his friend with a sharp sting in his voice.

Bittoo felt taken aback. Derk showed an unfamiliar new harshness, which caused the star tattoo on his friends face to twitch. He started to say something but decided against it.

"The mogur is speaking at this very season to the bands living on the east side of the Beaver Tail Mountains. He speaks on your behalf. By Creator One Breath, it's essential you assume your holy obligations as a tusu. If you don't, when all that Ceda predicts comes true, the people won't trust or follow you."

A lump in Bittoo's throat caught him off guard. He brought his children into the world and hoped for a much different future for them. Yet they'd be more comfortable in the role of a holy leader than he. Even though unsure as to what powers his daughter possessed, he felt confident she'd be powerful.

He clenched his teeth, his nostrils flared. *So this is your final trick. You failed in forcing me to take up the shaman path, so you use all my children as bait.* And his children would need him. Otherwise, by virtue of their young ages, they might fall into danger if practicing their skills unwisely. And they certainly needed someone to buffer them from the clansmen who distrusted him and the twins and now would probably distrust Caree.

Yes, his love for his children was the reason he'd take up the trail of a shaman—not because he wanted to or because he had any true bond with his spirit totem. If anything, he felt in bondage.

Ceda, the mother of all water beasts, had won—he certainly believed so. He'd been placed in a position where there would be little room to compromise—or was there? "I'll do this thing for the sake of Caree and the twins. I always planned to walk that path, but only for a short time—just as long as it takes to lead the people to this other land Ceda talks about and as long as it takes to call the fish to the empty waters. I don't know why she demands me to be a full time shaman."

Nothing more was said that night.

Something woke Caree. She sat up, wrapping her warm fur around herself. A chorus of snoring was going on in the lean-to. She thought the tones and rhythms funny but refrained from giggling. The fire looked dead. She heard a far away noise, but above the sleepers' racket couldn't identify its source. Standing, she stepped outside.

A lone wolf howled. She had never heard her wolves before but felt strongly that the howl came from the handsome black male that befriended her. He was calling her, his voice sounding desperate. The fur slipped off her shoulders as she made her way through the darkness. She stumbled many times, working in the direction of the agonizing cry. When the noise subsided, she stopped and waited.

Father Sun pushed a few dim rays over the mountains, permitting her to see the contour and outlines of the forest. Still, her wolf remained mute.

Yesterday, she experienced a strong connection with the attractive pair, and sensed that they felt committed and bound to her. The spirits had deemed it.

How she knew the male wolf was summoning her, and how she knew the wolves had a problem, baffled her—she just knew, for most holy ones possess an uncanny inner sight. But that inner wisdom had't dwelled inside her until after stepping into the amazing rainbow.

They were her wolves—a relationship of some type developing. But she worried, for now the only sounds issuing from the forest were the chirps and singing of wide-eyed birds, which she considered much more pleasing than the clatter of snoring left behind in the shelter.

Scanning the area didn't help. She saw nothing. Pain mounted in her chest and tears swelled. This was the first time the wolves needed her, and she couldn't find them.

Wearily, she leaned against a tree. So many things had transpired that her mind wandered. Another howl probed her to awareness. She listened closely, her sadness disappearing. Again, it was the male wolf, sending her a message. This one stated that all was well with him.

22

P lease don't expose me by telling our people that I see colors around them," Caree begged, her voice desperate.

Derk nearly ceased his breathing. He couldn't believe his ears. "Caree, you surely possess a valuable gift, even though I'm unsure of what it entails. Why not make your power known?" What bothered him the most was that Caree, just like her father, was refusing to exercise her powers.

Bittoo studied his daughter. She'd always been dear to his heart. Lately though, she had shown the strangest behavior. For many days she avoided speaking to the villagers, instead she sat cross-legged, out of everyone's way, and stared at them. And she kept leaving camp, spending a great deal of time by herself in the forest. Always ,she carried her long spear but used the weapon as a walking stick.

"You've remained secretive for almost two moons now. I respected your wishes, but I'm perplexed as to the extent of power the spirits gave you.

Can you tell us what they are?" Derk asked.

"We're a family of shamans. If you're troubled
by your new position, we could help," her father
stated.

"Are you afraid to be a shamaness? You're the
only female one in the entire six bands, although the
apprentice of the Horse Band is a girl."

"Remember, your brothers are also holy leaders.
You know they would see no harm came to you. And
Piika will forever be by your side once you become
a woman and take him as a mate. You're well protected."

"We've waited many days for you to open up
and explain what upsets you."

Caree was annoyed with the two holy men sitting with her at the sacred hearth. Both seemed nervous or anxious. They threw questions back and
forth at her but gave her no time to respond before
one or the other of them spoke up again.

Twisting up her facial features, she gave them a
look of silly disgust. In a breath of time, her antics
brought them to silent attention. "I only want to keep
quiet about my new knowledge, because something
terribly evil is going to happen. I hope to prevent
it."

"How did you come up with such an idea?" pried
Bittoo.

"Deep inside I sense it, but whatever will transpire isn't yet clear to me."

Derk stated his opinion. "We know you're endowed with wisdom sent by the sky spirits and can
see a person's aura. That's all we understand about
your newly acquired knowledge. You've been distant, almost like you're in a continual trance."

"Is that what the colors around people are called...auras? What else is known about them?" she prompted eagerly.

"I've heard of a shaman in time past who could tell if his people were healthy, depending on the color and specks in their auras. The information has either been forgotten, or the shaman didn't bother to share his priceless wisdom with other holy ones. The knowledge went with him to the Land of the Souls."

Caree felt tired. It was early morning, and she hadn't slept well. All night she tossed her soft bed furs off, only to grab them, cover up and repeat the step over. From some deep place in her being, grew a nagging suspicion that her father was in danger. It wasn't a nightmare, rather a knowing. One which hadn't provided her a single clue as to whether he was at risk now or many seasons in the future. But the warning gave her reason to remain secretive about her new ability.

"I have the insight to see if a person is healthy. I can identify where their old injuries were and locate any new illness and know if the person is in pain. Each color indicates something. Yesterday, Grandmother Leha treated a new born with her healing herbs, but only after I told her where the baby was hurting. The infant appeared much better by evening."

"By Creator One Breath!" was all Derk could utter. His eyes grew large. He was impressed.

"Why's it so important not to inform others? How does that figure with the reading of health problems?"

Caree sighed a gusty sigh before revealing more. "I can also detect the goodness of people by the shades surrounding them and tell how strong their energy is too, although energy is colorless and only shows like heat waves above a smoldering fire."

Bittoo's eybrows raised in disbelief. Actually, he accepted what his daughter was revealing, but it did seem astounding for her to be given such rare skills. He and his children were evolving into a powerful and dynamic family. A family of holy leaders who were being prepared. But for what? To go to a new land?

"Can you tell if someone is mean or evil?"

"I'm not sure. I watch people, and even their hues change. This happens when their moods change. I've observed them get angry when at first they were happy or at least content. I watch and realize there's some color to every feeling a person has. But no, I don't understand what color determines that a person is genuinely evil. Maybe as yet, I haven't seen anyone who's truly evil."

"Since you think something horribly vile will take place, are you expecting to find the evil one by the color which encircles him?" asked Bittoo, thinking his daughter very bright if that was her plan.

"Yes, I hope to. I'm thinking there'll be a different color around this person or persons, which up to this point, I haven't seen surrounding anyone. The villagers shouldn't know that I'm capable of doing this. Someone may interfere."

"I agree," stated Bittoo. "The less everyone knows, the easier it will be for you to find this wickedness. I've often pretended to be in a good frame of mind when I was truly feeling poorly. I wonder how that would affect my color. She's only learning this skill, and I suggest we keep our mouths closed, letting her do whatever she needs to do...the way she thinks is right for her."

Caree was restless and wanted desperately to leave. She stood, cocked her head slightly and addressed Derk in a firm voice. "You should ask grandmother for medicine. You have pain...." She closed her mouth without revealing more.

The morning was breezeless. A perfect day and exactly what Caree had waited for. She sprang down the path to the water's edge. She was correct—conditions appeared ideal. The lake looked absolutely calm without the faintest of ripples. She selected a place to kneel and peer into the clear water. Her reflection gazed back at her. Curious as to the color of her own aura, she had decided the only way to find out was at the lake.

Many seasons had slipped by since she saw her image. She was startled to see how her appearance had changed. Before, she looked like a child, now a woman smiled back at her. Guilt flooded her. Yes, she certainly did look like a woman, one who already achieved womanhood, yet she was still remaining quiet about her moon bleeding.

Briefly, she forgot why she was there. She became preoccupied studying her face. Would anyone think her pretty—would Piika think so?

Shaking her head, trying to concentrate, she fixed her eyes on her likeness then slowly allowed her gaze to become unfocussed. This was how she observed the beautiful rainbow colors, flowing around others, and this was how she hoped to see her own aura.

Disappointed, and after what seemed forever, she

raised her head. Her neck had stiffened. Rolling her head in a circular motion, she stretched the taut muscles. She spotted her father on the opposite bank of the lake. Of course, he was much too far away to make out his features, but up to this point, he was the only person she had witnessed surrounded by a silver blue light. It was these dazzling colors she saw all the way across Frozen Duck Lake.

She stood, walking the murky edge through grass and weeds, which continued to look fresh and green as their thirsty stalks sucked up water from the lake. The air felt cool along the shoreline. She would rather linger and stray to the other side, gather cat tails sprouts and catch up with her father. But she was concerned and wanted to return to the tree she once climbed in hopes of finding her wolves, although it didn't seem too likely they were there. She hadn't encountered them since the day the magnificent animals joined with her in the rainbow. They were probably raising a family somewhere secluded. She'd very much enjoy meeting the young ones.

She gave one last glance at the glorious, blue silver hue rising from her father. Even though he reluctantly walked the shaman path, the colors around him and even her instincts said he was the most holy of all. She felt privileged to be his daughter.

"Ya, Ho!" Reem yelled at Caree who wearily climbed the path back to the camp.

Reem's face was covered with joy, making it obvious to Caree that her friend had something quite special to divulge. Even though the two girls were close friends, Caree had been aloof for a considerable length of time.

"Ya, Ho," Caree replied, waving up at her friend

who waited at the top of the embankment. She thought Reem overly attractive, so did her brothers, Braaz and Jarkoo. The boys forever followed the two girls around, but usually remained out of sight—or they thought they stayed out of view. She and Reem usually spotted them.

"I began my moon bleeding! Oh Caree, it's so wonderful! I'm a woman now!" Reem blurted loudly. "You're the first to know...except mother found out."

Caree felt as if she'd been slapped hard across the face. She was envious and angry at herself for feeling that way. Her woman's flow began two moons earlier. Now however, since Reem was considered a grown-up, Reem would probably think her still an immature child. She dismissed her bitter thoughts and pretended to be pleased for Reem. "I'm happy for you, except soon you'll be required to leave Frozen Duck Band and live at the Bear Hunter's Camp with the mate your parents selected."

Reem's expression lost its brilliance. "I'm undecided whether I even like him. He came through with the Bear Hunter Band on his way to the seal hunt, and he'll be coming back here on his way home. He didn't look very strong. Did you notice him?"

"No, if I did, I didn't recognize him as your future mate. When he gets here, point him out." Caree knew seeing the man could be very helpful, since she possessed the capability to read his aura.

"I'll be sad moving to another village, away from you."

"How fortunate you're not moving on the east side of the Beaver Tail Mountains where we'd hardly ever visit. Because Aunt Mupo and Aunt Teaa took mates and moved to the Fur Seal Band, I seldom see them."

"I must go, mother said I could come tell you, but she insists on talking to me about women things."

Caree watched her friend return to her earthen lodge. She couldn't comprehend what any mother might convey to her daughter about womanhood. But the gossip was that each mother took her daughter aside for a supposedly important talk. In each pit house, everyone lived in one large room. Anything that takes place in a lodge a girl would've already seen or heard. Walking in bewilderment, she turned this over and over in her mind until she found herself away from the village and standing at the base of the ancient fir tree.

As before, she climbed carefully, though she didn't venture so near the top like the last time. She gazed toward the narrow canyon running between the two mountains but was unable to spot the trail Nonetheless, she was familiar with the area and knew its general location.

She stared, putting one hand above her eyes for shade. She saw a very unusual thing. Far-off, a mass of colorless heat waves rose smokeless just above the tree-tops. She studied the pass but nothing else appeared out of the ordinary. Her foggy mind couldn't make out its meaning. She remained still and watched intently, but other than the waves moving just a tiny bit in her direction, nothing more transpired.

Deeming it wise to tell her father or even Derk, she began her descent. Let someone else decide if this strange happening is important. Half-way down the old fir, it dawned on her. The oddity was people

—people in the pass—the currents of heat waves were coming off them. There must be many bodies, grouped close together, trudging along the wide trail in Whistling Wind Pass, sending up a tremendous flow of wavering air. Her new powers allowed her to see it.

Her twin brothers were coming home. They'd arrive in the village before nightfall. Piika was coming home! Her face flushed.

She was thrilled, so thrilled she trembled throughout her entire small frame. Using extra caution, she placed her shaking feet onto the limbs below her. Taking a final plunge, she jumped to the ground.

The black wolf pup scrambled behind his mother, who leisurely napped nearby. A monster had just leaped out of the tree and attacked him. He growled, yipped and attempted to raise his guard hairs in order to make himself look bigger and threatening while waiting for his mother to take charge. But she was ignoring the danger, putting them both at risk. Nudging her, he received no response.

He darted back, further into the forest, keeping his mother and the enemy in sight. The unfamiliar animal that had bounded out of the enormous tree was a strange looking creature. It had four feet, but walked on only two, and it appeared almost hairless.

Sitting on his haunches, he raised

his small head and let out a pathetic immature howl, desperately hoping the call would attract his father. He knew better than to believe his plea would scare off this intimidating foe.

The peculiar monster had bent at the knees and crumpled to the earth. Ugly noises came from its mouth, ones he wasn't accustomed to. He felt so frightened he hadn't, until now, noticed the rank, nasty odor it threw off. His mother had awakened; he felt relieved. Horrified, he watched as she worked her way over to the sitting creature. They were touching! His mother was licking the monster's head, and the fiend was touching his mother with a bare front paw!

The beast leaned against the tree. He couldn't imagine how that was possible. If he sat down on his tail and leaned against anything with his front feet in the air, he'd probably fall over sideways. Maybe the deformed creature was capable of this feat because it was tail-less. Now, his mother was resting her head on the animal's stretched out hind legs.

Still untrusting, he slowly made his way toward them. His mother looked at him, then plunked her head back down on the monster. She intended to sleep right there. Creeping low to the ground, he approached the two.

Caree wanted to giggle, but dared not. Such an action would probably send the little wolf high-tailing it back into the woods. What a beauty the youngster was. Black like its father with a large splotch of white on the neck and chest and at the tip of each paw, which the whelp clearly inherited from its mother. Apparently, its parents hadn't informed the little one about her, their human friend, or surely she and the pup would be buddies by now.

She felt very saddened that the pair had only one offspring. At the high meadow, she remembered caressing the mother wolf and feeling a whole litter of wiggling unborns in her belly. Small packs of wolves weren't safe. There was safety in their numbers, just the same as with humans.

Immediately, she understood the meaning of the desperate howl which the father wolf sent her, the very same night the three of them sat in the rainbow. He told her that his pups were stillborn. His last howl was another message, indicating that this fine pup had been born alive.

For a while, she hadn't moved a muscle. Her nose itched, and she was about to sneeze. The little one stood close enough to see it was a male—gangly, developing fast, and with enormous overgrown paws.

The pup was sniffing at her feet and her legs, nearly to her knees. Seemingly afraid to explore any further up her body, it backed up and timidly lay on the ground next to his mother, yet still out of Caree's reach.

Ever so softly, she began to talk. "You're a smart one to be leery of those you don't know." She cooed to the restless whelp in a gentle tone, but he remained wary. She remembered her uneaten piece of roasted duck, still clinging to the bone. With slow graceful movement, she dug it out of her leather satchel. The aroma of the meat caught even the mother wolf's interest. Caree wasn't sure if the pup was too young to chew and eat the meat. She placed the morsel on the ground very near him. He eagerly snatched the duck and darted away.

As much as she hated to abandon her wolves, she wanted to be in camp when her brothers and Piika returned. She ruffled her hands through the female's thick white fur and noticed for the first time the slight tinge of gray at the ends of her hair.

After taking only a few steps, the black male wolf crossed her path. "Ya, Ho. You have a son to be proud of," she declared with enthusiasm as he disappeared back into the brush.

She continued on her way. "I must give my wolves names," she muttered aloud to the deaf forest. "Maybe 'Night Wind' for the black one and 'Snow Gust' for the white female. Both are appropriate names for two beauties which the sky spirits sent. I'll need to ponder long and hard for the perfect name for that fiesty little one."

23

The weary man placed the fallen medicine bag on the very top of the over-sized grave. He tightly wrapped its leather strap around a rock then secured the remaining three satchels in the same manner. Tears rolled down his dusty narrow face and into his beard, creating beads of muddy drops, working their way through his bushy chin hairs and onto Mother Earth.

Looking at the burial site saddened him enormously. He'd been very fond of Har, his two brothers and Barc. All four had treated him fairly, many seasons ago, when he lived at Frozen Duck Camp. It was evident, back then, that he hadn't treated them well.

Froom sat down hard, letting his mind drift far back in time when one act of violence altered his life forever. And worse, the act drastically changed the life of his wife, Patee, and also of their daughter. His disturbed mind wasn't thinking rationally when he took matters into his own hands. He nearly slaughtered Bittoo, the most holy of all, believing the boy had been disrespectful toward Ceda. And believing if Bittoo weren't destroyed, the boy would bring the horrid wrath of the water deity down on the entire village and possibly the whole clan.

Being so sure he was doing the correct thing in order to save his people, he brutally clubbed young Bittoo and carried him onto the ice to dispose of his limp body in the center of the lake.

But the great mogur had stepped in and put such dire fear in him that he fled into the Beaver Tail Mountains and lived pitifully in a cave for the first winter. Later, he moved to an isolated spot south of Frozen Duck Lake where he kept a close eye on his wife and daughter who dwelled in Lant's earthen lodge at the Spear Creek Village. As a young boy he felt like an outsider, now he knew he was.

Even after his first attempt, when Bittoo was still young, he tracked the boy through a blackberry thicket, again with a burning drive to murder him. He waited until having the perfect shot, except when raising his spear thrower, he spotted a lone mountain cat also stalking Bittoo. A strangeness came over him. He distinctly heard a husky, yet female voice from out of nowhere say, *"stupid man,"* and in that speck of time, he made the split decision to save rather than destroy the young shaman.

However he'd misjudged, thinking the powerful feline was ready to leap for the boy. He threw his spear just ahead of the cat. But the animal hesitated after she caught his scent and his weapon went flying past Bittoo, just missing him. Going in different directions, both he and the she cat swiftly bolted from the hidden valley.

Yes, something came over him that day, he realized the voice that called him 'stupid' was holy. Even more, the earlier words the disfigured mogur once said to him rang truthful—the boy held a position and duty to help the people of the clan. Should he again undertake to murder Bittoo, his wicked soul would walk Earth Mother for an eternity and never be permitted to enter the Land of the Souls, this he knew for sure.

He spent most of his adulthood in seclusion, always watching and spying on the six bands—mostly from afar, watching over his woman and his daughter. That's how he saw his little girl grow up, never being able to hold her and never being able to sleep next to his lovely Patee. And now his daughter had taken a mate, and proved to be a stunning woman whose stomach protruded with an unborn in her belly. How desperately he wanted to go home and be forgiven, and grow old among the people. It seemed an impossible dream, but it was his dream.

Not long ago, he closely observed Har and his three hunting companions when they met their tragic death on Beaver Tail Mountain. Tam had expertly herded the goats to a place where the animals could be ambushed. He even knew where the men spent the night and had remained close by, wishing he could join them.

He was in jeopardy when the first quake hit,but was further down the mountain than the others and reached safety. After the first avalanche of snow and rock, he went back to find the four men but found only corpses. Frantically, he dug Har's lifeless body out of the rubble and while doing so, almost got caught by Bittoo, Gaaf and Piika who also looked for the hunting party. He escaped with Bittoo's dog on his heels but later returned and buried the bodies. It took him clear into the next day to construct a common grave for all four bandsmen. Luckily, Raccoon stayed with him and kept vigil over the corpses at night, so he could sleep.

After burying the men, he struck out for Frozen Duck Camp through a dangerous short cut. Another tremor hit, and he tumbled from the cliff top, landing wedged between two boulders, crushing his right arm and many ribs. His mission seemed too important to let his injuries deter him. Gritting his teeth, he wasted little time tying stout leather around his chest and painfully maneuvering his way to the village with Bittoo's dog tagging along beside him. Even at the village, the canine didn't leave his side.

He was disturbed with the happenings at Frozen Duck Band. Certainly, Bittoo wasn't safe. Just recently he realized that someone was clearly out to kill the tusu. He had observed Luun, the mogur's apprentice, hiding at the edge of the forest for almost an entire night. After Bittoo and his children entered their lodge, Luun grew furious and broke a spear, leaving the splintered weapon on the ground.

He had retrieved the two pieces and studied them, and saw the mark which identified the spear as his. Shocked by the realization, he carefully sneaked into camp and quietly rummaged through Luun's quiver, finding five spears—three with his own familiar marks carved into them and two with Luun's marks. Curiously, he stole the three deadly weapons, returned to the grave site, and pondered over their implications. He came to a ghastly conclusion—Luun intended to murder Bittoo and blame the savage act on him.

Now it was up to him to protect the mighty shaman from the apprentice and, if possible, expose the treacherous man. He no longer wanted the People of the Ancient Humans to think he remained a threat to Bittoo, and he surely intended to prevent anyone else from slaying the holy leader.

Later on, when he sat by the peaceful grave, Bittoo came back, this time with four others. Since the tremors had subsided they returned to bury the bodies of their loved ones. Frightened, and with just enough time, he tied Raccoon to a tree and disappear down the mountain.

Two moons had passed and again he sat at the gravesite. "I'm sorry, Har, that long ago I nearly killed your son," he shamefully uttered aloud. "Does this resting place suit you? I dug the hole with respect and reverence." He raised his head and with renewed strength rose to his feet. "I make a solemn promise to you. I won't let your son be murdered."

After placing his right arm through his pack, he adjusted it against his shoulders. His ribs on both sides pained him, plus his left arm was still left stiff and nearly useless.

He proceeded in the direction of Frozen Duck Camp, knowing the group coming from the Great Sea with their packs laden with seal meat and pelts were well ahead of him. He had initially followed them to the Great Sea, and from high on a cliff spent much time watching the hunters and his woman and daughter who were also in the Fur Seal Camp. But mostly he rested, allowing his ribs to partially heal.

He headed toward the hazardous short cut, wanting to arrive in Frozen Duck Village before the exhausted travelers straggled into camp. He would locate Bittoo and Luun. The vicious apprentice also journeyed with the hunters and would soon be in the village. Deliberately, yet cautiously, he meant to watch them both. He aimed to keep his promise to Har.

Winded of breath, Froom arrived at the lake where he caught sight of a large, black wolf milling in the underbrush, watching Caree's every move. Other people and even small children were unknowingly closer to the wolf, but the animal seemed only concerned with her.

To him, this oddity was just another strange thing which only happened to the family of Bittoo. Not so long ago he decided that Bittoo's look-alike sons, their appearance unusual in itself, had something very odd going on between them. Many times overhearing them talking, the boys said identical words at the same time. There was a tremendous amount of power in that family—power he didn't comprehend.

So lost in his thoughts, he failed to see the magnificent, black wolf until it circled him and lay down in the green foliage just a spears throw away. He swallowed hard but didn't move. The wolf looked content with one keen eye on him and another on the lodge Caree entered.

"Ya, Ho," Froom whispered. The wolf's yellow eyes caught Froom's brown eyes. The two locked in a stare. Finally, the wolf licked at a front paw. Froom took a step backwards; the animal remained calm, even uncaring. He took another step and received the same response from the large animal. Sensing a trusting manner about the wolf, he turned his attention toward the village but was unable to locate Bittoo. He eased away from the wolf, making his way to the west side of the lake where he saw someone standing on a knoll clear across from him on the south bank.

The revulsion which grew inside him since first encountering Ceda, his spirit guide, was an overwhelming feeling—one Bittoo worked hard to overcome. He sat opposite the village on the bank of Frozen Duck Lake, staring into his clam shell filled with clear water. His intense dedication had come to no avail.

He closed his lids tightly, let out a dreary sigh, then reopened both eyes. Instantly, he was blinded by Sun Father's golden sparkle spread over the surface of the lake. Reaching down, he patted Raccoon who had faithfully remained by his side the entire day. The dog licked at his hand while wagging her tail, sending a flurry of dust into the air.

As before, Ceda was ignoring him. Seldom did he beckon her, and rarely did she respond to his infrequent calls. Always, he found difficulty summoning her with a respectful heart, even so, he was trying to change the way he felt toward her. The mother of all water beasts resented his attitude. It frustrated him, since now, he was at least ready to consider any message from her, yet she remained distant.

Her avoidance merely reinforced one of his ideas, the one he liked best. Maybe he'd only be needed when the existence of the clan became threatened— with the exception of the time he helped the great mogur by taking him to the middle world to be healed.

Ceda must have thought it very important to keep the mogur alive. Possibly, back then, she was trying to keep Luun, the mogur's successor, from becoming the spiritual leader of the Bear Hunter Band. Luun, a nice enough man, just didn't seem to understand the ways of the spirits. True, he showed devotion to the mogur. Perhaps, he still needed time to grow into the role of a holy leader.

There was no clarity to Ceda's plan, and he couldn't help but be frustrated with her all over again. As Father of all Shaman, he had absolutely no idea what she expected of him, nor what direction to steer.

At last Ceda had forced him into shouldering at least some duties by bestowing his three children with knowledge and wisdom which mere men didn't possess. Wanting to protect them if it ever became necessary was his true reason for trying to summon her, except she was stubbornly refusing to send him images in his shell.

He grasped the shell container by the edge and brashly tossed the water over the ground. He bent his knees, squatting down and scooped up fresh cold water into his ritual clam shell. The liquid wasn't the sacred water of the sea. Surely, his spirit guide wasn't particular whether the water was salty or not. After all, long ago, she twice visited him right here, submerged in this deep lake which drained from white snow and blue glaciers directly off the Beaver Tail Mountains.

Picking up his sacred seal skin blanket, he vigorously shook the pelt then spread the beautiful white fur nearer the lake's edge. He rested the clam shell in front of him and again sang his chants in a voice grown rattled and faint. With eyes cast downward, he waited for a vision to take place in his hallowed shell. He sang with an earnest devotion which he was unaccustomed to, yet hoped that such reverence would strengthen his cause.

Frightened by something, Raccoon scrambled to her feet then firmly and protectively planted herself between her master and the lake. She growled with a deadly seriousness, taking the tusu by surprise.

Bittoo jumped to his feet and stared into the glazing water. He saw nothing other than its blinding sheen.

"Stupid boy."

The startled dog rushed for the trail, away from the voice, coming from the water, stopped abruptly and turned back around, keeping her distance.

"Stupid boy. Look at me," rose the words blaring straight from the water.

Bittoo's legs nearly went out from under him. He trembled violently while his pulse beat in his ears. He was surprised to see Ceda appear as she did twice before when he was only an adolescent. He had expected her to send him pictures in his ritual shell.

Her brief statement brought back raw resentment. She not only called him 'stupid' as she did when he was young, but even though his children were almost grown, she again rudely addressed him as a boy.

"Boy, I am Ceda!" said the spirit guide, bursting into chilling laughter.

He listened to the hysterical cackle until, the tone shifted, and her laugh became a teasing giggle.The change put him somewhat at ease.

"So, now you finally call on me."
Bittoo became tongue-tied. He did't know how to answer the deity's question without stirring anger in her. And in the past when she showed her wrath, it frightened him even more.

When Sun Father drew behind a heavy mass of billowing clouds, it allowed him to view his elusive spirit guide. She looked enormous, her guise was that of a massive salmon.

Seeming to understand that he could now see her, she dove in and out of the lake, like a fish attempting to swim upstream, jumping a waterfall and heading for its spawning grounds. Her antics amused him and also gave him time to sort his thoughts.

"I'm now ready to follow your counsel," he admitted humbly to the mother of all water beasts, who had vanished underneath the water and was nowhere in sight.

Her frenzied maneuvers created waves of rolling water, lapping against the embankment where he stood.

Out of nowhere, in front of him, her huge head emerged. She looked at him, face to face. *"You still remain disrespectful. You call on me only when you're troubled. Are you now prepared to assume your duties?"* The questions issued from a mouth which didn't move as she talked.

"I'm...ready," stammered Bittoo softly. He felt positive that anything he said to Ceda she already knew, and getting him to answer was her way of provoking him into speaking his mind aloud, causing him to feel deeply humble.

"Your footsteps are already flanked with the lineage of shamans trailing behind you. Your children are mighty, and the rivers of their blood will also leave generations of holy ones. Your offsprings' powers are many—you also have varied power, though only one sole purpose. You're the keeper of the people and when the time proves right, you shall carry them to safety where there are no salmon."

"Is the time soon?"

"When you see the spirit of the wind. Be concerned with the teachings and discipline of your children. Bring about their strengths and win over the people, so they'll follow your lead."

"You finally forced me into the role of a shaman by giving my children mystical power. You were crafty,"hesaid as his resentment mounted.

"You give me credit, however the merit isn't all mine. Creator One Breath guided the sky spirits and the mammoth spirit to make sure you followed the trail of the shaman. Only through your children could we ensure you take the holy path. Have you filled your medicine bundle with power objects from the water?"

His hand flew to his bulging medicine bag. The leather pouch hung from his neck, stuffed with many small items from both fresh water and salt water.

"You remain stubborn!" Ceda snapped. *"You continue to wear your childhood nose ring and sickness bag to keep you safe from dark demons. You had your vision quest when you were young, and I declared myself your spirit guide...the one keeping you safe from black spirits...but I guess you continue to believe I'm a threat to you. You wear them for protection against me!"*

"Yes," was his brief reply.

"Its a sacrilege and disgraceful. You mock me!"

Bittoo remained quiet, his teeth clenched tight.

He would not give up his nose ring and be at her mercy. There was a long silence.

"You must concentrate on what I instruct." Her voice sounded serious. ,She continued with an urgency. *"Be alert. You have a friend who is your enemy and an enemy who is your friend."*

Swimming backwards she lowered her big form into the depths of the lake and disappeared.

Bittoo remained, waiting for her return, hopefully with an explanation of the sinister warning she spoke.

***

His identical twin's voice seemed to mask the sounds coming from the spirits. Bear Claw wondered if he really had ventured into the Land of the Souls and come back. Maybe he experienced a dream. He couldn't remember seeing his brother Eagle Shadow there, so perhaps he actually did die and traveled to the afterworld—by himself. Once his mind cleared, possibly he could determine where he had been!

***

24

Caree zipped into camp, yelling at the top of her lungs, informing the residents of the coming of the seal hunters. She then disappeared into the lodge and vigorously brushed her long, brown hair with a large thistle burr. With great care, she twisted and tied small strands around slender bluejay feathers. She was positive the shimmering feathers had been left on the ground by the sky spirits just for her use.

Sanee allowed her daughter to wear a new, yet unfinished, leather tunic. The shoulders and yoke area were plain and only needed decoration for the final touch. The hairless, deer hide retained a strong pleasant fragrance which would diminish the longer Caree wore it.

She pretended to be minding the hearth, but watched Caree's preparations out of the corner of her eye. Caree's efforts were a bit amusing and also disheartening. Her daughter was growing up, she was rapidly losing her little girl. She hadn't seen Caree take such care in getting ready for anything.

Caree's Great Aunt Kata and Grandmother Leha had both been grinding dried corydalis bulbs to make flour, however their movements had ceased, and they turned their gray heads in Caree's direction. Kata lovingly treated Bittoo's and Sanee's children as if they were her own. Her and Cir's only child was stillborn, and Creator One Breath hadn't sent them more.

Entirely absorbed with what she was doing, Caree failed to notice the three interested women. When finishing her grooming, she fled the lodge like a sudden passing storm.

A few at a time marched into camp—tired but happy—especially those who lived at Frozen Duck Camp. The others from the Bear Hunter Band and the Spear Creek Band had further to go before reaching their villages. Even so, those people seemed grateful to spend the night with a few more comforts than they experienced on the trail.

Jarkoo and Braaz, both burdened with fat, heavy packs came into view first. Caree saw Piika behind them. She flew to the backside of a domed roof, wanting to watch Piika without being seen. She was unsure as to her motive, but her heart began to beat fast, and the blood in the rivers of her body throbbed. She inhaled and exhaled slowly. With the turning of his head, she knew he was searching the encampment for someone—probably, his parents. So many people staggered into camp that she soon lost sight of him in the crowd.

A male voice from behind her said, "Ya, Ho, Caree."

She jumped and screamed at the same time. "Why do you scare me like that?" she blurted sternly at Piika. Instantly, she felt sickened to have talked in such a manner.

"It's nice to see you even if your tone is harsh. I brought you a present." He thrust a small newly made pouch in her hand and stomped away.

Gathering strength, she held back her tears. Piika had walked away from her because her words stung. But maybe her outburst didn't matter, afterall she was unwilling to reveal her moon flow secret and receive him as her man.

She had lied to herself in an attempt to feel better—for it was the natural course of things—to attain womanhood or manhood and then take a mate. Sometimes without thinking she gave in to her newly acquired emotions, other times, she fought them.

Reem rounded the domed roof. "There you are, I've been dashing all over, trying to find you."

"Ya, Ho," Caree said to her friend.

"He's here, the man from the Bear Hunter Band whom I'm betrothed to. Please come see him. He looks like a weakling to me...even though he was hefting an oversized pack when he came into camp."

Reem groped Caree's free hand and dragged her half-way to the other side of the village. They remained at the fringe of the crowd, weaving in and around the pit houses.

"Do you see him?" Caree asked.

"Yes, yes, there he is...over there," Reem claimed,

pointing her finger at a young man who was resting his lean frame against a tree on the outskirts of camp.

She started to walk away, heading towards the stranger, but Reem grabbed her by the new tunic and brought her to a stop.

"I don't want to go any closer," Reem protested with panic in her shrill voice. "If we approach, he may talk to me. Just tell me what you think of him."

Caree saw a very thin man. Somewhat good looking. He was coughing and appeared to be spitting after each heaving motion.

She stared at him, but instructed her eyes to become unfixed on the stranger. His overall aura looked favorable, showing him to be a gentle and trusting person, however a massive dark brown blotch covered the top portion of his body in the area of his chest. She hung her head. She couldn't reveal this information to her friend. As yet, only a few knew she possessed this type of insight, and it was best her gift of knowledge be kept secret.

She felt cursed rather than blessed. With such wisdom, she was unable to inform Reem that her betrothed was deathly ill.

"He looks nice. My guess is that he'll treat you kindly. His cough probably needs attention," suggested Caree, hoping nothing she said sounded like her information came from the spirits.

Reem gave her a big hug, one that showed deep devotion and love for her dear friend. "I also was thinking the same thing about him. Perhaps I'll stroll over there, and he might speak to me."

Before Caree turned and went back to her lodge, Reem saunter over to her would-be mate in a very seductive, hip swinging, manner and engaged the man in conversation.

Sitting on her bed furs, Caree opened the leather bag Piika had thrust at her. She turned the pouch upside down, spilling the contents on the ground. She was entirely alone. Where everyone had gone, she was uncertain, but their absence was probably due to the arrival of the twins and so many of their friends.

She looked at the baubles which lay in the dirt. There were two bracelets made from the rims of clam shells. She placed them both on her slim wrist. The adornments not only fit perfectly, they'd been carefully smoothed so as not to gouge or scratch her soft skin. There were two handfuls of flat shell pieces, beautiful pinks, blacks and blues, obtained from the inner surface of colorful shells, and each one drilled and ready for stringing.

She whipped off her clean leather garment and slipped back into her old worn one. It fit snug through the chest, much tighter than the reindeer frock she removed. On a woven mat, she lay her new one out smooth and dumped all except the bracelets onto its wide front yoke. She busily arranged them in a variety of patterns, attempting to create a design for the unfinished piece. She delighted in the way the shells enhanced the golden hue of the bodice. Her heart swelled with love for Piika who had patiently made them for her.

She was attempting to thread sinew through a bone needle when Gaaf's family and the women of her lodge came single file down the stout ladder. Their arms were over-loaded with bundles of bed furs, floor mats and preserved food—a complete household of items. She sat with her hands in mid air, the needle still waiting to be joined with the thread. She gawked at the procession.

Piika was with them. When he deposited his goods on the earthen floor, he shot a glance and winked at her. Confused about what was going on, she didn't respond to his teasing gesture.

"What's the matter?" asked her mother. "You look as if you see a spirit."

In order to find her tongue, Caree shook the fuzziness from her head. "Where did all that stuff come from?"

"Everything belongs to Gaaf and his family. Did you expect them to move into our dwelling without their goods?"

The news so startled her, she flung her sewing into the air. "Move to our lodge? Who's moving into our lodge?"

A frown crossed her mother's brow. "Gaaf and his family are going to live with us. Your father asked them, but Piika's parents waited anxiously for his return. They wanted his opinion about it."

"This is the first I've heard about this new arrangement." She jumped to her feet, dumping her unfinished frock and beautiful shells to ground. "What about my opinion?" she blared. "Who asked me what I thought?" She scrambled up the ladder and in semi-darkness went straight for the ancient tree and her wolves.

The instant Caree reached the top rung, a set of yellow eyes spied her from the underbrush. The wolf had waited on the outskirts of the village at the spot where Luun once stood waiting to ambush Bittoo.

When Caree approached the trail, Night Wind promptly followed her, undetected.

Sobbing, Caree slumped against the rough base of the stately fir. She felt consumed with shame, confident of having just made a complete fool of herself in front of Gaaf and his parents. She probably hurt their feelings and most likely caused them to think she didn't care for them. Piika especially must be feeling badly. Maybe, he even thought she didn't wish to be his mate.

It seemed too complicated to sort out. She wanted Piika as her man, but not right now. Feelings inside her stirred for him, feelings she kept trying to dismiss. How could she ever ignore those unfamiliar emotions with handsome Piika sharing the same dwelling? He brought her such wonderful presents from the Great Sea. How she loved those trinkets which looked so attractive against her clothing. But could she keep her woman's bleeding a secret with so many living in the lodge?

She shuddered to think something ghastly might really happen to her father. She knew of his destiny —to lead the clan to a new and strange land. At present, no one knew what that meant, and certainly no one wanted to go anyplace. Yet she was confident her wonderful father would undertake an extremely important and probably difficult task which would somehow rescue and preserve the people and all those belonging to the Clan of the Ancient Humans.

Oh, so badly she yearned to close her eyes and go back to an easier time. A time when her father was safe, when she hadn't been thrown into the role of a holy one, and a time when she was younger with no moonflow and no disturbing thoughts about Piika.

She wiped her swollen eyes and raised her head. At a distance, she made out the outlines of the three wolves. Unaccustomed to this type of behavior from her, they watched intently, but seemed undecided whether to approach. Even the young pup appeared to be waiting for some kind of cue from her.

By nightfall, Piika was pacing inside the pit house.

"My grandaughter will return," Leha said with a mischievous grin swamping her mouth. The older woman remembered being crazy in love with Har when they were but the same ages as Caree and this fine young man, Piika. Sometimes betrothing a boy and a baby girl when the girl was first born didn't always work out. Occasionally, later in life, the two refused to be joined. When such a thing happened, the bride gifts were immediately returned to the groom's family, often causing bad feelings between the two families. But long ago she decided that Caree and Piika made a proper match.

Sanee's thoughts weren't the same as her mother-in-law's. It would be a disastrous turn of events for her daughter to decide not to become Piika's mate. Piika's father was Bittoo's prized friend and lifelong guard. And now, both families planned to live together. How could they reside in the same pit house with Caree being so ill-mannered? Caree hadn't been herself, acting strangely for far too long. As her mother, she should understand why the girl's actions were so peculiar—but it remained a mystery. If only her daughter confided in her, instead the girl remained remote and solitary.

"Sit, before you wear a trench in the floor," Piika's mother advised her son as she patted the mat beside her. "Something very special transpired while you were away. Caree was chosen to be a holy woman, a shamaness."

Awe spread over Piika's face. He was speechless. With a heavy sigh his entire stance relaxed. Maybe Caree's annoying manner was the result of her new position.

Kata's kind eyes enveloped Piika. She read his troubled thoughts and added, "She'll make a dynamic holy woman after she comes to grips with the situation. Caree was given this gift unexpectedly. All of us were there, all of us saw the marvel, and that's why I can tell you that the girl was given a tremendous power. But she struggles between three identities: childhood, womanhood and shamaness. Allowances and patience are required of you. Patience is required of every single one of us."

Outwardly, Piika didn't show his zeal, inwardly, he felt overjoyed. Two summers had elapsed since he'd been overly drawn to this girl. Always, he tried hard not to reveal his feelings. He was forever wanting to court her, pick her a blossoming herb, carry her heavy baskets, but he dared not. She needed time to mature. And if he had showed any interest, Caree would have probably spurned him much like she did today. But now, there seemed a strong possibility that her tantrum had nothing to do with him and nothing to do with his family moving in. "It's dangerous for Caree to be out after dark in the woods. We should light torches and look for her."

Gaaf, listening to the conversation decided the women had explained the situation well. His son

looked greatly relieved until now. "She's well protected in the forest, the wolves are with her."

"Wolves...what wolves?" His eyes buldged.

Late that night and with the help of Night Wind,
Caree returned home. Quietly, she stepped through
the sleeping people and over to her bed furs.

Earlier that day, she'd been in her lodge when
Luun, the mogur's apprentice, came into camp and
entered Derk's shelter. She remained sleeping the
next morning when the vile man left, along with
most of his bandsmen for their home at the Bear
Hunter Camp.

She didn't see him, or witnessed his aura. If she
had, she would've observed a startling vivid color
—one unfamiliar to her, one so terrifying she'd have
understood her own prediction—the source of evil
that stalked her father.

25

Braaz and Jarkoo peered down at their sleeping sister. The twins smirked at one another in a way which suggested they hadn't quite decided whether to wake her. Yesterday, when returning from the Great Sea, they went directly to Derk's dwelling and met with their father, Derk, the mogur and his middle-aged apprentice. They came home with their father very late and Caree, along with everyone else, was already asleep. Why she now remained tucked in her warm bed furs, unmindful of the activities around her, they could only guess.

They planned on leaving with the men of their lodge to hunt at a newly burnt out area of the woods, an area bound to attract grazing deer with its first covering of thick, grassy sprouts.

Both had fared well at the seal kill where they speared the crafty animals on the thick ice flows. Their Aunt Teaa and Aunt Mupo had worked the skins for them, even removing the long hairs on the pelts, leaving the short desirable ones. And their uncles helped, so they, with no experience, would be successful. But still, more winter stores were needed.

Since their grandfather and uncles, each an expert hunter, perished in the snow and rock slide, obtaining enough winter food to last them past the time of the Starvation Moon might prove difficult. Before winter was over, there could be ten hungry stomachs going without food. One good thought flowed in the minds of the men—if the stores ran out, there were no young children in the lodge who would starve.

Piika sat on thick furs at his newly assigned sleeping place. He was spying on the twins, deeply hoping their silly antics would wake Caree. He cared for her more now than before he went to the Great Sea with her brothers. But he also felt sorry for the girl, since all at once so much had happened to her. If all those things happened to him, he couldn't deal with the suddenness of it all. Now with her new status she needed added protection.

Tucked away in his pack was another present for her, which at first he planned on saving and giving to her after she became his woman. But his hunch lead him to believe she'd be pleased to receive it now rather than later, and he so wanted to please her.

Now that she was a shamaness, their lives together wouldn't be as he once thought. He was curious about the mysterious wolves that the sky spirits sent to make sure of her welfare. The new power she received while entering a rainbow also intrigued him. He, too, waited for her to begin the day.

Caree pretended to be fast asleep, keeping her eyes tightly shut, rolling to her side and pulling the bed fur over her head. She yearned to talk to her brothers and find out about their seal hunting adventure and learn any news concerning her Aunt Teaa and Aunt Mupo.

Tears streamed down her checks. She brought her hand to her mouth in an effort to stifle the high pitched noise rising from her throat. If possible, she'd remain hidden under her sleeping robe until the men departed. Mostly, she was avoiding Piika's penetrating gaze. She had lashed out at him when he stole up behind her and presented her with the shell adornments. And she was embarrassed for making a fool of herself, hurting those she loved, which certainly made them feel unwelcome at her lodge.

The twins gave up their quest to wake their sister and hurriedly put their hunting packs together. Both were anxious to be gone, for they'd decided amongst themselves to finally divulge to their father, Gaaf and Piika, their remarkable ability. It'd be a surprise, and if all went as they hoped, their skill would be of great benefit on their hunting trip.

Caree lay still, listening for signs indicating the men's departure. Her emotions seemed as ragged as pieces of scrap leather torn to bits by ravaging dogs. Her stomach churned, she felt close to throwing up. Her earlier behavior proved obnoxious and shameful, and if she didn't apologize soon she'd make herself ill.

She heard muffled footsteps treading up the ladder. Thinking now might be her last chance to let everyone know she was sorry, she jerked her robe from her face and in a choked voice stammered, "I want all of you to live here. I really do." She paused, gulping in needed air. "And Piika, I love my shells!"

Gaaf set a quick pace while remaining silent most of the day. Bittoo followed him, the twins and his son Piika brought up the rear. Life was as it should be, yet seemed very odd, indeed. He loved Piika, loved him maybe more than he loved his own woman. But Piika was also a guard for Bittoo's family of shaman. Always, and if necessary, Gaaf would give his life for any of the holy ones, as would Piika.

He shuddered to think that such a dilemma might arise where it'd be necessary to choose between his son's safety and that of Bittoo's. He knew who he'd be required to choose, for the Clan of the Ancient Humans was in dire need of Bittoo. Hopefully, such a day would never occur, and he reasoned it probably wouldn't. A very long time had elapsed since Bittoo was in danger, and back then, hot tempered Froom was the culprit. He could think of no one else with reason to harm his friend. If danger ever arose, it'd most likely be in the form of an accident such as the terrible avalanche that took their fathers.

For the entire day, Piika's light steps matched his mood. The last words Caree spoke when he departed the pit house rang happily in his ears. The shamaness wanted him to live in her dwelling, and she liked the colorful sea shell ornaments he gave her.

He didn't relish leaving her behind. Either he should've stayed with her, or persuaded her to come with them. But Caree was needed to pick berries and would travel with others of the village to the thickets.

No one except her strange wolves watched over her, and he held little confidence in a pair of wild animals he'd not even seen. But the lodge was desperate for more winter stores, and so he made no objections about the arrangements.

Bittoo remained baffled by the message Ceda had given him: *'You have an enemy who is your friend and a friend who is your enemy.'* As a member of the hunting party he needed to concentrate, having other things on his mind put everyone at risk. But dismissing his spirit totem's disturbing words seemed impossible. Her unusual and unexpected warning was unclear. Why did Ceda talk in such a vague manner? Why not just come out and name his enemy? Would he be required to always be on the look out, watching his friends closely?

It seemed unbelievable that any of his bandsmen might be his enemy. Gaaf, his truest friend had stayed quiet all day long. Surely, Ceda hadn't been warning him about Gaaf. So who was this enemy she spoke of? The problem had plagued him since he faced the sea deity the day before. The dilemma was driving him senseless, he almost wished Ceda hadn't divulged the information. Who could he trust now? And was this vile person an enemy to his children, too? The questions went unanswered in his spinning head.

And Ceda had again scolded him for continuing to wear his childhood nose ring. She didn't say a single thing about Jarkoo and Braaz still wearing theirs. But she wasn't their spirit guide, so perhaps she didn't care whether they wore the loop through their nose. He wouldn't give up his nose ring or his sickness bag, it was one thing he wouldn't do for Ceda. It was his only protection against her. And why wouldn't he need protection from her, she was always demanding, explosive and sometimes threatening.

So involved were Bittoo and Gaaf in their own serious thinking, neither of them noticed the sly glances and gleeful twinkle in the eyes of Jarkoo and Braaz, who were both finding difficulty in keeping their secret to themselves. Hopefully soon, conditions would allow them to demonstrate to the rest of the hunting party.

The five males arrived at the makeshift camp before nightfall. Each had been there before and were struck with sudden grief. Barc, Har and his brothers used the site two days before they were crushed in the dreadful earthquake. It was the same encampment where Gaaf, Piika, and Bittoo stayed when they went searching for the old hunters. And all five spent the night at the very location while on their way to bury the four dead men.

In the early morning, Gaaf and Bittoo added dried wooden twigs to the near dying embers of last night's fire. Both men had ceased their gloomy thoughts, turning their attention to the days hunt.

"We had a night visitor," Gaaf claimed, pointing to the ground near Bittoo's feet.

Bittoo knelt, examining the dust. "A single wolf. Does it belong to one of Caree's wolves?"

"Maybe, but as yet, I haven't studied or even seen them leave tracks. This one is smudged, not clear...maybe your dog followed us."

Bittoo placed more wood on the blaze, opened his pack and withdrew a small buckskin satchel. "Raccoon has a mind of her own. Remember when she spent four days with the man on Beaver Tail Mountain...the man who fled from us. She might have stayed even longer with him, whoever he was, if the man hadn't tethered her to a tree."

With a disgusted expression, Gaaf peered at his friend. "You know full well Froom is the man you talk about...the very same person who buried our fathers and your uncles."

Bittoo ignored Gaaf's remark. He placed a small piece of reddish-brown ochre on an indented rock. He chose another smaller stone from Mother Earth, and with pressure, rolled the little rock back and forth over the soft ochre until it became crushed powder.

"Froom did a fine thing," Gaaf persisted. "I'll always be grateful to him for tending to my father's body. He kept all four bodies from getting ravaged by animals, and he sent them to the Land of the Souls much faster than we would've been able to. Surely, the man isn't totally wicked...possessed by black demons?"

Bittoo was absorbed in mixing his face paint. He heard, but ignored his friends' words.

"Froom risked his life to stay on the mountain when a giant fish was still causing earthquakes. He might have gotten himself killed...just like the others."

Mist appeared in Bittoo's eyes. He turned his face in an effort to keep Gaaf from seeing. He recognized the brave deed Froom did, and he gave it much thought. Raccoon didn't have to stay with Froom after the avalanche, but for some unknown reason the dog remained with him. Either Raccoon really liked the man or felt a desire to remain near the lifeless bodies of the four men she knew so well.

He drew a circle of red paint around the tattoo on his right upper cheek bone. Sometime soon he'd trim or cut his whiskers as other holy men do so their shamans' tattoo can be seen clearly. He sensed his friend staring at him, waiting for him to comment. "Sit. I'll smear the red, sacred paint of the spirits on your forehead. It will help us on our hunt." Mingled with tears his grey eyes filled with deep pain.

Ignoring Gaaf's penetrating gaze, he began a high-pitched chant that woke Piika and the twins. Reverently and quietly, the three joined the two men around the firepit, allowing him to smudge the wet ochre over their faces. He abruptly stopped his song just as he put the last holy mark across Piika's chin.

"You must all ask your totem helpers for guidance and protection. And call on the spirits of the deer, so they'll enter our hunting territory. You must tell the agile deer, when they find themselves at the ends of our spears, they won't die, but live within us. Tell them that we desire and consider it an honor to eat their flesh and wear their hides."

The hunters began their songs—their eager voices raising and lowering, asking their spirit brothers for a favorable hunt. Bittoo heard Jarkoo and Braaz's distinct identical words as the pair sang in unison, slightly drowning out Piika's and Gaaf's appeals.

His heart swelled with love and pride for his sons. He was confident their strength came to them because they were nearly identical. The twins endured as two individuals, yet they seemed as one. In all six bands, never before had twins been born. The people of the Clan of the Ancient Humans continued to fear his sons—no one understood them —but then, no one tried. Even he didn't fully understand them, but then, he wasn't afraid of them either.

Unsure of his powers and unsure of Ceda, everyone shunned him too. Soon though he'd bend to her will and win his clansmen over. And when he did, he intended to make certain each and every person accepted his three children as holy leaders. If it weren't for them, he'd walk away and never follow the shaman path. He was furious, mostly because Ceda still manipulated his life—now more than ever before.

"Father," the twins asked together. "Are you ready for the hunt?"

Lost in his thoughts, Bittoo hadn't heard when the chanting ceased. "Yes, I'm ready." He looked to Gaaf for a hunting strategy.

"I'll take the twins with me. You take Piika with you. We'll cut north through the forest, make an arch and enter the burned out area heading south. You and my son go east up the trail and when reaching the charred woods, turn north. Hopefully, we can drive the game between us, in our human snare."

Jarkoo spoke up. "We'd like to..."

"...separate. One of us going with father and the other with you, Gaaf." Braaz finished his brother's request.

Piika, Bittoo and Gaaf starred in shocked wonderment. To their knowledge, the twins had never been apart. Always, each boy stayed in view of the other one. What would happen if they split-up? Would they be in danger, or could it possibly be a bad omen where their hunt was concerned?

Bittoo's face went pale. He cleared his nervous throat before speaking. "Have you boys been apart before?"

Braaz answered his father. "We separated many times when by ourselves. I went my way and..."

"...I went mine. My brother and I've been given another unique gift. We worked hard on it, though. The new skill didn't come easy," added Jarkoo excitedly.

The twins' flashed glances back and forth between each other and their father. Jointly, they attempted to clarify their reasoning. "If we're together, we're unable to show you. For it to work, one of us needs to go with father and the other with Gaaf. We believe the hunting will be more successful if we do. Our grandfather and great uncles are now in the Land of the Souls, so there are less hunters in our lodge. Creator One Breath gave us this power so none of us will go hungry during the time of the heavy snows."

All morning, Bittoo walked ahead of his son. Not a single thing out of the ordinary had happened. He grew skeptical about the twin's new and important claim. Perhaps today wasn't the day for them to reveal their secret. Realizing he no longer heard Braaz's or Piika's footsteps behind him, he turned around and watched.

Braaz seemed to be concentrating—on nothing that Bittoo could see. His son's eyes widened, his pupils enlarged, his temples pulsated. Bittoo swallowed hard and also remained still.

Braaz's muscles became rigid. He viewed a scene from far away, a place such a great distance that only a flying bird could've witnessed. He took in shallow spurts of air, his nostrils unmoving. The sight was evolving in his mind, sent to him by his twin brother, Jarkoo. Ever so slightly, the corners of his mouth curled. His eyes grew bright and his shoulders went limp. He felt exhausted, but he and Jarkoo had done what they hoped to do.

"Are you ill?" asked Bittoo.

"Jarkoo and Gaaf are fairing better than we are. They found musk deer."

"How do you know this?" Bittoo inquired while scanning the region as far as he could see. He squinted, straining his eyes. Gaaf and Jarkoo were nowhere to be seen. Bewildered, he fixed his glare on Braaz.

"I saw them in my head," Braaz revealed proudly.

"How?" Piika demanded of the twin.

"I'm unsure of how it happens, it just does," Braaz responded. "My eyes grow foggy, and then vague images come before them. I remain quiet and think hard in order for the picture to become clear."

"Where do these pictures come from?" his father inquired.

"Why, Jarkoo sends them to me! And I can pass impressions on to him. But of course, I wouldn't do such a thing right now, because he's busy on the trail of the musk deer he saw."

"Tell me everything that came into your head," Bittoo requested.

"I didn't see Jarkoo because it's as if I was observing through his eyes and seeing exactly the things he sees. My brother stood at the north end of the burn, on a rise, scouting the green meadow below him. I noted two handfuls of the tiny deer scurrying through the char. But there was grass for them."

"Can you tell if they killed any?" asked Piika, who sounded amazed by Braaz's account.

"They are engrossed in either stalking, killing, or gutting the animals. Jarkoo will let us know by sending another image. Or I can convey one to him, however he would need to stop what he's doing and concentrate, just as I did to obtain a clear picture."

Bittoo was impressed—the twins power of insight was very helpful indeed—something that all might benefit from. He shook his head in wonder. "We best keep heading north. Maybe we'll find game before we meet with Gaaf and Jarkoo."

They spread out in a line, keeping one another in view while cautiously and quietly marching in the direction of the two remaining hunters.

Braaz was pleased with himself. Both he and his brother feared that something might go wrong where they'd be incapable of showing anyone their new power. He kept noticing his father and Piika throwing him sideways glances as if each of them waited for yet another vision to take place. He chuckled to himself, hoping soon he'd be able to oblige the curious two.

Under the burning heat of Father Sun, the trio advanced northward. An array of wildlife inhabited the lush green meadow, which expanded much further than the eye could see. Squirrels and birds made their nest in partially burned out trees. There were skunks and porcupine burrows along with ground squirrels. The flowering purple clover attracted bees in abundance. But there were no deer.

Braaz gave a signal to stop and each remained in his place to rest.

Again, Bittoo and Piika watched him closely.

Braaz's eyelids closed while he attempted to make his mind blank. Jarkoo was conveying another picture. When he opened his eyes, both of his hunting companions stood by his side. "This time I saw the back of Gaaf. Only not much of him is showing. Jarkoo walks behind him."

"Why can't you see my father?" pressed Piika.

"He carries two musk deer on his back," Braaz informed his listeners.

"Are you sure they're musk deer?" inquired Piika.

"Oh yes, they have gray-brown coats with creamy spots. If Gaaf doesn't readjust his load, I think he's going to get his back punctured by one of the tiny deer's canine type teeth."

Piika gave a halfhearted laugh, but stopped quick when hearing a dog barking in the distance. "Was that Raccoon?"

Bittoo shook his head. He listened intently, but the noise didn't repeat. "Which way did the sound come from?"

Both Piika and Braaz pointed to the northwest.

"It's a roe deer, making the sound of a barking dog," Bittoo said, his voice sounding shaky. "Maybe we'll also have good fortune."

Braaz thought his father was joking with them.

Doubtful and with one eybrow raised, Piika glared at Bittoo.

Bittoo answered Piika's silent question. "The deer make a barking noise for only two reasons. One when its rutting, and the other when its distressed."

Making very little sound, they struck out to find the source of the barking. The last time Bittoo saw a roe deer he'd been an adolescent. He thought that perhaps they'd run into red deer this day, but never did he feel lucky enough to encounter the rare roe deer. He scoured the ground for evidence that might indicate the deer had passed through the region.

The blood flowing in the rivers of his body ran with excitement. Maybe his sons and Piika would get a chance to see the elusive animal—and some-day relate the event to their children. For sure, the scarce deer would soon be extinct on the island. But then, he thought they already were.

Halting, he examined a newly made trail. The path wasn't overly worn, just used a couple of times. Some of the grass was stomped down while other grass blades were bent. "Can you send an image to your brother?" Bittoo asked.

"I see nothing important to send him," Braaz re-plied.

"See this trail? Look at how it slightly arches in both directions. It seems early in the season, but there's a roe buck making a circular path around a doe, it's the stag's way of pursuing her. If we wait here long enough, the buck will make another round on this path. And you can bet the doe is somewhere inside this ring. I'm guessing if you send your brother the image of this circular trail, he'll be bewildered, but when Jarkoo explains what he sees to Gaaf, Gaaf will remember from his childhood and understand your meaning."

Braaz did as his father instructed.

"Keep a sharp look-out," Bittoo stated. "This time of year the roe deer are yellow and twice the size of musk deer."

26

She felt tired, somewhat frightened, and beginning to believe she had made a terrible mistake. But the young woman was determined and obstinate—such was her nature. Maybe she was a little too determined this time. Either she could turn back or go forward, but each way measured about the same distance. Alone and caught in the middle, Teaa wished to be at one end or the other of Whistling Wind Pass.

Three nights earlier under the observant eyes of Moon Watcher, she crept from her home and out of the Fur Seal Camp. The first evening, staying alert, she skirted around the trails which led to the Reindeer Village and the Horse Village. Her keen hearing saved her from being observed. Twice, she eluded groups of clansmen on the main, heavily used trail.

Her sister Mupo also dwelled in the Fur Seal Camp with her mate and son. Their father Har had paid the bride price for both his daughters. The betrothal gifts went to two families, living at the Fur

Seal Camp. This clever arrangement insured that when she and Mupo became mated, they wouldn't be alone in a strange village and even able to help one another in times of crisis.

And crises occurred—too many of them. Now, her plan was to return home. Home to where she was born and home to her mother, Leha.

She had looked forward to her father and her mother showing up at the seal hunt, but instead just her twin nephews came.With Jarkoo and Braaz came the horrifying news that her father, Har, and both her uncles had been crushed to death in a landslide of rock and snow.

The twins had told a mysterious story, which they gladly, although discreetly, shared. While on their vision quest, they visited the Land of the Souls, even though at the time, neither of them realized they were in the afterworld. Not until receiving the news of the four tragic deaths, did they understand.

Knowing her father lived in the Land of the Souls comforted Teaa—still, her mother's arms around her would prove even more comforting. She needed her mother and felt confident her mother needed her.

And she wanted to talk to her brother—indeed she did. It was time he took up the trail of a shaman and take it up seriously. His spirit guide was right —Bittoo is stupid.

A twinge of movement in her lower stomach took her by surprise. "Yes, little one," she said lovingly. "I'll always comfort you." It was the first time her unborn had moved and the first time she had spoken to the life inside her.

Although only early afternoon, her feet resisted taking even one more step. Easing down in the middle of the path, she glanced around for a place to stay the night. She sat perched on the edge of a mountain. On one side of the trail loomed sheer basalt cliffs, dropping straight down into what looked to be the bottom of the earth. On the opposite side of the path rose an upward sloping bank with shrubs and a scattering of young pine trees, each attempting to gain a stronghold in the rocky soil. Behind the bank, healthy large pines grew lush.

Somewhere, up in the thick trees she hoped to find a protective niche where she, along with her unborn baby, would escape the strong night winds which often blew through the pass. "You hang on tight," she advised the unseen one within her. "Your mamma is going to find a nice warm camping area for us to rest until tomorrow."

She rose and walked just a short distance until thinking she found the easiest way up the embankment to the forest above. After taking just one step upward, she was forced to grab a low growing bush. Hesitating, she caught her breath, fumbled for another handhold and pulled herself closer to her destination.

Near the top, her pack caught on a pine sapling. With hands still clutching a scrawny scrub, she wrenched sideways in an attempt to free the bed roll. With her right hand, she released her hold and wiggled her arm and shoulder through one of the leather straps. She yanked at the left side, and the strap came untied—the bundle, went flying, causing her to lose balance. Quickly, digging her feet into the soil, she sent a flurry of loose rock across the path below and down over the cliff.

She made her way back down to retrieve the bed roll. Hugging the bank, she slid swiftly downwards on her front side, skinning her face and arms, and gaining a mouthful of dirt. With a severe jolt, her body collided with the hard ground. Until gathering her wits, she remained in a squatting position, spitting out the mud that invaded her mouth.

Her pack was nowhere in sight. She looked up at the ridge, frantically hoping the bundle had gotten tangled in another bush on its way down. Angrily, she kicked the nearest stone, sending it plunging over the steep cliff, knowing full well the rock was joining her bed furs at the bottom of the earth.

Discouraged, she clambered back up the slope, looking for a sanctuary. She wandered through the trees until coming flush with a sizable hollow in the side of an outcropping. A large boulder, jarred out of its resting place, had left an ideal area for a human to camp. The hole housed a deep layer of pine needles. To make a comfortable sleeping cushion, she scooped the dried needles away from the center and into a long, wide pile. To her amazement, she discovered a fire ring. At least one other person, probably many seasons ago, also stopped here, built a fire and cozily spent the night.

Exhausted she took stock of her meager possessions. Her sleeping fur and the dried horse meat strips were forever lost over the jagged bluff. Tied to her waist was her woman's knife and a rawhide bag housing her fire starter kit, a length of tendon sinew, a bone needle and an awl, plus a lock of her mate's raven black hair. She judged her belongings to be a pitiful assortment, for tonight she'd neither eat of the salted horse meat nor sleep curled up in her bed robe.

Far off, she heard the noise of running water. Exploring eastward, she found a clear gurgling of cold water, spouting lazily out of the ground. She reached down and scooped a handful of the refreshing liquid, gulping it down with speed, then washed her bruised hands and face.

On the way back to her hideaway, she picked up an armload of broken tree limbs and one straight stout branch. She spied strawberry plants littering the hillside and held back tears when discovering the plants were eaten clean of berries.

She surveyed the trees , making an unattractive face as she did. Tonight she'd eat a meal of green pine nuts and young pine needles. What edibles would Mother Earth provide for her in the following days? Hopefully, the food would be tastier than what her mouth was about to consume.

After kindling a warm fire, she peeled the bark from the lengthy stick, and with her woman's knife sharpened one end to a sharp point. She lay on the cushion of prickly needles thinking how ironic that a single type of pine tree could offer her food, a bed, heat and even a weapon. But she dozed off before eating her meal of pine needles and roasted pine cones.

She woke, startled. Something had awakened her —probably an animal foraging. Her fire had dwindled to a few burning embers. Hurriedly, she took fistfuls from her bed and threw the dried needles onto the coals, then added twigs and heavier wood until the fire burned freely. She hadn't heard or seen anything suspicious.

She stood and stretched her aching, cold body and brushed the needles from her hair and clothing. "Are you as hungry as I am, little one?" she asked of the sleeping unborn in her bloated stomach. She moved her stiff neck back and forth, working out the kinks.

A short distance from her bed she viewed a peculiar sight. A flying squirrel lay stretched out on the ground, unmoving. She prodded the reddish-brown rodent with the pointed end of her newly made spear, then rolled the body over, exposing its white underbelly. The creature lay lifeless, but to her touch the furry animal felt warm. It was a pretty little thing. She would've enjoyed seeing it glide through the air. Outwardly, nothing seemed wrong with the squirrel, other than the small, tasty animal was very much dead. She guessed it had died of an unknown injury, but how mysterious that it showed up at her camping spot and right when she was in need of food.

Famished, she gutted, skinned, roasted and half-ate the carcass in great speed. She badly wanted to devour the entire cooked squirrel but using self-control, she placed the uneaten portion in her leather bag.

After going a short distance, she found a discarded spear, lying in the middle of the trail. It bore a long, slender obsidian point, the kind that easily shatter. The weapon with its spearhead was one that a person, like herself, without much strength, could easily plunge into an animal.

Out of a sense of kindness, she abandoned her own crudely made stick at exactly the spot where she found the new spear. Someone may come along who could use the implement, but she doubted any one would really think hers useful. She carried her new weapon, using it when necessary, as a walking staff.

She traveled all morning and even though seeing or hearing nothing, a nagging feeling that something watched her, grew stronger with each short,
tired steps.

By mid afternoon, she caught a fleeting glimpse
of movement in the trees. Her heart pounded. Frightened, she kept her eyes fixed in the area where the
flash of color appeared, while also looking for a place
to retreat. Why would a wild animal stalk her most
of the day without attacking?

Plodding along, she kept her eyes working and
her ears strained. She had almost reached the trail's
summit. Soon, her pace, for the most part, would be
downhill.

Her eyes glowed when she witnessed a reindeer
hide spread out directly in her path. On top of the
furry pelt, lay a buckskin bundle. Bone tired and
breathless, she sat on the much welcomed skin and
hastily opened the small container. The satchel held
a few roasted corydalis bulbs and three hunks of
freshly cooked venison. To her amazement, the food
looked more than enough to last till she arrived at
Frozen Duck Camp.

Her mind raced. Someone was out there. Whoever it was, the person probably meant her no harm.
In fact, this elusive person, who certainly must be
male, seemed to be looking out for her welfare. His
kindness touched her deeply, she felt like weeping.
But she'd be embarrassed to cry in front of a stranger,
and her hunch was that he still lurked somewhere
close by.

Her back and legs hurt. She dragged her newly
acquired belongings to the side of the trail. No longer
was it necessary to strike a fire for warmth, she now

owned a warm bed fur. Uneasy though, she prepared a large stack of wood, enough to provide light until morning.

Hearing a rustle in the brush, she yelled out a lie. "I know who you are, so come out!" She remained dumfounded and as yet couldn't even begin to guess who the stalker might be. She tried another approach. Because of her family, she held status. "I am Teaa. My father was Har of the Frozen Duck Band. My mother is Leha and my brother is Bittoo, the great tusu and Father of all Shamans!" The words no sooner jumped out of her mouth than she regretted having said them.

"I know who you are, Teaa! You forgot to mention that Mupo is your older sister!"

Her eyes narrowed, and her hands flew to her face. The voice seemed older, but she recognized its treacherous sound from her early childhood. She remembered the man's violent deed and still had nightmares about him. He was the lunatic who clubbed her brother over the head when Bittoo was just an adolescent.

The blood drained from her face. She was speechless. Ever so slowly, her hand crept toward the spear.

"Don't be afraid! I'm leaving!"

As he left, he made a loud spectacle of himself, trampling westward through the woods and allowing himself to be seen. With a huge sigh of relief and a leery smile, she watched Froom depart. Desperately, she hoped he'd be true to his words, but her trust was shallow.

With her back against a tree and the reindeer hide draped over her clear up to her chin, she'd slept fitfully throughout the night. As long as she sat in an awkward position, she could depend on herself to wake up, and then, ever so often, add wood to the fire.

There were no signs of Froom during the night. She racked her brain trying to remember even the smallest details. The vile man had sported a bushy face, his left arm hung stiffly and at a strange angle. His dress looked as ragged as the mogur's of the Bear Hunter Band, with an odd grouping of skins and furs tied together, dangling uncut at the bottom of his tunic and pants. Yes, Froom was someone to be feared, and he looked the part.

She turned the reindeer hide over, exposing its hairless side. Removing her woman's knife, she cut a running slit at both ends. Without long straps, she had no easy way of carrying the robe. Except for holding the spear, she was determined to keep her arms and hands free.

After knotting the food bundle to the thong around her waist, she slid each arm through the freshly made cuts in the hide. As long as she remained careful, the armholes wouldn't rip. Her idea pleased her. It was even more comfortable than the back pack she started her trip with, the one which caused her shoulders and back to hurt and now lay at the bottom of the earth.

The day went fast for Har's daughter. She met no unwelcome nor unexpected visitors. She walked downhill at a speedy track with just enough soft breeze through Whistling Wind Pass to keep her cool while wearing the loose robe. At first her mood was high, for tomorrow, at dusk, she'd be home with her mother and brother. But as the day progressed, she became sadly aware of her loneliness.

Tucked away in the soft suede bag hanging from her waist was a lock of hair which once looked so handsome on her man. After her twin nephews returned to their home at Frozen Duck Camp, her mate ventured back onto the ice flows, this time by himself. Being late in the season, the unstable ice proved shifty and soft, and he fell through. His body had surfaced, washing ashore the following day.

He had been a kind and proud man, who now camped in the Land of the Souls. For certain he lived there with her own father and uncles. However she intended to ask Jarkoo and Braaz if they would return to the cave of their vision quest where they visited the Land of the Souls and find out for sure. She'd feel at peace if they discovered her man residing in that holy place with her father.

Her sorrow was overwhelming, and more so since she deliberately hadn't told her handsome mate she carried an unborn in her belly. Her fear stemmed from the fact that her sister Mupo lost two unborns long before their birthing time. So she schemed to keep the news a secret until her swollen stomach gave her situation away. If she lost the baby before anyone discovered her condition, there would be less grief since no one anticipated the coming of the child. Now, she regretted not sharing her news with her loving man.

Bringing her legs to a screeching halt, her eyes nearly popped from their sockets. Just off the trail, at the next bend, a large brown bear tore away at a decaying tree. The massive animal stood on her back legs, pulling away rotten hunks of bark and pulp. Bawling in the center of the path was a lone cub. Judging by its small size, the cub had been born during its mother's last hibernation.

In slow motion, Teaa sidestepped behind the nearest tree which lacked the girth to hide her. The she bear stopped her efforts and turned in the direction of the young woman. The gentle wind betrayed Teaa, blowing from west to east, carrying her scent toward the vicious bear. The beast sniffed at the air as if getting a fleeting whiff of something totally undesirable. 'Creator One Breath,' Teaa screamed in her mind, 'let me get home to Frozen Duck Camp!'

From the corner of her eye she spied Froom cautiously working his way through the lush green foliage. He held his spear thrower loaded and raised. Her relief was short-lived. Because of his injured left arm, could he possibly get more than one shot at the creature? Such a feat would take quickness and agility if the huge bear rushed him.

The beast turned her attention back to the task of stripping apart the rotting tree, while the little cub made unhappy noises, running around in confusion. With both front paws, the giant bear sent the tree crashing. Masses of bees swarmed, attacking both animals, and challenged the mother bear to the rights of the hive. Wildly, the cub fled through the underbrush.

Angered, the insects focused on the she bear's eyes, nose and ears, stinging and covering her brown face with a solid deep layer of yellow and black bodies. Blindly, she batted and swatted at her face, but the raging bees were determined. Feeling overpowered by the tiny insects, the huge beast yielded and lumbered through the woods in the general direction of her offspring.

Relieved with the outcome, Teaa slumped to the ground. Again, she wanted to burst into tears but didn't care to let Froom see her weep. He seemed truly a good and courageous bandsman, even though he hadn't kept his word about staying away. He had given her food, a weapon and a robe. And just now, the brave man put his own life in danger and positioned himself between her and the powerful bear.

She turned her head. He was no longer in sight.

"Ya, Ho, Froom! Thank you! Thank you!" she shouted gratefully. But the only response was her own voice, echoing off the cliffs of the Beaver Tail Mountains.

27

Bittoo entered the smoke-filled lodge. His grey eyes were easy to read. They marked him as a man who worried and carried a heavy burden.

"How's your sister?" Derk asked politely.

"Teaa remains unconscious," Bittoo informed his holy teacher. The creases in his brow deepened. "Did you see her come into camp?"

"I saw her reach the edge of the village. She smiled a pleasant greeting and promptly crumpled to the ground."

"She's been in that state since last night." Distressed, Bittoo shook his head. "She's been much too long lying there between the world of the living and the world of the dead."

"Call on your spirit guide," Derk suggested. "Ceda may surprise you."

In one graceless movement, Bittoo slumped downward onto a pile of furs. He sat quietly at his rightful position on the west side of the sacred fire.

Derk felt badly for his friend. Surely, the family of the Father of all Shaman had experienced much too much grief in such a short time. He was reluctant to interrupt Bittoo's thinking, yet he had a great deal of pressing things to discuss. "Will Jarkoo and Braaz join us?"

"No, I sent the twins with Piika. They look for Teaa's man. I don't know why my sister came into camp by herself. He must be on the trail." Bittoo paused before pulling the remaining thought from his mouth. "He's either hurt or dead."

"Teaa has always been a strong-willed one. I can't help but laugh when remembering the time she slid down my lodge ladder, got back on her feet and thrust your childhood sickness bag at me. She showed no fear of any of us shamans, not even the scary-looking mogur. Teaa was less than four summers old then, and she fought for you, not wanting you to die. You should do the same for her, although I truly sense your sister will pull through this ordeal."

Bittoo waited before looking directly at Derk. The muscles around his mouth quivered. "Caree says she sees colors around her Aunt Teaa's stomach that indicate she carries an unborn in her belly."

"What else does Caree see?" Derk asked, hoping to learn if the girl had even more insight about her aunt's condition.

"She sees nothing out of the ordinary, but refuses to leave Teaa's side."

"Caree's probably correct." Derk shuddered, thinking about the alarming news Caree had given him. He pushed her prediction from his mind. "How's Leha doing?"

"Mother isn't taking this well. Father died tragically, and now she's afraid of losing her youngest daughter. The women sooth her, yet all of them are fearful."

"I saw groups of people collecting outside your dwelling."

"Most everyone in the village remembers Teaa especially her pranks and her cunning little mind. She still has many childhood friends. There's also a crowd looking at the deer we killed."

"You fared well?"

"Jarkoo and Gaaf speared three musk deer. And thanks to the twins, we ambushed and brought home four roe deer. Our bandsmen are excited. Few have seen such animals, they're astounded that the vanished deer have returned. I heard some of them saying that the spirits sent the deer to us because we're a family of shamans. That's really funny since nearly everyone avoids us and doesn't treat us like shamans. And so far, they don't realize that Caree is a shamaness, but still the people of Frozen Duck Lake are in awe, standing out there caressing the yellow skins of the roe deer as if the hides are magical."

"Perhaps the spirits did send them to you. Anyway, it's good the people think so. Everyone needs to trust you. Before that happens, they need to believe you have real power. How did the twins aid you in ambushing the deer?"

"Oh, those boys surprised us," Bittoo said, his eyes sparkling. "They've been hiding a startling ability of theirs. If the twins are separated, they can send pictures of what they see through their minds. When we ran across a tell-tale sign belonging to the roe deer, Braaz concentrated hard and passed the image to Jarkoo. As soon as Gaaf was told, he knew its meaning; he and Jarkoo came to our aid. They came from the north, we came from the south, and we caught the roe deer between us."

"By Creator One Breath," stammered Derk. "By Creator One Breath!" he laughingly shouted.

Bittoo showed a wide grin and chuckled at his friend's cry of surprise.

"I'm just saddened that I won't be here to see your family of shamans in their glory."

"Where are you going?"

"Your daughter saw the color of my illness—the brownish spots of death. They live around my chest. I thought the ailment was my own secret, but with her power, she saw the sickness in my aura."

Derk's information seemed more of a blow than Bittoo could handle. Making not a sound, he drew the sacred shell from his satchel then did an unusual thing. He placed dried cedar in a bowl he had only used with water then reached into the fire pit and plucked out a small wooden limb which burned at one end. He set the smoldering stick to the cedar, and bent low at the waist to lightly blow into the container. The cedar lit, sending a funnel of scented smoke into the air. He stood, holding the shell, circled Derk and forced the cleansing smoke to surround his revered mentor.

He inhaled the hallowed smoke before giving the shell's contents to the sacred fire pit. Filling the bowl with water, he settled himself. He would wait for Ceda. Wait all night if need be. He required her counsel.

Derk was genuinely sorry for having told Bittoo his sad tidings. So much depended on immediate decisions which the two of them should make. Yet Bittoo was attempting to summon the water deity. He observed Bittoo's solemn face as his friend glared into his beautiful clam shell.

Shortly, Bittoo's eyes moved as if he were closely watching something. He smiled, then looked at Derk. "I saw Teaa! I saw her—in there!" he exclaimed, pointing at his sea bowl.

"What did Ceda unveil?"

"Teaa! Teaa, moons from now, during the time of the heavy snow. She layed in my lodge being tended by all the women. She was having a baby! Does the vision mean what I think?"

Many seasons ago the sky spirits gave Derk the gift to interpret when they presented him with a sky rock. He gently caressed his star, knowing he'd soon undergo the painful task of giving it up. "Yes, she will live," the shaman revealed.

"Men witnessing a birthing is taboo."

"Not if your spirit helper sent the image. And you weren't really there, because the birthing hasn't yet occurred."

Bittoo looked at his friend. "I didn't see you in the water. I could try again."

"That's not necessary. I already know, plus Caree confirmed it. The time has come for me to tell you about my dreams. My dreams are many, and I've much to take care of in a short amount of time."

Bittoo wanted to get up and slip out so he wouldn't have to hear what Derk was about to say. Nonetheless, he understood that sometime soon he'd be the lone shaman of the Frozen Duck Band. Desperately, he sought Derk's advice and guidance. He nodded, implying he was ready to listen. Sinking comfortably into the pile of furs, he intended to pay strict attention.

"My dreams aren't visions like yours; they come when I'm asleep. As you know, sometimes the images are vague and other times vivid. But this gift from the spirits allows me to decipher. When I'm incorrect about what I've seen, it's because I'm strong-headed and desire to interpret a certain way. Does what I say make sense?"

"Yes, however this is the first time you've admitted to any fault."

"Hopefully, what I reveal isn't just my explanation rather it's that of the spirits." He observed Bittoo's thoughtful grimace. "Froom clutters my sleep. If things aren't smoothed over with him, I fear he'll continue to invade my slumber."

Bittoo opened his mouth to object, then firmly closed it.

"The dreams take me back to when you were young and with Gaaf on his vision quest. I received a very clear picture. You were being stalked by both Froom and a mountain cat. Froom saw the cat and knew the vicious animal was ready to leap. Instead of throwing his spear at you, he aimed for the feline, but missed. His weapon almost killed you, but that wasn't his intention."

"Why would he change his mind?" Bittoo asked, his voice full of turmoil.

"Because at the last instant, he heard two distinct words. He heard a voice shout, 'stupid man'."

Bittoo's neck and face turned red. "You mean to say Ceda, my spirit helper, spoke to him? Can I believe such a thing?"

"You can believe she saved your life and altered the way Froom thinks of you. That was the last time he attempted to harm you. No longer was he your enemy."

For a while Bittoo remained speechless. He pondered the shaman's message. "Teaa brought a spear with her. When she fell to the ground, the point shattered. I looked at it. The stalk bears Froom's marks...three slashes and one dot. I think Froom murdered her man, somewhere in Whistling Wind Pass."

Derk didn't respond to the accusation. Instead he continued on. "The other dream concerning Froom seems to deal with an event many seasons in the future. A group of clansmen are on the coast. I didn't recognize the exact spot, but there were dead bodies floating everywhere. Froom pulled Caree from the cold water. That's all I saw." He stopped briefly. "I have this terrible dream over and over...too many times to ignore it. Now that I've told you, I hope the nightmare stops."

"Ceda gave me a frightening message when she last appeared. She said I have a friend who is my enemy and an enemy who is my friend."

"Heed her words," the shaman said slowly and deliberately. "Be cautious. I haven't experienced any dreams about this friend who's actually your enemy."

"I do heed her words. I'm suspicious of nearly everyone, but accuse no one...though my mind and heart remain convinced that Froom is my enemy."

In despair, Derk hung his head.

Bittoo felt guilty for causing the shaman to be sad, even though he stayed firm in his position. He approached the problem from a different angle. "If not Froom, then who?"

Derk sensed he had failed in persuading Bittoo. Yet he knew for sure that Froom would make a valuable ally. If his own health were better, he'd track the man down. At the very least, he would keep a vigilant watch for the elusive mountain man. His hunch was that Froom lingered close by, keeping an eye on Bittoo. "I'm sorry...I don't have the slightest hint of who your enemy could be, but it's not Froom."

While listening to Derk, Bittoo continued to peer into his vision shell, but it remained empty of images. He felt unprepared to be the primary holy leader of Frozen Duck Band—he hated the whole idea. Just recently, he'd been struck with a wonderful idea, one that would solve everything, and he felt freer than before when first encountering Ceda. He'd watch over his children and guide them while they grew into strong and powerful holy leaders. And after Derk went to the Land of the Souls, the twins and Caree could take over the shaman duties for the Frozen Duck Band.

"Bittoo, don't look for the solution through Ceda. My coming death is the solution...the way it should be." He failed to disclose the remaining truth. Yes, his death was Ceda's doing. She had manipulated again. Sure, Bittoo would help his children become shaman, but would Bittoo really walk the true path? His dying was Ceda's only way of pressing Bittoo into his dutiful role as the holy leader of the village. Explaining this to Bittoo might bring disaster upon the Clan of the Ancient Humans, for Bittoo would feel responsible, turn against Ceda again and forever turn down his role as shaman, as the great tusu. But then, he knew his friend Bittoo too well, maybe Ceda would never fully get the upper hand.

Setting aside his sacred shell, Bittoo gave his friend his complete attention.

"The mogur remained with me while you were on your hunt. Not returning to the Bear Hunter

Camp when his apprentice left gave us time to determine the course of things. Once you took him to the middle world where the spirits healed his health and his disfigured face."

"I can take you there!" Bittoo interrupted happily, excited because a visit to the middle world might restore the shaman's health as well. "I should've thought of it earlier!"

"I communed with my beloved sky spirits. They decreed my death," Derk lied. His sky spirits had nothing to do with his upcoming death. "I'm going to live in the Land of the Souls. Remember though, my sky rock and owl claw amulet go to Caree, for her gift of colors also comes from the powerful sky spirits."

Resting his head in his hands, Bittoo softly sobbed. His heaving chest sucking in gasps of air gave him away. Derk left his place at the sacred fire pit and placed his arm across Bittoo's shoulder. They both wept. They both wept for a long time.

Darkness had swallowed up the rays of Father Sun before the two shamans regained the composure to proceed. The coals of the hearth were almost dead before Derk noticed and renewed his fire. While he did, Bittoo fondly watched the man. "What did you and the mogur discuss?"

Smiling at his friend, Derk related the information. "It was a difficult trip for him, but he went to the seal hunt to confer with the three shamans who live on the east side of the Beaver Tail Mountains. He went on your behalf. All of them respect the mogur, his influence is great. His powers have always been the strongest of any of the soothsayers.

Each one considers him to be their spiritual leader, not just of the Bear Hunter Band, but of the entire clan.

"Forever, he'll be remembered as such," Bittoo said, agreeing with the shaman.

"It's you they'll always remember. The mogur and I are only instruments to see you obtain that high status. You and your family of shamans will be the substance of the stories which will go on forever in the minds of our people and of their descendants."

"I long resisted that belief, yet recent events altered my thinking. I wish you could stay and guide me."

"For many seasons I stayed and did just that. Bittoo, you aren't as weak as you seem to think. You lean too heavily on me. I should have leaned on you."

Bittoo made no reply. His fingers went to the ivory nose ring his sons had carved for him.

"The eastern shamans know little of you, as does most everyone else. Nevertheless, they still marvel about the mogur's unscarred face. He convinced them, such as it should be, that your abilities, not his, brought about that miracle."

"I was just a boy when that happened. That was my first and only deed."

"Now, two things need to happen. The first is to show our villagers that instead of being leery of you, they should support you as they do me. Second, once you've accomplished the other, you need to expand and make followers of the entire clan."

"What does the mogur's suggest?" Bittoo probed. His interest was intense, for anything that might protect his children could be beneficial.

"Very soon, in our band, we'll hold counsel. This will include all of the villagers. Since Barc and Har died in the avalanche, there's only one elder...me. So counsel will be with everyone in the camp. I'll talk to them and so shall you. We can introduce your sons as holy leaders. I intend to assist by quieting the rumbling voices of the disbelievers. The gathering is intended to be much more than a counsel. We'll call on our totems as we often do around our sacred fires. Have faith, Ceda will guide you."

"I have yet to know any of our people who would want to sit around a sacred fire pit when the shamans call the spirits to join them. They'll be terrified if dark demons appear."

"Oh yes, they'll be frightened, but it's necessary."

"It also seems necessary to inform them about Caree's ability. My daughter also requires acceptance."

"Ah, yes, but we must exclude her. She still hunts for your enemy. At this time, it's best no one knows she sees the colors surrounding them."

"What's the second thing you suggest?"

"We mean to hold the sacred bear ceremony here and soon, not waiting until after the run of the salmon. You'll conduct the rite in the mogur's place."

"They'll be furious and afraid with those changes," argued Bittoo.

"You have the blessing of the mogur, so they must allow it."

"But if the mogur doesn't perform the ritual, then it's Luun's rightful duty as the mogur's successor."

"Luun will accept the decision," Derk responded firmly. "He has always gracefully accepted the mogur's decisions."

"Ya, Ho!" Caree's shrill voice burst through Derk's earthen dwelling. "Father, Aunt Teaa is awake! She calls for you, and it sounds as if she's been stung by a wasp."

Caree broke into laughter and headed for home with Bittoo behind her and the shaman behind him.

"How is she?" Bittoo inquired when he caught up with his daughter.

"She seems fine, but for some reason Aunt Teaa is mad at you," the girl replied.

"Where's her man?"

Abruptly, Caree ceased her laughter. "He lives in the Land of the Souls," she said somberly as she grabbed the first ladder rung into the lodge.

"I knew it!" cried Bittoo angrily. "Froom has killed him!"

"I heard that!" came a loud but hoarse female voice. "Did you forget brother, that my hearing is excellent?"

"I forget nothing, Teaa. You spit like a she-cat!" Bittoo's smile grew broad and mist came to his eyes. He was pleased with what he saw. The women had washed and dressed his sister in a fresh garment. Her appearance showed no signs of injury other than bruises and scrapes.

"Froom did not kill my mate." Teaa sat up, positioning herself so she'd be at eye level with her kneeling brother. "If not for that wild looking man, I'd be dead, and also this unborn I carry. My carcass would be in Whistling Wind Pass and surely half-eaten by bears!"

"Sister, you need rest. You get too excited," Bittoo declared softly. He'd heard enough concerning Froom for one day—from the shaman and now his angry little sister. But his heart was full of love for her, it always had been.

"You must listen," Teaa persisted.

The women of the lodge, and even Derk, took a couple of steps backwards. They watched with amusement. To themselves, each one thought how refreshing it was to have Teaa home. Always, she had gotten her way with Bittoo, being the only person who ever stood up to him until getting her point across or his resistance down.

"Rumors come back to me that I'm stubborn. Ha! Have a look at you. You're the most stubborn one in the family of Har," Teaa spat. "If you don't listen to me, I'll stand in the middle of the village and shout my opinion so the whole camp hears."

Teaa's sharp words brought giggles from the women. Promptly, they raised their hands to their mouths, stifling the noise.

"I will hear your words but don't expect me to change my mind."

"That's fair," Teaa said. However, she had full intentions of altering Bittoo's unfavorable attitude about the mountain man. If not tonight—she'd try until she did.

'Ouch!' cried Eagle Shadow and Bear Claw as the sharp pain hit them both.

Guilt seized Eagle Shadow—for in the confines of their shelter, he'd accidentally jabbed his ailing brother in the ribs. But even so, a sliver of hope pierced his thoughts because his brother had, if only briefly, returned to consciousness when screaming. Did this mean Bear Claw was gaining strength? Would his twin brother live?

He tried to focus in order to hear any utterance Bear Claw might relay. His mind faltered—what actually transpired? When sharply gouging his twin, they both had screamed out in pain. Yes, he experienced the same pain in his ribs— he had felt his brother's pain.

Did he hear a faint chuckle coming from Bear Claw?

***

28

Late the next morning, Piika, Jarkoo and Braaz emerged from the forest with Mupo, her mate and their son Aroo. Speedily, the group made their way to Bittoo's lodge. Mupo descended into the earthen dwelling first. The others followed her, hampered with clumsy oversized packs on their backs.

Mupo rushed to her sister, embracing the young woman so stoutly that Teaa lost her balance. "You look unharmed," Mupo told her, "but you might have died out there on the trail by yourself! What were you thinking?"

"I..."

Mupo, the typical older sister, cared for Teaa, sometimes even being overly protective. She gave Teaa no time to reply. "The first day you were absent, we thought you went to gather sea weed. The second day, we knew something dreadful happened to you. We scoured the beaches, then the cliffs. Not until the night of the second day did we realize your favorite bed fur was missing, and you must have gone home to our mother."

Teaa watched her sister, knowing she had caused Mupo much concern. She expected Mupo and her family to eventually hunt for her and felt not the least bit guilty for running off. She looked at her nephew and smiled a healthy open-mouthed smile.

Aroo's hands moved fast, and Teaa read their every gesture. She and her mute nephew had grown close—both a little on the mischievous side. She winked at him, pleased he was happy to be at Frozen Duck Camp among so many relatives.

"Stop using your scolding voice," she demanded of her sister, whose chastising tone sounded only a pitch above her normal voice. Her eyes scanned the bundles that were being laid near the hearth. Just the bulk of them suggested Mupo and her family planned to stay until after the time of the heavy snows. "We're all here, at the home of our birth. I need mother, and she needs me. And both of us need you! How else would we have gotten together if I hadn't struck out on my own?"

Those of the family of Har who remained in the pit house sucked in air and held it. Teaa was up to her old tricks. Since childhood, Teaa had been a schemer. When she thought no one paid attention to her suggestions, she schemed. Yet each time her plots proved beneficial, and everyone was content with the outcome. Again, Teaa had outwitted them, and the family couldn't be happier.

"It's a good time to be home," Teaa added. "Our brother needs us too."

Piika and the twins peered at one another in bewilderment. Teaa's statement indicated something was wrong.

"Another reason I came home...I need to talk some sense into my brother. It's time he acts like the great tusu that he is. His people have lived frightened of him and Ceda far too long. And now look, his children posses magnificent powers that could be helpful to everyone if only Bittoo would...," Teaa grouped for words. "He leaves his children out there dangling, not knowing what to do with their powers. I hear rumors, and if Bittoo doesn't take responsibility, Frozen Duck Band will dissolve...people are going to move away and live among the other bands."

Mupo nodded her head. "I heard that rumor too. Some villagers at the Fur Seal Camp are talking about it."

"Where's father?" asked Braaz.

"He's making a sacred fire pit on the banks of the lake," answered Caree, who'd been studying Piika closely ever since he entered the shelter. His eyes caught hers for a brief instant. Embarrassed, they both looked away.

"Outside in the open? Why?" asked the twins, their voices sounding as one.

"Much was decided while you were gone," Caree
stated. "Father and Derk can explain it best."

"You're a shamaness...," commented Braaz.

"....aren't you helping them?" finished Jarkoo.

"No," stated Caree. "The people don't know of
my gift. I won't participate."

Hastily, Braaz, Jarkoo and Piika headed up the
ladder. They made their way toward the southern
edge of the camp. Flurries of smoke rose from every
lodge, yet the village looked nearly deserted.

Indeed the people of the Frozen Duck Band were
afraid and suspicious. Derk informed them of a
meeting between the villagers and the shamans,
suggesting the holy men's purpose was to call upon
the spirits, with all men, women and children in attendance. It was unheard of. No one had ever been
present when shamans performed such a ceremony.
And no one desired to be.

At dawn, terrified of the proceedings, one family had departed for the Spear Thrower's Camp. The
remaining bandsmen also wanted to steal away and
avoid the strange ritual. Although fearful of what
lay ahead, they were even more fearful of what
might befall them if they didn't stay. Many were
unwilling to risk the vengeance of the shamans' spirit
guides. But most of all, no one trusted Bittoo or his
spirit helper, who often foretold such sinister news
as the destruction of the clan. They didn't want to
be in Ceda's presence, but they didn't desire wind-
ing-up on Ceda's bad side either, so they stayed.

With a wish for protection from forces which
might invade the event, they prepared for the ob-
servance by readying their very best clothing. To

their garments, they attached animal claws, teeth and talismans, representing their individual totems. Milkweed and fresh ashes from the woman's hearth were added to the children's sickness bags, which dangled about the youngsters small necks. Their nose rings were polished, and in some cases replaced in hopes the new loops would possess more power than the old ones. Even the littlest children, not realizing the exact nature of the problem, understood by the bizarre actions and peculiar glances their parents gave one another, that something mysterious was in the air. Curiously alert, with eyes wide, they watched and waited.

At a distance, two men surveyed the shaman's work. Their faith in Derk had never wavered, but today both were having serious doubts.

"It doesn't matter whether we agree with this new undertaking of the holy ones, we're obliged to back them," stated the hunter.

"You're wise in your young seasons," whispered Coort, whose knowledge portrayed itself by the furrowed lines in his face.

"Ya, Ho," hailed Piika, as he and the twins briskly passed by the two onlookers.

"Ya,...Ho," replied Coort, his words stumbling awkwardly off his tongue. Neither he nor his companion had seen the trio until they were upon them.

Dirty and tired, Bittoo rested on the ground beside Derk, whose strenuous labor left the older man looking exhausted and pale. "Excellent. We did a fine job with the outer circle around the sacred fire pit."

"Yes, the spirits will honor us with a visit," claimed Derk. He clutched his left arm and forced a broad smile.

A few paces away, Jarkoo, Braaz and Piika watched bewildered and speechless. They could see that the new circular pit was for a shaman's fire, but they just returned from Whistling Wind Pass and knew nothing of the reasons for this revered hearth.

Bittoo noticed his sons' surprise. "Come, I'll tell you what we're doing. You're as much a part of it as Derk and I." He rose and pushed for home with quick long strides. "I'm glad you're back, although amazed you returned so soon. Your Aunt Teaa has revived. Her mate died on the melting ice flow, and since you wouldn't have known that, I expected you to walk clear to the Fur Seal Camp before you found out."

"We intended to go all that way if need be, but we came across Aunt Mupo and her family traveling through the pass, looking for Teaa. Now our lodge is bursting with people. It will be a cheerful winter," said both twins, with blended voices.

In the lodge of Har, somber faces prepared for the ritual. Tonight, they planned to wear all their finery. The women adorned themselves with strings of shells, bone and amber beads.

With pride, Caree wore her new frock, now decorated with the colorful shell ornaments Piika gave her. Her Aunt Teaa and Aunt Mupo brushed her long, glossy hair. On each side they twisted beads of walrus tusk into her brown locks. She sensed that Piika carefully watched her and approved of the way she looked.

In an attempt to make himself heard, Aroo slammed a piece of firewood against the shelter's massive support pole. Everyone stopped short and stared at the boy as his hands signaled a message.

"You're right, I hear the shaman calling, too," responded Teaa.

Bittoo's family and friends took a breath of time to compose themselves. One by one with Bittoo in the lead and his sons behind him, the procession walked proudly from the dwelling. With heads held upright, they made their way to the ceremony.

Bittoo and the twins followed the path down to the lake's edge where Derk continued his loud chant. The remaining family members joined the villagers on the ridge, overlooking Frozen Duck Lake, the burning shaman's fire and the four holy leaders.

Some spectators sat while the rest stood. Everyone was mindful of the curled ritual sticks which Derk and Bittoo had driven into the ground.

Earlier, a whispered rumor spread through camp: The shamans would release yellow pebbles into the flames—the soft rocks that choke the air with a pungent odor and thick smoke. Always, when holy leaders executed their indoor rituals, this action indicated they were performing a rite and weren't to be disturbed.The people waited—waited for this sign which would allow them to scurry back to their dwellings and conceal themselves for the night, while the shamans commenced with the unfamiliar counsel without them.

Derk positioned himself between the gigantic sacred fire and the ridge, and peered up at the uneasy assembly. The soaring blaze sent an eerie red reflection across the lake, brightening both the shore where he stood and the bluff above. The immense size of the fire was intentional. The villagers might prove skittish if the area surrounding them wasn't lit. For himself, he felt sorely disappointed. Although the night looked clear with just a scattering of clouds, the brilliant fire doused any chance of seeing the stars. And he yearned to see his sky spirits twinkling their magic down on him.

Parts on his fur tunic had cleverly been shaved away in shapes of six-sided stars, much like the tattoo on his cheek. The yellow painted designs came to life as he moved. With his spear throwing hand, he firmly gripped his beautifully carved walking stick, and with his left hand tossed branches of mugwort onto the flames. The plant, known to be stronger than any evil, the bright fire and the ritual willow sticks were all expected to ward off black demons. Hopefully, they would settle the alarming doubts in the minds of the villagers.

He began the ritual by shouting an accusation which shocked his audience. "You and I allowed dark demons in our bodies! We lived with them inside us, controlling our actions for many turns of the seasons! Tonight they must leave!"

Gasps went through the crowd. Those sitting, jumped to their feet. Most looked as though they wanted to flee, but at the same time, appeared numbed in place by the shaman's dreadful statement.

Derk thought this method the last and only chance he'd have to sway his beloved people. "A very long time ago, we were given a mighty holy leader. He was blessed with powerful abilities beyond your understanding, and therefore you were afraid of him."

"You've always been our spiritual leader. We followed you faithfully!" yelled an unflinching voice.

"Yes," responded Derk. "Wrongly, I allowed you to do so."

"You haven't done anything wrong nor did you do us an injustice," rebutted another bandsman.

"I don't have the power that Bittoo possesses."

"We never complained. Always, you seemed close to the spirits and your sky people. We shared with you our stores and our fresh kills. We are pleased with all you do for us," spurted a voice in the crowd.

The man's remark brought overwhelming warmness through Derk's frame, for he also felt he'd served his bandsmen well. Still, he had't done enough. "I kept you to me when there was another you should depend on, and that was evil of me!"

Bittoo's clenched his jaw tight. *What special abilites do I have? None. I'm ordinary. It's my children who have geat power.* He agreed with his shouting neighbors; Derk was a superb shaman. If the fault was anyone's, it was his own. Never had he shown an aggressive nature and pursued the trail of the shaman. Before him stood Derk, shouldering the blame. He stayed quiet, restraining himself, as Derk earlier instructed.

"Long ago, Ceda called Bittoo a great tusu and gave him the title of Father of all Shaman. We went against him and against her. I, for one, am ashamed for continuing as shaman of the Frozen Duck Band, defying such an important deity. She rules the water creatures and is a strong spirit which none of us dare to neglect any longer. Once Ceda swore to cause

famine and death by not allowing us to catch her
water children. Heed her words!" Derk proclaimed,
with sweat rolling down his face. "She doesn't speak
idly! Sooner or later, she'll make do her threat!"

Derk's ghastly claim caught their attention.
Nearly every person nervously fingered their amu-
lets and leather medicine bags while listening closely.
Perhaps the shaman's message held something that
deserved consideration.

Caree, her Aunt Teaa and Piika clustered at the
side of the crowd. The light was fair but not bright
enough for the young shamaness to make out the
true colors surrounding anyone except Derk, her
father and the twins who all stood near the sacred
blaze. She felt Piika's warm breath sweep across her
face and the back of her neck. It caused her mind to
wander, even though her eyes remained alert.

Twice she blinked, leaning forward in an attempt
to believe what she was seeing. Heat waves fluttered
off her father, yet none was present around Derk,
Jarkoo or Braaz. She jabbed Piika and pointed at the
lake. A swell rose in the water and ever so slowly
was gaining height and moving toward the shore.

"It must be Ceda," Teaa whispered to Caree.
"When only a child, I saw her send a geyser of water streaming from the center of this lake."

Derk felt it, as he always did when in the presence of spirits. His flesh rolled, the hairs on his body
stood up, and the shaman's tattoo on his cheek
twitched wildly. Inwardly, he braced himself, not
knowing which invisible had arrived.

With their backs to the lake, the four shamans
couldn't see, but the stunned villagers saw the approaching water. Believing Ceda was coming to
punish them for rejecting her wishes, the horror

stricken spectators tried to escape. But their arms and legs had grown too heavy. No one seemed capable of moving. They sat as though in a trance, imprisoned in their own stilled bodies—except their minds continued to think, their eyes continued to watch and their ears continued to hear.

Unbelievably, the wave stopped in mid air. Just a spear throw away from the shoreline, the immense frothy breaker, high enough to wipe over the shore, the ridge and the entire village, loomed while the onlookers remained fixed. The crest of the water curled over, as though waiting for instructions to continue and destroy.

In their standing posture, the four shamans who still faced the crowd seemed stuck to Mother Earth - completely ignorant of the impending flood. As were the villagers, the holy men were helpless to move.

From the belly of the wave, an entity emerged. Ghostly in appearance, the foggy, transparent figure left the lake—not touching the ground—to install its fish-like form directly in front of the tusu.

Bittoo recognized his spirit helper, but as always he feared her. He feared what the mother of all water creatures might do. She hovered so close, he sensed the two of them had become one. Her odor was the strong stench of the village during the time of the Salmon Moon.

"There's a lineage of shamans before you who are blessed by the most revered of your deities. Even Creator One Breath sanctioned them. You remain foolish," Ceda informed the people who watched her, knowing they could see Bittoo's form through her filmy image.

Seemingly uncomfortable out of the water, Ceda

withdrew to the security of the wave. Retreating backwards, the swell receded, losing height until becoming tranquil with the blue green water of Frozen Duck Lake.

The villagers shook their heads, looking at one another, trying to understand. They remembered seeing a tremendous swell bearing down on them. And by the light of the sacred fire over the water, they viewed the huge sea-like wave when it died out. They didn't remember seeing Ceda's image. But even so, the incident, which they couldn't recall, was solidly fixed, far back in the recesses of their minds.

The event held the same effect for Derk and the twins. They acted as if in a stupor. An unknown amount of time had been snatched from their memories.

Bittoo remembered. He remembered how Ceda looked, he remembered how she smelled and word by word he remembered her brief message.

Derk forgot what he had last been telling the people. His pause was drawn-out before he began again. "You've long been fearful of Bittoo's sons. Neither one of them is dead as some of you cruelly accused. Even if one twin is a spirit, he'd be a righteous one rather than a dark demon. But they're alive, they're healthy and are a part of Ceda's prediction...they're Bittoo's offsprings, the beginning of a lineage of shaman."

Derk ignored the murmuring of the crowd. "I want a couple of men to light torches and take one of these boys with you, out of sight from the rest of us. Everyone will see what a wonderful gift these twins command. This is a demonstration, not a trick, so you choose which twin."

Two men stood, looked at one another and

shrugged. Neither man knew which twin was which, so the older man called out one of their names. "Jarkoo!"

"We must remain very quiet...even you three who are leaving us," Derk added.

Jarkoo trod up the path, trailing behind the two men. The trio made their way through the domed roofs of the pit houses and into the trees.

Quickly and quietly, Froom ducked behind a tree as the three males brushed past him. So far, the night had proved inspiring. Flat on his stomach, hugging the soil, he witnessed the display and watched Bittoo's spirit guide come forth from the lake and address the villagers. He knew he wasn't alone in watching the apparition. Caree's three wolves had stole into camp.

He reflected on the events of the night until Jarkoo, and the two villagers passed by him again, returning to camp. They halted at the edge of the ridge and leered down at Bittoo, Braaz and Derk.

"Braaz told us where you three went and what you did," cried Derk. "One of you men tell us your version, so we'll find out if your account matches Braaz's. Remember though, Braaz did't follow you, he stayed with us the whole time.

The man cleared his throat and spoke loudly for all to hear. "We cut through camp, not taking the trail. After we broke though the forest into a dense area, we veered east until coming upon the half eaten carcass of a reindeer. It'd been dragged through the underbrush and apparently, hurriedly abandoned when we approached. We found tracks, a clump of golden fur caught in a low branch and deadly claw marks and puncture wounds on the deer. Every sign told us that the reindeer was the property of a mountain cat. Not wanting to run into the wild animal, we found our way back to the village."

No one spoke. What had taken place seemed truly a miracle. Almost word for word, the man's description proved the same as the one Braaz told them.

Much had come about this night—too much to digest all at once. With drooping shoulders, the people of Frozen Duck Band slowly retreated to their shelters.

29

With soft footsteps, Teaa stepped up the ladder. She carried two reindeer hides, a sharp woman's knife, sewing items and the lock of her dead mate's hair in a satchel tied to her waist.

She caught sight of Caree as the girl slipped into the woods, then as a childhood friend headed her way, she dodged behind a drying rack. Glancing back at the forest, she no longer saw Caree, but out of the corners of her eye, spotted Aroo trailing her. She should've guessed that with his keen hearing he'd catch her sneaking from the lodge. Deciding he'd be of help, she signaled for him to join her. "Want to go on another adventure? We can't tell anyone."

It would be like old times in the camp of the Seal Fur Band when she fetched him, thought Aroo. They'd wander off taking risks, such as climbing the most remote and hazardous reaches of the towering cliffs for bird eggs. Always, they found chancey things to occupy themselves. His Aunt Teaa was more like an older sister to him. He smiled with excitement showing on his young face.

"Good," Teaa replied to Aroo's silent enthusiasm. "Caree disappeared into the forest, right over there. We need to find her."

Aroo nodded, took the heavy pelts from Teaa's arms and led her into the woods.

She tugged on Aroo's arm. "Has anyone told you that a family of wolves tags along with Caree when she tramples around in the forest?"

Aroo stopped and closely studied his aunt's face to determine whether she was teasing him. He swallowed hard when realizing the woman was serious. They walked as quietly as possible and every so often stood idle while he listened for the sounds of Caree's distant movements.

When they stopped for the fourth time, the blood drained from his face. He wanted to turn and give a warning to his aunt but was afraid to move.

Just observing his posture, Teaa understood they were in danger. She, too, remained still.

A deep growl came from behind them and another somewhere in front. Although neither could see the animals, both recognized the sound as belonging to wolves.

At other times when managing to get her nephew and herself into a situation which proved too risky, she'd been consumed with guilt. She knew Mupo would never forgive her if something dreadful happen to Aroo. Except each time, they had gotten free of their dilemma and never mentioned it to anyone. Now the same guilty thoughts raced through her mind.

"Ya, Ho," Caree greeted from a branch high in a tree.

"Ya, Ho," repeated Teaa. "Can you call those wolves off us?"

"Probably not. But they'll most likely back down when they see we're friends. So far, they don't know if you mean me harm."

Strangely, the first wolf to emerge from the undergrowth was the normally timid pup. The curious little whelp headed straight toward Aroo. Without hesitation, it sniffed around the boy's ankles and up his leggings.

Aroo crumpled to the ground and extended his palm. Rather than smell the boy's hand, the spindly, playful creature tore into Aroo's fur sleeve, pulling and growling in unison. In a blink of the eye, both the pup and the boy went rolling together over elegant green ferns and cool damp moss.

Caree left her lofty perch and stood with her Aunt Teaa, watching the two youngsters while they played. "I thought all three wolves were mine, yet I believe I've just lost the loyalty of that one," she laughed as Night Wind and Snow Gust appeared behind her.

Teaa spied both wolves. Her mouth dropped. Fear spread over her, along with admiration for the magnificent pair. "Do you think they're spirits?" she whispered. "I've never seen such grand wolves before."

Caree didn't respond. She had no answer to the question. It was something she continually pondered.

Aroo joined his aunt and cousin Caree. He was interested as to why Teaa needed to track Caree and why the whole thing should be kept a secret. All three sat on Earth Mother. The whelp lay next to Aroo while its parents rested behind Caree.

"Did you trail me on purpose?" Caree asked.

"Yes, but if Aroo hadn't aided me, I wouldn't have found you." As she spoke, Teaa couldn't help but keep her eyes on the wolves. "I have an idea which requires your help."

Teaa was Caree's favorite aunt, mostly because the woman remained youthful in thought and behavior. Never around Teaa was there a boring day. Her aunt treated her like a best friend rather than a child, and she treated Aroo the same. "Of course, I'll help," Caree promised, anxious to know what Teaa planned for the three of them.

Impatiently, Aroo's hands flew into motion. His palm gestures fluttered through the air, so fast Caree couldn't catch their meaning.

"Aroo, you're too smart. Yes, this does have something to do with Froom," Teaa said.

"You leave me in suspense," muttered Caree

"Have you ever seen Froom?"

"No, not unless I saw him and didn't know it was him."

Disappointed, Teaa continued, "I really hoped you'd seen the man and read the colors around him." She paused as if in deep thought. "Would you like to see him?"

Caree became as speechless as her mute cousin. She reacted by slightly tilting her head.

Noting Caree's hesitancy, Teaa continiued. "I think Froom is truly a good man, regardless of his conduct so long ago. Who else could've buried Har and the other hunters? And he watched over me in Whistling Wind Pass, putting himself in danger to protect me. I wish to find him, give him a gift and ask for his support."

First Caree gave her aunt a suspicious look, then her expression brightened. She chose her words carefully. "I could determine what type of man he is if I saw his aura." She nodded her head up and down as the idea came together. "And maybe settle the differences between my father and Derk, concerning Froom...and even between father and you, Aunt Teaa."

If she judged the colors around him to be evil, then perhaps Derk and Aunt Teaa would no longer insist that Froom be allowed to return to Frozen Duck Band. However, if she saw only goodness in his aura, then it would be necessary for her father to honor Derk and Teaa's request. "I like your scheme, but how do we find him? Last I heard he lives somewhere between the lake and the Spear Creek Camp, though no one knows exactly where."

"See this? This pelt is mine. The other fur I sort of...awe...borrowed from the pile around the hearth."

"Why bring them?"

"Caree, you and I together could sew Froom a tunic. Like the one Aroo wears today. Simple enough that we can cut and stitch the garment in a very short time. I'm grateful to Froom for all he did for me, and I saw his clothes. They looked hideous and shoddy, made without a woman's touch."

Caree remained baffled. "But why do you want his help?"

"You say your father's life is in danger. Ceda said that your father has an enemy. I can't believe that person is Froom. Whether my brother knows it or not...or even cares, I think Froom is his friend. My brother needs an ally, and the mountain man is skilled and can help. Any number of people might turn against your father. He needs Froom."

"I'll help sew the garment. However, if no one else knows where Froom lives, what makes you think we'll find him?"

"Ah, that's the beauty of my plan." Teaa's face glowed. "This reindeer fur belonged to Froom, the hide he left for me in the middle of the trail in Whistling Wind Pass. It's my belief the pelt holds Froom's scent and when your special wolves get a whiff of his odor, they'll lead us to him."

Caree was amazed by her aunt's cleverness. "Just like father's dog. No one gives her anything of ours to sniff since Raccoon already knows how we smell, still she tracks us through the woods."

Aroo clapped his hands before making signs with them. Just to see the wild mountain man would make the adventure truly the best one ever.

"No," Teaa replied to her nephew. "We won't go until tomorrow. Today, Caree and I stay here, making Froom's tunic. You return to camp and should anyone ask, tell them you saw Caree and I together with her wolves. Then they won't worry, nor will they come looking for us."

Attempting to make his clothing presentable, Froom cut another ragged piece of fur from the bottom of his tunic. The frock's hem remained lopsided and uneven, but he guessed at night no one would notice.

When at the gravesite, he had sworn an oath to Har, stating he wouldn't permit anyone to kill his son. Now he felt a great urgency to mingle with the people in Frozen Duck Camp with the goal of preventing Luun from killing Bittoo. Luun was surely coming, coming for the bear festival, and probably coming for Bittoo and already might be on his way.

If only he could speak to someone and inform them about the marks on the spears in Luun's pack, which he found four moons ago. But Luun was a holy man and he an outcast. Who would believe him if he said Luun intended to murder the tusu and blame the hideous crime on him? Whatever happened, he didn't want to be forced to kill anyone. A confession out of Luun would be best, but that seemed impossible.

With considerable regret, he rubbed his painful left arm. Although still able to grasp with his palm and fingers, ever since his accident, the arm remained stiff and inflexible. His ribs remained bound with leather.

To lessen his aches, he scooted nearer his cooking fire, allowing the heat to enter both his chest and arm. Building a smoldering fire was the first task he performed many seasons ago when looking for an adequate shelter. He built fires at three different caves and found all of them unacceptable. But this one, inhabited by a variety of animals before his arrival, proved ideal. When he struck a fire, the smoke didn't leave the dwelling in one heavy burst, rather its bellowing clouds filtered through the back of the cave. When he went outside to look for the smoke holes, he couldn't find them. And all the time while living there, no one had found him or his cave.

From his stash of cobble choppers, he withdrew an obsidian core. A sizable chunk had broken off his skinning knife. He'd reshape the point if the rock wasn't fractured. Still, the stone looked too tiny to use as a knife. He preferred the weapon wide and

long. With his left hand holding the cobble and resting on his leg over a thick swatch of hide, he struck
the rock with a hammerstone and began to make its
shape. When finished, he tested the sharpness by
lightly running his finger over the knife's edge.

Tomorrow, if clansmen from other bands were
already arriving at Frozen Duck Camp for the bear
ceremony, he'd slip in among the crowd, blend in
and attempt to keep Bittoo safe.

Few bandsmen had seen him since he was a
young man. Those who got a recent glimpse, saw
him with an unruly beard and tattered clothing. He
planned on entering camp with a changed appearance, so as not to be recognized.

Taking a spear thrower and his new knife, he
briskly deserted the dwelling for the cool water of
the lake. He waded up to his knees before sitting
down, surrounded by the refreshing mountain water. With the black obsidian blade, he scraped the
unruly whiskers from his face, allowing the clumps
of matted hair to float on the lake's surface until they
sank.

It was nearing the end of the hot season when
most men hadn't started their winter beards, and he
didn't want to stand out. With a clean face he viewed
his reflection. His eyes grew large with horror. He
didn't know the ancient stranger who stared back at
him. Old, the man looked old and tired far beyond
his seasons. With his narrow face, he wasn't sure he
even resembled other bandsmen. He splashed water on his cuts while vowing not to feel sorry for
himself.

He heard loud giggling voices coming from the
trail. If the intruders stayed on the path he wouldn't

be seen. But should they veer off toward the lake, they'd surely spot him. He grabbed his clothing and spear thrower. Slowly, so as not to cause sizable ripples in the water, he moved into a dense growth of cattails.

"And next I told your father that if he didn't permit Froom to live in our camp, I'd give my unborn the name 'Froom' whether it's a girl or boy."

Caree held her sides and continued to laugh.Though not a sound issued from Aroo, his mouth flew open, showing his white teeth. His posture indicated he also thought Teaa's words comical.

"What did my father say to that?" Caree asked.

"He turned red, so very red...puffed up like a chipmunk with nuts stored in his cheeks and stomped away."

Caree laughed so hard she began to cough. She could envision her father doing exactly that.

Teaa rested between the fresh green branches of a newly fallen tree. "I do hope those wolves aren't leading us on a dead end chase." She wiped the sweat from her neck.

"They took off like shooting stars when Aroo let them sniff the finished tunic. At least I think they've been going in the right direction. It's rumored he dwells south of the lake."

"Well the next question is, are we going to find him and also have enough time to get back to camp before nightfall?"

"We're lucky to have only dodged one group of people from the Spear Creek Band on their way to the bear ceremony. Tomorrow there'll be hordes of clansmen from the other five bands on all the trails."

Night Wind paced. The male wolf seemed impatient for the three humans to follow him. The pup had stayed close to Aroo, but Snow Gust was no longer in sight.

"I think you deserve to name that pup," Caree said to Aroo who responded with a grin. "Look, Night Wind is heading off the path." Caree extended her hand to Teaa, drawing the woman to her feet.

They followed the wolves through the underbrush, not once finding a single track or sign which might suggest anyone had recently been in the region.

Aroo led the way just behind the animals. Unable to keep up, Teaa and Caree lagged after him. Scratched and scraped, the females kept going until they ran smack into Aroo who hunkered down behind a stump. He pointed to a cliff, then put his finger to his lips.

Caree and Teaa spotted nothing unusual. They were peering at an ordinary rock bluff with trees growing from its base and a few dislodged boulders.

Although the pup was still with them, the adult wolves were missing. Teaa suspected some kind of unknown danger until she spied Caree's two wolves emerging from behind a boulder with their noses rooted to the ground. The animals turned around and disappeared the way they came.

Curiously, the three rose and slowly advanced toward the cliff to find the wolves and see what interested the pair so.

"Look!" Caree exclaimed.

"By the spirits," said Teaa. "A cave...smartly hidden behind the fallen boulders. For sure, someone lives here."

"For sure, Froom lives here," Caree stated softly, yet alarm sounding in her voice. She tugged on her aunt's sleeve in an attempt to draw her from the entrance. "The coals are hot. He must be close."

"Close, but not here," Teaa muttered as her eyes adjusted to the darkness.

A drying rack leaned against each side of the narrow dwelling—one with a musk deer hide stretched to the frame, the other bare.

Aroo walked through the small cave with thoughts of becoming a hermit and living by himself in such a place. There were birch bark containers, paunches but no baskets. He discovered a horde of jasper, chert and obsidian. In between a folded hide, he found handfuls of finished spear points.

Sticks of varying lengths leaned against the cave's wall, all in stages of being prepared as spears. Some were stripped of bark and rubbed down with a coarse volcanic rock until the shafts were smooth and perfectly rounded.

Whether the cave went further back into the mountain the intruders couldn't tell, for a large pile of stacked wood obstructed their view. They found dried and pulverized bulbs and roots, a flat mortar and pestles, two quivers, a pair of roughly constructed knee high boots, two piles of various animal pelts, claws and other talisman items. They didn't see the man's meat stores.

"It's not proper to disturb his things," Teaa told Aroo when seeing him rummaging through Froom's belongings.

Laying their gift on a heap of bed furs, the discouraged woman sat beside the garment and absently played with the seed and bone beads which dangled loosely about the neck.

Deeply upset, Teaa couldn't bring herself to speak. She loved her brother so, and sensed that his life was about to be shortened. She felt desperate to find Froom and enlist his aid. If only she had the slightest hunch who Bittoo's enemy was, she could watch that person and warn her brother. Feeling as though she'd failed him, she dropped her head and exited Froom's cave.

30

Caree filtered back and forth through the village, observing the hordes of clansmen flocking in from the two trails leading into camp. She found reading their individual colors difficult with so many bunched tightly in groups. Frustrated, at seeing their auras mixing together in dull shades which she was unable to interpret, she headed toward Derk's lodge to inform her father of her dilemma.

Today she would've rather been alone with her wolves in the forest. Earlier this morning, when she awoke her woman's flow had started. The day before, along with her Aunt Teaa and cousin Aroo, she had walked a very long distance, hunting for Froom. The rugged march caused her moon bleeding to begin, and she'd soiled her bedding—so heavily, someone else saw the stains. Beside her sleeping furs, an unknown person had placed a handful of cotton grass for her use. Her womanhood was no longer a secret and shame still overwhelmed her, but the desire to help her father drove her to hold her head up high.

Discouraged, Caree entered Derk's shelter. She was completely unaware of Piika who had dutifully watched over her throughout the afternoon and now hunkered outside, waiting to follow her when she emerged.

"Ya, Ho," muttered Derk with a smile that matched his weak voice. He patted a spot next to him and Caree eased down. "I'm glad you visit us."

Many emotions ran through the girl—disappointment, because, so far, her new ability wasn't helping her father. Sadness, because she'd seen the colors, indicating Derk was going to die. Already, his strength was fading. Upset, because someone discovered her soiled sleeping fur, and proud, because this was the very first time she'd been invited to sit at the shaman's hearth.

"This is your true place," Derk said. "You'll always be on the east side of the shaman's fire pit where I've been stationed throughout my seasons, because your gifts come from the sky spirits as mine do."

Caree regarded her father and brothers who remained still, yet appeared pleased."My gifts are weak. They're no help in the darkness of the night nor in the daytime when people don't move away from one another. Father, I'm failing you."

"No such thing," Bittoo spurted sternly. "If you can't detect my enemy, it's the way the spirits have decided. You're not doing anything they haven't decreed. And if the sky spirits decide you should find the evil one, they'll allow you to find him...nothing more...nothing less. All you can do is continue to hunt for him."

Lovingly, Derk watched the young shamaness. He would've liked to teach her about the sky people and all that he knew. As with her father, she possessed stronger abilities than he himself. This was truly a powerful family sitting around the sacred hearth with him, and he savored the privilege of being in their midst. But the privilege would be short lived. He cupped the crusty stone in his hand and under his breath said a farewell to the star he'd found when only an adolescent. "This is your sky rock," he said to the shamaness. With tender care, he placed it in Caree's lap.

She opened her mouth to say something but remained quiet.

"Caree, you have the sight of auras and within them you see many things, including a person's health. Some sicknesses can be cured when caught early. You and your Grandmother Leha make a good team. She was taught by her mother and holds the knowledge of healing herbs. Learn her secrets and your talents will be twice what they are."

Caree fingered the round contour of the sky rock while nodding in agreement. She understood what was happening. Derk was giving her advice, probably the last he'd ever grant her.

Derk removed his owls foot amulet and placed it around Caree's neck. Then he untied a leather bundle and with affection separated the contents. Long ago, he showed the collection of power objects to Bittoo, but this was the first any of Bittoo's children had seen them. "All belonged to past shamans. For safe keeping, I present these holy relics to your father. He'll explain their meanings at another time. My meaning is to give Caree the healing rocks to aid her with her task."

Caree laid her hand over the many smooth stones just deposited in her care. She felt a shock in her finger and swiftly pulled back her hand.

"That pleases me," Derk conveyed. "You have the identical reaction your father had when he first touched them. They hold power for you. Keep them with you until you venture into the Land of the Souls."

Caree found her voice. "These stones are red."

"They're red with the blood of the holy one who first used them." Derk leaned very close and whispered in Caree's ear. "Perhaps, the blood on the rocks will persuade your woman's blood to flow."

Startled by Derk's statement, Caree jumped to her feet, dumping her newly acquired treasures. She headed up the ladder. The four holy ones stared after the fleeing girl. Not hearing the words Derk had whispered, Bittoo, Braaz and Jarkoo had no idea why the girl bolted.

Caree reached the top of the crude ladder and spied Piika sitting cross-legged beside the lodge. Her heart exploded with love and shame. In a fit of tears, she backed down the steps, settled on the fur and gathered her rocks.

Her head was lowered, and the men failed to see the tears streaking down her cheeks. First, she brushed the damp hair from her face, then lifted her head, looking each one directly in the eyes. Finally, her gaze rested on Derk. She took a deep breath before speaking. "During the time of the Seal Birthing Moon, I became a woman."

Even though those in the shelter remained silent, much ran through their minds. Why hadn't Caree disclosed this information long before now? Every girl they ever knew boasted when becoming a woman.

Caree must have her own reason, which was good enough for Bittoo. "Daughter, we'll keep your secret, if that's what you want."

"Someone knows already, but I'm not sure who."

"Ya, Ho. Ya, Ho," came the mogur's tired voice.

Bittoo, the twins and Caree peered at the main smoke hole. Derk did not.

Springing to their feet, the four holy ones stepped toward the ladder to assist the old mogur. Derk did not.

When returning to the sacred hearth, they found Derk fallen across his sitting fur, clutching his chest. Strained words uttered from his mouth. "By Creator One Breath." His body went limp. His breath was gone.

Caree scooted near Derk's body and cradled his head in her arms, gently rocking back and forth, choking in her grief.

In defiance of lurking evil spirits, Bittoo threw mugwort on the fire. Without being asked the shamans took their places around the revered blaze. Full of great respect, they sat for the very last time and shared silent counsel with Derk.

When the scared fire died out, Bittoo rose and stood by his daughter. "You have work to continue." He didn't specify what her job entailed, because the now present mogur was unaware that she read auras.

Caree carefully placed Derk's head on a pillow of soft furs, collected her rocks and scurried from the lodge.

Piika stood when seeing Caree reach the top
wrung. He grinned heartily, saw her expression and
his smile vanished. "What...?" He caught her as she
crumpled in her tracks. With Caree in his arms, he
slipped to the ground.

Their eyes met in a brief embrace before she expressed her sorrow. "Derk's soul left him. It lingers
near his body, waiting for a proper burial."

Holding Caree tightly, Piika rocked her back and
forth until her sobbing ceased. "I must continue looking for father's enemy."

"I'll stay with you." He took the rocks from her
and placed them in the bottom of his quiver. The
two walked away, closer than usual, with Piika guiding her through the crowd by touching her about
the waist.

Behind them, unnoticed, came Aroo, weaving in
and out among the people, holding his own quiet
watch over Caree. He felt nearly as fond of his cousin
as he did of his Aunt Teaa. He'd seen Caree when
she left the shaman's lodge and then witnessed her
crying, except he hadn't been close enough to hear
her voice. And with her head bent down he couldn't
watch her mouth form words. But he knew something was very wrong.

Caree and Piika walked to the outskirts of camp
where a bear cage was being built. Gaaf stood talking with the men at the empty structure. With his
back to the clansmen, but facing Aroo, Piika softly
whispered to his father. "Derk has just died. His was
a natural death."

Gaaf let out a huge sigh, his stance sagging. He
leaned heavily on his spear before pulling himself
out of his sadness to take charge of the situation.

"I've been here since Bittoo went in the shaman's lodge. Everyone in the family knows to come here and tell me if they learn anything unusual which might be damaging to Bittoo. So far, they report that there's much tension in camp, and everyone's talking about Bittoo and the twins. Some are very determined to follow Bittoo while others are still uncertain. Clansmen from the other five bands are curious as to what happened at the counsel when Jarkoo and Braaz demonstrated their new power."

Caree discovered Aroo standing at a distance and motioned for him to join them. When the boy stood by her side, she addressed Gaaf. "Has there been talk of anyone planning to harm my father?"

"No, nothing," Gaaf replied. "It could go either way, I suppose. You three remain near the bear pen until the next family member reports, then tell whoever it is to stay right here, so as we previously planned, there's always someone stationed at this spot getting reports. Then keep looking yourselves." Without waiting for a response, Gaaf departed.

"Coort," Piika inquired of the old story-teller, who was securing poles with wet, dripping rawhide strips. "Where's the sacrificial bear?"

Coort quit his work to answer Piika. "Only a few from the Bear Hunter Band have arrived, the rest are on the northern trail. It seems the brown bear is finding the tasty corydalis bulbs in the high meadow irresistible. When Luun and the others try to prod the beast along, the animal gets mean. I think the travelers are pulling up the entire field of plants and placing them on the path, hoping the thick-headed animal will pursue the line of bulbs and devour each one...all the way into Frozen Duck Camp."

Coort's amusing account caused the bystanders to chuckle. "Well," declared one man. "It's a good thing that the bear festival takes place tomorrow rather than today, or we'd be celebrating without a bear."

"Very good," giggled Caree as she peered past a stranger leaning against a fir tree and into the swaying brush. She guessed that one of her wolves was keeping its eyes on her every movement. Aroo also looked at the stirring foliage and by the light in his eyes, she knew he'd rather disappear into the woods to find the pup than stay in the village.

The brightness on Aroo's face disappeared. He stared directly into the stranger's brown eyes. Aloof from the others, the man seemed distant and wasn't mingling.

Sensing the boy detected more than most, Froom shifted his eyes from Aroo. Before doing so, he caught a look of recognition cross the boy's face, and knew he'd been discovered.

Caree saw the newcomer and Aroo locked in an uncommon gaze. She unfocussed her eyes in order to observe the man's auras. The colors surrounding the stranger took her by surprise, she stumbled backwards, clutching at Piika for balance. Before muttering an explanation, she looked over at the man, however he was no longer in sight. "Do you know that clansman? The one that stood against the tree."

"I didn't recognize him, though right now, I don't recognize quite a number of people roving through our camp. Aroo, is he from your band?"

The boy shrugged his shoulders and shook his head at the same time, then slipped away.

"What did the stranger's colors suggest?" asked Piika.

"He had a mixture of colors. Basically, he showed pink, indicating he's a good, wholesome sort. But as I tried to concentrate, the pink turned to orange and then red."

"Do you know what the change means?"

"I've seen children's auras turn just like his when they became angry and determined to get their own way. Usually, it happens when another youngster does something wrong to that child. Once, I saw the identical thing between adults. However, when the problem was finally settled between them, the orange hue disappeared. This man holds a grudge of enormous size. His orange changed to red. He's angry and bent on doing something about it. Yet basically, he's kind."

"Aroo, can you find the man and stay close on his heels?" Piika asked, but just as he finished his request, he realized the boy was missing.

Froom roamed through the village, avoiding anyone who might want to talk. He hadn't come up with a story about himself that seemed convincing. If someone were to ask him where he came from, he'd need to pick the name of one of the six bands. Should he choose the same band that the person belonged to, that person would know he lied.

He wore the reindeer tunic which Caree, Teaa and Aroo had left in his cave. Thinking they might be able to identify their work, he removed the adornment from it, attached a fox skin off one shoulder, which somewhat covered his stiff arm and wore a fox tooth and badger amulet around his neck. He felt naked without his whiskers and even in the heat, his bare face seemed cold.

Since Luun remained on the trail, posing no immediate threat, he ventured into the woods in an attempt to stay out of sight until the man with the bear arrived. Something in the back of his mind nagged at him, even though he couldn't figure out what. Surely, when Caree had looked at him, she saw something and also the boy's expression seemed to show he saw right through his guise. But how could either one identify him, since neither had ever seen him.

Well hidden among the undergrowth, he closed his eyes. He slept fitfully until a loud commotion coming from the village brought him out of his restless sleep. His eyes fired open, his brow wrinkled. The racket didn't cease. The entire camp was in an uproar. On his hands and knees, he slithered through the cool ferns and scratchy brush. He exited his secluded hideaway and came into a clearing, finding himself face to face with the black wolf he encountered once before, the boy who earlier this day stared at him and a young strapping wolf. He guessed they were three of the six intruders who had discovered his cave and left their prints in the soil. Apparently, the uninvited trio had been watching him sleep through the dense growth.

"You know me, huh, boy?"

Hesitantly, Aroo bobbed his head up and down.

"How did you know?"

Aroo remained still.

"Are you afraid to answer? I won't harm you." He pulled himself up and sat across from the boy and the wolves. He wanted to return to camp and learn of the disturbance, except he wasn't quite sure whether this young, shy adolescent and his two companions were keeping him captive. He tried again. "Do you know what's going on in the village?"

Aroo shook his head to indicate, 'no'.

"Can you keep a secret?"

Again, Aroo nodded, only this time in the opposite direction.

"Good," Froom replied, wondering if the boy was ever going to speak up. "I'm here to help your Uncle Bittoo, but if anyone finds out my true identity, I won't be allowed to stay and aid him. Do you know he's in danger?"

Aroo gave a stiff smile.

Froom felt himself losing patience with the strange boy who wouldn't answer him. "You could help me."

Aroo's fear let up. He knew the man's identity by the amulet he wore. He'd seen the talisman when nosing through the belongings in the cave. This was the man who gave his Aunt Teaa food and the same one she hoped to enlist to save her brother. This was Froom—the mysterious mountain man.

"I really do need you," coaxed Froom. "Do you trust me?"

Aroo grabbed his throat and opened his mouth as if trying to form words.

In a breath of time, Froom thought he understood. "You can't speak. How do you communicate?"

The boy's hands jumped into motion.

"Ah," said Froom, although he didn't comprehend any of the gestures."Show me your sign for Bittoo."

While the unconcerned wolves watched, Froom drilled Aroo. And the boy taught him simple hand signals.

"How many people know your language?"

Aroo held up three fingers.

"Do most people in Bittoo's lodge know your language, even just a little bit?"

Aroo motioned 'yes'.

"Don't tell anyone about me. First, we must discover what problem goes on in camp. Around the clansmen, pretend you don't know me."

Aroo gave his sign for Caree, and then all ten of his fingers fluttered under his eyes.

"Caree cried? Your cousin was crying?"

Aroo was pleased, his new friend understood him.

31

Feeling grand and overly important, Luun reached the outskirts of Frozen Duck Camp. His chest stuck out like a strutting bird, his sharp definite steps mimicked a wild prancing stallion. He gave instructions for his bandsmen to stay behind both him and the sacrificial bear, so he might be the first one the villagers saw.

His furless reindeer frock was cleverly trimmed with fox and wolves tails, and he presented a striking, awesome figure. Such was his goal—to stride into the village and give the impression of someone all-powerful, who many would decide to follow and few would dare to confront.

Before the bear ceremony reached its completion, Bittoo would be very much dead. The ancestors once decreed that if anyone killed a sacrificial bear before the given time, such person should be buried in a most disgraceful manner, underneath the lifeless body of the sacred beast. But if the bear destroyed someone, the animal should be slain and dumped beneath the individual it killed.

He wasn't particular which way it happened as long as Bittoo's body lay beneath the ground with the bear. Then with so much shame falling on Bittoo's family not a single person in the Clan of the Ancient Humans would appoint the twins as holy leaders. His plan was cunning, however should it fail, Bittoo would still die with a knife twisted deep in his back.

He tugged at the leather thong attached to the bear's collar. If only the animal would snap out of her laziness and be just aggressive enough to put on a show for the spectators. But the sluggish brown beast had gorged herself on corydalis bulbs and was determined to stop in her tracks and nap.

Only a few children had come near to get a look at the bear. The adults with long saddened faces didn't seem interested in his procession. And why hadn't anyone greeted him further down the trail as was the custom in times past when Frozen Duck Camp held the ceremony?

Slowly, he walked among the pit houses where people seemed busy with their own affairs and continued to ignore him. He spied Derk's lodge but saw no smoke rising from the shaman's smoke hole. A holy man's fire never died out, even if it required someone else to stoke the blaze in his absence. A shaman's hearth was left to die only when its owner died.

Jerking his head around, he angrily found two columns of grey smoke, rolling from the domed roof of Bittoo's lodge. His teeth clenched as he doubled-up his fist. What he saw implied that Derk lived in the Land of the Souls, and Bittoo was now the shaman of the Frozen Duck Band—a higher status than he himself held.

In frustration, he kicked at the ground. He saw a boy watching him closely as if trying to sum him up. He made a hideous face, but the boy remained steadfast and continued to study him.

His grand entry had failed. Feeling miserable and let down, he swore by the spirits to get even. When departing from the wretched camp he'd leave with much fanfare—he made that promise to himself. Frustrated, he handed the drowsy bear over to a bandsman and stormed toward Bittoo's dwelling.

"Ya, Ho," Luun said, as calmly as possible before going in.

"Ya, Ho," replied numerous voices.

He stopped at the base of the ladder. The size of the group stunned him. Maybe two handfuls of people gathered at the woman's hearth and four males at the shaman's fire. The mogur and Bittoo huddled by the sacred blaze—that, he expected. But Braaz and Jarkoo were also stationed there as though the two were newly assigned to the positions of holy men.

Aroo came bouncing down the ladder and slammed into Luun's back, sending the man sprawling. The apprentice, no longer holding his temper, raised his arm, threatening to strike the boy. "Watch where you're going, you black demon!"

Before Mupo could defend her son, Teaa exploded at the man she'd never seen before. "You dumb frog! I'll throw this hot bear grease on you if you hit my nephew!" She held her arm back ready to heave the hot liquid—container and all.

Rather than backing down, Aroo boldly glared at Luun in defiance. Everyone else seemed shocked and fixed in place.

Bittoo's mood flared, but he dared not show it. The only right person to settle this outburst was the mogur, Luun's mentor, otherwise there'd be more bad feelings.

The mogur rose. He appeared tired and found the situation unforgivable. For certain, upon returning home, this time, he'd strip Luun of rank and declare the man unfit to ever become a shaman. But for now, there were endless duties to fulfill. Should Luun even guess about being dismissed, he might cause problems which the mogur didn't care to deal with at this time. "You can't disrespect the family of Har."

Pretending his actions embarrassed him, Luun glanced at the worn old mogur whose days were no doubt limited. But still, the youngster's behavior seemed totally out of place, along with the sassy woman who stood ready to scald his flesh. "That boy should apologize."

The mogur winked at the adolescent, then spoke to his assistant. "That boy is Aroo, Bittoo's nephew. He's unable to apologize. He can't speak." Inwardly, the mogur chuckled. He had seen the youngster make himself understood and knew Bittoo's nephew perfectly capable of rendering a silent apology.

Teaa lowered her arm and stood by Aroo. "You called my nephew an appalling name. Are you willing to open yourself to the mercy of the spirits who watch over him?"

Luun felt not the least bit threatened by any spirit which looked over the boy. Yet he needed everyone to think highly of him, so later, none would suspect him of any wrong doing. He took his quiver from off his back and by the strap, handed the leather case to Aroo. "You may find an antler tine for my weapon's bag." Someday, he'd give the boy what he deserved, but in the meantime, he hoped to satisfy everyone by bestowing a great honor on the youngster, allowing Aroo to take charge of his weapons.

Jarkoo and Braaz said nothing. They looked at one another with loathing in their eyes for the man who nearly attacked their cousin. They caught an identical flash of disgust in their father's expression.

"Come," suggested the mogur. "We...we have a great sadness. Never can we join in wise counsel with Derk around his sacred hearth. When we reach the Land of the Souls, then we shall resume our role with our dear friend."

"Ya, Ho," interrupted the medicine seer from the Spear Creek Band. He descended into the lodge and over to the fire pit. Tears formed in his eyes, for he also observed Derk's smokeless vent and witnessed groups of sorrowful people with food offerings, waiting outside the shaman's dwelling. "We've lost a valuable...a dear..." His lips trembled as he fidgeted with a grey wolf hide, absently smoothing the already smooth pelt. He settled on the south side of the flame and stared heavy-hearted at the empty spot which Derk once occupied.

Aroo looked for a hook for Luun's quiver. Many empty tines jutted from the sod and antler ceiling. He could have his pick. But curious about the heavy bag, he searched for a place where he might easily rummage through the contents without getting caught. Luun wasn't even watching to see where his weapons were put.

Teaa understood what Aroo was up to and relished the idea of digging through the quiver herself. She pointed to a sharp antler sticking out above her sleeping furs. When the leather case hung where she instructed, she covered the satchel with a hide.

Aroo gave Teaa a quick wink and mischievous smile. Inwardly, he snickered then exited the dwelling. He scurried across camp, stopping only when reaching the bear cage. Through the log slates, another boy poked at the creature with a long, sharp branch. To Aroo's regret, the sleeping bear didn't wake.

He saw Froom leaving camp by the trail that eventually led through the Beaver Tail Mountains. Once the man was out of view, he followed. He ventured a short distance and found Froom waiting for him.

"The noise we heard in camp came from the people when learning of Derk's death. Derk once helped to save your Uncle Bittoo from getting murdered. He was brave and his wisdom great. He'll be deeply missed. Tonight, at his mourning, I'll pay tribute to him. My idea will surely speed his journey to the afterworld. I could use your help."

Aroo made a sign.

"Someone else? Who?"

His hands made the shape of a woman, then Aroo moved his palms in a hump formation at his waist.

"Teaa? You want Teaa to come with us?"

Aroo nodded vigorously.

"She'll be helpful, except she must promise not to tell." Froom paused just long enough to place his spear between himself and the boy. "These three dashes and the dot beside them are my marks. I cut them into the shaft. If I lost this spear and someone found it, they'd know the weapon belongs to me. If I find a spear with different marks on it, I could figure out whose it was."

Although already knowing about a person's property marks, the boy patiently listened.

"I may be wrong, but I suspect that Luun isn't trustworthy. If you get a chance look in his quiver, see what marks are on the wooden shafts. Check each one, not just a single weapon. Be very, very careful...don't get caught."

Aroo bounced in his seat and grinned from ear to ear, wanting to explain that he already planned to look through Luun's weapon bag and knew exactly where it was.

"Tell me," prompted Froom. He watched intently as the boy tried to communicate. "Sorry, I don't understand."

Aroo shrugged his shoulders as if his account was unimportant.

"You and Teaa get away, right when Derk's body is brought out, hug along the east bank of Frozen Duck Lake until you find me."

While returning to the village, Aroo passed near the bear pen and noticed Luun engrossed in a flashy narration about one of his hunts for bear cubs. The boy remained half hidden, thinking the unfeeling man with his outlandish story showed bad taste—dishonoring Derk and the people of Frozen Duck Band.

Aroo wandered through the crowd, then slipped into the pit house. The earthen lodge was quiet and empty of everyone except his Aunt Teaa.

"I waited for you and didn't peek in Froom's quiver for fear someone would enter and see me. I'll keep a lookout while you go through the satchel...if you'll do the same for me." She frowned. "What are you telling me?" She knew full well what her nephew's hands were saying, but to her surprise she hardly believed his news. Her voice rose. "You saw Froom!"

Aroo held up two fingers.

"Twice? We still need him. Where did he go?"

Aroo threw up his arms.

"You're not sure? Maybe Caree's wolves can find him."

Aroo grabbed his aunt's shoulders and eased her onto the bottom ladder rung.

"All right, I'm listening." She watched the boy as his hand motions spoke. When he finished, her head spun with the enormity of his message. "But first, look through Luun's belongings."

Teaa climbed the ladder, stationing herself so no one could climb over or around her. She sang a little song to her unborn who chose this time to flutter and squirm in her belly.

A stern voice startled her. "Are you going to move, so I can get my quiver?"

"Why do you need your weapons?" she asked Luun, hoping to stall the brute, giving Aroo time to put the leather case back on its hook.

"And why are you so sassy? If you were my woman!" Luun snapped his mouth shut. This woman inflamed him beyond what he could bear.

Teaa's first impulse was to claw at Luun's eyes. But like the bully standing before her, she held back her temper. "Does anyone take their weapons to

Derk's farewell? He's dead. You want to kill him again?"

"Woman, you are addled. Now move!"

Teaa's hand flew to her mouth, smothering a giggle. She lowered her head and slowly descended the wooden steps in front of the repulsive man.

Aroo had quickly replaced the satchel, but it still swayed with the slightest of movement. He sat innocently by the woman's hearth, drawing pictures with a stick in the cold powdery ashes.

Luun saw his case hanging off a curved tine. Tonight, hopefully without offending anyone he'd sleep outside—away from this mindless woman, the stupid boy playing in the soot and especially Bittoo. While all this and much more pressed heavy on his mind, he failed to notice anything amiss with his leather case. He grabbed the quiver, slung the bag over his right shoulder, ignored Teaa and Aroo, and stalked out.

Teaa slunk down beside Aroo at the hearth. She shook her head and sucked in a massive amount of air. With blown-up cheeks, she exhaled. "That was too close."

The twig Aroo played with twitched in his hand. He trembled with the knowledge that he almost got caught snooping in Luun's things. Dropping the stick, he made a statement with his hands.

"I agree," responded Teaa. "Our adventures here are much more exciting than those we experienced at the Fur Seal Band... more dangerous, too."

She watched Aroo talk with his hands, at the same time, she talked with her mouth. "We'll ask Caree to go with us. She can see the aura around Froom, and then we'll know if what he plans to do is good or evil. Luun has strange markings on his weapons? Well then, that fits his strange character. I agree, it's time to leave and find Caree."

Clansmen were camped in the center of the village, between the lodges, around the outskirts and even on the bank overlooking Frozen Duck Lake.

Many days ago, word spread that the mogur and Derk were calling for an early bear ceremony. The entire Clan of the Ancient Humans thought such a thing odd. But what seemed even more peculiar, Bittoo would direct the rite which had forever been the sole privilege of the shaman of the Bear Hunter Band. Those who hadn't heard about the twins' vision power before reaching Frozen Duck Camp, learned the news once they arrived. All were hoping for a demonstration.

Teaa shuddered as she twisted through the chaos of strangers. So as not to get separated, she held tightly to Aroo's tunic sleeve and pulled him along through the maze until arriving at the entrance to Derk's lodge.

Just as they reached the dwelling, Derk's corpse was being lifted, feet first, out through the sacred smoke hole on a ladder, with elaborate prayer sticks fastened to each end and talismans dangling from the rungs.

They came across Caree as she exited the pit house. Unable to read auras among the multitude of people, she spent the balance of the afternoon in mourning with others, preparing Derk's body for its journey to the afterworld.

Teaa whispered into her niece's ear. Caree's eyes flared as she caught her aunt's meaning. "Yes, I'll go."

Not until the trio walked beside the lake did they realize Piika lagged behind them. Caree turned and convinced him she didn't need protecting.

Uneasily, but with respect, Piika agreed to Caree's wishes. He scrambled back into the now deserted camp and headed westward, following the people and the dead shaman.

When he came upon the ridge where the bones of the holy one were to be buried, he climbed onto a low branch and beheld the splendid site—a striking place for anyone to rest, either alive or dead—a view of the entire lake. He squinted, trying to see if Caree remained on the far bank of the lake. Since darkness had nearly set in, he couldn't see much of anything at such a great distance.

The heart of Earth Mother had been scooped out, leaving an empty hole, large enough for the remains of three humans, rather than one. Uneaten burial food lay heaped in the grave, ready for Derk to take to the Land of the Souls and share with loved ones there. Nearly every thing Derk owned lined the inside of the burial vault.

Beside the deep hole was a mound of loose dirt covered with fragrant branches of sweetbriar and white flowering umbelli plants. Wrapped snugly in a woven grass mat, lay Derk's motionless frame resting on layers of soft foliage. The magical plants housed the ability to ward off black demons attempting to capture a dead man's soul and prevent it from entering the afterworld.

Piika was amazed to see every single shaman belonging to the Clan of the Ancient Humans present and stationed around the splendid formation. Six holy leaders in all, and seven apprentices. Each shaman was accompanied by one apprentice, except for Bittoo with two—his twin sons. Piika looked forward to the day when Caree could take her rightful place next to her father and her brothers.

In his lifetime, he couldn't remember seeing all the shamans together in one place. Surely, Derk would consider it a very great honor—the entire spiritual force of the clan taking part in his farewell. Even so, the holy ones hadn't come for the funeral. Most were on the trail headed to Frozen Duck Band for the bear festival when the blood flowing in the rivers of Derk's body ceased to pump.

Four rings surrounded Derk and the empty cavity in the ground. The widest and outer ring consisted of birch bark torches placed near one another and pushed securely into the dirt. From Piika's vantage, the torches appeared as a solid circle of fire. The seven apprentices made up the second circle. Between them and their mentors was another ring, a circular row of beautifully worked prayer sticks— each one with delicate curled shavings decorating the sides, and like the torches, the pointed ends were driven firmly into the soil.

As if on cue, the six holy men began their hypnotic chants. No two voices sang the same words, and no one's words were of the clan's language. The strange songs were separate—each primitive and known only to the shaman who herald the verse—a mysterious clash of voices that only the spirits of both good and evil could comprehend and be drawn to.

The assembly of people quieted, every one fearing the appearance of demons. Some thought they might get a glimpse of Derk's soul hovering nearby before it gained admittance into the Land of the Souls. They stood still, bracing themselves, holding their breath; nonetheless, their eyes stayed active, darting, not willing to miss a thing.

The three shamans who lived near the Great Sea unfolded a heavy fishnet with stone weights tied to its edges. Their chanting didn't waver as they veiled the mesh over Derk's shrouded corpse. The webbing was a very special gift from the holy ones. Not only did the fishnet prevent black spirits from coming near Derk, the net would accompany him to the home of his ancestors and be a useful tool.

The apprentices advanced toward the mound. Braaz and Jarkoo, one on each end, raised the corpse by the ladder poles and held it above the awaiting pit. Earth Mother beckoned for the bones of their revered leader, and the twins gave her what now belonged and was a part of her. With taut muscles, they gripped the leather cordage and slowly released the strapped form into the hole.

A frenzy of wailing rose from the clansmen. Those of Frozen Duck Band were torn by the absence of their beloved shaman. Their high-pitched cries became choked by their uncontrolled sobbing, which drowned out the shamans' magical songs.

In a near trance state, Bittoo, the mogur and the medicine seer moved to the edge of the pit. Each had removed cold ashes from Derk's sacred hearth, and by the handfuls scattered it into the hole and over Derk's frame.

Without warning, a frigid wind burst into their mist. The force came from all four directions and clashed against itself, becoming a whirlwind above the burial opening. The air scooped up the hallowed ash, pulling the discarded soot up through its funnel, turning the whirlwind into a morbid, black mass.

The strong wind caused the clansmen to drop to the ground. Not even the holy ones knew whether the presence was vile or righteous. The six shamans struggled to remain on their feet. Each took their position around the pit—the same stations they kept when sitting in counsel at a sacred hearth.

Three shamans stood to the south, two to the north and standing by himself to the west was Bittoo. Together the holy men made up a very strong force, but not until they took their rightful places did they see the void. Not one of them received their power in the east—from the sky spirits. Derk alone had held that powerful place.

The empty spot left a weak opening for any force to appear. Bittoo didn't see his daughter among the mourners. It would've been a two fold-gain if she stood to the east. First, filling the gap and, if the entity seemed evil, her presence could strengthen the shaman's circle and diminish the power of the black whirling force. Secondly, after she performed that duty, all the clan would understand that his daughter was a shamaness.

He glanced at the mogur whose face looked tense. Any other time the great man would take charge of such an important matter, but the shaman of the Bear Hunter Band didn't step forward. A silent communication ran between them—he understood the mogur's reasoning. The man was giving him his rightful due as the tusu and Father of all Shaman. But he couldn't live up to the honored titles unless his powers tested stronger than the force that hovered above Derk and his open grave.

What mattered most was that before him hung an entity that might prevent his beloved shaman from joining the ancestors. The phantom whirlwind housed a force which refused to identify itself and therefore deserved to be crushed.

Piika understood the problem. He climbed down from the tree and worked his way through the people. He knelt on the outside of the ring of torches, removed his quiver and with respect placed Derk's sky rock on Mother Earth.

Bittoo observed him, but with no idea as to what the young man put on the ground. Piika had nearly broken through the circle and defiled the ritual area. Bittoo held tremendous trust for the Gaaf's son and felt on this critical occasion, he'd take a chance.

He pulled a chant from his mind. One he remembered hearing from Derk's lips. As he strode over to Piika, he sang the almost forgotten words. What he saw brought tears to his eyes, his voice broke into a sputtering of tones. He felt the force of energy as he lifted the star and laid the sacred rock to the east where its owner would have stood.

All directions were represented—three by shamans and one by a divine rock which once dwelled with the sky spirits.

Everyone in the Clan of the Ancient Humans felt it. The hair on their arms rose. The air became full of an energy usually only produced by lightning. The tunnel of wind released its hold, and the ashes floated downward onto Derk's waiting corpse.

A show of lights caught the people's attention. In the darkness toward Frozen Duck Camp, volleys of bright streaks arched into the night sky, then plunged into the lake. Their reflection in the water gave off a spectacular double image. The man-made showers continued, mimicking the falling stars that lived in the heart of their dead shaman.

The closing tribute quenched the last bit of life from the vanishing whirlwind and became forever imprinted in the hearts of the Clan of the Ancient Humans.

Across the lake, Caree, Teaa, Aroo and Froom stood proud.

***

Eagle Shadow paused. Had his brother heard anything, or had all his silent words—the story he'd been telling—floated through the stillness?

He was very, very tired, deprived of sleep. But should he sleep? He desperately wanted to remain alert for whatever destiny might befall his weakened twin. His sibling could recover. But if Bear Claw left for the Land of the Souls, he wished to remain awake and watch his brother's spirit depart. And maybe then his identical twin would be less frightened.

'I read your thoughts,' Bear Claw murmured, the words not rolling off his lips, but only passing through his mind. 'I've already visited the Land of the Souls. If you hadn't been so busy with your story, perhaps your spirit would've gone with mine. Though I tried to focus on your words and am sure it was your voice running through my head that brought me back. If you had stopped talking to me, it's likely I wouldn't have found my way home.'

Eagle Shadow was at loss for a response. His mind reeled with happiness. His brother had returned!

'Go on with your tale, I intend to listen. Someday you may be known as a great story-teller. You have a better memory for it than I do.'

'I'll continue for a short time, then we both can rest.'

***

32

In order to light their way home, the men had removed torches from the sacred ring burning around the burial mound. The closer they ventured toward the village, the livelier their steps became.

This night, they actually witnessed a black demon in the form of a dust devil, intruding on the funeral ceremony. Most judged the form to be a demon because when confronted by Derk's powerful star rock and the unknown lights over the lake, the presence lost its strength and vanished into the night. And now, looking back on the incident, they realized that the vile whirlwind attempted to steal the ashes that came from Derk's sacred fire pit. A shaman wouldn't like to enter the afterworld without them. If he did, no one in the Land of the Souls would recognize him as a holy man. Derk's restless spirit may have forever walked between the two worlds, searching for his sacred ashes.

Everyone was pleased to be making distance between themselves and Derk's remains. It pleased them too, that tonight, they'd participate in the bear festival. Such a ceremony would surely over-ride the horrifying ritual they just observed, and prove their loyalty and devotion to the bear deity and Creator One Breath. Revered and familiar spirits would be watching the celebration. And when those spirits arrived they'd feel safe again.

Rushing into camp they scattered, scurrying, making ready for the night's festivities. The women completed the cooking, which they started earlier in the day, and produced an enormous amount of food, even though for the first time in their remembrance, the annual ceremony lacked the fresh salmon normally served. The men readied their weapons and raised the altars. With everything completed, the men, women and children stood outside Bittoo's dwelling in eager anticipation, waiting for the shamans to emerge and open the ceremony.

Bittoo showed himself first, dressed in finery befitting an esteemed leader whose totem was Ceda, mother of all water creatures. His garments were mostly sealskin, but his boots and the sleeves of his frock were made from the skins of salmon which still bore the intricate patterns of the fish.

When he walked, he walked noisily. Strand after strand of shells, sharks teeth, and walrus-tusk beads clad the front of the tunic and reached to his waist. Attached to his leggings were pieces of flat colorful shells, each secured by a length of leather fringe, tied and knotted through a center hole. Most trimmings on his clothing had been gifts from the villagers— ones he received when just an adolescent, after Froom nearly killed him.

He stood proud and strong. His appearance didn't match his inward mood. He felt uncomfortable, taking charge of the event and being thrown into such an important role—it wasn't his place to do so. Yet the mogur and the healing seer insisted that when the festival was over, it would set good in the minds of the people belonging to Clan of the Ancient Humans.

The crowd parted, permitting Bittoo, the shamans and their apprentices to make their way to the center of the camp and the altars. The procession moved slowly and regally, ever aware of the important occasion.

Although unable to see her father, the noise arising from the crowd, suggested that he was making a dramatic impression. Caree could hardly wait to tell her family, especially her father, that she was partially responsible for shooting the spears of fire into the air to honor Derk. Her Aunt Teaa walked to one side of her, but Aroo and Froom had disappeared into the crowd and most likely struggled toward the heart of the village where the high shrines were raised.

The tall altar consisted of a line of six stout tree trunks sunk and secured deep into the ground. Each hardy post forked near the top and all but one fork held a bleached animal skull. Mountain cat, wolf, deer, horse and fox—all stared down on the celebration with vacant, joyous eyes. Decorated spears, suspended from pegs, patiently waited a turn to participate. The split in the highest pole lay empty. The shrine was righteously adorned and resembled a massive ritual stick, taller than three men, layered with fancy rows of curled shavings clinging to its sides. A large woven collar, dangled near the base, awaiting the honor of embracing the neck of the sacred bear.

Bittoo skirted the bonfire and stood with both feet planted solidly in front of the stately altar. The remaining five shamans took their places, standing by themselves in reverence before a holy shrine.

Bittoo began the prayers. The soft voices of the other shamans joined in, as did the muffled beating of drums but neither drowned Bittoo's pleas. He withdrew the bear collar, gripping it firmly in his hand, then turned toward the bonfire and addressed the blaze. "Grandmother Hearth, soon we send the great bear to its ancestors. We request that you help her deliver our messages, so always we'll be endowed with the meat and hides of the bears which keeps us from perishing. No more do we put our infants on the snow in the time of the Starvation Moons. It's because of you, Grandmother Hearth. In the past, you helped give our message to the noble one...the mighty bear deity."

Inside he shook, outside he appeared almost calm. The heat of the fire and this new awkward role caused sweat to form on his brow. If only he could see the mogur's eyes and maybe catch a hint of silent approval in them—but the brightness of the roaring fire blinded him.

He sat cross-legged, face to face with the flames of Grandmother Hearth. After settling himself, the remaining holy leaders joined him. In honor of Grandmother Hearth, everyone in the crowd removed their weapons and laid them on Earth Mother.

Someone thrust a wooden bowl of food in his hand. As custom prescribed, the leader was the first to be served. He threw an offering of bear fat into the flames. The respectful gesture paid homage to Grandmother Hearth and was the awaited signal for the clansmen to seat themselves. Like schools of fish, they bunched tightly together.

Luun stationed himself behind the mogur who sat beside Bittoo. So far, Bittoo had conducted himself in a fitting manner, and the people of the clan seemed impressed. Luun was furious, envious and thirsting for revenge. Instead of reciting chants, he glared at the back of the tusu's head, incapable of concentrating on anything but Bittoo's upcoming death. Bittoo didn't deserve to lead the ritual.

He hadn't raised this bear to turn the beast over to someone from another band. By the time of the next bear ritual, he'd have that honor. At dawn he'd send Bittoo to the Land of the Souls. Then surely, at the next bear festival the old mogur would turn the honor of conducting the important ceremony over to him.

Froom maneuvered among the swarm of bodies until he installed himself directly behind Luun. He observed the vile man and detected tenseness throughout his evil frame. He gave a slight smile. A nervous man was apt to make serious mistakes. And he wanted Luun to make a mistake—he was counting on it.

He squirmed until getting so close, his breath breezed across Luun's neck. The sight of Luun's quiver sent rapid pulsating blood through the rivers of his body.

Earlier, Aroo cleverly rummaged through Luun's quiver and reported back to him. After Derk's burial, the mute boy carefully described its contents, even drawing the marks in the dirt. As suspected, Luun had scratched Froom's marks on some of the spear shafts. And now, for sure, Luun intended to do something wicked, making him look like the guilty one. But he had his own plan—from a stash of spear heads, knife points and wooden shafts he hid in the forest, Teaa, Caree and the boy had quickly worked with him to copy the ones seen in Luun's satchel.

He preferred to exchange Luun's leather bundle with another, but Luun's bag looked too fancy for him to copy. It would've been easier to slip-in one complete bundle for another. Instead, he would secretly exchange the spears and the knife in Luun's quiver with ones he made. If he managed to do it, Luun's satchel would be packed with new weapons, weapons with only Luun's marks on them. Then, whatever wickedness the apprentice was up to, could no longer be blamed on him.

By chance, the opening of Luun's quiver lay facing toward Froom. He positioned the flap of his bag against Luun's, moved his hand into Luun's quiver then slowly pulled out a short spear and hid it under his own satchel. Three times he repeated the process until, by Aroo's earlier account, only one remained—a knife bearing forged marks on the short handle. He couldn't feel the sharp weapon—it had to be laying deep inside the quiver, lodged underneath Luun's leg.

His mind raced. The feasting would continue until sunrise, and possibly he'd find the opportunity to remove the knife. But before that happened, what if Luun ran his hand over the bundle and felt its flat emptiness?

There seemed little choice. He placed the four new spears with Luun's marks into Luun's leather pouch, then deposited the four he stole into his own satchel. With Luun's quiver once again full of weapons, it was doubtful he could sneak his hand in the bag and rummage into the depths of it for the missing knife. He did the only thing that came to mind. He added the knife he had crafted. Luun's quiver now held two knives. One with Luun's marks and one with his. The compromise raised a gnawing sensation in his gut.

Luun patted his satchel. He heard someone behind him expel a huge sigh, but thought little of it. He resisted the temptation to take the knife from his weapon's bag and direct the sharp point into Bittoo's ribs. Driving the weapon into Bittoo would be so easy. His dream though was to see the tusu buried either below or above the sacred bear. His scheme gave him a healthy appetite, and he gorged on the roasted tubers and strips of beaver meat that was passed to him. He even smiled at the boy who handed him the food.

Aroo wanted to heave. With all his effort, he restrained. If only he possessed some type of noxious herb which he could've sprinkled in Luun's bowl before handing the vessel to the ruthless man. Yet at the same time, he refrained from silently laughing. He had observed his friend Froom exchanging the spears in Luun's satchel. Although it wasn't necessary, he had been prepared to divert Luun's attention, but Froom very cunningly completed his task without any help. Aroo was uncertain what might unfold this night, but guessed the evening would prove exciting. Smugly, he sat back and watched Luun, knowing sooner or later the man would be surprised with the contents of his quiver.

The clansmen ate and sent good tidings to the deities far into the night and until Sun Father poked his first ray over the Beaver Tail Mountains and gave consent to continue the sacred festival.

Bittoo rose and with elaborate arm gestures, thanked Grandmother Hearth for allowing the six bands to feast around her warmth. He treaded eastward toward Sun Father and the bear cage, with his clansmen following, the quietness feeling as heavy as thick fog.

When he arrived at the cage, the brown beast was just waking. He raised his voice and addressed the sacred animal. "Thank you for visiting the Clan of the Ancient Humans. The people of the Bear Hunter Band took excellent care of you. They were honored to do so. Be gracious and advise those in the afterworld of our kindness. We appeal for more visits from you and from many other esteemed bears. Please repeat my message when presenting yourself to your ancestors. Give messages to our ancestors."

The unimpressed bear ventured to the side of the pen. Sensing the stranger with the unfamiliar voice carried a morning fish for her, she reached a large paw through the logs of the enclosure. Swiftly, Bittoo took a step backward, out of range of the long black claws.

Luun smirked. He knew why the animal so boldly swiped at Bittoo. The bear caught the lingering odor of fish on Bittoo's sleeves and salmon skin boots. Unobserved, he removed a knife from his quiver and slipped the weapon in his leather waist thong.

The men crowded near the wooden pen while the women formed an outer ring. In unison, everyone danced in place while dispatching prayers to the spirit of the bears, informing the deity that soon they'd send the caged bear to them.

The mogur took the collar from Bittoo and handed it to Luun. Luun shot him a look of disbelief. Since Bittoo led the ceremony, then fastening the leather choker around the beast's neck was Bittoo's duty—one that would put Bittoo at risk. Luun's eyes flashed in bitter resentment, and his lips parted on the verge of making a sharp protest. But he obeyed, extending his hands through the pen and securing the leather band as the mogur instructed.

He had reared and pampered the bear from the time it was a small cub, and the creature was accustomed to his presence. After attaching a strong cordage strap to each side of the collar, he coaxed the creature from its pen. "Don't let me down," he whispered to the animal.

Agitated, the bear tossed her broad head. She'd been left in a pen in a strange place, hadn't been offered food since arriving, and the noisy mob around her was shouting and flinging their arms in wild gestures.

Luun held one leash and presented the other to Bittoo. With the bear between them, each wrapped his end many turns around his hand. The creature strained in Bittoo's direction, and Luun gave a hefty yank on his strap. With his eyes, Bittoo thanked him for keeping the beast at a distance.

Luun acknowledged Bittoo's thanks. Perhaps, it was a little early to let the bear loose on Bittoo. At this point, the animal seemed much too docile to be certain she'd carry out his plan. He wanted Bittoo dead not maimed.

The medicine seer had seen the sacred bear veer toward Bittoo and was grateful for Luun's fast thinking reaction.

Froom also viewed Luun's response, yet wasn't as gullible as the seer. He'd seen Luun's expression of hatred and caught a glimpse of an obsidian knife tucked into Luun's clothing. The man planned to do something totally evil. But did the knife in the apprentice's waist strap carry his marks or Luun's marks scratched into it? He himself carried a blade in a case sewn into the top of his boot. Purposely, he hadn't carved any identifying marks on its handle.

With Aroo at his side, Froom steadily pushed through the mob, trying to place himself at the front edge of the gathering, near the brown bear and the two who held her.

As the clansmen continued to the center of the village, they chanted the songs of their totems in rhythm to the cadence of drum beats. When standing at the empty beckoning shrine, each voice finished with a request for help from the revered bear deity.

Bittoo and Luun passed Grandmother Hearth's dying coals and stood proudly with the bewildered bear between them. Bittoo gave the leather thong to his son, Braaz. When he did, Jarkoo positioned himself beside Braaz in case his twin needed help holding back the strong bear. It was customary and an honor to assist with the leash.

Froom cut from the crowd and stood next to Luun. The apprentice looked him over. He wasn't familiar with the man whose narrow face was streaked with cuts from either an angry mate or from scraping his whiskers. Even so, the stanger's arm sat at an unsual angle, maybe the man wasn't very strong. He nodded, a motion indicating he accepted the stranger's aid.

Froom was thankful to be close enough to the dangerous man to put a knife in him if necessary.

Graciously, the medicine seer presented Bittoo with a lavishly curled prayer stick designed especially for the ceremony. Bittoo walked around the bear, waving the ritual stick in the air, purifying the animal for the journey to her ancestors. The beast thrashed her massive head back and forth in confusion.

Six marksmen, one representing each band, removed the decorated spears from the shrines. Unarmed, holding only a prayer stick, Bittoo stationed himself between the men and the great creature. With muscular arms, the marksmen threw a shower of stunning points at the startled beast. The dull spear points bounced off the thick furry hide. With her fang-like teeth, the riled bear snapped one of the shafts in half. She reared on her hind legs as a second rain of blunt weapons swished through the air.

Anticipating the animal's movement, the men aimed high, and all the weapons struck around her neck and face. One pierced her right eye and for an instant lodged in the socket. Maddened and in pain, the once calm bear tried to throw her bindings loose. Blood ran from her eye.

The first bawling noise from her told everyone that she was in distress, the next—a roar echoing off the Beaver Tail Mountains, informed them that she was to be feared. The animal began to walk upright toward the marksmen who stood ready with one last volley—this time a volley of needle sharp weapons.

In desperation, both Jarkoo and Froom dug their heels into Earth Mother, hanging onto the leash with all their might.

With his prayer stick, Bittoo remained between the enraged beast and the marksmen. To see the sacred animal hurting, saddened him. He didn't relish sending an injured bear to its ancestors, especially a creature with only one good eye. The animal might inform the deities that the people of the Clan of the Ancient Humans didn't treat her kindly. He raised the carved ritual stick to once again cleanse the now disfigured bear.

Although everything was happening fast, Luun saw it going better than he anticipated. The bear needed little coaxing. She headed directly at the marksmen—Bittoo stood in her way. Bittoo showed no signs of fear, but rather continued to mouth a sacred chant as though transfixed, unaware of any danger.

The entire crowd watched in silent horror while the monstrous bear strained, tugged, trying to reach her attackers. Braaz and Jarkoo wrapped their end of the leash around the tallest altar post and held on to both the pole and the thong.

Luun and Froom hung tightly to their leash. Yet Luun, who stood in front of Froom, pushed forward in Bittoo's direction rather than pulling back on the cordage. Luun released one hand, and drew out his knife.

Blood from the wounded eye washed into the bear's mouth and spilled back out through her teeth

as red frothy slobber. Partially blind, the beast continued toward Bittoo. Her massive paws supported
ten sharp claws, all striking out wildly in front of
her. The savage creature had no idea what held her
from reaching the men who wounded her.

To everyone else it looked as if Luun was trying
to hold the bear at bay and was willing to kill the
hallowed creature if she dared to assault Bittoo.

Froom knew differently. Aroo knew differently.
Caree and Teaa who had just pushed their way to
the front of the terrified mob, knew differently. Luun
would destroy their beloved tusu if the beast did
not.

Froom released his grip on the leash and at the
exact same instant stuck out his leg, placing his foot
infront of Luun. Luun went flying, then tumbled
head-on, landing at the feet of the vicious bear.

***

'You're finished?' Bear Claw asked in disbelief.

*'Yes! No! I'm too anxious to hear about your
journey to the Land of the Souls.'*

*'There's not much to tell. I think I was there for
a short amount of time...only because I remember
so little. But first you must complete your story, then
I'll explain.'*

*'The sacred bear mauled Luun. He got torn to
ragged bits. Except, as she killed him, he used the
knife he intended to apply on Bittoo and stuck the
blade deep into the beast's heart. Both of them died
shamefully...both were given a dishonorable burial.
The sacred bear was buried first, because the animal destroyed a human. They threw Luun's corpse*

in on top of the massive creature, since Luun killed
her in a way which wasn't the custom.'

The twins sent thoughts back and forth through
each other's minds as they attempted to envision
the morbid scene.

Bear Claw finally spoke up. 'Has anyone else
ever been buried in that manner?'

"I haven't heard of any other. We should remember to ask,' suggested Eagle Shadow.

'Is your story about Bittoo finished?'

'Not really, there's much more. His is a powerful
lineage, and Froom is an important man too, one
that will change history. But now, it's your turn.
What did you see in the afterworld?'

Groping for his mental voice, Bear Claw began
slowly. 'It's difficult to describe. Everything was
beautiful beyond words, even more so than the silent words that you and I communicate. It seemed
wonderfully peaceful. I felt healthy and strong and
sensed many things all at once. I saw a single spirit
and even a pair of twin spirits. Before me stood a
line of many regal clansmen, and with my ears I
heard the magnificent sounding voice of Creator One
Breath. And then a holy man, one of our ancestors,
whose garments were of seal fur and fish skin
pointed toward the clansmen and said to me, "They
are your LINEAGE...a Trail of Shaman."

***

GLOSSARY

The following information is attributed to the Ainu peoples and are facts woven into this fictional novel LINEAGE: A TRAIL OF SHAMAN. From band to band and island to island, even today the Ainu differ in their practices. Included in the book is additional data derived from other populations who are reviving their old ways. At some time in history, I feel that at least part if not all of these beliefs and customs were intertwined with all peoples and are a part of everyone's history.

LANGUAGE:

AINU WORD	MEANING	USED AS
Ya, Ho	Words used to drive away evil spirits	A greeting
Ainu	Human	Clan of the Ancient Humans
Tusu	Shaman	Shaman

COMMON FEATURES:

Light skinned
Thick and sometimes wavy hair
Brown hair common
Men usually grow beards
Eye color varies—either brown, grey and occasionally blue

BASIC INFORMATION:

Hunters, foragers and fisher peoples
Made and used birch bark torches
Gather a variety of edible plants including leek, berries and corydalis bulbs
Made and used some obsidian implements
Keep dogs

CLOTHING:

Made from a variety of animal pelts such as reindeer and fur seal pelts
During cold weather, two sets of clothing were worn. The inner garments were often worn with the fur on the inside and the outer garment's fur on the outside
Some festive clothing, including shoes, were made of salmon and/or trout skin

SPIRITUAL BELIEFS AND PRACTICES:

Supreme Being
Bear Deity
Sky Deity
Sea and Water Deity
Good and evil spirits
Believe in spirit helpers
Hearths belong to the women, as Grandmother Hearth (Deity) resides in them—the exception being the shaman's hearth
Children wore a sickness bag, consisting of milkweed and hearth ashes as protection against evil

Some Ainu men continue to wear talismans
Tattoos are thought to frighten demons
Women tattooed their lips and often their arms and
    hands prior to marriage, indicating their readi-
    ness to serve their husbands to be
The Ainu used the technique of tattooing, described
    in this novel, until the introduction of razor
    blades
Spirits are believed to crave trance-inducing herbs
Mugwort is thought to be the oldest plant on earth,
    therefore stronger than any evil
Earthquakes were thought to be caused by a large
    underground fish shaking its tail

BEAR DEITY:

Still practiced today and possibly the oldest contin-
    ued belief and ritual world wide
Brown bears are sacrificed in elaborate ceremonies
Sacrificial bears are raised from cubs
Bear cages were built identical to description in
    novel
The main purpose for sacrificing bears is to send the
    animal to the afterworld where it will relay mes-
    sages to its ancestors and encourage others of
    its species to return to earth and provide meat
    and hides
During the winter, dried coyrdalis bulbs were fed to
    captive bears
In earlier times, if a person killed a sacred bear, other
    than ritually, he was also killed and buried un-
    derneath the animal. If a bear killed someone, it
    was slain and placed in a grave underneath the
    human's body

The bear is sacrificed at dawn

Shaman wave ritual sticks at bears to purify the animal

Large forked poles or trees are made into altars and an animal's skull is lodged into each bifurcate

The main altar resembles a large ritual stick with curled shavings clinging to it. Until the bear is sacrificed that fork remains empty, awaiting the bear's skull

Dull decorative spears are thrown at the bear before it is killed with sharp ones

SHAMANS:

Ainu continue to rely on their shamans

Disposition to be a shaman appears to run in families

Shamans are known to visit the afterworld and return

Sea water is often drunk in rituals

Prayer sticks made of green willow are used in rituals

Bear's gallbladders were used for medicinal purposes

AFTERWORLD:

Ainu call the afterworld either the Land of the Souls or the Land of the Dead and believe the place a reversal of their life on earth

The dead can't interact with mortals who visit them in the afterworld

FUNERALS:

Funeral feasts are held with the expectation that the
   newly deceased will take the banquet to the
   afterworld and distribute the food gifts to the
   family members of the ones on earth who prepared the meal
Ashes from the hearth are removed after an individual dies
Bodies are removed head first from the home
The deceased were wrapped in grass mats
Fishnets were sometimes draped over the corpse as
   protection from evil spirits and also for the deceased to take and use in the Land of the Souls
Bodies are buried in Mother Earth
The plants of sweetbriar and cow parsnip (umbelli)
   were used at funerals to expel demons

The following information is attributed to the ancient KENNEWICK MAN SKELETON found at the
Columbia River in 1996. The italicized words are
facts woven into this novel.

Long narrow face and head/deep contours
Prominent nose with high bridges
Unhealed fractured ribs
Atrophied left arm
aproximately 5ft. 9in. tall/ 45-50 years old at death

ORDER FORM

Name_____

Address_____

City State Zip_____

Phone_____

Enclosed is my check or money order for $23.45
($19.95 for *LINEAGE: A Trail of Shaman* and
$3.50 for Shipping & Handling)

Send to: Spirits Talking Press
P.O. Box 927
Molalla, Oregon 97038